THE FOLLY

FOLLY

Lydia Bennett

NEW ENGLISH LIBRARY
Hodder and Stoughton

British Library C.I.P.

Bennett, Lydia
  The folly.
  I. Title
  823 [F]

ISBN 0 450 57454 7

Printed and bound in Great Britain for Hodder and Stoughton Paperbacks, a division of Hodder and Stoughton Ltd., Mill Road, Dunton Green, Sevenoaks, Kent TN13 2YA (Editorial Office: 47 Bedford Square, London WC1B 3DP) by Clays Ltd., St Ives plc.

If thou remember'st not the slightest folly
That ever love did make thee run into,
Thou hast not loved.

As You Like It, II.iv

Prologue

'. . . once . . . twice . . .' The auctioneer's hammer gave a prosaic thud. I rose, walked to the table and signed the papers which made my folly irrevocable.

Then I went downstairs. I walked through the public bar and stood in the archway leading to the lounge. The lounge was full of people chattering in their thick Yorkshire accents. Other people were pushing past me, coming from the auction room. My new neighbours. They stared at me with open curiosity. I stared back as calmly as I could.

Finally I saw the familiar red spiky hair of Effie. She was at a small table in the middle of the room, looking distinctly disgruntled. I wove my way through the crowd and sat down opposite her.

'Well!' said Effie. 'And where have *you* been?'

'Upstairs,' I said faintly. 'Buying a farm.'

'Ha ha. Charlotte, I've been here half an hour fighting off the local yocals to keep this crummy table. Another five minutes and I'd have been mobbed to death.'

'I'm sorry.'

'Apology accepted. Right, what'll you have to drink?'

'Drink?'

'You know: liquid. In a glass. Usually alcoholic but not necessarily.'

'Oh. Yes. Mineral water, I think.'

She peered at me, her face suddenly softened with concern. 'Charlotte, I hate to be rude, but you look ghastly.'

'I feel ghastly.'

'Look, I'll order us some food as well.' She stood up.

'I don't think I could eat.'

'Oh yes you will. I'm not having you drop dead on me halfway down the A1. I'll get you a salad or something.' She gave a little wave and disappeared into the crowd.

The sunlight slanting through the window was suddenly blotted out. I looked up to see the cause: a man, standing beside me and looking down on me with an amused expression in his bright blue eyes. He had bright blond hair to go with it, and a matching bright blond beard. He was a big man, powerfully built. All he needed was a horned helmet and a shield to turn him into a Viking.

The Viking thrust out a huge hand. 'Richard Staveley. Your new neighbour.'

I took the hand with some trepidation. 'Neighbour?'

'Graegarth Farm. We share a boundary: your west, my east.' The hand was hard but warm.

'Oh. Yes. Pleased to meet you, Mr . . .'

'Richard. Richard Staveley. There aren't many of us up there in the hills. We get to know each other pretty well, uh . . .'

'Charlotte. Charlotte Venables.' I smiled. 'Of Cappelrigg Farm.'

He smiled in return. 'Mind if I sit down? Just until your friend comes back.'

'Please.'

He sat down. Even seated he was big, overwhelming the little table. He leaned forward. 'If you don't mind me saying, you don't look much like a farmer, Charlotte.'

I looked steadily at him. 'You mean I'm not a man.'

His smile broadened. 'I mean you don't look very . . . well . . . tough.'

'I'm in the prime of life. I have perfect health. I work out in a gym three evenings a week and what's more I'm a farmer's daughter.'

His eyebrows rose. 'Where from?'

'Sussex. My father had four hundred acres on the Downs. It was a mixed farm, including sheep. And cows.' I leaned forward in imitation of him. 'I've had my arm elbow deep into a cow's backside,' I smiled, 'calving. I know what I'm doing, Richard Staveley.'

And, suddenly, I did.

2

1

Well, yes . . . I was a farmer's daughter, but not the sort accustomed to remote farms in one of the wildest upland regions of England. My father had been a gentleman farmer, and the land he worked was soft, fertile, easy. Most of it was arable, field after hedgeless field of lush corn. True, there was also some livestock: a herd of dairy cows in the water meadows, a flock of placid Downs sheep who cleaned up the stubble after harvest. But the work was mechanised and much of it done by farm labourers.

Despite this, I did have some experience of farming. Dad – unusually for a farmer – believed that a woman could run a farm as well as any man. In any case, I was an only child; there was no one except me to inherit the farm. So on weekends and during school holidays, I trailed after Dad as he did the rounds, learning the business. I was apprenticed in the calving sheds, spent whole nights in the fields at lambing time. I learned to drive a tractor, and although I didn't actually repair the farm machinery myself, I learned how to detect what was wrong and what needed doing.

There was another, less practical, reason for Dad's insistence that I work on the farm. He'd had to work his way up from his first small farm to his present position as country gentleman. He knew how to work and he wanted me to know, too. He wanted me to know where our money came from and the comfortable lifestyle it bought. He'd seen too many spoiled children of other landowners taking their life for granted, whining if ever they got their hands dirty. I knew this and seldom resented my chores.

Mine was an unusually happy childhood, with all the freedom that four hundred acres, two loving parents and a respected position in the community could give. I spent much of my time outside, childish games by the river and in the copses giving way later to gymkhanas and fox hunting. I had my own pony from an early age and looked after it myself. I did everything except the shoeing, for it and for the larger ponies that followed, right up to the big bay hunter that was my last.

I seemed to live a charmed life. I was reasonably attractive, intelligent, well-off if not downright rich, and loved by nearly everyone I knew. Sometimes it made me uneasy. There was something uncanny about my consistent good fortune. Surely, if one was so blessed from birth, one would have to pay for it later? Sometimes I woke up in the early hours of the morning, at the frightening moment of transition between night and day when the earth held its breath, and I held my breath, too, waiting, wondering if this would be the moment when my luck would turn.

But it held, right through school and university. My parents didn't mind at all that I wanted to study English rather than a more practical subject. 'Plenty of time to be practical afterwards,' they said. Mum in particular was pleased. She enjoyed reading, regretted not going to university herself, and had even taken a few courses with the Open University.

I went to Sussex and loved it. At university, as at school, friends were important to me, and as home was so near, I often brought friends home for happy weekends in the country. They were amazed at the tidy flourishing farm, the warm welcome from Mum in the big farmhouse kitchen dominated by the ever-warm and comforting Aga. 'You're so *lucky*, Charlotte!' they exclaimed. I agreed, sometimes a little nervously.

And still my luck held. I'd been Treasurer of the local branch of the National Union of Students. I seemed to have a useful mixture of caution and boldness with money. Soon after graduation, one of my classmates got a job in the City. A few months later, I followed her. I arrived in the City at just the right moment. Luck again. Within a few years I'd earned enough to buy a tiny luxury flat in the Docklands.

Then came Effie, Effie whom I almost missed because of her bizarre appearance. How could someone who looked like that be an interior designer? I'd never known a woman as tall and thin as Effie. She was so thin that, seen sideways, she almost disappeared. She compounded the effect of her height by wearing high-heeled shoes with everything, and she compounded the effect of her violently red hair by wearing the most shocking shades of pink.

But even here I was lucky. The same intuition that told me how to play the market told me Effie would be better decorating flats than decorating herself. That, plus high recommendations from friends, decided it. I looked round my flat, which the builders had made into a sleek, sterile machine, and told Effie what I wanted. 'Something soft and homey,' I said. 'I'm losing touch with my roots.'

It was a crazy thing to ask of Effie, New York born and bred, urban to her bright-pink varnished fingertips. But, like the occasional risk I took in the City, this one paid off. The flat, when Effie had finished, was a gentle welcoming place into which I could sink after a hard day at work. In the process, Effie had become my best friend.

True, when it came to men my luck faltered. Lucky at money, unlucky at love. I'd always had boyfriends, but not once had I been swept off my feet. I didn't mind too much. I certainly didn't brood about it. Not for me the anxious preparation, the half-living of a life while waiting for Mr Right to fill it out, make it complete, provide the perfect ending. I intended to live my life to the full, right now. If someday a man came along to share it, so much the better, but I was too shrewd a businesswoman to gamble on such an unpredictable element.

And then my luck failed in the most dramatic way possible. My parents were killed in a motorway accident. My first reaction was not grief but rage: how *could* they be robbed of a peaceful old age? They of all people. Those that the gods love best die young? I didn't believe it. I didn't believe in God either, not anymore. The last weak shreds of childhood belief crumbled as I thought of the brutal treatment meted out to Mum and Dad. All the theological arguments used on such occasions were meaningless, life itself was meaningless.

As the rage turned to grief and the first awful year wore on, my senses became dulled. What energy I had left burrowed deeper and deeper into the single question: What *is* the point of it all? The more I thought about my own life, the less substance it seemed to have. If I died tomorrow, what would be left to show for it?

Not surprisingly, my work suffered, too. The delicate balance between boldness and caution was gone. I had survived the October 1987 Crash only to find my own fortunes diminishing now. I hesitated, fumbled, kept changing my mind. I began to lose money. I didn't care. Nothing I bought with it seemed to matter anymore.

At the end of the year, Effie decided on drastic action. We drove up to the Scottish borders for the May Bank Holiday weekend to stay with some friends of hers. It was marvellous: peace, quiet, a lovely old farmhouse snuggled up against the edge of a huge forest. Plain food, gentle people, real conversation. The whole weekend was as refreshing as the cold clear water coming up from their well.

And I did feel refreshed, that last morning, when I wandered into the forest for a walk before breakfast. It was one of those perfect mornings, with the mist rising slowly from the forest floor to meet the shafts of sunlight boring through the green canopy. The collision between the two set off sparks of gold which bounced off every surface. I was leaning against a large spruce, luxuriating in the wild *son et lumière* when I heard the voice:

You must change your life.

I froze, my back pressed against the rough bark, my feet planted firmly on the needle-strewn ground. Hearing voices is definitely not a part of my life. A year ago my reaction to this one would have been brusque enough. But not that morning. That morning I fused with the tree, stopped breathing and waited.

Around me, the forest in its green-gold glory was pulsating with life. My own life was suspended, while visions of the world I was returning to superimposed themselves on the glittering greenery. My flat, my job, the circle of friends, the hectic social life – all of it was drained of colour, leaving a flat grey shadow through which the sunlight crashed.

And then another voice: Effie, calling me in to breakfast.

I walked slowly back to the farmhouse, brooding on the warning. It wasn't the first time either. The first time had been when I'd commissioned Effie to turn my sterile flat into what I now saw was a pale imitation of the Sussex farmhouse which had shaped my life. Even before my parents had died something had tried to tell me I had strayed too far from the centre of things, moved too deeply into an alien lifestyle. Somehow I must find my way back again. Today was my thirtieth birthday, too. A picture of my future flashed through my mind with alarming speed: myself ageing, the bright life in London turning increasingly stale as it continued year after year, dragging me towards a solitary death as pointless as my solitary life.

But I was both too old and too young for that kind of questioning. Such brooding belonged to the intensity of adolescence or the reflectiveness of old age. I was beginning, today, the prime of my life. This was the time to live, not to question that living. I shook off my unease and went back to the house.

None the less, the unease returned as we drove back south in Effie's little white Porsche. Everything that flashed by was suffused with green: the countryside, of course, but also the tedious little towns, all of it strained through the green-gold filter of the eerie morning forest, a wild, disjointed kaleidoscope of green. By the time we stopped for lunch in Kirkby Langham, my mind was so fragmented that I couldn't think clearly about anything.

We parked the car and walked up the High Street. There was an estate agent's near the pub, not a modern one with revolving drums full of enticing pictures, but an old-fashioned one with just a few brochures in the window. We stopped for an idle look.

'Cappelrigg Farm. What an odd name,' said Effie.

'Rigg means ridge. I'm not sure about the Cappel – chapel, perhaps?' I said vaguely. Then I saw the picture.

It was beautiful. A plain little stone farmhouse hugged by the green leaves of ivy and clematis and roses begging to get through the mullioned windows. A stand of trees behind leaned protectively over the house, almost brushing the mossy stone-flagged roof with another helping of greenery.

In the front, hens snoozed in the cobbled courtyard. A sense of peace and calm radiated from the picture and filled me with longing. My mind, confused all day, skimmed the details. The auction was this morning, in the meeting room above the Golden Oak just down the street. I looked stupidly at my watch. Right about now, as a matter of fact. I shook my head to dispel the pain of longing.

'You too?' said Effie. 'This heat's turning my brain into a fried egg – do you have any aspirin?'

'Aspirin?' I echoed.

'Little white things you swallow to make headaches go away. Charlotte, wake up. You look like a zombie. Look, there's a chemist across the street – I'll nip over and then meet you in that cute old pub for lunch.' She peered at me. 'The sooner you get out of the sun the better.'

I nodded and watched my friend play hara kiri with Kirkby Langham's traffic as she zoomed across the street. Then I entered the Golden Oak.

2

'Golden Oak?' said Richard. 'I suppose it's from the Druids – the oak is their sacred tree.'

'Oh, come on,' said Effie impatiently. 'I know you Brits go back a long way, but you can't tell me this pub's been here for two thousand years.'

Richard smiled. 'No, but the Druids have.'

'There aren't still Druids round here?' I asked.

Richard shrugged.

Effie watched him with visible irritation. She'd obviously been annoyed to return with our drinks only to find this stranger parked on her chair. Richard had sprung up immediately, introduced himself and managed to find the only other spare chair in the pub. He'd brought it over and then joined us. He'd joined us for lunch, too. Now we were having a coffee.

'There's a fad for reviving ancient customs,' said Richard.

'Hippies at Stonehenge,' Effie snorted. She looked pointedly at her watch. 'Charlotte, we ought to be going. It's a long way.'

'But I want to see my farm before we go!'

'Then we've *really* got to get moving,' said Effie.

I ignored her. 'Did you know the people who lived there last?' I asked Richard.

'Like I said, Keldreth's a small world.'

'Then you know why they left?'

Richard shrugged again. 'Usual reason: husband dies, wife can't manage on her own.'

'No children?'

'Too young to work the farm.'

'Then their father must have died young,' I said softly. 'What did he die of?'

'Boredom, most likely,' said Effie. 'And so will you if you bury yourself in this godforsaken place.'

9

I laughed. 'You really are the most urban person I've ever met.'

'Thanks be to God.' Effie pushed back her chair and stood up. With obvious reluctance she put out her hand. 'Nice to meet you,' she said to Richard. 'Hope to see you again sometime.'

'I'm sure you will,' he said.

We were all standing now, saying our goodbyes. Then Effie and I were back on the street, back in Effie's car, driving through the countryside.

'You don't like him,' I said.

'Viking thugs aren't my line.'

'He's not a thug. I think he's charming.'

'So was Attila the Hun on good days. Charlotte, you're not seriously thinking of working this stupid farm yourself?'

'I've got to get back to my roots.'

'This isn't your roots. This is darkest Yorkshire.'

'It certainly isn't the Sussex Downs,' I agreed.

Kirkby Langham was situated in a large and fairly flat vale which was, judging by the fields whizzing past, pretty fertile. But now we reached the northern edge of the vale and began to climb a steep switchback road. The landscape changed dramatically. From open farmland we moved abruptly into a dense forest which looked as if it continued right to the top of the hill and beyond. The air changed just as abruptly from the heavy heat of the lowlands to the cool fragrance of forest.

'Just smell that air, Effie! How can you bear to go back to London?'

'Easy. I like my comforts.' She changed gear and crept round a hairpin corner. The road was only just wide enough for one car. 'What kind of a crazy road is this anyway? What happens if I meet something?'

'That's what all those little lay-bys are for.'

'Looks like I'm about to try one out. There's a filthy great tractor hot-footing it towards us.' She swung the car into the lay-by and turned the ignition off. 'Charlotte, it's time for a talk.'

'I know. I'm sorry we couldn't talk at lunch. But I really did need to get to know Richard better. He *is* my nearest neighbour.'

'More pity you. Never trust a man with a beard – they're hiding something.'

'Honestly.'

'Please tell me this isn't for real, Charlotte? Please tell me it's a joke?'

'It's no joke, Effie.'

My words were nearly drowned by the tractor which was now chugging past us, pulling behind it a laden muckspreader. Bits of manure dropped onto the road. Effie grimaced. The farmer smiled and raised one hand in greeting and thanks.

'The natives are friendly,' I tried.

'That's real friendly shit he's just dropped onto the public road.' The stench of manure and diesel replaced the cool medicinal smell of the trees. Effie turned in her seat to face me. 'Just let me get this straight. You saw the picture of Cappelrigg Farm in the estate agent's window and it "spoke" to you. Right?'

'Right.'

'You took note of the fact that it was being auctioned in a few minutes, and without saying a word to your dearest friend, you marched in and bought it. Right?'

'Right. Wrong. Oh, Effie, I don't remember!'

'You've just bought a two hundred acre sheep farm and you don't remember???'

I said nothing.

'And stop sulking. Charlotte, for once we have to be serious. Has it occurred to you that this is a more than averagely long commute into the City?'

'I'm leaving the City. I'm leaving London.'

The words, as I said them, felt unreal. I felt unreal. I felt like a ghost floating above the remains of a previous life which hadn't been mine.

Effie shivered. 'Hey, I'm sorry I'm playing the heavy. This really means something to you, doesn't it. Why don't I shut up and just let you tell me everything, right from the start.'

I told her everything. As she listened, Effie shivered again several times. She couldn't pretend any longer that this was a joke or that an absent-minded mistake in the auction room had led me into this. She, too, could see that something was driving me towards Cappelrigg Farm. 'I know it sounds crazy,' I finished, 'but I'm *meant* to go to Cappelrigg. Don't you see?'

Effie sighed. 'Then we'd better have a look at this place.' She eased the car out of the lay-by and continued the tortuous drive up the hillside.

When finally we reached the top, I gasped. 'Oh, Effie, look! It's like another world!'

Keldreth was, in effect, a huge hidden plateau perched above the vale. Where we were, at the lip of the steep wooded hillside, was slightly elevated. From it the land dipped very gradually to a gentle fold running east to west, then rose again northward in a series of irregular hills to the base of another steep hill. This hill, however, was not wooded. It was more a cliff, a wild tumble of rocky outcrops interspersed with heather and bracken, broken here and there by a precarious tree whose roots must have anchored themselves beneath the rocks. The sun glinted off a profusion of waterfalls looking from this distance like long thin strings of tinsel on a Christmas tree. It was breathtakingly beautiful and so dramatic in its untamed grandeur that I couldn't help seeing it as the setting of a nineteenth-century romantic novel – Hardy, perhaps, or one of the Brontës. We had bought a map of the area before setting off, and I knew from it that what lay beyond would be even more spectacular: the North York Moors, stretching for mile upon mile, vast, lonely, uninhabited except by grouse and curlews.

I could feel a hectic flush rising in my cheeks as I took in the spectacle. Some small rational shred of me from my former life had almost hoped that the landscape of my new home would be ugly, or at the very least boring. I had almost hoped I'd be repelled by it and return to London. I could see now that there was no chance of that. This landscape was special, it wouldn't wear off in a few months or a few years. It was a landscape one would grow into, become a part of. I knew with absolute certainty that, once settled, I would never leave. Never.

Effie started up the car again.

The plateau itself was a jumble of fields and woodland, the latter dominating the part we were in just now. That, too, was strange. I'd expected a bleak network of fields full of sheep, but the large tracts of forest enhanced the wild beauty of the backdrop behind it. The road headed north in a series of curves to accommodate the undulating land. Then it dipped down slightly to the fold and we came to a crossroad.

Two weatherbeaten signs pointed left to Cappelrigg and Graegarth. Several others pointed right to equally strange names. Straight ahead, however, the road continued behind a pair of high forbidding gates. One sign on them said THE FOLLY. The other said PRIVATE. Neither was very reassuring.

'So this is where the squire lives,' Effie mused.

Richard had said little about the owner of The Folly, but I'd got the impression that Mr Farleton was a man to be avoided. Clearly he took pains to be avoided: the high gates continued in a high forbidding fence running east and west for a long way. Behind it a whole forestful of trees leaned over as if trying to escape, their crowns joining with those on the other side of the road to form a canopy over it. The canopy was densely and darkly green. Another green canopy loomed over the private road leading to The Folly. I knew from the view we'd had at the edge of the plateau that interspersed among the stands of trees were open fields, but they were invisible from here, giving the impression of one vast forest.

'Has a thing about trees, does your squire,' said Effie. She looked at me. Something about my appearance must have alarmed her. 'Charlotte,' she said nervously, '*say* something.'

'It's magic,' I breathed. Then, a little louder, 'I'm sure there are dryads and water sprites here, hundreds of them, and elves, too.'

'I think your water sprites are culverts carrying some very mundane water under the road. Charlotte, wake up. You've gone all funny on me again. I don't know you when you're like this.'

I shook myself and smiled at Effie, trying to give some semblance of normality. 'Do you think Cappelrigg will be as magical as this?'

'I doubt it, but there's an obvious way to find out.' She turned left and drove under the canopy for some time. Above the soughing of the trees and the hum of the engine I could

13

hear the water of a beck running alongside the road, no doubt carrying off all that water from the falls that draped the distant and now invisible hillside to the north.

'Bogland,' said Effie cheerfully. 'Your sheep will be riddled with liver fluke and foot rot or whatever it is sheep get on boggy land.'

'How do you know about that, Urban Effie?' I smiled.

'Even us city slickers know a few things, hard though we try not to. Friends,' she explained. 'The ones we've just been staying with, if you can remember back that far. Their smallholding was pretty soggy, too, remember? Hence the huge Forestry Commission holdings. The land's not good for much else.' She glanced briefly at me. 'Hey, you're supposed to know all this. Some farmer you are!'

I laughed. 'I'll learn.'

The trees stopped suddenly, the high fences turning away from the road at right angles with the captive trees continuing on for the entire width of the plateau. The fence here marked the east boundary of Cappelrigg Farm.

'Well, here we are. Chez Charlotte,' said Effie.

I gazed at the land ahead of me. 'I just can't believe this is mine.'

There were trees at Cappelrigg, too, but most of them were tucked away in the corners of fields and in other places where machinery couldn't go. The rest was open pasture full of sheep sheltering from the sun behind the dry-stone walls. I could see the panting flanks of the nearest ones. I hoped they wouldn't get sunstroke. Those sheep were mine now. I'd bought them after the farm itself because they were 'heafed': born and raised in these fields and so better suited to the land than any outside stock I could buy in.

'*My* sheep,' I murmured in wonder.

Effie drove on. Up ahead was a particularly large grove of trees far to the right of the road. As we drew nearer I could see glimpses of stone through the leaves. At last we were parallel with the grove. The road went on ahead, but to the right was a long gravelled farm track; at the end, the house, tucked in among its trees and looking even more picturesque than in the estate agent's window. If the whole plateau was like another world, this grove containing the farmstead was

14

another one still, this time gentle, friendly, protected by the huge amiable trees bending over it. To one side of the house was a large barn, to the other a single-storey farmbuilding, both built from the same stone as the house and forming, with the house, three sides of a courtyard.

'I'll get the gate,' I said.

Effie drove through the opened gate. As I shut it again, I stared at the perfect little set of buildings. It was as if modern life had passed it by, leaving it somewhere in the nineteenth century or earlier. No ugly concrete blocks, no corrugated asbestos roofing, no tatty sheds, just this perfect little jewel of serenity set among the fields.

'I can't believe this is mine!' I said excitedly as I got back into the car. 'Just think, Effie! If we'd stopped for lunch in some other town, or come to Kirkby Langham just a few minutes later, none of this would be happening!'

Effie said nothing as we drove into the farmyard. We got out and stood looking round at the hens scratching at the earth between the cobbles.

Hens?

'Charlotte, you didn't say you'd bought the poultry, too.'

'I didn't – they weren't even mentioned. How odd of the last people to leave them behind.'

'Charlotte, you did say it was Vacant Possession?'

'Yes, of course.'

'No way is this place vacant. Look.'

3

I looked. There were curtains at the windows. One window was open. Through the open doors of the barn I could see the back of a parked car. Effie was right, there was someone living here still. I tried to remember what the auctioneer had said as I signed the papers, but I'd been in too much of a daze to notice much. Also, the auctioneer had irritated me – one of those smooth country types sure of their place and good at making an outsider feel excluded. I'd been determined to show him a cool facade as I signed the papers, and determined, too, to treat his patter with disdain.

Suddenly I remembered that the woman who was undoubtedly inside the house right now was a widow. Her husband had been taken from her without warning, too young, and very recently. 'I think we should leave,' I said. 'Let the solicitors sort it out. I'm sorry I wasted your time, Effie.'

I followed her to the car. She turned it round the big cobbled farmyard and we drove fast down the gravelled track. Too fast.

'Effie!'

The brakes squealed as a cat shot across the track. I had just one glimpse of its body, twisted into a defensive posture, a crooked white patch on its terrified face, before it disappeared into the field opposite.

'Jesu,' said Effie. 'That's all I need to round off the day: a black cat.'

'Black cats are lucky in England,' I reminded her.

'I'm not English,' she reminded me.

We reached the end of the track to find a Land-Rover blocking our exit.

'Great,' said Effie. 'The Keldreth mafia.'

We got out of the car at the same moment the Land-Rover's door opened and Richard stepped out. And here something very strange happened. The whole day – the 'voice' in the forest, the trance in which I'd bought the farm, the unexpectedly occupied house – all of it floated away in one last wave, leaving me stranded on an island of calm. At the centre of it was Richard, his large body leaning easily against the side of the Land-Rover, his arms folded across his chest, his handsome face smiling at us with friendly amusement.

'You don't waste much time,' he said, the amused smile broadening.

'Who the hell is living in Charlotte's house?' said Effie, gesturing vehemently towards the farm.

'Noreen Jowett,' said Richard. 'She wasn't sure the farm would reach the reserve – she stayed on just in case. I'm sorry. I should have warned you. I didn't realise you'd be coming straight up here.'

Then why did he follow us? We'd left right after lunch. Richard must have followed us just a few minutes later. His eyes didn't leave mine all the while he addressed his remarks to Effie. In the open air, their blue seemed even more intense. There was sanity in those eyes, in his steady gaze. Everything about him was steady and reassuring. None of the men I knew in London were like that. Beneath their self-confidence was the innate nervousness of the city dweller. Richard was rooted in the earth. Like me. Like I had been and would be again. A sudden quickening of the breeze lifted a handful of his thick straight hair and let it fall again. The breeze cooled my face at the same time and I smiled up at him with childlike pleasure.

'How long ago did her husband die anyway?' Effie asked.

I was still basking in the warm reassurance that seemed to radiate from Richard. I scarcely heard the conversation, didn't really want to hear it. This was no landscape for words. The great sweeps of open land, the dense tracts of fragrant forest – it was all on a grand scale, making small and insignificant the doings of mere humans and most of all their foolish words.

I looked to Richard for confirmation of my thoughts and was startled to see him look down suddenly, as if lost for words. When he looked up again, he unfolded his arms and

17

put his hands in his pockets. He turned his head away and said to no one in particular, 'About a month ago – beginning of May.'

'How exactly did it happen?' Effie asked.

Richard hesitated for some time. The silence grew deeper. From somewhere far away, up towards the moor, I heard the rich trills of a curlew taking off. Starting deep down, the trills slowly ascended in pitch and intensity along with the bird itself, ending with the dark mournful contralto cry of *Courrr-li, Courrr-li*, as the bird, now visible, soared high above the land. A lonely sound, the sound of this landscape.

Richard was gazing towards the sound now, and I saw that he was older than I'd first thought. Early forties, perhaps? His eyes, squinting against the sun, were surrounded by tiny lines, and the rest of his face showed the years of working in this harsh landscape. There was a faint scar – two thin lines which failed to tan – running down one cheek. A farming accident, no doubt.

Farming accident. John Jowett?

As if reading my thoughts, Richard spoke at last. 'I suppose you'd better know – you'll hear it soon enough from the locals. Some of the versions are pretty lurid. You may as well hear it straight.'

He raised one arm and pointed to something behind us. We turned round and looked but there was nothing to see beyond the buildings except farmland stretching to the base of the hillside and then the steep rocky slope itself, ending in a ridge. 'Up there,' he said, 'beyond that ridge, is the moor. If you look hard you can just see the faint outline of the top, about half a mile back. There's a flat table of millstone grit. What you can't see is the circle of standing stones on it.'

I turned round to face Richard again. He gave me a faint smile and continued. 'You asked about the Druids. Well, that's where they had their temple.'

Effie turned round, too. 'No kidding?'

His arm swung round to point behind him now. 'And way back there, on the other side of the vale, there's another set of hills, and on the top of it, another millstone grit table.'

'And another lot of standing stones?' said Effie.

The curlew was now somewhere over the vale. I could barely hear the faint *Courrr-li*, barely see the tiny speck it had become. Behind Richard I saw only the edge of the distant trees and then an unbroken expanse of pale blue sky.

'Yes,' said Richard. 'There's a network of them all over Britain.' He paused again, looking at me.

I was suddenly aware that I hadn't said a word to him or to Effie since our encounter at the end of the track. Was that why he was staring so? I cleared my throat but still no words came. A landscape without words. I felt I could stand there forever, my mind and my body just absorbing the warmth emanating from Richard and from the sun. For one absurd moment they fused in my mind: Richard's face, shining out from the golden aureole formed by the hair and beard, and the sun, giver of warmth and life. I tried to shake off the comparison, turn him back into a Viking; better still, a local farmer, my neighbour. But the trance-like state in which I'd bought the farm had gradually returned in Richard's presence, blotting out my reason. It was totally uncharacteristic. I'd always been so much in control of my life. Intelligent, sensible, clear-headed. This giving up of control was alien to me. And yet, it felt so warm, easy, inevitable.

'You've heard of ley lines?' Richard was saying.

'Vaguely,' said Effie.

'Some people say the temples are all connected by lines of energy – ley lines. Rather like the ancient fairy paths of Ireland.'

'Come again?' said Effie.

'Straight lines between the hilltops where fairies had their meeting places,' Richard explained. 'The lines are always straight, like the ley lines – something to do with concentrating the elemental forces. At certain times of the year the fairies march along them, and legend says that anything in their way will die. It's nonsense, of course, but the ancient Celts and Druids must have picked up the idea; at certain times of the year they gathered in their hilltop temples and harnessed the energy of the ley lines. Some say that they drew into themselves ancient wisdom, others say it was just a fertility cult. Anyway, the first of May – May Day – was important to the Druids. So they got together and, well, did whatever Druids do on May Day.'

'Like?' said Effie.

'Like sacrifices,' said Richard. 'In the beginning, human ones.'

'Charming,' said Effie.

Richard gave a wry smile. 'In the *very* beginning, a huge wicker basket shaped like a human and stuffed full of sacrificial people. Burning the basket was the centre of the ritual. Nowadays they make do with hens.'

'*Nowadays*?' Effie's voice was incredulous. 'You're not telling me they still do it?'

Richard shrugged. 'Here and there.'

I let the words drift meaninglessly over me. There was power in this landscape. I could feel it, it was almost palpable, radiating out from Richard and the sun, filling me with such strength that if I stood there much longer, soaking it in, I might explode from the sheer magnitude of it. It was so wonderful, this letting-go of control. I smiled happily at Richard.

But something was wrong. Richard wasn't smiling. He was staring hard at me. Above me, Effie's words echoed:

'Richard, this isn't Wales. And what's all this got to do with Mr Jowett's accident anyway?'

Still looking at me, and frowning intently, Richard replied. 'There's a ley line running straight through Cappelrigg Farm. John Jowett had his accident on May Day.'

4

The next few weeks passed in a blur as I tied up the loose ends of my old life and tried to prepare for the new. Only one moment stands out: pausing in front of a full-length mirror before going to my farewell party and being shocked by the stranger staring back at me.

The stranger was as urban as Effie. She was tall and slender and wore a dramatic black and white dress to match her dark hair and pale skin. The skin seemed thin, almost translucent, stretched so firmly across the fragile bone structure. Everything about that heart-shaped face was small, precise, fragile. Above it, however, was a sumptuous crown of plaits, aggressively old-fashioned and increasing the sense of drama. The only colour in this stark black and white landscape was a pair of very large and very dark blue eyes, almost violet, staring at me with unmistakable mockery. The mouth suddenly turned down at the corners in a rueful smile.

You? A farmer?

The party – in Effie's flat – was marvellous, but I wished desperately that evening that there were fewer mirrors. Everywhere I turned, this streamlined stranger kept mocking me. And she was right. Everything about me was designed for city life: first nights at the theatre, Covent Garden, expensive restaurants, preview parties in art galleries, exclusive shops whose owners greeted me like one of their own. Which I was.

I hadn't realised until that night just how many friends I had. I also hadn't realised how little they knew me. Everyone except Effie seemed to think I was buying a country cottage. It was understandable enough. Country living was fashionable. Everyone wanted a house in the country with two acres, three geese and a goat. Richard had said that the land the other side of Farleton Forest was full of tarted-up old farmhouses and architect-designed barn conversions, all of them owned by off-comed'uns who trudged round heartily in their wellies and played at miniature farming.

I wasn't playing. I don't know if Richard understood that, but my friends certainly didn't. They all promised to come and see me. We would have lovely country weekends together. Then, when I'd had my fill, I would return to the City and keep Cappelrigg as a weekend cottage. It was pointless to argue.

That night, I dreamt I was driving a tractor in my black and white evening dress. The dream was extremely realistic, right down to the landscape behind Cappelrigg. There was a dip in the land going down to a little syke which ran east to west. I was driving towards it when suddenly my foot seemed pinned to the accelerator and I was going faster and faster. I tried to scream but of course no sound came out. I just had time to glimpse Richard, standing to one side and bathed in a gold aureole like in a Russian icon, before my dress caught in the wheels. At the same moment, the tractor hurtled over the edge and started to somersault.

I woke up, still trying to scream.

*   *   *

And then it was the day of Midsummer's Eve and I was alone at Cappelrigg for the first time. The removal men had just left, after helping me distribute my meagre furniture. I stood in the doorway of the stone porch and watched as, far down the track, one of the men jumped from the van to open the gate, then closed it and climbed back in. The van turned left and started the long trip back to London, taking its noise with it. In the silence, the buzz of a fly beating against a porch window sounded unnaturally loud. The porch faced south and had obviously been used for growing things. The sills were ringed with the marks of vanished pots, a curiously desolate sight. The only contents of the porch now were my wellies and an old jacket looking lonely on its peg.

I went through into the kitchen. It, too, seemed bare. The large square room had swallowed up my Welsh dresser, small pine table and chairs. My fridge looked ridiculously small, a

22

Londoner's larder unsuited to the spaces of the countryside. Even the Aga failed to dominate the room as Agas should. What's more, it was cold – I hadn't had time to clean out the ashes and relight it. Still, it was potentially a wonderful room. A coat of white paint and some rough-textured curtains was all it needed.

I went across to the back window. The trees in the grove were now fully in leaf, even the stubborn ashes. A brisk wind was moving the branches in restlessly shifting patterns of greens. It would be marvellous to be a painter, to try and capture all the different greens. I flung open the window. The trees responded by flinging in a gust of cool fresh air. The kitchen seemed instantly to spring to life. No, I will not have curtains. I will keep the windows open in all but the coldest weather. The trees will furnish my house.

There was no corridor downstairs, all three rooms opening straight into each other. I went into the living room and was surprised to feel it welcoming me already. My tweedy sofa and chairs were grouped round the fireplace which backed onto the Aga wall of the previous room. They seemed to be waiting for me to light the fire and settle in for a good read. On the opposite wall, an open staircase climbed up and disappeared. The other walls were lined with my bookcases, also waiting. My imagination emptied the teachests, filled the bookcases, lit the fire, sank into the sofa. It would be a good room.

I went across to the windows and opened them both. Again the breeze billowed in, breathing the room to life. Through the branches came glimpses of the moor, its edge a sharp smooth whaleback broken here and there by rocky outcrops. The day wasn't clear; the flat summit Richard had mentioned was still invisible.

Midsummer. I wondered if the Druids would be celebrating tonight. The longest day, when the earth began its slow descent towards winter. I leaned out of the window. The sun was sulking behind a fat black cloud which spread a charcoal mat across my highest pasture. A moment later it popped out again, whisking the mat away and flooding the field with green-gold light. The light bounced off the fleeces of my sheep.

23

Fleeces. Shearing. They would have to be shorn soon and there was no one to help me. Everyone had said I was crazy to try and farm it alone. They were right, of course, but was craziness always such a bad thing? I reconstructed my previous life, so recently abandoned, and again saw the future I would have had, endless days filled with activity and yet empty, moving on to a meaningless old age. No, there had to be something more to life than pushing pounds and dollars and yen around the market. I would take my sheep to market instead. Shorn or not. Something would turn up.

I went to the other side of the room and opened the windows there. Then I stood in the doorway of the end room. In the past, the end room would have been for best, the parlour and dining room for special occasions. I had no need for a 'best' room. I had no need for so many of the things that had crammed my life before. In the weeks that followed the auction, a plan had unfolded in my mind. It was devastatingly simple. I would strip my life bare. Then, bit by bit, I would assemble a new life, testing each element to see if it really mattered. The house I stood in now was the first part of the process. It, too, was bare. After all, what did I need? Somewhere to lie down, somewhere to sit. Food, drink, warmth, protection from the weather. My last weeks in London had been an orgy of throwing out everything that wasn't essential. Television, video, stereo, microwave, dishwasher, computer, all the technological clutter of my life had gone. My wardrobe had shrunk to jeans, sweaters and a few dresses just in case my new life required me to be respectable once in a while. Here and there I had wavered. I'd kept my tiny fridge. Also my books. I hadn't read anything but financial reports for years. With no social life to distract me, I would read, and think, and become – what?

My friends had been confused and who could blame them? I was jettisoning something they were working hard to achieve. My action threatened their own lives and they needed to misunderstand. I was 'going green', I was becoming a 'nature freak'. One ex-boyfriend even called me a nihilist. I couldn't explain, didn't even try, except to Effie. She didn't understand (neither did I), but she loved me enough to be patient. 'You *will* let me visit you in your hermitage?' were her last words before I left. Her voice had been uncharacteristically timid, and for one awful moment I had questioned what I was doing.

Then I'd remembered another moment: standing at the end of the track and watching the strong lines of Richard Staveley's face melt into those of the sun, a great golden disk radiating power into my body until I felt I would burst with it. It had shaken me, that moment, but at the same time it compelled me.

Richard. I would phone Richard and ask him about the shearing. There would be contract shearers, and he would know how to get in touch with them.

But I couldn't phone him. The phone hadn't been reconnected. Suddenly a swarm of urgent tasks filled the empty house, each demanding priority. There was too much to do at once, Effie had been right, I should have taken things more slowly.

And then, like magic, a curlew soared overhead, trilling its ancient song and sweeping aside my panic. The sound was a benediction. I closed my eyes in gratitude, letting the sound surge over me in great waves. *Courrr-li, Courrr-li*. The upbeat at the end was brisk and made me smile. I shook the last shreds of panic away, shut the end room door and started up the stairs.

Suddenly another sound shattered the air: the jagged whine of a chainsaw ripping through the curlew's cry. It was coming from somewhere behind the house.

My trees. My precious grove of trees.

I hurried back down the stairs and to a back window, but the trees were untouched. The fresh green leaves continued their dance with the naïve delight of children just released from school, waving their branches. Look at me, look at me.

The sound of the chainsaw intensified. I squinted at the forest beyond my east boundary but there was nothing to see. I barely knew the layout of my own land. Wasn't the dip down to the little syke lined with trees? I tried to orientate my eyes and ears, focus on the source of the chainsaw. Yes, it could very well be coming from somewhere near the syke. In which case, someone was cutting down one of *my* trees.

I rushed to the porch for my wellies, then ran out and round to the back of the house. There were boulders strewn among the trees. I threaded my way between trees and boulders and entered my nearest field.

Irritation grew into anger as I hurried across the field. Mrs Jowett – or someone working for her – had taken the hay off it and other fields very recently. It must have been done after the ownership had legally passed to me. She had evidently sold the hay to some other farmer. In any case, there was no sign of it at Cappelrigg. I would have to buy in hay for the winter. I could afford it, but that wasn't the point. The point was Mrs Jowett. It was a mean thing to do, especially after the high price I'd paid for the farm.

I went through into the next field. This was the one with the dip – I could see the tops of the trees ahead. There was no motion in them other than that caused by the wind, but the sound of the chainsaw was nearer now, seeming to come from the east end of the dip. I veered towards it. Sheep started up at my approach and trotted away to stare at me from a safe distance. No doubt Mrs Jowett would have shorn the sheep, too, sold their fleeces, if they'd been ready. But the yelk hadn't risen, the fleece wasn't ready to come off.

I tried to sympathise with Mrs Jowett and her unexpected widowhood but her behaviour made it difficult. Her meanness acted as a warning, too. I was an outsider, farmer's daughter or no, and the locals would be watching me, waiting for me to make a wrong move. That was one reason why I couldn't take legal action over the hay. However much I might be in the right, it would antagonise the locals, make me seem all the more the arrogant outsider bullying the locals who had a special right to be here. It was an elusive right I couldn't buy along with the land. I would have to earn it, and that in turn made me even more resentful.

I had reached the eastern edge of the dip before I remembered the nightmare. I looked down. The little syke chuntered on peacefully towards the forest. Beside it, the trees rustled. No nightmare material here. It was a magical place, private, tucked out of sight from the open land that surrounded it. It was almost like a miniature valley. The trees growing here were all small – hawthorn, hazel, willow – scaled down to blend with the diminutive syke.

I clambered down. Immediately the wind dropped, and even the sound of the chainsaw diminished. There were boulders here, too, with patches of flowers springing up between them. A sweet smell rose to meet me from a carpet of bedstraw that foamed round the base of a rock, the tiny flowers looking even more fragile against the hard grey stone. There was tormentil, too, its leaves a crisp green, its flowers bright yellow and turned up like little faces soaking in the sun. Sentries of purple foxgloves stood to attention beside the rocks. A huge bumblebee buzzed loudly in the amplifier of one flower and then popped out again to fly lazily about looking for another, spoiled for choice.

The chainsaw stopped. I could feel the tension draining away. I sat down on the slope. I eased my back down onto a blue duvet of speedwell. I closed my eyes against the sun. My back hurt because I'd been shifting furniture. I'd been shifting furniture because my house was in chaos, as was my farm, and I smiled to myself because it didn't matter anymore. Nothing was urgent. Time stopped in my tiny valley and I stopped with it, turning my face to the sun with the tormentil.

The chainsaw started again. I frowned and sat up, the spell broken. The sound was closer now. I stood up, then went further down the slope to cross the syke. The water was too low to threaten my wellies. The other side was steeper. I climbed up it between the rocks and trees, trying not to step on too many flowers. At the top, I looked round.

The ground here was much higher – perhaps the rigg that had given my farm its name. From it I could see most of my land. The house and buildings looked surprisingly low down. The whole plateau, which seemed to undulate gently with little change in level, actually rose, so gradually that it was difficult to notice, to meet the base of the cliff leading up to the moor. I could see the other clumps of trees on my land now. None were threatened with the chainsaw.

Without really thinking, I began to move towards the chainsaw's noise. It brought me to my east boundary. On the other side of the high stone barrier the forest trees rose like a great green wall. They were serious no-nonsense trees, unlike those of my grove and the little valley. We mean business, we work for our living.

Curious, I looked for a way over the wall. I knew from the map that the whole plateau was criss-crossed with ancient footpaths connecting all the farms with fine disregard for the modern road. They were public rights of way. There must be a way over. Finally I saw the jutting stones of a stile. I climbed it and dropped down to the other side.

The temperature dropped with me, the high green canopy shutting out the sun. Here and there a gap appeared and a golden ray slanted down through it to light up a patch of ferns or spent bluebells. The footpath was clear enough. I started to walk along it. Above me the leaves rustled secretively, enclosing me in a cool green tunnel as private in its different way as the little valley. I continued for a while in what I took to be an easterly direction, though the density of the trees made it difficult to tell.

Suddenly the chainsaw was much nearer, coming from somewhere to the north. After so long in the city, I'd adopted the urban love of trees, precious islands of life. It seemed so awful to kill them. I knew I was being irrational. This wasn't London. It was a commercial forest and no doubt tended well. No doubt whoever was cutting them down had a right to do so. Still, I turned off the path and plunged into the forest, following the sound.

The trees here were closer together, but the thicker canopy they formed excluded even more light, inhibiting the undergrowth and making it fairly easy to walk. I remembered the dense conifer forest of the borders where, just three weeks ago, the insistent inner voice had told me to change my life. This forest, though equally dense, was different. There were conifers here, too, but mixed in with them were hardwoods – all different species, all different sizes. How odd. Richard had said it was a commercial forest, but surely the varying sizes and species would make them difficult to harvest efficiently? Surely commercial foresters grew their trees uniformly to make it easy for the machines to get in?

My thoughts and my walk stopped abruptly. An impenetrable mass of greenery was blocking my way. I looked closer and saw it was the top of a fallen birch, its leaves already wilting. I looked about for a way around the tree. Making a wide half-circle, I came to its severed trunk. It had been felled with the chainsaw. It was a relatively small tree, its trunk only a few inches in diameter. A thinning, of course, and of course it was right to thin out the trees and allow the others to grow. Anyway, it was none of my business.

The chainsaw was very close now. As I made my way towards it, there were more and more felled trees, their butchered trunks oozing sap. There were voices now, men, shouting above the scream of the chainsaw. Their voices were as harsh and ugly as the chainsaw. The sound was deafening now, so loud that I had to put my hands to my ears.

Suddenly the noise snapped off. There was a moment of eerie silence. Then a new sound, high up and sinister, a strange sort of crackling. It crescendoed with terrible speed, thundering now, and I looked up just in time to see a huge green wave bearing down on me. A harsh shout – 'Look out!' – was too late. The tree crashed down with all the inevitability of a nightmare in which the dreamer runs to escape but stays rooted to the spot. There was one last moment of clarity, and then a dark, green world turned black.

5

'Jesus, Davey! You've gone and done it this time. Is she hurt bad?'

'It was only a sapling. Where're you going?'

'To be fetching a doctor, just in case.'

'All she needs is water. Take my hard hat. The syke's just over there – I think there's enough in it.'

'You're a hard man, Davey.'

'Just get the water.'

As I came to, masculine voices shouted above me. It took me a while to reconstruct what had happened. It took me even longer to realise that I was pinned beneath a fallen tree, quite possibly injured. If so, the company I was in was hardly reassuring.

The voices stopped. I struggled to open my eyes just in time to see a pair of muscular tanned hands reaching towards me through the tangled branches. I shrank away, but they weren't coming at me after all. The hands grasped the trunk of the tree, heaved it up and with a massive thrust pushed it to one side. A shower of debris and dirt, released by the violent movement, fell onto my face and in my eyes. I shut them again in pain.

There were footsteps now. For one awful moment I understood the terror of the newly-blind, the utter helplessness of not being able to see what threatens. But I couldn't open them. Couldn't. The pain was too great.

Then a deluge of water hit my face with such force that my eyes jerked open involuntarily. The first thing I saw was a large, deeply tanned face surrounded by a mass of tangled black hair. The eyes staring out of the face were also large and very dark brown, almost black. And they were hard, unbearably hard, gleaming chunks of coal spitting sparks at me. I flinched as much from their aggression as from the pain in my own eyes.

'It's all right,' he said shortly. His mouth was hard, too, and the severe planes of his face. His cheekbones made me think of the rocky ledges in the cliff. Oh, he was part of this landscape all right. Born to it. Carved from its own stone.

'It's all right,' he repeated, his voice authoritative and utterly unkind. 'You're not hurt. Just a few scratches.'

I glared up at him, anger overcoming my fear. 'How do *you* know I'm all right?'

'The tree's only a first thinning,' he said abruptly. 'Be grateful it wasn't bigger.'

I pushed myself up into a sitting position, wincing with pain. '*I* should be grateful? *You'll* be grateful if I don't sue! There are regulations about this kind of thing, you know!'

'Oh Lord, one of those,' he muttered over his shoulder.

Behind him I could see the other man, older, with reddish hair also untidy but grizzled with grey. His face seemed a little less unyielding than the younger man's, but I was too furious to notice much more.

'Yes, one of those,' I retorted. 'One of those despicable townies who know their rights and intend to use them! One of those inconvenient people who know the regulations!'

He had been crouched over me. Now he stood up and gave me a hostile stare. 'I'm well aware of the regulations. I'm also aware that you're trespassing.'

I stood up, too. I wasn't going to let him look down on me, literally, damn the pain. 'Trespass is neither a criminal nor a civil offence,' I said coldly.

'Neither is thinning trees.'

'Plonking them on passers-by is.'

'Give me strength,' he muttered again over his shoulder. Then, facing me, 'I did not "plonk" it on you,' he said through clenched teeth.

'Property owners are legally liable for any damage to people who injure themselves on their property, trespass or no. Negligence. You've heard of negligence?'

'I yelled a warning,' he said stiffly.

'Too late.'

'What the hell do you expect me to do?' he exploded. 'Post

31

a ring of sentries with trumpets around each tree before I fell it?'

I tried to make my own eyes as hard as his. I put my hands on my hips and leaned forward aggressively. 'You *could* apologise.'

He leaned forward in mockery. 'You *could* apologise for trespassing.'

We stood for what seemed a long time in silent confrontation. Above us, a pair of robins chittered at each other as if mocking us both. He was a tall man, and big in every way. Face and body both would have seemed heavy if they weren't so obviously sheer muscle. He must have gone into forestry in childhood, like miners' sons sent to their fathers' pits to become hardened before their time. I tried to judge his age. Forty? There were thin hard lines etched into what little I could see of his forehead beneath the mass of hair. His skin was coarse, too, almost leathery, long years spent in hard outdoor labour. One or two strands of silver glinted in his hair.

And then the inevitable happened. As I scrutinised his appearance, waiting for him to give way, I realised that he was likewise scrutinising mine. And with a shock of humiliation, I knew what he saw. The falling tree had pulled apart my crown of plaits and the water had plastered loose strands of it over my face. My face was streaked with sodden swathes of dirt, my clothes were covered with debris. I brushed ineffectually at some twigs, then tried to wipe my face with one sleeve of my shirt. The sleeve was dirty, smudging my face even more.

And then the final humiliation: I saw the corners of his mouth begin to rise. I froze. Then I gathered myself into one last attempt at dignity. 'Very well,' I said, 'if you're not prepared to apologise, perhaps your employer will. I'll be in touch with Mr Farleton shortly.' A bluff, of course – no way would I expose myself to his employer as well. I gave a curt nod and turned to go, stumbling over the fallen tree.

'Footpath's that way,' the forester pointed.

I wheeled round. 'I'll walk where I please.'

He shrugged. 'Suit yourself.' He bent over to pick up his hard hat. 'Just don't expect us to come looking for you when you get lost.' He rammed the hat onto his head and walked over to where the other man leaned against a tree.

I hesitated, then stormed off in the direction of the footpath. Within seconds I was out of sight of them both. Within minutes I was lost. The sun, which might have given me a clue, had clouded over, and it was beginning to rain. I stopped to think what to do. Then I heard the voices resume, closer to me than I would have expected.

'Davey, Davey,' said the voice with the slight Irish accent. 'You've the tact of a rhinoceros. Would it have killed you to make just a wee little apology to the lass?'

'What for?' said the forester's voice.

'It makes life that bit pleasanter for us all to be on goodday-to-you terms with our neighbours,' said the Irishman.

'I don't want to be on any terms with Yuppyville,' said the forester.

'She's not Yuppyville. That was Charlotte Venables – she that trounced us at the auction.'

I caught my breath. There was a pause from the two men as well. Then the forester's voice said incredulously, '*Her?*'

'The same,' said the Irishman. 'As you'd have found out if you'd taken the trouble to ask.'

'*Her?*' the forester repeated. '*Farming Cappelrigg?*'

'Right first time. And she'll have tough enough a time of it without a myrmidon like you giving her hell every time she sets a dainty foot off the public.'

The forester muttered something I couldn't hear, which was probably just as well. Then there was a pause, after which his voice continued, sounding oddly serious and not at all sarcastic:

'That's real land she's playing with, Brendan.'

'*Mea culpa,* Davey. I should have bid higher.'

'It's not your fault,' said the forester. 'You were given a ceiling and you stuck to it.'

I thought back to the auction. I'd taken a seat near the front and hadn't seen the people who had bid against me. It hadn't even occurred to me until now that there must have been locals who wanted that farm, perhaps wanted it very badly.

'No, you did right to stop,' the younger forester continued.

'The land isn't worth what she paid for it. And she wouldn't have dropped out at the next bid, or the next. I know that type – she would have pushed it right up to Mayfair prices.'

'Can't you forgive and forget, Davey? The deed's done, the land's hers. Why not let bygones be bygones and all that? She seems a decent enough girl.'

The younger forester snorted.

It was raining harder now. I wanted to leave, but if I moved, the underbrush would give away my presence. The first humiliation was bad enough without being caught spying as well.

The Irishman was raising his voice. 'For God's sake, boy, unbend a little! Pride's got a place and all, sure enough, but not when it works against the very thing that matters most to you.'

'Could we finish thinning these birches?' said the younger forester.

'That's it – change the subject. You've got a great way with the deaf ear, and the stubbornness you've got on you would make a mule look saintly. Why it is we put up with you the good Lord only knows.'

And then, mercifully, the whine of a chainsaw. The younger man had clearly started it up to end the argument.

Under its hideous noise, I crept away at last.

*   *   *

I stumbled through the forest looking for the way home, burning more with shame than with the few scratches from the fallen tree. The rain was waking me up and making me see the whole awful scene in a new perspective. Who *was* that harridan who had screamed abuse at the forester? If that was the new me, I'd better sell up and go straight back to London. Of course the forester was a boor, of course everything I'd said about liability was true. But that wasn't the point. Of all things, I detested self-righteousness most. I had oozed self-righteousness. And childishness. Was that it? Did stripping my life and starting at the beginning mean becoming a child again?

By the time I got home it was raining hard. I regarded it as divine retribution.

I spent the rest of the afternoon being aggressively practical. Lighting the Aga. A bath. Unpacking. Cleaning. Eating my first meal at Cappelrigg: a sandwich and a cup of tea.

In the evening I lit the living-room fire to air the house. With the fire crackling on one side and the rain hissing down past the windows on two others, I felt enclosed within the elements. There'd been rain enough in London, but somehow this was different. Up here on the exposed plateau, these things grew in scale. The sky, too, felt higher, larger, uninterrupted by buildings, while the earth stretched away endlessly to dimly seen horizons.

Earth, air, fire, water. The four elements. One could hardly get more basic than that.

I finished unpacking my books and arranging them in the bookcases. In the last box were some mythology books I'd forgotten I had. Two of them were from the same series and had similar cover illustrations: one of a Viking god, one of a Celtic hero. For one unnerving moment, as I lifted them from their box, I saw two other faces instead: Richard Staveley and the forester. I had to blink several times before the faces turned back into anonymous cover illustrations.

I poured myself a whisky and took the books to the sofa for a closer look. I remembered the last time I'd seen Richard, glowing golden against the sundrenched landscape. A Viking god might well have looked like that, minus the scar down his cheek. And the forester, his dark head looming down at me, his tangle of black hair merging with the birch leaves in a kind of wreath, his eyes a primeval black. It was, I realised in retrospect, an extremely handsome face, heavy with the dark secret strength of the Celts.

That he was a Celt I was sure, just as I was sure that Richard had descended from the Vikings who had driven the Celts further and further west. The history of Britain portrayed in two men. I could picture the forester ranging restlessly across the steep darkly-treed slopes of Wales, while Richard belonged to the open space of the lowlands and the sea where the sun could reflect its own. Broody, too, the Celts. And short-tempered.

No, I didn't want to think of the forester. With luck his temper would soon get him sacked. I wished him ill. I wished never again to encounter that concentrated knot of dark angry energy.

I banked up the fire and went to bed.

My bedroom was a big airy room over the kitchen, facing north, as did all the upstairs rooms, with the corridor running along the south side of the house. It was eleven o'clock. I was tired but not sleepy, which didn't bode well. It still wasn't quite dark outside, and wouldn't be tonight. The strange half-light of Midsummer's Eve streamed in through the big windows. Far off to the left I could see pale golden patches which must be the windows of Graegarth, soft and friendly in the floating blue of the incomplete night. To the right loomed the forest, black.

I was glad to have no curtains. I didn't want to shut myself off from the magical landscape outside. The rain had diminished to a drizzle. I opened the windows. A damp acrid green scent floated in from my grove of trees. It took a while to reach me because the air was so still, the drizzle scarcely moving, a thin hazy veil suspended outside in lieu of a curtain. Smiling, I turned off the light and went to bed.

Clean sheets, clean air, a life swept clean of all but the basics. Bliss. None the less, I lay awake for some time as, one by one, strange sounds crept in to fill the silence: a creak here, a drip there, an unplaceable little scuffling noise. It was difficult not to feel anxious, my first night in my new house. I had sole responsibility for the place now. Was that drip a water pipe needing attention or just the plop of a raindrop on a leaf outside? Was that creak just an old oak beam settling an unmeasurable fraction further? Had I stoked the Aga enough to keep it in for the night? Had I remembered to put up the fireguard in the living room? (I nipped downstairs for a look. I had.) Somewhere far away a lamb, now too big to need its mother, cried plaintively for her regardless. I waited for the gruff answer of the disgruntled ewe and listened as the distance between the two noises diminished and finally ceased.

6

Who ever catches the moment between wakefulness and sleep? I didn't. All I know was that some time in the night the landscape outside slid into the landscape of dream. I was back in the City, back at my office, fiddling with the computer in an effort to make it divulge some vital piece of information. The dream was extremely realistic, right down to the clothes: one of my sharp-edged black suits with white touches; then an outrageously huge multi-coloured scarf and equally outrageous earrings. Effie, who had toyed with the idea of becoming a psychologist before deciding to furnish houses rather than strip minds, had pointed out that my appearance sent out contradictory messages. The hard suit said *You'd better take me seriously, chum*, while my quaint hair said *I'm just a sweet old-fashioned girl*. In between, the scarf and earrings signalled unpredictability – 'the gypsy in your soul,' she said. I didn't need Effie to tell me. My appearance, like my 'cautious boldness' tactic, was designed to back things all ways. It was my way of surviving in what I now saw as an extremely hostile environment, one I should never have gone into in the first place.

The dream continued, my efforts becoming increasingly frustrated until finally I jabbed a key so violently that the whole office exploded, myself with it, and I was suddenly on the trading floor dressed only in a slip. Nobody seemed to notice. Trading went on as usual while I scuttled about looking for shelter among the human tree-trunks. Which suddenly turned into real tree-trunks. I was in a forest, now completely naked but unconcerned. Eve, I suppose, unaware that I should be searching out a fig leaf. And the forest was certainly Eden, as unrealistic as the previous part of the dream had been real. My dream forest defied all laws of nature. The trees, every sort imaginable, displayed their tender springtime leaves, full summer clothes, brilliant autumn colours and sculptured winter silhouettes all at the same time, in the way only dreams and madmen know.

And suddenly, there was Adam, also naked, smiling at me from a wreath of foliage which merged with his curly black hair so effectively that it was impossible to tell what was hair and what was leaf. He opened his arms. I floated into them. We made love. This, too, was extremely realistic, except that the intensity was greater than I'd ever experienced in real life. Above us, birds twittered and a jolly owl screeched with vicarious pleasure.

Gradually, however, the owl's screech dominated and I became aware that I was waking up. I embraced all the more passionately my Adam, desperate to maintain the dream's magic.

Futile. I woke up, furious, in the spartan bedroom of Cappelrigg Farm and stared straight at my dream owl outlined against the open window. *Ke . . .wick!* I was too angry to be startled, let alone afraid. I lay quite still while my eyes carved out the bird's shape from the sky behind. *Ke . . . wick!* A female, yelling for her mate, waiting for his answering hoot. Something like this had happened only once before, in Sussex, when a barely-fledged owlet had mistaken my windowsill for a branch and perched, waiting for food. It was as magical as the dream itself but real, utterly real. I breathed as shallowly as I could, anxious not to disturb the bird. I could see only her outline, but the memory of countless photographs etched in the ancient face with its mixture of calm and cruelty softened by the delicate face feathers. Welcome home, I thought. And my first night, too.

Finally a distant *Who . . . ooo . . . ooo* wavered through the still air. The owl turned her head sharply, then lifted off and with a powerful flap flew into the night. Where she'd been I could see the faintest of auras. The aura, reddish in colour, persisted long after the bird had gone. Puzzled, I got out of bed and padded barefoot to the window.

It was, the clock said, two o'clock, as dark as this transitional night would ever be. Through a gap in the motionless trees, the aura led my eyes up to the top of the moor. It was a fire, too distant for the flames to show, but unmistakable.

Midsummer's Eve. I remembered Richard's talk about the Druids. The fire was located just about where the flat table he'd mentioned would be. There could be no other explanation. I envisaged a bunch of middle-aged children prancing around the fire and felt irritated. Who needed these tired reminders of ancient ways when the real thing perched on the windowsill?

I was about to return to bed when another sound caught my attention, one of the unidentifiable scratchy noises that I'd heard earlier. I was so awake now that I might as well investigate. I threw my dressing-gown over my pyjamas, climbed into my wellies and went outside.

The drizzle had stopped, leaving a squeaky-clean scent. I breathed it in drunkenly and went to the back of the house. The noise grew louder, then stopped. Suddenly a shape shot across my vision at ground level. I just had time to identify it as a cat before it disappeared round the side of the house. I followed it. There, crouched in the doorway of the barn, was the cat: black, with a crooked white patch on its face. Presumably the same cat Effie had nearly run over the day we first saw Cappelrigg. Mrs Jowett must have abandoned it. I crouched into a harmless position and called to the cat. It shrank further into the shadows and disappeared, no doubt half wild by now.

I went into the house and returned with a saucerful of milk, setting it just outside the porch. Then I went back to bed. This time I was both tired and sleepy. I was out within minutes, but not before a brief rerun of my dream flitted across the screen behind my eyes and I realised with a shock who Adam had been.

*   *   *

The next morning the milk was gone. Near the saucer was a faint human footprint. There were more prints – still faint – beside the house, and the grass in the grove looked trampled.

I didn't have time to investigate further. These were hectic days. Mrs Jowett had stripped the farm as thoroughly as I had stripped my life. I had to refurnish it from scratch, taking care to accumulate only the essentials. I made lists ('v. urgent. urgentish. possibles?'), rushed back and forth between Cappelrigg and Kirkby Langham, buying up the basics. I had the phone reconnected. I sold some shares, bought a brand new Land-Rover. On one trip to Kirkby I noticed, in the estate agent's window, blurbs for several farm dispersal sales coming up in July and August. I scribbled down the dates.

I put a For Sale in the local paper for my car. In the same paper a group of contract shearers offered their services. I arranged for them to come, relieved that I wouldn't have to ask Richard's advice. This was my life I was rebuilding, I had to do it myself, alone.

None the less, not long after the shearers arrived, Richard drove up and came round to the pens behind the barn. Immediately everything shrank. The shearers became midgets fussing with toy sheep while I, tiny Tinkerbell, groped with shears suddenly grown huge and clumsy in my miniature hands. Richard loomed above us, a golden giant emanating vitality.

'Bush telegraph,' he explained before I had time to ask.

I nodded to hide my confusion: pleasure at seeing him, embarrassment at having him see my first attempt at shearing in many years. He reached for my shears. I drew back. 'Go play with your own sheep,' I scolded.

He laughed, the sound bouncing off the back of the barn and filling the air. The fretful baas of the sheep diminished to a piping chorus beneath the recitative that followed: instructions on what I was doing wrong.

'Please,' I said. 'I have to re-learn this my own way.'

'Pretty hard on the sheep,' he said.

'They're tough.'

'So are you.'

The shearers were enjoying the performance. I handed my shears to one of them and led Richard round to the front where we could talk privately. 'It really is kind of you to come,' I said, 'and I do appreciate it. But I'm a bit rusty at this kind of thing, and I'd rather make my own mistakes. You do understand?'

He shrugged. 'Suit yourself.'

I hadn't expected someone so confident as Richard to

have such a thin skin. I smiled. 'I mustn't lose face with the shearers, don't you see?'

This he did see. With a graceful gesture, he shepherded me back to the pens. 'I'll keep my distance,' he promised.

He did, joining the other shearers instead and joking with them – they seemed to know and like him. By midday I felt competent enough to abandon the shearing and join the man who was bundling up the fleeces. Within minutes he had melted away and Richard was in his place, standing beside me. 'Please, Miss?' he said, mimicking the tone of a repentant schoolboy.

'Don't put me in roles that don't suit,' I said, but I couldn't help smiling.

He smiled, too, a great sunny smile which swept away the last vestiges of tension. 'All right.' He watched as I rolled and secured the dirty fleece in record time. 'Impressive,' he said.

'It's the bit I used to do when I was a child,' I explained. 'Dad was determined that I shouldn't become one of the idle rich. I did some shearing, too, but the sheep up here are different. The wrong size and shape somehow – they feel different under the hand.'

'Bred for the moor,' he said. His own hands had vanished in the matted wool of the next fleece. 'Tough. Like the people.'

I didn't want to defend my qualifications as a hill farmer. 'There was a bonfire up there on Midsummer's Eve,' I said instead.

No reaction at all. He finished the fleece and tossed it into the rapidly filling wagon.

'Did you see it? The bonfire?' I persisted.

'No.'

'Richard, *is* there a group of locals playing Druid?'

We were waiting for the next fleeces. The midday sun was beating down, cooking our bare arms. He looked straight at the sun before replying. 'There could be. Old Mrs Farleton started up a craze for that kind of thing – she was the one who discovered the stone circle.'

'How can you "discover" a stone circle? Surely it's obvious?'

'This one wasn't. The stones were displaced, some of them almost buried. Mrs Farleton fancied herself an archaeologist, she got the estate workers onto it. They heaved the stones back into place, and presto! – our very own ancient temple. It caused a bit of a stir at the time – not much else to think about, winter evenings.'

'When was that?'

'A long time back – twenty-five years, maybe more.'

He still hadn't answered my question. 'But you must know if there are "Druids" playing around there now?' I persisted.

He shrugged. Just then two more fleeces arrived. We each took one. As we started to push the bulky things into shape, his bare forearm lightly grazed mine – I don't think it was accidental – and a charge of electricity shot through my body. I knew I should pull back from the source, but I couldn't. Instead, I stood quite still, luxuriating in the sensation. The sheep pens were suddenly silent. Even the sheep seemed poised for something.

Then, 'Lunch!' called one of the shearers.

I withdrew my arm with some relief.

7

I dressed with as much care for my first farm dispersal sale as I did for a day in the City, though the costume was rather different: an old shirt, pale blue, one size too big, with open collar and sleeves rolled up to the elbow; an equally old and well-worn pair of brown twill trousers which, like the shirt, had been expensive when new; heavy black no-nonsense farm wellies. Casual wealth casually ignored: I am rich enough to know what's what, but I don't throw my money around, said my costume.

I knew this trick from my childhood. The truly rich, the old-money rich, were the most shabbily dressed landowners in the county. I also knew that the impression I made today was crucial to my entire future in Langhamdale. This was my first public appearance, so to speak, among my new colleagues.

The field marked off as a temporary car park was already full of Land-Rovers when I arrived. I parked my own, then strolled casually to the next field, marked off as a temporary saleroom. In it, a lifetime's accumulation of farm equipment was spread out for display.

I could feel the excitement as I approached the edge of the crowd. Greenbank was Farleton Estate's biggest low-land farm, just a few miles from Kirkby Langham. The tenant who was retiring, a Mr Somerthwaite, had a lot to sell. He was, according to Richard, a popular farmer. Everyone would want to give him a good send-off, bid the prices up to give him a good chunk of cash to begin his retirement.

These farm dispersal sales had been a feature of my child-hood, too, and I knew how they worked. It was like taking up a collection for a leaving-present, except that those who donated also got something in return: a baler, an electric fence unit, one of those Honda ATVs for shepherding that were all the rage but nobody wanted to buy new.

It was a ritual, the dispersal sale, as potent as any from ancient times. Here the locals gathered to renew old acquaintances and show solidarity. It was a trap for the unwary newcomer. More than once I'd stood beside my father as he bid up the price of something he had no intention of buying, tricking some outsider into paying more than the thing was worth. I would have to be careful today. It wasn't the money so much as the pride. If I lost face today, the stigma would stay with me for years.

As I squeezed through a cluster of people at the edge, I listened to a pair of large red-faced women, obviously farmers' wives:

'Keeping well, Molly?'

'Not so bad. Yourself?'

'Fit enough. Looking to buy?'

'Depends on price. Who's the new one?'

'Tenant? Over Wharfedale way, says Jim. Nowt else about him, though. Nobody knows a thing. Tight as a fish's ass, them Farletons, words were muck the land'ud be right clemmed.'

The woman roared at her own joke.

The field looked like a sculpture park, all the equipment cleaned up and displayed against the green grass. A brisk wind kept the flies at bay and hurled a succession of black clouds and white clouds across the sky for the sun's hide and seek game. Corresponding swathes of black shadow swept across the fields. One minute the stage set for the sale was spotlighted by a triumphant sun, the next minute the lights went out, plunging the crowd into semi-dark. It gave an extra sense of drama to the event.

Several people were grouped round a display of small tools. Off-comed'uns, obviously, trying hard to look as if they belonged. They were casually dressed, too, but in the wrong way. Their clothes were new, stylish, obviously bought at expensive 'country clothes' shops. I felt rather sorry for them but couldn't afford to be friendly.

I walked past and collected a lot sheet. I was so intent on reading it that I failed to notice Richard's approach until a shadow suddenly blotted out the sun, just as on that day at the Golden Oak. I looked up, startled, to see his crinkly blue eyes smiling at me and a woman by his side. He introduced us.

'Charlotte Venables. My sister, Jean.'

I wouldn't have guessed they were related. She was short and slightly plump, with a halo of light brown hair, cut short and curly, surrounding a lightly tanned face. Her eyes were light brown, too, and would have been pretty if it weren't for the tension around them. They were old eyes in an otherwise young face. She couldn't have been more than twenty-five.

I smiled warmly and put out my hand. 'It's lovely to meet you at last!' I laughed. 'It's ridiculous, isn't it? Nearest neighbours and we don't meet each other for what, four weeks?'

Her own hand was limp and her voice pale as she said, 'Yes. No garden fence.'

'Right,' I said, 'and somehow it doesn't seem good enough just to turn up and say "Hi, I'm your new neighbour," without some proper excuse. I thought about the old cup of sugar, but it seemed a bit feeble.'

She laughed a little at this, but it was the pale laugh of a ghost. What was wrong? I tried to remember what Richard had told me about her. Not much. Just that the two of them had worked Graegarth together ever since their father had died some two years ago. Was that it? Grieving still for her father? She was at least fifteen years younger than Richard. A late child, very probably a mistake. Resented by her mother and resenting everyone else in turn?

We started walking round the equipment. There was a chain harrow, cleaned up and gleaming against the intense green grass. 'Oh, look!' I exclaimed. 'Isn't it gorgeous? I've always loved harrows. When I was a child, Dad told me they were giants' chain-mail. I believed him, too.' I stooped down to inspect it. 'It's in good nick. I must bid for it.' I stood up again and smiled at Jean.

A pale winter smile barely illuminated her face.

I could feel my own resentment rising. For heaven's sake, I was trying – couldn't she make a little effort, too? It occurred to me that she might be jealous. Living in such isolation at Graegarth, she might be unusually close to her brother, wary of anyone stealing his affection. I made another attempt. 'Richard tells me you're the one who does most of the work with the animals.'

'I hate machinery,' she said suddenly.

The statement, so quiet and yet vehement, was startling.

'Jean, how about getting us a lot sheet?' said Richard.

The girl went off abruptly. As soon as she was out of hearing, Richard explained, 'John Jowett's death rather upset her. She hasn't driven a tractor since.'

'Oh, I see.' But I didn't. Nor did I have time to ask more. Jean returned and handed the lot sheet to her brother. 'Auctioneer's just come,' she said in her lifeless voice.

A burst of laughter rose as the auctioneer came into view, his arrival signalled by a volley of practised jokes. He was the same one who'd sold me Cappelrigg Farm, the main agricultural auctioneer for Langhamdale. Knowing all his well-worn jokes was no doubt part of being a farmer here, one of the things that made you an insider.

Then I froze. Two other men were walking past: the foresters from Farleton Estate. Of all people, the two I least wanted to see. I slipped away quietly on the pretext of inspecting a sheep rack. From behind it I watched them. So did everyone else. The younger one in particular was stared at intently.

The interest wasn't mutual. He concentrated on his friend or the ground, not even glancing at the crowd of people watching him. A big surly bear, I thought. Even the hair: a great mass of tangled black curls far too long for fashion. Did he ever use a comb? Probably not. He seemed as indifferent about his own appearance as he was of the crowd. His trousers were frayed, his shirt thin at the elbows.

The men passed, heading for the auctioneer's van, a mobile office that had no doubt accompanied him to every farm dispersal sale for many years. In front of it stood the auctioneer, his assistant and Mr Somerthwaite. Mrs Somerthwaite would be busy in the kitchen with the neighbouring farmers' wives, cutting hundreds of sandwiches and fuelling the tea urn. Mr Somerthwaite greeted the two men with pleasure and, strangely enough, respect. It all seemed very odd, but it was none of my concern. I was here to buy some equipment.

I strolled back from behind the sheep rack and told Richard and Jean that I wanted a closer look at some things before the sale began. I was glad to get away from Jean. She, too, was none of my concern. I didn't want to get involved in whatever it was that was troubling her. None the less, when the tide of people began to surge towards the van, I found myself once again beside them.

Black clouds and white clouds sped across the slatey sky. A black one paused, released a shower of rain, then scuttled away, leaving the sun to glitter off the last drops and hint at a rainbow. The auctioneer raised a threatening fist skyward. A ripple of laughter. Then a moment of intense silence before the auctioneer again raised his hand, this time in a sort of Papal blessing.

'Friends,' he began.

'Romans,' came a voice from the back.

Ritual laughter from the crowd. The auctioneer feigned hurt surprise, though it was obviously a part of his act.

'Countrymen,' a third voice contributed.

More laughter. More hurt surprise. A long pause. Then, 'As I was saying . . .'

The sale had begun.

*   *   *

'. . . Lot Seventeen. Nineteen eighty-five Massey-Ferguson 290 tractor, two-wheel drive, eight speed, ground drive, complete with MF 85 power loader, bucket and fork . . .' The auctioneer's incantation unfolded itself in layers of extravagant praise.

'That's the one,' I whispered to Richard.

' . . . virtually runs itself. The lucky buyer of this little beauty can retire for the day to the Golden Oak, leaving this magnificent machine to . . .'

'At least I think it's the one.' I consulted my lot sheet.

'So! Who'll start me off on this veritable Hercules of a tractor for your Augean shippon?'

Silence.

'Shy? Well then, how about fifty thousand? Cheap at the price.'

A concerted hoot of laughter.

'*Too* cheap?'

The hoot became a roar.

The auctioneer raised his hand. 'What? Oh, I see. The milk cheque hasn't come through yet. Feeling a little pinched, are we? Well then, forty-five thousand? Come on, raid the kiddies' piggy bank.'

Finally he capitulated and the bidding began in earnest. I put in a first bid, and then, a little hesitantly, a second.

Suddenly there was a flurry of activity and, to my utter horror, the older of the two foresters stood before me.

'Don't go any higher!' he was saying in his faint Irish accent.

I looked at him in astonishment.

'It's a dud,' he rushed on. 'It's John Jowett's tractor. Somerthwaite bought it cheap because nobody else would touch it after the – '

'I'm not superstitious, Mr . . .'

'Never mind names, just don't bid! Let it be!'

At that moment, somebody topped my second bid. I hesitated. Then, rather aggressively, I began to raise my arm to catch the auctioneer's attention.

The Irishman grabbed my arm down. 'For the love of God, woman, will you listen?'

I wrenched my arm free and spun round to face him. 'No, I will not listen! I had a good look at that tractor. There's nothing wrong with it and I want it!'

' . . . once . . .' the auctioneer's voice sailed over the crowd. He was looking at me. Richard joined in the argument, taking my side and making threatening gestures at the Irishman.

' . . . twice . . .' The auctioneer's voice was louder, a direct challenge to me.

I took a step forward and raised my arm. The Irishman grabbed it. I jerked my arm away and in a blind rage tried to hit him with it. He grabbed it before it could land.

Just then the younger forester arrived, and at the same moment the auctioneer's voice sang out: 'Sold! Mr Wadeson, you're a lucky man!'

I turned the full voltage of my rage on the younger man,

jerking my arm free at last. 'There! I hope you're satisfied, both of you! Mr Wadeson or whatever is one of your men, right? Mr Farleton put you up to this, didn't he? You deliberately – '

'Lady, will you listen – ' the Irishman began.

I cut him off with a violent gesture. 'Listen to what? Some sob story about poor Mr Farleton struggling to keep the stately home afloat? How desperately he needs a fifth or sixth or seventh tractor? Sure, *I'm* just a rich Londoner, *I* can afford to go out and buy a new one! I needed that tractor, you bastards!'

The younger man looked into space, as if the whole scene had nothing to do with him. The Irishman persisted:

'Lady, it was *you* I was thinking of, if you'll just – '

'Great! Thanks a bunch! In future will you kindly leave *me* to think about me?'

We stood frozen in a tableau, glaring at each other. Then, 'Leave it, Brendan,' said the younger man. 'Let's go.'

They left.

'Well, well,' Richard said admiringly, 'you do have spirit.'

I scarcely heard him. I was still shaking with rage. If I could have pressed the button to release an atomic bomb on that field, I would have done it. Some moments passed before the black cloud of my anger cleared and showed someone standing right in front of me, a strange and – it seemed to me – slightly malevolent little smile on her old-young face. Jean.

'You've met them before?' she was asking.

'Once,' I said distractedly. 'In the forest. They were rude then, too.'

'Maybe,' said Jean, her smile increasing a fraction. 'But they're not estate workers, you know.'

'So?' I said. I didn't know what she was getting at and didn't care.

'Not that it matters, but you ought to know.'

'All right,' I said impatiently. 'So who are they?'

The smile broadened. 'The older one is Brendan Iveson. He's the estate manager. He runs the whole of Farleton Estate.'

A chill began to creep up into my body. 'I see,' I said, trying to sound indifferent. 'And the other one?'

The smile was now unmistakably malevolent. 'That's David Farleton,' said Jean. 'You know – the squire.'

The chill was an iceberg now, rushing into my face and draining it of life. I felt as prematurely old as Jean looked. 'I see,' I said, with utmost control. 'Thank you for telling me.' I forced a smile onto my own face. 'Will you both excuse me? I'd like to have another look at that harrow.'

As soon as they were out of sight, I hurried to my Land-Rover and left.

8

Once again I fled a scene of humiliation. The fact that this time my anger was justified didn't help much. What embarrassed me was that twice David Farleton and his manager had seen me in a rage, out of control. Not myself. Perhaps I *had* been myself in London after all. Certainly I'd been in control of my life there. Here, in this huge rough landscape, other forces seemed increasingly to take control of me.

I felt increasingly alone, too. In stripping my life bare, I'd stripped it of friends. That frightened me. Effie was snowed under with work, couldn't get away for a weekend. We talked a lot on the phone, but it wasn't the same. I missed her. I missed all my friends and colleagues, though London itself seemed pale and shrunken as Keldreth swept across the canvas of my mind in big bold swathes of colour. Everything about the landscape seemed to be writ large, including the emotions it generated in me.

But, as the days passed, both anger and humiliation diminished. In any case, another busy period was upon me: the first dipping of the season. This time I worked alone – Richard didn't turn up. The jungle telegraph must have short-circuited and I was too proud to ask for help. It went surprisingly well none the less. It took a long time, of course, working on my own, and it was wet, messy hard labour. I didn't mind. In compensation for my loneliness, I was getting to know my sheep. Well, it's company of a sort, I suppose.

There was other company, too. A sheepdog. I bought him from a farmer who assured me Moss was the quietest dog he'd ever had. That clinched it. Ours had never been a doggy family – we liked our peace and quiet too much. One or two notorious farmers in Sussex had signalled their bad management with noisy dogs. The sound carried a long way and annoyed us. A well-cared-for dog was a quiet dog.

We hadn't needed a dog at all in Sussex, with no unfenced upland spaces scattering the sheep for miles. Our sheep were always in fields, it was easier to gather them by shaking a half-filled bag of sheepnuts. One of my earliest memories is an ocean of woolly backs converging on me at high speed as I shook the bag. Carrot rather than stick. But along with Cappelrigg I'd bought the sheep gaits which entitled me to graze a certain amount of stock on the open moor. I'd lose face with local farmers if I didn't use it. There was nothing for it but a dog.

Moss soon showed himself to be a treasure. He was young enough to run like hell, old enough to have dignity. In fact, he was a bit of an aristocrat – too contemptuous of the sheep to harry them with noise or nips at their heels. Once, too proud to bark at a maverick, he allowed her to wander some distance while he sat there exuding will-power. His face registered astonishment when he realised his tactic had failed and he had to run and round her up again.

It was usual to take sheep to the moor soon after dipping. There they would spend the rest of the summer, giving the fields a chance to rest and grow. But I kept putting it off. My farming background had adapted well enough to most circumstances here, but the moor was outside my experience. All that space, unfenced. I was terrified of letting my sheep loose on it. Would I ever be able to round them up again? Only one small dog stood between me and anarchy.

Finally, after spending a whole fortnight just practising with Moss, I decided it was time. On a beautiful morning in mid-August we set off. I kept to the back and left Moss to trot a continuous crescent behind his four-legged rugs, keeping them in a nice tight group. At last we reached the final dry-stone wall. On this side, the tidy parcelled pattern of farmland; on the other, the unknown. I tried to appear casual as I opened the gate and stood back to let Moss funnel his sheep through. Then I shut the gate again. Goodbye civilisation.

The quality of the land changed instantly. No intricate underground network of drains here, no annual mowing to keep rank grasses and weeds at bay, no land roller to keep it smooth. We crossed the rough bumpy strip of no man's

52

land and soon reached the bottom of the cliff. Someone, centuries ago, had laboriously carved a narrow green track up the side, just wide enough to take a peat cart, I suppose. It looked dreadfully precarious, the sort of track used for those glossy photos of cars that have brains as well as beauty and will stand you in good stead should you find yourself up a mountain track. The sheep seemed unconcerned, while I looked more and more nervously over the edge the higher we climbed.

And then the top and over the top. I gasped aloud, as mile upon mile of glorious mauve carpet unrolled itself before me, disappearing at last into the sky itself. The North York Moors, unbearably grand, the beauty so intense that my eyes blurred with awe. The meaning of life? The moor *was* its own meaning. I had seen moors before, of course, driven across them en route to some country weekend or other. But never had any of it seemed so wild and magnificent as this.

Moss took it in his stride, as did the sheep. I suppose it was their land. Certainly it wasn't mine, not for humans. I felt like an insect, no more significant than the ones churring away unseen in the heather beneath my feet. Or a giant, intrusively outlined so sharply against the sky. Insect or giant, but not human.

As I walked behind my flock, the empty moor began to fill with sound. Grouse shot up from beneath the sheeps' hooves and flew off low over the heather, leaving behind their weird laughter. The sheep baa-ed softly, just keeping in touch. The insects chattered away. Somewhere the gurgle of an underground stream briefly came to surface. And always, above it all, the curlews. The moor was teeming with life.

I called Moss to me and we stood together as the sheep, released from their keeper, began to meander away from each other and from us, spreading themselves across the heather in search of grazing. So grand. So peaceful. The City had never seemed more remote. I listened to the tiny insects and thought of my busy colleagues scurrying across the grey landscape of London.

Then an air force training jet appeared from nowhere and roared overhead. Well, even Eden had its serpent.

About half a mile ahead loomed the flat raised table

Richard had mentioned. I made my way towards it, Moss beside me. It was rough walking. My wellies kept slipping off the hummocks and into tiny black peat channels that twisted round the heather clumps. Here and there were black craters where peat had been extracted. There were boulders, too, half buried in the ground at odd angles and covered with lichens.

The edge of the table was a scree. I scrambled up it, Moss following. At the top was another surprise. The table, about half a mile in diameter, was truly flat. It was covered with a mixture of short grass and clumps of heather that had never been burnt off and so had grown into bushes. The handful of sheep who had been cropping the grass leapt away when they saw us. Moss watched them disdainfully, knowing they weren't our sheep and were therefore unimportant.

In the centre were the standing stones, about a dozen, widely spaced. They were whitish grey and had a scrubbed look about them. They were so evenly spaced and standing so vertically, like soldiers at attention, that the whole effect was oddly urban. It looked more like a well-maintained ancient monument than a wild moorland site. In lieu of groundsmen, the rain scrubbed the stones and the sheep mowed the grass. All that was missing was the ticket kiosk.

I threaded my way between heather bushes and went through a gap between the stones. A perfect little moorland pond was cradled within the circle, its smooth surface a black mirror refusing to reflect the sky. I suppose the peat beneath soaked up the colour and reflected back its own darkness instead. Around its edge were tall reeds, some of them wading right into the water. The whole effect was so civilised compared to the wild moor around it, rather like a landscape feature deliberately planned. The unnatural neatness of it all was oddly disturbing.

Moss was getting restless. He had been sitting beside me, but suddenly he shot to his feet and barked. The noise shocked me, it was so uncharacteristic. It also annoyed me. 'Moss!' I said, in my most authoritarian voice. He cringed, clamping his mouth shut against the whine that threatened to break through. I don't know if he was more shocked at my harsh voice or at his own loss of composure. In any case, he sulked, glaring fixedly towards one stone. I looked just in time to see a faint flash of a yellowish colour – a sheep, probably, its fleece stained by the peaty water. 'Moss,' I said (conciliatory now), 'You're right. This is a disagreeable place. Let's go.' As I turned, I noticed a large circle of burnt vegetation. Of course. The fire on Midsummer's Eve. So this was where they played at being Druids. Even that was neat.

But when we scrambled down off the table, the moorland magic returned. I didn't want to go back just yet. And so we walked on, in an easterly direction. And because I was curious to see how the forest would look from this height, we veered a little southward, too, bringing us once again to the edge.

We must have gone further east than I thought, for there below me was The Folly.

It was, in its different way, as startling as my first sight of the moor. Certainly the building itself was the most extraordinary I'd ever seen, a crazy jumble of square turrets and round towers, crenellations, eccentric chimneys, strange windows in improbable places. The windows were what puzzled me most. They didn't seem to be arranged in rows. They were scattered at random in a way that suggested that there wasn't any ground floor, first floor or second. Further, they were of different sizes and shapes and periods: tiny leaded casements, elegant sash windows, oriels, windows deeply recessed into Norman arches, gothic arches. There was even one of stained glass, long and narrow, which I doubted had any religious significance.

A pair of extensions were joined to the main building by two enormous covered archways to form a three-sided courtyard at the back. The extensions were just as bizarre. The eastern one appeared to be the former stable block, built to resemble a Greek temple. The other was more a mixture and had probably housed a wash-house, bakehouse and so forth, all of it quaintly medieval.

The only thing that unified this fantasy concoction was the stone from which it was built, the solid grey no-nonsense stone which said I was 'in Yorkshire, lass, and don't you forget it.' The ivy, too, made an attempt at reconciliation, wending its way indiscriminately over each period of architectural history.

The large stretch of ground between the courtyard and the cliff on which I stood was no less strange than the building. The cliff was evidently unstable and had throughout the centuries shed great boulders. These had been incorporated into a wildly romantic artificial wilderness. A waterfall had also been incorporated. This began in a boggy delta near where I stood and gathered itself to tumble in a picturesque series of waterfalls down the cliff and into a turbulent pool fringed with ferns and more boulders. From there it snaked through the tree-decked garden as a stream flowing beneath rustic bridges before disappearing into a cave or grotto. It must have gone underground after that and resurfaced in the centre of the garden where it formed a second pool. This one was placid, an innocent blue mirror smiling up at the sky and playing sweetly with the trailing foliage of a huge weeping-willow beside it.

I remembered the black pool on the moor. The one at the centre of this garden could hardly be more different. The wildness of the landscape below me was, at heart, just play. All the paths seemed deliberately to lead to the peaceful little pool, the centre of the mandala. There was calm, order and serenity here, despite the impish gestures and mock ferocity.

The air force training jet roared overhead again, reminding me how quiet the landscape had been. When it left, the waterfall resumed its crazy little tune. A second sound joined it – very like a horse whinnying from within the former stable block. It seemed improbable – what business would a horse have in this kind of countryside? Improbable but charming, a ghost of former times.

And then a third sound: laughter, gutsy and female. This was no ghost. As I watched, a kaleidoscope of colour burst through an open doorway and twirled across the cobbled courtyard. It was a large and gaudily-dressed woman, as vivid as a parrot or the stained-glass window winking down on her. A moment later a second figure exploded from the same doorway. Even at this height and distance I could see at once it was Brendan Iveson. He hurtled after her, his laughter as loud and lusty as hers. In the centre of the courtyard he caught up with her. His vigorous arm hooked her round the waist and swung her to face him, and he kissed her. She raised her own arms to draw his face more firmly down on hers.

I couldn't believe this was the same man who had so churlishly baulked me at the farm dispersal sale. I couldn't believe this was the 1990s. I was in a time warp. The Folly shimmered, dissolved, then reconstituted itself in a scene from the Middle Ages complete with steward and kitchen wench about to have a roll in the hay. I was right at the edge of the cliff, but I forgot entirely that I was an interloper clearly visible from below. I forgot everything in the bizarre enchantment of the scene.

It was Moss who brought me back to the present with a growl. I looked at him in surprise – what could he object to in the innocent play below? But he wasn't looking at it. He had his back to the scene and was growling at something else. I whirled round and saw Richard standing a few feet behind me.

9

In that first moment of relief on seeing Richard, I remembered Moss's bark by the Druid pool, and remembered too the sense I'd had of half-seeing something yellowish disappear behind one of the standing stones. Richard's hair and beard, brilliantly gold in the overhead sun. He smiled and in a few steps was beside me on the edge of the cliff, looking down at the courtyard. Below, the couple broke their embrace and walked back to the house, laughing and talking loudly. After a final peal of laughter from the woman, they disappeared inside.

Richard's face seemed oddly wistful when he turned to me. 'The place went downhill after the old squire died. It's a commune now.' Then he smiled again. 'But that's before your time – the commune craze.'

'Yes. I've sometimes regretted it – not being around when idealism meant something.'

He gave me a mock reproachful look. 'Strange talk from a City lady.'

'I'm not there anymore,' I reminded him. He looked more than ever like a Viking, with his straight blond helmet of hair and straight strong nose. His features seemed so firm and purposeful, as if anchoring the amusement dancing beneath the surface of his eyes. The laugh lines surrounding them were immensely appealing. It was easy to see why he got on so well with the locals.

Most of them, anyway. We struck out in a westerly direction. Several times he looked back towards The Folly, now disappearing from view. 'You don't much like Iveson, do you?' I said. 'Or Farleton?'

'Not much,' he said cheerfully. 'Neither will you, when you've got Cappelrigg running smoothly and start to get hungry for more land. He's bought up just about everything in Keldreth except our two farms.'

'Bought? I thought it was all part of the estate.'

'It used to be. But when the old squire died, his widow sold some of it to the tenants to pay the death duties. Then when she died, the son sold the family seat down by Kirkby. Farleton Hall. Have you seen it?'

'I think so. Just the entrance. I thought it was a country hotel.'

'It is now. David Farleton sold it to a consortium that turned it into a luxury hotel. Centuries of tradition gone just like that. You can imagine what people thought.'

'I can imagine. Were there any other Farletons left?'

'Just the younger brother, Hugh. Hugh didn't inherit – he had to go off and make his own fortune. David went to Cambridge and got in with an arty crowd. When he came back he had a band of hippies with him. They settled into The Folly. The rest you can see for yourself.' Richard waved an arm towards the forest.

At that moment, a large dark shape rose from its edge. It skimmed the tops of the trees briefly before disappearing again. I thought I glimpsed a forked tail but knew I was wrong. Kites were the only birds with forked tails and there were none in England. 'Not really,' I said.

Richard had been watching the bird so intently he didn't hear.

'No, I don't see for myself,' I explained. 'I thought the forest had always been here.'

'Forest? What, no, not all of it. Only the part nearest The Folly.' He turned his full attention on me again. 'The Folly was the hunting lodge,' he explained. 'But the new squire wasn't interested in hunting. Just trees. He waited for outlying farms to become vacant and then bought up their land for his trees. People didn't much like that either – destroying hill farm land for trees. If it weren't for your place and mine the whole of Keldreth would be one huge forest.'

I couldn't really see why it mattered to him. Unless, of course, he was already hungry for more land and had been thwarted by David Farleton in trying to buy some.

'Is that why he's so disliked?' I asked.

'Partly. And partly,' Richard smiled winningly, 'because David Farleton's a surly bastard.'

I laughed. 'At least you're open about it.'

'Why pretend? Nobody likes Farleton. Neither should you. He was the one who pushed the price of Cappelrigg so high.'

I stopped and stared at him. 'He what?'

'Didn't you know? He was bidding against you. He cost you a lot of money, did David Farleton. Through Iveson, of course. Boss man was away, but he'd left instructions for Iveson to bid high.'

'I see,' I said quietly. And I did. I was remembering the overheard conversation in the forest. I hadn't realised who the men were then. Now it all made sense. So that's why David Farleton was so furious with me. It had nothing to do with trespassing. I had bought an enormous great chunk of land that he wanted. I must have been the first person to get the better of him.

'I was bidding against you, too,' said Richard. 'Did you know that?'

'*What*?'

He nodded. 'I led you a merry chase for a while. But then Iveson went so high I had to drop out.'

He was smiling so good-naturedly, so innocently, that I had to laugh. 'I do like your honesty.'

He shrugged it off. 'Why lie? You'd find out sooner or later.'

Good point. I looked at him with open amusement. 'And your shrewdness,' I added. We set off walking again. 'Well, well, so it was the three of us, was it?' I gave him a penetrating glance. 'Then you must resent me as much as Farleton.'

'What for? You didn't cost me any money.'

'But I cost you the farm.'

'I wouldn't have got it anyway, with Farleton flashing his money around like that.'

'True.'

Moss was trotting sedately ahead of us. I suddenly realised that Richard had no dog with him. 'Have you come to check up on your sheep?' I asked.

He nodded.

'Without a dog?'

Clearly he hadn't expected this. He looked disconcerted for a moment. Then, as if making a conscious decision, he gave in to it. He raised his hands in the classic gesture of surrender and said, 'Caught. To tell you the truth, I just like being up here. It's not something a hill farmer should ever admit.'

'Oh?'

'We're supposed to be at war with the land, wresting our meagre living from the hostile soil and so forth. Also, we're supposed to be too busy to wander round for the hell of it.'

I laughed. 'Then I hope I never become a proper hill farmer. I hope I never fall out of love with this land.'

He moved a little closer and scrutinised my face. 'You're a strange lady, Charlotte.'

'Everyone's strange if you look closely enough,' I said.

'Why did you do it?'

'Do what?'

'Buy Cappelrigg.'

'A whim.'

'Women like you don't do things on a whim.'

'What do you know about women like me?' I said.

'If you mean London women, not much,' he admitted cheerfully.

'I meant, how do you know what kind of a woman I am at all? How does anyone know what kind of person anyone else is?' I smiled a little ruefully. 'I don't even know what I'm like. The human race seems so deeply mysterious to me. I despair of ever knowing anything.'

I suddenly remembered another occasion when, in retrospect, I had sensed an unseen presence. It was a hot day a week or two earlier, when I had wandered round the base of the cliff near my own land and come across a rocky pool. There were many of these picturesque little places, where the tiny waterfalls which decorated the cliff ended. Most were very small and, at this time of year, pretty low. This one wasn't. It was cool, inviting, surrounded protectively by gorse bushes. I had stared into it for some time. Then I had taken off my clothes, left them on a rock at the edge and slipped into the pool, allowing the pure water to dissolve some accumulated tension. I had floated about in the pool for some time, enjoying the sense of freedom. But as I started to put my clothes on again, I'd heard a scuttling little noise among the bushes. I had kept low and remained quiet for some time while the noise receded. Then I had resumed dressing and gone home. It hadn't worried me unduly – probably just a rabbit. Now I wondered.

Richard was walking very close to me now, our arms occasionally brushing. We had left the forest behind some time ago and were now parallel with my own land. We came to the edge of the cliff. The whole of Cappelrigg Farm was spread out beneath me, looking like a map done in relief.

'How exactly did John Jowett die?' I asked suddenly.

The question clearly took him by surprise. He hesitated some time before replying. 'There's not much to it. He was driving back from the fields one lunchtime and lost control. The tractor overturned and crushed him.'

'What about the cab?'

'It happened on a hillside. It turned over several times. Cabs can do only so much.'

I nodded. 'Was there an inquest?'

'Of course.'

'And?'

'Accidental death.'

'What about the tractor? What was wrong with it?'

Richard looked rather grim. 'Quite a lot after the accident. But Gordon Somerthwaite's a genius with tractors. He knew he could repair it and make a good profit. Iveson shouldn't have interfered. Gordon knows what he's doing, that tractor was better than new. You would have got a bargain and Gordon would have got decent payment for his labour.'

'I meant *before* the accident. There must have been something wrong with it before the accident.'

'Why?'

'Because everybody I've talked to says John Jowett was a pretty sober type, not the kind of person to hurtle down a hill at high speed.'

'I don't suppose he did.'

'Then there must have been something wrong with the tractor.'

'Eh? You've lost me there,' he smiled.

'Because – Oh, never mind. It doesn't matter.'

The green track was some way off, so I started down the cliff where we were. It was laced with tiny sheep paths no more than six inches wide and petering out in the most inconvenient places. Boulders jutted out and added to the difficulty. Here and there the cliff had crumbled away, leaving gaps to jump across.

I reached the bottom with Richard close behind. Together we walked towards a stile in the boundary wall and climbed it. As we crossed the upper field, I looked round with proprietorial satisfaction. 'He seems to have left the farm in good nick,' I said. 'And the house, too – I mean Mrs Jowett.'

'They were old-fashioned farmers,' he agreed. 'Decent sort, on the whole.'

'Where exactly did it happen?'

'I'll show you.'

We went into the next field, and with the lightest possible touch on my elbow he steered me towards the fold of land running east-west with the syke at the bottom.

'Here?' I said. 'Surely it's too steep.'

'Further along.'

We walked along the ridge a little way and came to a place where the ridge lost some of its sharpness and went down to a little ford.

'There,' he said.

I looked at it in silence for some time. 'Yes,' I said at last. 'I suppose it's possible, just. Even so . . .'

'You're forgetting where we are.'

I looked up at him, questioning.

'The ley line,' he said. 'We're standing on the ley line. John was on it, too, when they found him. There was nothing wrong with the tractor or with John. It was – '

'Oh, that,' I said scornfully. I turned and went down to the ford. 'I don't believe in that nonsense, and I don't believe you do either.'

He caught up with me at the ford and turned me round to face him. I was startled at the physical contact, but before I could say anything, he went on. 'Yes you do, Charlotte.

Because I saw you at the stone circle. You sensed it there. You shivered and you said out loud that it was a "disagreeable place".'

'So,' I said quietly, 'it *was* you.'

He nodded. 'It wasn't the first time either. I've been following you around for weeks, Charlotte. Do you know why?'

I smiled. 'To save me from the Druids?'

'Can we just forget about the Druids for a minute? Charlotte, I've been trailing after you for weeks like some idiotic lovesick puppy. Me! Big strong Richard Staveley, reduced to – '

'I'm sorry. I had no idea. I didn't mean to – '

'From the first moment I saw you in the Golden Oak. I'm trying to say something, Charlotte, in my clumsy way. I'm trying to say – '

'Richard, please – '

He tightened his grip on my shoulder. 'Will you listen to me, Charlotte – '

'Let go of me!'

'Charlotte!'

The next thing I knew, I was pinioned to his chest like a piece of flimsy wood in a vice and he was kissing me.

10

Richard's action took me wholly by surprise. Nothing in his previous behaviour had prepared me for it. When finally he released me, my first thought was that I must extricate myself from this situation with tact. Richard was my only real neighbour, I couldn't afford to alienate him. Further, I did like him, even if not in the way he might wish. There was a force in him which was attractive. I had a horror of lives lived vaguely and without direction. The sense of energy in Richard was extremely appealing. In time, this admiration could turn to something more.

But not now. Now I had to gather up the memories of previous awkward encounters and find a way to subdue Richard without damaging his ego. I didn't like doing this because it meant acting a role, and I would have preferred being honest.

None the less, I think we had come to some kind of understanding by the time we resumed our walk towards the house. I hadn't rejected him, but neither had he relinquished his interest in me. We had come from opposite extremes to meet in a compromise which was surprisingly comfortable. I felt able to invite him in for a coffee without too much sense of embarrassment.

It was a good move. He looked round my stripped house (bare white-painted walls, quarry-tiled floors, minimal furniture) with surprise. It gave me a chance to explain a little, and to soothe his wounded ego.

'I wasn't entirely happy in the City,' I said as we sat at the kitchen table. 'That's why I came here. An experiment, if you like. To strip my life bare and discover if I can what it is that *does* matter.'

His handsome blond head nodded, taking in the surroundings. 'So men are one of the items to go, along with the curtains?' he said with a rueful smile.

I laughed. 'Something like that. I need to be cautious.'

'I think I understand.'

Perhaps he did, perhaps not. In any case, he did understand that my rebuff of him wasn't personal. It was men in general, not Richard specifically, being held at bay.

When he left, I made him promise that he wouldn't follow me round anymore. 'After all, I do like your company,' I said. 'Why waste it?'

That seemed to satisfy him. I watched him disappear through the gap between the house and the shippon on his way home across the fields. Then I went back inside and collapsed with sudden exhaustion on a kitchen chair. I hadn't realised the whole encounter had been such a strain. Solitude. It did things like that, turned an unexpected kiss into something more important than it was. In the evening, I broke my solitude with a phone call to Effie.

'He's after your money,' she said.

'Thanks.'

'Seriously. However delectable you may be, it's really your money he's after.'

'I'm too young to have a gigolo.'

'If I weren't rushed off my feet with the Hargreaves commission I'd whiz up there and rescue you.'

'I don't need rescuing.'

Effie wasn't listening. 'Look, why don't *you* whiz down *here* instead? Give yourself a break. There's nothing much doing on the farm right now, is there?'

That was true. There was nothing keeping me at Cappelrigg. I couldn't even pretend I was needed to look after the wethers I'd left in one field to fatten up for the autumn sales. The field was well-fenced and well-watered. If I was prepared, like any other farmer, to leave the ewes to their own devices on the moor, I couldn't pretend that the sheep in the field needed me. Then I remembered.

'Moss.'

'Who the hell is Moss?' said Effie.

'My dog. My sheepdog. Who would feed him? I can hardly ask Richard to do it, can I? Not if I want to cool things down and stay independent of him.'

66

'Take him to a kennel.'

'I don't think one does that with sheepdogs,' I said mildly. 'And there are the hens now, too.'

Silence. Then, 'Charlotte, I despair of you. You don't *want* to come south, do you? Moss is just an excuse. So are the hens.'

I protested, but later that evening I wondered if Effie was right. There might be something I could do with Moss and the hens. The truth was that I didn't feel ready to revisit my old life. I needed to settle something with myself at Cappelrigg first, though I didn't know what.

Also, I had to admit that the landscape exerted a strange power over me, held me in thrall. It wasn't the ley line – I refused to take that seriously – it was the whole of this wild isolated plateau. I felt as deeply bound to it as if I had been born and raised here. And yet, I hardly knew it.

And so, for the next few weeks, I wandered the land incessantly, trying to learn every inch of it. And not just my own farm either. As August moved into September, I began walking more and more in Farleton Forest. I had a map showing all the public footpaths. Day after day I walked the land. Night after night I studied the map, trying to fuse map and memory into a single picture.

It was on one such walk that I met David Farleton for the third time, on a magical misty morning in mid-September. I'd been awakened before dawn by Moss barking. The noise was so unusual that I was out of bed and into my dressing-gown almost before I was awake, assuming the worst. Sheep rustlers. A fox trying to get into the hen hut.

It was still dark when I arrived in the yard in dressing-gown and wellies. But as my eyes adjusted and I zeroed in on the sound, the colour shifted imperceptibly into charcoal. And against it I could see two darker shapes: one large, one small; one barking, one spitting. I moved closer still and two heads turned towards me, flashing their white markings. I recognised the smaller one as the cat. After a few days of accepting the milk I provided, the invisible cat had disappeared altogether and I had stopped setting out the milk. Now it had returned to its old home and was indignant to find its place usurped by a dog. This was high drama in

67

my farmyard, a territorial dispute of great import. I was not amused.

'Shut up, the pair of you,' I said crossly, still woozy from my bed.

A shocked silence. Then a whine from Moss, and the cat shot across the yard to vanish into some bushes. I had a feeling it would be back, and so I went to the kitchen and filled a saucer of milk.

But as I set the saucer down beside the porch, the sky lightened just another fraction to reveal a duvet of mist laid across the land, and at the same moment, a scent of air fresher than any I'd ever experienced wafted across me. I couldn't go back to bed, not on a morning like this.

I went inside and, not bothering to do up my hair, simply exchanged my dressing-gown for jeans and a sweater and returned to the yard. Moss looked up expectantly.

'No, Moss,' I said. 'This isn't a morning for dogs. The fairies would get you.'

I half believed it. There was a touch of magic about the place. I experienced it as I glided across my fields, wide awake and yet at the same time sleepwalking. In one field the backs of the wethers floated above the mist like woolly ice-floes in a calm sea. They were silent. The whole world was silent, holding its breath, waiting for a miracle.

And then, as I approached the edge of the forest, a robin slit the fog and through the opening poured forth a solo of ineffable beauty. It finished with a flourish. After a brief pause, a second robin lustily produced a rival song. The contest had begun: who was to be the Mastersinger of Farleton Forest? Soon melody and countermelody were weaving through the tops of the trees. Then a second pause, and suddenly the chorus welled up, as soft as the mist itself, underpinning the clear voices of the soloists. And then, chorus and soloists merged into a single sound containing all the harmonies of the universe. But so softly, as if afraid to damage the yet-unborn day.

I climbed the stile and entered the forest. Immediately the day regressed into near night as the trees closed in above me. But the path was clear enough, I needed little light to see my way. And as the chorus subsided into the softest pianissimo and died away altogether, the sound of hundreds of tiny wings replaced it as the birds flitted about secretively high in the canopy. At the same time, a scent rose from the forest floor, the dark acrid scent of autumn, of green things making their last effort before submitting to the winter. It was, I think, the first time I truly felt the cycle of the seasons, poignant and beautiful. I also felt my own mortality and, strangely, didn't mind too much.

The mist was thicker here, trapped by the tree trunks which rose above the billowing mass like the legs of primeval beings. It *was* a primeval forest that morning and I was the first human ever to walk the earth. The earth itself was new, forming itself from the grey breath of an unseen god beneath the forest floor. I stopped thinking and gave myself up to the sensation. I knew, vaguely, that I was floating in a north-easterly direction, towards The Folly which I had before avoided – the mist was paler in the east and provided its own compass – but it didn't matter. Nothing mattered except this effortless floating along the silvery pathway.

I could have walked forever that morning, walked clear round the planet, oceans and all, and perhaps I would have done if a stone wall hadn't loomed in front of me and blocked my path. Instead, I climbed the stile, perched on the top of the wall and gazed out on the world beyond.

An impenetrable curtain of pale grey clothed what must have been an open field carved out of the forest. I blinked, not trusting my eyes, but the curtain stayed stubbornly in place. I was both seeing and not seeing, a disconcerting sensation. And I had been wrong about the forest. The formation of the world wasn't taking place there but here. Somewhere, hidden deep within the luminous mist, I could feel a force moving to create something out of nothing. It would be the very first act of creation, and I would see it. I held my breath, fearful of disturbing the great work. All my senses were alert now. I would have heard a leaf fall, if any of the trees behind me had dared. But none did. Nothing stirred.

And then, so quietly that I almost missed it, the first faint rumble, a little like distant thunder almost beyond the range of human hearing. I strained to hear better. It was no delusion; I could *feel* it now, the earth trembling a fraction. The mist was moving, too. No longer a solid curtain, it was breaking up into swirls of slightly different shades of grey, like a great slab of marble dissolving.

And as I watched the formation and dissolution of the patterns, it seemed that one part of it, right in the centre, began to take on substance. The centre seemed to glow, a more silvery colour than the rest, shimmering against the muted backdrop. It seemed at the same time both lighter and darker than the rest, but if I looked at it directly, it disappeared. I could only see it by gazing somewhat to the side and catching it unawares.

And then, at the same moment, the rumble increased and the earth trembled more distinctly and the glowing centre began to take shape and I was aware of movement, the shape moving towards me, coming to me out of the mist, drawing into itself the thunder and the movement of the earth. And then, in one last mighty surge, everything went silent and still again, and I saw, outlined against the mist, the first horse ever to stride out upon the earth.

It was utterly magnificent, a massive creature shining grey. It was standing quite still now, watching me from a distance as if startled to find itself sharing the land with another living being. Then it gave one toss of its huge head and stepped forth grandly. After all, what did an animal like that have to fear? It moved towards me slowly and yet so confidently that I thought of a monarch who knows for certain that anything in its path will step aside. As it approached, its features became clearer: the arched neck, the fine ears pricked forward and alert, the creamy mane and tail foaming against its sleek mother-of-pearl coat. Closer still and I could see the long Roman nose and then the dark intelligent eyes gently questioning my existence. It was a mare, and both her size and the silky feathering of the lower legs told me she was a draught horse, but one so finely formed as to suggest a mythical creature rather than an animal bred for the plough. She stopped a few metres away, raised her head a fraction higher and blew softly.

I stretched out a hand and whispered, 'Queen of horses, come closer.'

She stepped forward and reached out her great head towards my hand. Her muzzle was soft on my palm, and I could feel the warmth as she breathed in and out rapidly. She was investigating me and at the same time nibbling at my palm in the hope of a treat. In compensation for my empty hand, I moved it up to rub the soft hairy groove of her throat. She half closed her eyes in pleasure. If she'd been a kitten, she would have purred.

'You beautiful, beautiful creature,' I breathed, still not quite believing she was real.

At the sound of my voice, she opened her eyes again and took another step forward. Raising her head higher, she nuzzled my face. Her breath smelled of fresh green grass. With both hands I stroked her cheeks and then her neck, warm and silky beneath her creamy mane.

Her muzzle moved on to investigate my neck, sweater, jeans, right down to my wellies. She must have been reassured, because she lowered her head to the ground and I heard the sound of a mouthful of grass being torn off neatly. She shifted her massive body to one side, the better to reach another patch of grass.

She was now parallel to the wall on which I sat. It was a high wall, but even so her back rose a good foot or so above it. Her smooth coat seemed to gleam, as if lit from within, and on it sparkled tiny diamonds of morning dew. I ran a hand along her back. She looked up expectantly.

Was it the dreamlike unreality of the morning, or was it some madness in myself? Her head was up now, her ears swivelling round, alert, waiting, as if in invitation. How could I resist? I did the only thing possible. I eased myself up on the wall and with one swing of my leg I was on the horse.

A shiver of surprise rippled through her. She swung her head round and sniffed at my knee. Satisfied, she gave a graceful toss of her head and stepped off smartly away from the wall.

We were striding across the field, each effortless step eating up the ground. This was no plodding draught horse. However large her body, her spirit was larger still and gave a zestfulness to her movements. She was as awake to the magic of the morning as I was, tossing her great head and

71

sniffing the air with almost girlish pleasure. I leaned forward slightly and ran my hands down her neck – dewy on one side but warm and dry on the other where the mane covered it.

She took my action as a signal, and before I knew what was happening, she had made a smooth transition from her earth-eating walk to a springy trot. I moved my knees higher to absorb the bounce of her step and at the same time grasped a mass of coarse mane in each hand. Briefly – and belatedly – it flashed across my mind that I must be mad. Bareback, yes, I had often ridden bareback and had no difficulty maintaining my seat. But with no bridle? I was completely at her mercy. And yet, the moment I realised this, I relaxed. She had too much dignity to take advantage of a foolish thing like me. I relinquished all control to her, and in my exhilaration I leaned against her neck and inhaled joyously the clean horsey scent of her mane.

And again, with no discernible transition, we were cantering across the field, through the swirling grey mist that had seemed to spawn her and which seemed to be her element. I sat upright again, as steady on her broad back as if I were in an armchair. And again her grace surprised me. How could such bulk move with such ease? There must have been nearly a ton of muscle and bone working beneath me, but all I was aware of was a smooth vast shape gliding across the land as if the earth were cotton wool.

She was going faster now. My face was bombarded by a million tiny particles of dew and I could feel my hair flying out behind me like a banner. Faster still and the wind began to whistle past my ears, and now I could hear the deep low rumble that had signalled her approach, as her great long legs thundered across the earth awakening the gods who had created her.

And then the gods disappeared and *she* was the goddess, self-born, who had awakened this day that was the beginning of all time, the first day of the new world that was flying past me, faster and faster, and I leaned low and buried my face in her mane. I was wild with excitement, and she was wild and the mist swirled wildly round us both and the wind rose and beat her mane into a thousand whips that stung my face, the wind a hurricane now, screaming past my ears, shrill.

And then, suddenly, she swerved so abruptly that I had to cling hard to her neck, and she was thundering across the field in another direction, running towards the wind that was shrilling so painfully. And I began to wake up and realise that it couldn't be the wind making that noise. There was no wind at all, only the stirring of the air as it parted to make way for her. There was no wind, and yet the sound shrilled across the field, louder now. And at the same moment that I began to understand, with a sickening wrench of fear, what the noise might be, the noise stopped and with it the horse, and there, dark against the high dry-stone wall, stood David Farleton.

Dark his outline and darker still his face, as if all the thunder of the horse's wild run had gathered into that single face that stared up at me with unspeakable anger. I could feel the blood drain from me, leaving me cold and shivering. My shivers were the only motion in that awful scene. Both he and the horse stood quite still, waiting. I clenched my teeth to keep them from chattering with cold and fear. He was holding a halter in one motionless hand. It was all over, the wild exhilarating gallop through time, the first morning of the earth's creation. All gone. Instead, a rich landowner come to claim his property.

It was the horse who broke the spell. She reached out and nuzzled his face – so handsome and so hostile. Her gesture was not placatory, just friendly, and for one moment I thought she might soften his anger. He raised the hand not holding the halter and ruffled the hair between her ears. But the gesture was absent-minded and his eyes never left mine. His eyes were as black as his hair and bored steadily into mine, still waiting. He was evidently too proud to speak first.

So was I, though in my case it was guilt that made me search for justification. It was obvious even to someone like me who knew nothing of draught horses that this one was extremely valuable. I had wantonly flung myself on her and urged her to race across a fog-bound field. Who knows what stones or molehills might have felled her? She could have broken her leg, she could have been killed. At the thought, tears pricked behind my eyes – remorse, belated fear, and love for the beautiful mare who had given me this precious morning.

But I couldn't feel a shred of remorse for trespassing on his property, both land and horse. And she *hadn't* been hurt. Even now she was snorting with a pleasure which I was sure had more to do with our shared flight than his hand caressing her ears. She had *wanted* to run, had run across the field by herself to greet me. We had been conspirators, she and I, sharing the wild joy of being alive on such a day. It was he who was the intruder, sullen in the offended pride of ownership. There was no way I would apologise to a man who regarded this great mare as nothing but property to be defended against me.

He must have sensed my own stubbornness and, knowing that I wouldn't break the silence, broke it himself. '*Get off*,' he hissed through teeth as tightly clenched as my own.

I slid off and stood before him. I looked directly into his eyes. 'You have a talent for destroying magic,' I said quietly. 'There. Take your property.'

Then I turned and walked across the field. I didn't look back, didn't want to see him clamp the halter on her and lead her away.

The mist had cleared a little and I could see ahead of me a wall with a stile. I headed for it, hoping it was the same one I had climbed before. Otherwise I had no idea where I was. The mist and the wild run had disoriented me, and until the sun rose – if it rose – I would be unable to get a sense of direction.

I reached the stile and went over it. The path on the other side looked the same, but then, one path looked much like any other. I started down it, not much caring, conscious only of a sense of falling from grace, being expelled from paradise – fallen angel, greedy Eve. The mare and I had experienced something special, and now it was over.

I was conscious, too, of a residual fear – the harm I might have done her. All my rationalisations couldn't cancel that out. The tears that had threatened finally came. As the mist slowly lifted, I replaced it with one of my own and stumbled along with my face streaming.

The path seemed to wind more often than I remembered. I don't know how long I'd been walking when I saw another bend up ahead and heard from somewhere beyond it a voice calling. The last thing I wanted was to meet anyone, friendly or not, but the trees on either side were too dense to allow an escape. I wiped my face with the sleeve of my sweater and smoothed the disorder of my hair as best I could. I turned my face into a mask of indifference, then walked calmly round the curve.

There stood David Farleton, holding his horse by the halter and blocking the path. Behind him, I could see another man running towards us. One way or other, I was in for a confrontation. I took a deep breath, preparing at last to apologise – not for using his property but for putting the mare in danger. But before I could speak, he said, 'I'm sorry.'

My jaw dropped. If he'd raged at me I might have known how to react, but this apology, wholly unexpected, floored me.

'For destroying the magic,' he said, repeating my earlier words to him.

Behind him I could now see that the man running towards us was Brendan Iveson. 'David!' he was shouting.

David Farleton seemed not to hear him. 'It's the last thing I want to do,' he said. 'Destroy magic. Here.' He made a slight gesture towards the forest around us and then let his hand settle on the mare's neck. And I realised with a shock that he loved her. His anger hadn't been proprietorial, as I'd thought, but delayed panic. He must have been terrified when he'd seen her hurtling across the field like that.

Controlling my tears, I mumbled my own apology. I don't know what I said, and I don't suppose the words mattered. A little hesitantly, I reached up and rubbed the mare under her throat. 'She *is* magic, isn't she?' I said.

Then, to my utter amazement, he smiled. Not a very big smile, granted, but it was the first time I'd seen him smile at all, and the transformation was stunning. 'Yes,' he said, 'she's magic.'

11

'David!'

The shout jerked us both out of our trance. I'd forgotten all about Brendan Iveson running up the path towards us, and I don't think David Farleton had noticed him at all.

'David!' he called again, closer now. 'Where the hell have you been, and us with our breakfast ossifying on the table and Belle fit to fry you up in the stead of it?'

In reply, the horse swung her massive hindquarters round to block his path.

He put his hands on her rump and shoved hard. 'Shift your arse, you old devil!'

She raised her head high and looked down on him disdainfully as he squeezed past.

'And don't you be giving me any of that, you witch,' he muttered up at her.

And then he was standing in front of us, his breath rasping, clutching his side after the long run. His face was nearly as red as his hair and beads of sweat stood out on his forehead. He was so agitated that I wondered if he'd expected to find David Farleton on the verge of killing me. But of course he knew nothing about the wild ride. He must simply have noticed that his boss was late coming back with the horse and gone to investigate. He looked at me, at David Farleton, at me again, back and forth as if trying to take a reading. Finally he let his arms drop foolishly by his sides and said to his boss, 'Sure and this is a pleasant enough spot for a morning's chat, but your breakfast's getting cold.'

It seemed a feeble remark under the circumstances.

David Farleton nodded but made no move to break up the tableau. The last shreds of the morning mist swirled above our heads, seeking a way out of the confines of the forest path. The air was so still you could hear a pine needle drop, but none did. The whole of Farleton Forest was holding its breath, waiting for the next stage in a drama whose first act Brendan Iveson had patently missed.

'If it's all the same to you, I'd appreciate some illumination as to the meaning of all this,' he said peevishly.

The spell was broken at last. As if the mist had been the only thing holding me up, my knees suddenly went soft and I had to concentrate simply to remain upright. The interrogation was about to begin. I turned to Brendan Iveson. He would have to know sooner or later, I may as well do it myself.

'I've done something rather awful,' I said. My voice was shaky, as if the tears that had dried from my face had moved to my throat instead. 'I went for a walk,' I continued uncertainly, 'and when I came to the field, and sat on the wall, the horse . . . came out of the mist, up to the wall, and she . . . ' My voice faltered. I took a deep breath and continued, 'I don't know how it happened, but then I was on the horse, and we were flying across the field . . . '

Iveson stared at me as if I were insane. I didn't dare look at the other man.

I took another deep breath. 'And Mr Farleton was . . . understandably upset.'

And then the impossible happened.

'No harm done,' said David Farleton.

No harm done? I could have killed his horse. And, given his reputation, I hardly dared think of the form his revenge would have taken. Iveson shifted his stare to his employer, obviously as stunned as I was by his reaction.

Delayed shock was catching up with me. I was shaking badly now. 'What can I say? I'm terribly sorry. I won't . . . I won't be bothering you again. I'll keep off your land.'

I turned abruptly and walked away. All I wanted was to get away from the two men and sit down somewhere on the forest floor to recover unseen. Just before I disappeared round the curve, I glimpsed David Farleton manoeuvring the huge horse around on the narrow path and heading back home. He had clearly forgotten me already, preoccupied with the simple job of taking the horse back to the stables. I'd been let off lightly.

Out of sight, I walked as quickly as I could, just in case he changed his mind. Running away from my shame once again.

Not fast enough. Footsteps behind me. Then Brendan Iveson, grabbing my arm.

'Did you ever hear of such nonsense, and with the footpaths public and all? And I'll not be letting you flounce off into the forest in the state you're in. You're coming back with me for some breakfast.'

I searched his face in utter bewilderment. Had he, too, forgotten what had just taken place? Had he forgotten, too, that the last time we'd met he'd also grabbed my arm and prevented me from buying a tractor I badly needed? I felt like Alice just gone through a looking glass peopled with creatures constantly changing their shape.

'And a fine thing it would be if you lose me the chance to make my own amends,' he added.

I tried to focus my eyes. 'You?'

'The same. For acting the lunatic at that dispersal sale.'

So he did remember.

Then he smiled. 'Will you trust me with having a reason? And to tell it to you while we walk back to the house?'

Without giving me a chance to reply, he tucked my arm in his and steered me firmly back up the path. I had no strength to resist.

'You see,' he began, 'if I'd known you'd be bidding for that tractor, I'd have looked you out before and tried to explain. But it happened so fast that . . . '

His voice trailed off, and I realised that he was less sure of himself than he pretended to be. The thought that he was human after all, a little bit fallible, was comforting.

Up ahead, David Farleton was walking his horse homeward. The scene was absurdly idyllic: the narrow path, shot with silvery gold light where the sun managed to squeeze through the mist; a few gilded leaves drifting slowly down in the still air; the horse herself magnificent in her gleaming mother-of-pearl coat. Her owner dark and tousled and totally unpredictable, as much a part of nature here as the horse and the trees and the mist.

'You see,' Brendan Iveson began again, 'the tractor's more

than a dud. It's lethal. It killed John Jowett, and when I saw you raising your arm to bid . . . '

My mind suddenly jerked into clarity. So it wasn't just my imagination. There had been something wrong with the tractor. But why should David Farleton's estate manager care who bought it? I looked at him closely. He was in his early fifties, not much younger than my father had been when he'd died. The comparison wasn't as absurd as it might seem. He was looking at me in a way that reminded me painfully of my childhood.

'D'ye see, lass?' he went on. 'I meant well and all. And truly we didn't want the tractor for ourselves. You see that lump of horseflesh up ahead? That's our tractor, and there's more like her back at the stables.'

I smiled faintly. 'Rather a beautiful tractor.' My mind was busy reconstructing the scene at the dispersal sale. The more I thought about it, the more it seemed that his intervention hadn't been aggressive after all, just clumsy. I had misinterpreted, and had reacted badly.

'Indeed and she is – and safe with it,' he said.

I considered his words. 'But Richard Staveley said there was nothing wrong with the tractor.'

For a while, silence. Then, 'Well now,' he said slowly, 'you'll see by now, with the layout and all, that Cappelrigg and Graegarth are out on a limb, so to speak, that side of the forest?'

I nodded, wondering what on earth he was getting at.

'And with our friend up ahead there being a mite on the surly side,' he continued, 'and with everyone else up here off-comed'uns, well, you'll see that the two farms are thrown together a good deal?'

Again I nodded.

There was another long pause before he continued. 'Well, so John Jowett and Richard Staveley were always taking help off of each other, things like this or that little item goes wrong with the tractor, they helped each other out.' Then, choosing his words with obvious care, 'I'm saying that a certain number of Richard Staveley hours went into that tractor, and he'll maybe be feeling a trifle touchy about it.'

I thought about this a while. 'Pride?' I suggested.

'Something like that. And just a bit of responsibility with it and all. In a general kind of way, you'll understand.'

And, finally, I did understand. Poor Richard. How awful, forever to be wondering, and never to know, if some small neglected detail – a bolt forgotten, perhaps – had flung his friend and neighbour to his death. No wonder he was touchy about the tractor, and anxious to defend it.

'So you'll see,' Brendan Iveson was saying with some of his former cheerfulness, 'that I got a little rattled at the dispersal sale and neglected the needful. Such as saying that I'm Brendan Iveson – Brendan to you, I hope – and that it would be a fine thing from my point of view if we could be friends . . .'

He stopped, turned towards me and put out his hand. At that moment I felt such a surge of affection for this clumsy but well-meaning man that I could have hugged him. Instead I took his hand firmly and said, 'Charlotte Venables – Charlotte to you – and it would be a fine thing from my point of view, too, if we could be friends.'

He squeezed my hand so vigorously that I feared for the bones. His whole big face beamed pleasure and relief. I thought once again of my father and wondered if Brendan had children. If so, I envied them.

'Right, then, that's settled,' he said. 'And him up the path there, that's just plain David – we've got no time to be fussing with surnames. And when we get home there'll be the wife, Belle, to give you breakfast, only don't be letting on that you know she's the wife because she likes to pretend she never did such a bourgeoise thing as marry the likes of me. And then there'll be the lads, too – students. They that give us the slave labour to run the place – '

I laughed. 'I'm not prepared to see you as a slave-driver.'

'Oh, we're hard masters, and that's the truth of it. You can ask the lads themselves.'

And at that moment, the last of the mist cleared the tops of the trees, and the sun slanted through in an explosion of golden searchlights that bounced off the horse's flanks and gilded her halter. Already it seemed a lifetime ago that I'd been on her, flying wildly across the field.

'I'm thinking you'll be knowing a thing or two about horses,' Brendan said.

I looked up guiltily.

He brushed away my guilt with a conspiratorial wave of the hand. 'To be riding Olwen with no bridle,' he explained.

I nodded. 'I've had horses since I was a child. But I never – did anything so . . . rash. I don't know what came over me this morning.'

'Leave it be. No harm done. To her . . . or yourself.'

It hadn't really occurred to me that I had endangered myself as well as the horse. It seemed astonishing that this man whom I barely knew should be the one to think of it. I was touched, and a little embarrassed. I changed the subject. 'That's her name? Olwen?'

'You've not heard of the Celtic giant, Ysbaddaden, and his daughter Olwen? King of the giants he was, which makes Olwen a princess. And doesn't she know it, the minx.'

I laughed. 'She is rather splendid!'

'Ah, but you should have seen big daddy!'

'Her sire? Don't tell me he *was* called Ysbaddaden?'

'The same. The biggest toughest Shire in the whole of Britain. You'd not be riding *that* one without a bridle.'

He gave me a sideways look that had more than a touch of admiration in it. I realised that despite everything, he was impressed with my wild ride. That made me feel a little better about it. Had David also felt a touch of respect for my nerve? It might explain why I'd been let off so lightly.

Up ahead, Olwen was nibbling gently at David's ear. He pushed her huge head away. Undeterred, she poked her nose under his armpit and flung his arm up. He pushed her away again.

I touched Brendan's sleeve. 'Look!' I whispered. 'She's *flirting* with him!'

She pretended to eat a wayward clump of his hair. He tugged at her own forelock in revenge. She shook her head, her mane rippling in a creamy wave shot with silver. Then she rubbed her cheek against his shoulder.

'Shameless hussy,' said Brendan. 'And he's no better.'

'He does seem terribly fond of her.'

'Crazy about the nag. She was all but sold two years ago.

Sure and he pulls out of it at the last minute. Cost us a bob or two, that did. We had to keep the lad on at our own expense while we trained him up with a different horse.'

'What exactly do you *do* at The Folly?'

'Do? Breed horses. Train them. Train the men to work them. Plant trees. Harvest trees. That's about it. You'll be seeing soon enough, once you've got some breakfast inside you. Look – we're home.'

The path widened. A moment later we were out of the trees and I was staring with open wonder at the front of The Folly.

12

Home, Brendan had said. His home. But it was uncanny, the powerful sense of homecoming that *I* felt as I stood in front of The Folly. And yet it could hardly have been more different from the Sussex farmhouse of my childhood.

Here, the great green forest, already flecked gold and russet, swept up the land to end in a gravelled semi-circle. Beyond it, a few low steps led to a broad terrace running along the entire front of the house. The steps and the terrace were flagged in stone which glowed grey-gold in the sun. The house itself glowed the same colour in the few places where the ivy allowed it to show through. The ivy was stupendous: thick, lush, intense green, as if the trees, thwarted by the gravel apron, had leapt across the space to re-establish themselves in the form of an ivy forest. Here, as in the back, the windows were placed with curious irregularity and displayed every period of architectural history, as did the towers and turrets which finished off the extraordinary building. Disneyland with class. Certainly it was like nothing else I'd ever seen.

So why did I have such a strong sense of *déjà vu*, of instant belonging, as I stood in that gilded bowl of sunlight?

Suddenly a rainbow of colour exploded from round the side of the house, defying the green-gold decor of The Folly. Belle, no doubt, trailing behind her three boys in their late teens or early twenties who must be 'the lads', all of them striding across the gravel to meet us. Belle stopped in front of David and issued some indignant words on the wickedness of blackened bacon. The lads grinned shyly to hear the boss upbraided. Olwen flicked her tail indifferently to dislodge a fly. There was shouting, laughter.

Home.

David handed Olwen over to be led to the stables. I detected a touch of reluctance in relinquishing her. The little procession made its way across the gravel: Olwen, flanked by her three young courtiers, taking their noise with them. Then Belle caught sight of me. Despite her considerable size, she was beside me in an instant, her hand outstretched, her broad face beaming a welcome.

'You must be Charlotte! Thank *God* we've met at last! I'm Belle. You *will* stay for breakfast, please? I can't *tell* you how *good* it is to see a face without whiskers!'

With one strong wave of a hand she shooed Brendan and David towards the house, then linked arms with me.

' . . . absolutely *ridiculous* not to meet sooner, and us next-door neighbours! Breakfast first – you must be *perishing*! – and then we'll show you the house and stables and all that, and . . . '

I listened contentedly to her rhythmic speech speared with emphases, while luxuriating in the strange sense of homecoming. It wasn't so much knowing that Belle and I would become friends; more, that we were friends already. Of course I had seen her before. She was the bright parrot, the medieval kitchen maid who'd kissed Brendan so lustily in the courtyard. I could see now that this exotic bird was in her early fifties, like Brendan. Her plumage today was a scarlet jumper, a voluminous patchwork skirt in bright primary colours, thick purple stockings and a pair of heavy brown clogs of the sort worn by Lancashire millworkers in the last century. Above it was a strong happy face full of large features. Everything about her was generous, including the wild frizz of hair in which the original gold was now colonised by big helpings of silver.

She was not at all like my mother, or Effie, or any of my other women friends. And yet, I *knew* her, and it seemed the most natural thing in the world that we should link arms and stroll round the side of the house behind the others, chattering as if we had a lot to catch up on.

At the back, we passed under a monumental stone archway which connected the main building to one of its extensions. It was the stables, from which had issued the phantom neighing of a ghost horse, that morning I'd inadvertently spied on it.

No ghost horse Olwen, now being led to her box for her morning feed.

We went into the house through a small dark room (formerly the gun room, Belle said) where we pulled off our wellies and clogs before passing through into the kitchen.

And what a kitchen! I'd seen such rooms before, meticulously restored in stately homes, but I'd never seen one in such obvious use. It was a huge, square, high-ceilinged palace of food. It faced north, but the windows were so big that light flooded in to bounce off the fresh white walls and illuminate what must have been a whole year's supply of onions and garlic hanging from the ceiling. Equally generous masses of herbs were hung to dry, and the oak shelves were full of home-bottled fruits and vegetables so colourful as to make Belle's gypsy dress seem almost subdued. Another splash of colour came from the rag rug in front of a huge double Aga which itself was almost dwarfed by the inglenook in which it stood. A row of antiquated servants' bells hung above an inside door. A grandfather clock occupied one corner. A big grey cat snoozed on the rug while pans above it exuded the wonderful scent of imminent breakfast.

'Shift,' said Belle, prodding the cat with a bright-stockinged foot. The cat glared, then jumped onto a cushioned chair by the grandfather clock, while Belle took up her place before the Aga. It was hard not to see the Aga as an altar with Belle as high priestess. 'Sit anywhere you like, Charlotte,' she said. 'We're awfully informal here.'

'Can I help?'

'Bless you, no. Everything's under control.'

I raised a sceptical eyebrow, remembering the severe ticking-off she'd given David.

She read my meaning and laughed. 'Oh, that! I just read the riot act from time to time to keep the men in line.'

The room was filling with men, not in line but in rowdy disorder, sitting down at random round the big oak table which was the centrepiece of the marvellous room. I sat down, too, just where I was, and listened peacefully to the shop-talk which swirled round me: breechings and bearing reins, logging arch and sledge, skidding, brashing. Arcane language, all of it, and I should have felt excluded but didn't. I felt I was simply a part of the place, comfortably taken for granted. Brendan was beside me, David across from me. The students were scattered about, occasionally glancing at me with amiable curiosity.

A giant teapot appeared, then giant toast racks and giant pots of marmalade. Everything was so *big*: Brendan, David, Belle, the horse, the cat, the kitchen. I was a fairy tale child who had wandered by mistake into friendly giantland.

Brendan poured the tea – 'Put some of that down the inside of your neck, lass' – while Belle produced huge plates heaped with enough food for . . . well . . . a roomful of giants. She sat down at last and there was a pause in the chatter as we shovelled in the first mouthfuls. I was terribly hungry. I hadn't realised it till then. In the new silence, I heard the soothing tick of the grandfather clock.

'Isn't this the nice state of affairs!' said Brendan suddenly. 'I clean forgot the intros!'

He introduced me to the students. They were graded in size, as if the longer they lived at The Folly the larger they grew. Paul was the senior, a stocky lad from the Lake District. He'd been sent by the National Trust, which had large woodland holdings in the area, and he was due to return there at Christmas with his horse Gerda.

Next in size and seniority was an Aberdonian called Simon, red-haired and freckled as every good Scot should be, except that he wasn't Scottish. His sponsor was the Forestry Commission, which, I gathered, had sent students to The Folly before.

A rather smallish Bavarian called Wolf was the new boy, sent by the German equivalent of the Forestry Commission.

It was all rather confusing, this talk about sponsoring bodies and horses that were discussed as if they belonged to the students. When finally I managed to ask some questions, there was a brief silence. The students seemed surprised that I hadn't heard about their work. But the silence from the others had a different quality, full of unspoken tensions at odds with the easy-going kitchen.

Belle sprang from her chair. 'Seconds, anyone? David, you tell Charlotte what we do while I get some more food.'

The seconds were not quite due. It was obviously an excuse to put David on the spot. It was obvious, too, that he knew it. He was watching me across the table. I suddenly realised that he hadn't said a word to me since our encounter on the path. His manner was not unfriendly, just private.

'Are you really interested?' he asked finally.

I thought he was being sarcastic, querying my silly female curiosity. Then I saw how serious he was, and with a shock I saw, too, a touch of shyness. Shyness, in this rich landowner who'd yelled at me for being squashed by a tree he'd felled, who'd been white with fury when he told me to get off his horse. Richard's opinion of David Farleton was unprintable. Few people I'd met in the area had a good word to say for him. He was arrogant, bad-tempered, possibly a little bit insane. So who was this quiet gentle man gazing at me across the table?

'Yes,' I said, 'I am interested.'

A diffident shrug, and then he began.

'It's very simple. Most foresters grow just a few species, and they plant all the trees at the same time. They clear-fell at the same time and then they start all over again. It makes a mess of the land and the wildlife. All we do is try to keep a continuous forest. We have more species, and they're all different ages. We harvest each tree individually, when it's ready. That means we can't clear-fell. Heavy machinery is out of the question. Even a tractor would damage the younger trees hauling out the older ones.'

He broke off to take a bite of toast, but his eyes never left my face. He was testing me, and perhaps also testing himself. Even chewing he was handsome. I'd forgotten how handsome that big dark head with its mass of wayward hair was, probably because our previous encounters had been so fraught. There suddenly rose in my mind the memory of my dream on Midsummer's Eve, when we'd come to each other as Adam and Eve and made love. I tried to control the colour that crept into my face with the memory.

'Olwen?' I said. 'She's the answer?'

He nodded. 'And all the others. Horses are easier to manoeuvre in a thick stand, and they don't compact the land.'

'They don't break down either,' said Paul.

'Or depreciate,' said Simon.

'And they make the new horses to replace,' said Wolf.

Again this sense of unity, of a group of disparate people gathered together because they believed so intensely in what they were doing.

'There's nothing new in any of this,' said David. 'It's the way forestry used to be done. We're just bringing it back.'

Why was he so self-deprecating? It was clear to me already that what he was describing was rather special. 'It sounds marvellous,' I said to David. 'Why isn't everyone else doing it?'

He shrugged. 'They're beginning to. The problem is that there aren't enough horses; that's why we branched out into breeding. Then we discovered that no one knew how to train the horses we bred, so we started doing that. Then we realised that not many people knew how to use our trained horses, and so we started taking on students. Then we pulled the whole lot together and started calling ourselves a school. That's about it, really.'

He returned to his plate, dismissing the subject and me along with it. Again, not unfriendly, just cautious. And private.

Belle got up again to make some more toast. I saw a warning glance at a student who seemed about to take up the story. Clearly she wanted David to do the talking.

'How does the school work?' I asked him.

He looked up, as if surprised to see me still there. 'It's straightforward enough,' he said at last. 'The owner of a forest buys one of our young horses and sends a student to us. The student and the horse are trained together, so that when they go back to their forest, they go as a team that's used to working together.' Then he smiled, and again I saw the heavy forbidding face transformed. The dark Celt took on a touch of the leprechaun as he said, 'The school's a fraud, of course. We just use the students as slave labour.'

The kitchen exploded into life again as the students agreed and described how dreadfully they were exploited. It was clear that they didn't mean a word of it, but they were enjoying their act so much that I played along with it. It took me a while to realise that David had engineered this scene to get himself out of the spotlight. All the while, my mind increasingly circled in on the bigger questions left unanswered. Why did no one locally seem to know about the work done here? It was the kind of thing the media jumped at these days when everybody wanted to be thought Green. It was almost as if the locals didn't *want* to know, as if they preferred to cling to their hostility. Which begged another question: Why was David so disliked? And why did he do nothing to counter this hostility?

And then a second explosion, as something raced up my leg and landed with a soft furry *plumpf* on my shoulder. I jerked my head round and stared into a pair of intense violet eyes only inches away from my own. The eyes belonged to a kitten and took up most of its face. The rest of the kitten was a fluffy grey, a little darker than Olwen but equally unusual and very beautiful.

'Well!' I said, 'And who are you?' though its relationship to the big grey cat now sulking on a chair was obvious.

David was smiling again. 'A good mouser, if her mother's anything to go by. Take her with you – souvenir of The Folly.'

'You don't want her?' I said in astonishment. She was the most exquisite kitten I'd ever seen.

'We have too many already. She's the runt of the litter, but she'll do well.' He drank the last of his tea. Breakfast was over.

Then an odd thing happened. His tea mug stopped suddenly on its way down to the table. He leaned forward and looked intently into my face, then the kitten's, then mine again. It was a look of wonder, unexpected in such a rough man. Then, 'Your eyes are the same colour as hers,' he said. 'Exactly the same. Take her.'

Then he was gone, and with him everyone else except myself and Belle. The ticking of the grandfather clock was deafening.

'Well, well,' said Belle at last. 'It's been a good few years since that one noticed the colour of anyone's eyes.'

I rubbed my face against the kitten's fur, partly to escape Belle's scrutiny and partly for the sheer luxury of it. I'd forgotten how soft a kitten's fur could be. She inched a little further towards my neck and settled down against it as if I were a hearth rug.

'Belle,' I said quietly, 'why is David so disliked?'

She whirled off her chair and went to the Aga. 'More tea?'

Her action threw me. I'd been so sure that this was a person I could speak to freely. 'Are you changing the subject?'

She turned to face me, smiling broadly. 'Lord, no! Just settling down for a nice long talk, I hope!'

She returned to the table with the pot and poured us each a big mugful. The last thing I needed was more tea – I was awash – but there was something comforting in the ritual. It occurred to me suddenly that she might have been an actress. I don't mean that she was phoney, but there was something bigger than life, dramatic, about even her simplest movements. Also a grace, an at-homeness in the body which I associated with the theatre. Her voice, too, seemed designed to project across bigger spaces even than the kitchen.

'You must know the way they talk,' I added.

She sat down again in an elegant swirl of skirts and leaned her elbows on the table. 'I do. They've been talking that way for two decades.'

'Why? And why does nobody seem to know what goes on up here?'

'It's a long story, Charlotte, and you shall hear it all.' There was a pause while she collected her thoughts. Then the soliloquy began.

'When we first came here, all of us, and started this work, the locals regarded us as freaks. We were hippies, back-to-nature fanatics, fringe lunatics. David didn't care and neither did we. We were all mad with enthusiasm. We felt we were starting a revolution, and to hell with public opinion.' She smiled ruefully. 'Big mistake, that. The selfishness of the righteous. Anyway, David started with a built-in handicap: he wasn't like his father. People had adored the old squire. David wasn't like that. He detested the role of "young squire" and refused to play it.

'The first thing he did got him off to a bad start: he sold the family seat and moved up here. Centuries of tradition gone, just like that. Then he started planting up the land with trees. More tradition gone. Worst of all, he started buying back some of the land east of us and planting more trees. People felt that the whole structure of the community was being threatened. It wasn't, of course. People who'd done farmwork before worked with the trees instead. But David was too stubborn to explain any of this. To him, it was blindingly obvious that if this poor-quality land was turned over to trees, it would actually be producing something useful. At the same time, the land would gradually recover from the strain of forced farming, wildlife would flourish, and so forth. It was a Utopian vision, really, ahead of its time.'

'So *why* didn't David explain?'

'Yes, well, there the locals were wrong: David *was* a true Farleton, every bit as aristocratic as his father. But while his father loved playing the squire, David loved work. And he does not, as the phrase goes, suffer fools gladly. Because the rightness of what we were doing was so obvious to him, he assumed it was obvious to everyone else. It wasn't. And so began the downward spiral.'

There was a clatter of hooves on cobbles outside. Through the big open windows I saw a huge black Shire going past, harnessed up and pulling behind it a contraption which I presumed was for hauling logs. Paul walked behind, holding the long reins. Behind him was David. He didn't look towards the kitchen, his attention was fixed on the horse and the boy. A fanatic. Belle continued her narrative undisturbed, merely raising her voice a fraction to compete with the noise outside. To her this magical sight must be commonplace.

'You probably don't realise,' she said, a little tentatively, 'that David has another side to him. There's a part of him that's extremely vulnerable. Yes, I know – you'd never guess, the way he acts. So when his . . . personal life started to go wrong, the locals were delighted. Serves him right and all that. David pretended not to notice, not to care, but he did. He was terribly hurt.' She raised a hand as if to fend off criticism. 'I'm not making excuses for him or for the rest of us – just explaining. Anyway, that was the last straw. After that, he shut himself off completely. The ghetto mentality.'

'But *now*,' I said. 'What about *now*?'

Belle sighed. 'Exactly. Suddenly the Green Revolution was here, and we were right at the heart of it. Hippies turned prophet. Or would have been. But by then David was so bitter and angry about the way the locals had treated him that – ' She smiled hopelessly. 'Well, you can see for yourself. While the rest of the world is busy catching up with us, we sit here in our ghetto. Do you know, *twice* this autumn we've had the media phone us begging for a feature – the BBC and then the *Guardian*. Would his lordship budge? Not likely. He hasn't let anyone except forestry people onto his land for I don't know how many years. Apart from the public footpaths, of course, and now he's wanting to close *those* down.'

She stopped, as if wanting to say something and then deciding against it. The noise in the courtyard had faded away. There was nothing but the ticking clock and the purring kitten, snuggled up against my neck.

'So you can imagine,' Belle continued, 'how stunned I was when I saw you out there on the gravel this morning!'

'It was Brendan who brought me.'

'I know. I realised a second later. He's a cunning old thing, my Brendan, don't you believe those innocent blue eyes.'

I laughed so hard I nearly dislodged the kitten.

'But David didn't object, that's the real shock,' said Belle. 'So naturally I pounced on you: an emissary from the outside world! Quite apart from being dead nosy, of course, and wanting to get to know you.'

But we knew each other already, had known each other all our lives, as if I'd been leading a parallel shadow life in which Belle, David, Brendan, The Folly, all played a leading role. I couldn't shake off this sense of utter *belonging*.

Belle was suddenly serious again. 'Charlotte, you do know where all this is leading? I don't want to play games with you. Let me be straight. *We need you*.'

'Need *me*?' I sat up with such a jolt that the kitten fell off onto my lap.

'You could be our link with the outside world,' she said.

'*Me*? But I'm an outsider myself.'

'Yes and no. After all, you are a hill farmer. Charlotte, if only you would come and see us from time to time, casually, just be around the place. I know David would come to realise that people aren't automatically hostile to him, aren't waiting to laugh at him, if he makes the odd mistake.'

'Yes, but – '

'And David senses something in you, I'm sure of it. You're the one person who might get through to him.' Then she laughed. 'Oh, don't worry – I'm not trying to matchmake or anything daft like that. Just, well, friendship, I suppose.'

The kitten was staring lugubriously at me from the exile of my lap, trying to make me feel guilty about tumbling her from my shoulder. There were other things I felt much guiltier about. Belle was being honest with me, I had to reciprocate. I fondled the kitten absent-mindedly and said slowly, 'I'd love to help if I could. But I'm the last person he would trust.' Taking a deep breath, I told her about my wild ride that morning and the angry encounter with David.

As I talked, Belle's eyes grew larger and larger. When I finished, she began to chuckle. 'Well, well, well. But that just proves my point, don't you see? If he's prepared to forgive you after *that*, well! Look, forget about David. Just come and see *me*, please? And Brendan, and the lads. You'll be a breath of fresh air to us all.'

'I don't need persuading,' I said simply. 'I'd love to come.' I pictured the lovely walks through the forest to The Folly, lovely long talks with Belle. There was one public footpath which led directly –

Public footpath. My mind reverted to an earlier part of the conversation. 'Why is he trying to close the footpaths, after all this time?'

'Ah.' She looked furtively towards the courtyard. There were noises issuing from the stables – Brendan and Simon and Wolf laughing – but the courtyard was empty. She leaned across the table and lowered her voice.

'There is a reason. David would be appalled if he knew I was telling you, but . . . '

She paused, a picture of fraught indecision at odds with the easy manner she'd displayed until now. I was touched that she should even consider telling me something which could get her into trouble with David. I decided to rescue her. 'That's all right. Don't tell me if you don't want to.'

'Oh, Charlotte, I really am in a quandary.' She did indeed look terribly distressed. 'The point is, it's something that we really do have to keep quiet about. It really is rather important, it's not just David being bloody-minded.'

'Don't worry about it, I really – '

'But I'd hate you to think I didn't trust you, don't you see? Charlotte, if I tell you, would you promise – really promise – not to tell *anyone*?'

I contemplated her words – I don't make promises easily. The only person I might want to tell would be Effie, and I didn't think Effie would be all that interested in the intrigues of Keldreth.

'I promise.'

Belle's relief was palpable. 'You see, I haven't been entirely honest with you. There's something else we do up here that nobody knows about.' She leaned forward further still. 'For several years now, we've been – '

'Charlotte!'

We both jumped and looked guiltily at the window. There was Brendan, his open, good-natured face contrasting with the atmosphere of conspiracy in the kitchen. As the waves of guilt reached him at the window, he looked puzzled. 'Sure and I didn't mean to play the fox at the hen party,' he said uncertainly. 'Myself and the lads only wondered if you'd be liking a look about the stables before we're off . . . '

I got up quickly. The kitten took the opportunity to race up my sweater and settle herself on my shoulder again. 'Oh. Yes. Of course,' I stammered. How much had he heard?

Not much, I decided, for he grinned at the kitten and said comfortably, 'For sure you'll have to be taking that feline home with you, the way she's taken you over and all.'

Belle had got up, too. We moved closer to the window, the kitten clearly enjoying being the centre of attention.

'Yes, you must take her,' said Belle. 'You don't have a farm cat, do you?'

I explained about my here-today gone-tomorrow black cat and said I'd like the kitten to be a house cat anyway. 'I don't think Moss – ' I broke off, horrified. 'Moss! My dog! He's been tied up all morning with nothing to eat. And the hens. They're still locked in their hut. I really must go home. Can I come back another day and see the stables?'

There was a flurry of protest: couldn't the dog and hens wait a little longer? But I'd been irresponsible enough already this morning, with my wild ride on Olwen. Reluctantly, they let me go.

'But you will come back soon, won't you?' said Belle. 'Soon?'

13

I wanted to. I would have done, but one of the busy seasons of the hill farm calendar was suddenly upon me, with three different things demanding my attention almost simultaneously.

First came the compulsory autumn dipping for sheep scab. I couldn't risk being caught out by the inspectors, not in my first year. Rounding up the sheep from the moor with only myself and one dog proved a nightmare. It took ages, and at the end of it my legs felt as if they'd walked hundreds of miles. Was it really worth it, all this effort, for the scanty grazing on the moor? The dipping itself was as long and laborious as it had been the first time. Clearly it wasn't something that got easier with practice. One person alone was just not enough to run a hill farm during the busy seasons. I would have to hire labour the next time.

Right after dipping came the sales. Load by load I bundled into the trailer my wethers and those ewes too old for the harsh climate of Keldreth but with another year or two of good lowland lambing left in them. Off to market we went. It was a world of its own, and I didn't know it at all. I had to learn from scratch as I went along. Some of the sharper farmers took advantage of me. I didn't earn as much that season as I should have done. I thought ruefully how much easier it was to sell money than sheep.

Well, I would have to make up for it the next year, and the first step towards that was now due: tupping time. Some hideous but sweet-natured Leicesters and a handsome Swaledale did the honours. Day after day they strode into the fields with raddle harnesses on their chests to delight the ewes and, I prayed fervently, to plant a lovely set of twins in each. I planned it as carefully as I could, the different coloured dyes indicating both the father and the date of the deed. It was important for my first lambing season to

96

be well spaced, I couldn't afford to be caught in a rush at that crucial time.

It was late October by the time each of the chosen ewes displayed the tell-tale dye on her rump and I could relax a little. I felt tired and yet exhilarated. This was it: the end of one farming year, the beginning of another. There was little for me to do between now and spring except landwork and minor repairs, and there weren't many of those, thanks to John Jowett's care. I felt like celebrating. I would celebrate. I would phone Belle and invite myself to The Folly. My hand was actually reaching for the phone when it rang. I picked it up.

'Boo,' said a familiar voice. 'I'm coming up to haunt you.'

'Effie!' I cried. 'Where have you been? Your answerphone has been giving out the most extraordinarily mysterious messages for weeks.'

'I'm a mysterious lady.'

'But where have you been?'

'Everywhere, and that's God's own truth. I've had a bitch of a time, but I've got a breather now. I thought I might turn myself into a witch and fly up on my broomstick to see you for Halloween.'

'Great! Effie, you couldn't have timed it better – I've just finished with the dipping and the sales and the tupping, and – '

'Spare me the gory details. Just get some ice ready for Friday afternoon. The Porsche and a bottle of champers will be whizzing their way to you.' A pause. 'You *do* have ice?'

'Of course.'

'A fridge?'

'Certainly.'

'Electricity?'

'Naturally.'

'Hot water?'

'Definitely.'

'I'll make that two bottles. How's your thug?'

'Richard? I haven't seen him for ages.'

'Good. If I catch him anywhere near you I'll turn him into a toad.'

'Effie, you really are – '

'Gotta go – I've got a thug of my own coming round to take me out to dinner. See you Friday! 'Bye!'

*   *   *

Effie stood in the middle of my living room, appalled.

I'd tried so hard to make the house as welcoming as possible. I'd picked the last of the autumn roses from the trellis against the wall. I'd lit a big lusty fire in the living room, tending it carefully to make sure it would be at its roaring best just as Effie arrived. I'd set the kitchen table in advance, got a sumptuous meal brewing to fill the house with succulent fragrances. I'd – well, there wasn't much more I could do. Effie was right. The house was bare.

She took in the living room with one glance. It didn't need more, there was so little to see. Just white walls and a polished wooden floor, a sofa, two chairs and some bookcases against the walls. No carpet or rugs, no tables, no pictures on the walls, no houseplants, nothing but the fire and a few flowers to make it feel lived in.

'Minimalist, yes – I don't go for a lot of clutter myself,' said Effie at last. 'But this is ridiculous!'

I bowed my head, feeling like a nun in my cell being scrutinised for the first time by an outside world I'd almost forgotten. 'You'll get used to it,' I said uncertainly. 'It's very peaceful, really, having so few things.'

Her gaze stopped at the windows: stark squares of twilight against the pristine white walls. Nothing to mediate between inside and out. 'Oh, Charlotte, you *must* have curtains at least! How can you sit here at night with people strolling right up to your windows and gawping at you?'

'Effie, this isn't London – there *aren't* any people here.'

'What about those Druids?'

'There aren't any Druids.'

'There are. You said so yourself. You saw them on Midsummer's Eve.'

'Oh, those. That's miles away. You don't honestly think they've got a telescope trained on my windows?'

'What about Richard? You said yourself he skulked around the place.'

'Not anymore.'

'How do you know? He could be a really expert skulker by now. Look, I've got a darling little couple in Devon who do the most marvellous rugs and wall hangings – handwoven, any size, any design, no two alike, each one a little jewel. How about I commission a set for you? Put them on the walls by day and the windows by night. They really are gorgeous. Cost the earth, of course, but you've never been stingy.'

'Effie, I don't *want* anything on the windows! I don't *want* to shut out the countryside!'

'It's shut out anyway at night! You can't see anything but a horrid black hole! The place could be crawling with psychopaths and you wouldn't see them, but they'd see you all right!'

'That's ridiculous, there aren't – '

'Yes there are! The moors are crawling with them, everybody knows that! First thing they do when they escape from prison or whatever is head for the moors and then sneak down to some unsuspecting – ' Effie stopped.

I stopped, too, suddenly hearing in retrospect the winding up of the decibels. Decibels equals argument. We were heading for a row. We'd never rowed before. The nearest we'd ever got to a row was a desultory disagreement about which restaurant to go to, which play to see.

'Oh, Effie,' I said.

She nodded sadly.

And then, right on cue, a small grey comet shot into the room and climbed up her pink trouser suit. Effie caught the kitten halfway up and held it before her with both hands. 'Well! So this is your *souvenir de folie*?'

The tension fell away like magic, as if the kitten had brought with her some of The Folly's own enchantment. It *was* odd. Twice the kitten had chosen to befriend a stranger rather than her owner: first me at The Folly, and now Effie. Cats didn't do that, it wasn't in their nature.

'She *is* rather gorgeous!' said Effie. 'Have you found a name for her yet?'

'*You* choose,' I said.

It was a peace offering. It was also, I realised, an attempt to involve Effie in my life at Cappelrigg. I'd been alone long enough, stripped bare for four months now. It was time to start rebuilding, and to reconcile elements of my old life with the new. The kitten was doing just that. She scrambled up the rest of Effie and settled on her shoulder.

'I'll take her if you like,' I offered. 'I really must break her of the habit of treating people like trees.'

'Don't you dare,' she said.

She bent her head slightly to make her neck a welcoming cave into which the kitten crept, purring. Effie rubbed her face against the kitten, almost purring herself. It was a strange sight: Effie's spiky red hair against the kitten's downy grey fur. Tough, brittle, sharp-tongued urban Effie gone soft over a kitten.

'Tarzan,' Effie murmured.

Well, it wouldn't have been my choice. But, 'All right,' I said. 'Tarzan it is.'

A log settled into place with a whoosh of sparks and the fire blazed up. I could see it reflected orange in the indigo square of one window. 'Effie,' I said suddenly, 'about those rugs for the windows. I think I *would* like them after all.'

She saw immediately the significance of my olive branch. 'Right,' she said. 'Champagne time.'

*   *   *

We had champagne with the meal, too, and it deserved it. I'd always loved cooking for guests and been quite good at it. Now, four months of spartan eating ended in style. Star of the show was a chicken, one of my own, so free range she was usually out of sight and stuffed full of the good food with which I pampered my hens during their brief but happy lives. Effie didn't even recognise it as chicken, it was so tasty.

'Good meal?' I prompted when, later, we settled into the sofa in front of the fire with the rest of the champagne.

'Fabulous. You always were a brilliant cook.' Effie stretched extravagantly.

'Warm enough?' Rain was streaming down the uncurtained windows, but inside the fireplace was roaring.

'Wonderful. I'd forgotten how luxurious a real fire is.' She rubbed her face against Tarzan's soft fur.

'Kitten not bothering you?'

'I adore her. Watch I don't kidnap her.'

'More champagne?' Without waiting, I topped up her glass.

'You're spoiling me.'

She did look a picture of contentment, her long thin body curled into a corner of the sofa, champagne glass in one hand, the other stroking the kitten. I scrutinised the picture like an art dealer to confirm its authenticity. Good. Everything in order. The time was right.

'Splendid!' I said brightly. 'So you won't mind too much if I mention something just a teeny bit annoying?'

'My shoulders are broad,' she said magnanimously.

'We're invited to tea at Graegarth tomorrow.'

She sat upright, toppling the kitten but expertly saving the champagne. '*Tea*?' Her face grimaced like a monkey's. '*Tea*?'

''Fraid so.

'Your Viking thug giving a *tea* party?'

'Mrs Thug. His mother.'

'Yuk.'

'I tried to get out of it. She phoned yesterday. I said I couldn't possibly, that I had an old friend coming to stay, but – '

'A little less of the "old," please.'

'A young friend coming to stay. "How delightful! Do bring her along!" I did try, Effie.'

'I appreciate.'

'It's only for a couple of hours . . . '

Effie gave a sigh of resignation. 'Can I bring a hip flask?'

'Well . . . '

'Not even a hip flask?' She sank into gloom. She sighed again, looked mournfully at Tarzan, then at me. 'What did she sound like?'

I hesitated. Then, 'Frankly, rather awful. Very *refained* voice. Imitation County. I've always wondered why Richard had no trace of the local accent. Jean, too. Now I know. She drilled them from birth. Actually, I'm rather glad it's come when you're here. I'd like your expert opinion.'

'Designer or psychologist?'

'Psychologist. You have a knack of seeing through to the heart of things.'

'Flattery, my dear.'

'I know. It gets me everywhere.'

Effie laughed. 'Okay. Fill me in.'

I settled in, knowing I'd aroused her curiosity. If there was anything she loved more than her creature comforts, it was a good mystery. 'It's Jean,' I began. 'There's something wrong there. She's quite a pretty girl, and you can see she used to be a chirpy easy-going sort. It's still there, like a faded aura, but covered over by a dark film. I have a feeling that she's had some kind of a shock and hasn't yet adjusted to the new person she has to become because of it. Do you see what I mean?'

'Sort of. Portions of two different people floating around and competing for space. What d'you suppose did it?'

'I haven't a clue. I haven't even met the mother or seen where they live. But Jean seems barely under control. I don't think this is going to be quite the tame little vicar's tea party you imagine.'

'Good! Bring me my fiddle and my opium pipe and I shall give it my full attention.'

I laughed. 'You see? Flattery does get me everywhere.'

14

Effie did her best to enter into the spirit. She wore the most subdued clothing she'd brought with her (the shocking-pink trouser suit), she deleted some of her more bizarre make-up, she brushed her red spikes down sufficiently to resemble a torpid porcupine rather than one poised for attack.

I tried, too. I chose a fairly respectable shirtwaist dress which, though fashionable, wasn't obtrusively so. I even scrubbed out the Land-Rover in Effie's honour, annihilating all traces of sheep and dog.

We set off in style, with forced good spirits. We ignored as much as possible the drab rain which streamed past the windows and curtained the landscape in grey muslin. I'd never been to Graegarth and was, of course, dead curious. If a house displays the personality of its owner, how much more so a farm.

The signals given off by Graegarth were distinctly ominous. The dry-stone walls had collapsed unheeded in so many places that it would have been a nightmare trying to repair them now. Instead, great tracts of rotten wooden posts and rusted wire spanned the lengths between the remains of the old walls, punctuated here and there by a propped up bedstead or sheet of corrugated roofing.

Beyond the risible boundary walls was the land itself, the sour peat waterlogged despite the dry summer, its surface covered with ugly clumps of reeds between which mangy sheep and bullocks nibbled what grass they could find. In the drier places, thistles replaced the reeds. Great fistfuls of burrs stuck to the fleeces of the sheep.

Three centuries of farmers had carved a passable hill farm out of this land. What had destroyed it? The grants and subsidies were twice as high as on non-hill farms, and sheep and beef were less demanding than any other form of farming.

Apart from a few busy times, most of the year was free for patching walls, draining the land, repairing outbuildings. This land was, beneath its awful surface, identical to that of Cappelrigg and Farleton Estate. Yet John Jowett and David Farleton had made their land decent enough.

Even someone as irredeemably urban as Effie must see that something was badly awry with Graegarth. I dreaded her response.

'Makes the Bowery look quite smart,' she said as we rattled our way across a broken cattle grid into the farmyard.

The farmyard was a wreck. Not one of the original stone outbuildings remained. All had been replaced with tatty new ones of concrete and asbestos and corrugated roofing. The Land-Rover's wheels churned through a sea of mud and slurry. I parked as close to the house as I could, and Effie and I jumped directly from the vehicle onto a clean concrete apron in front of the house.

We'd been so busy negotiating the muck that we hadn't really seen the house. Now we stood before it, and I for one had difficulty concealing my amazement. The house was a neat little oasis in the middle of a rural slum. It was the only stone building left and was punctiliously cared for. A varnished front door, heavily studded as if it were a pub, led into the porch. Beside it a scalloped sign in rustic style announced GRAEGARTH. A brass carriage lamp hung above it, competing with two hanging baskets. The doorbell was also brass, well polished and incongruous in its surroundings.

We didn't have a chance to use it. The door popped open and there stood Mrs Staveley, corsetted into a tweed skirt and twinset with a string of pearls. Above it a meticulous head of salon-blue waves surrounded a plump and pleasing face. The face smiled a greeting and with motherly clucking urged us into the house 'quickly, before you're soaked, you poor things.'

We shed our coats in the porch before being whizzed through the kitchen. Clearly the kitchen was not for visitors, though it seemed eminently respectable: bright, clean and modern, crammed with all the latest gadgetry. The vinyl floor-covering gleamed and the overhead light glinted off a multitude of chrome controls. It looked like a spaceship.

We were ushered into the living room. It, too, was crammed. There must have been a dozen little tables, each displaying a careful arrangement of knick-knacks. Electric candle-style lamps ringed the walls, competing for space with pictures that showed country life at its most idyllic. The pictures almost obliterated the floral wallpaper. The thick carpet was floral, too, and on it stood a whole shopful of reproduction furniture, all of it beautifully polished.

Mrs Staveley indicated a battery of ruffled chintz chairs in front of the log-effect electric fire, and we sat down.

'The children will be down shortly,' she smiled. I pictured a scrubbed procession of cherubs before remembering that 'the children' were Richard and Jean. 'Having a little wash after their day's work,' she explained. 'It's so difficult to keep clean on a farm,' she added.

Well, yes. On this one.

We scarcely had time to begin a conversation before 'the children' arrived. One look at Jean told me she wished herself a thousand miles away. I didn't blame her. I wondered how the five of us would survive the next hour or two.

Richard, however, seemed undaunted. I admired his ability to manage, such a big vigorous man, in a house so uncompromisingly feminine. It must take extreme physical control to avoid sweeping a tableful of clutter to the floor each time he passed through the room. In fact, he manoeuvred his way to us with the grace of a lion and sat down between his mother and me. Jean, a poor attempt at a smile on her young-old face, sat at the end, next to Effie. Seated, we formed a precise semicircle in front of the fire.

Mrs Staveley said to Effie, 'It must be lovely for you to have a friend living in the country. Somewhere to come for a breath of fresh air.'

The room was stifling.

'Marvellous!' said Effie. 'And all that open space!' She looked brightly round the crowded room. If we'd been at a table I could have given her ankle a sharp kick.

Mrs Staveley didn't notice. 'Yes, and the silence!'

On cue, a barnful of dogs started howling.

This time she did notice. She laughed. 'Well, more or less! Still, at least it's a natural sound.'

I had my views on that but kept them to myself.

Just as the conversation threatened to expire, Mrs Staveley ordered Jean to put the kettle on. Jean's relief at even a temporary absence was manifest. Why had Mrs Staveley convened this awkward little gathering? I knew from my farming childhood that such events were rare. Newcomers were welcomed discreetly, indirectly, not with tea parties.

The conversation turned to Effie's job. Mrs Staveley was thrilled to discover that Effie had done the houses of some fairly famous people. Effie dutifully 'revealed' a few of their quirky ways, though none, I noted, that couldn't be gleaned from any magazine.

Then the spotlight was on me: my farming background, my job in the City, my intentions for Cappelrigg. The atmosphere hotted up at this point. It was understandable that they would want to know more about their new neighbour, but the intensity of Mrs Staveley's interrogation startled me.

Jean arrived with the tea, wheeling in a hostess trolley heaped with food which had obviously been arranged in advance by her mother. Mrs Staveley distributed the goods with queenly aplomb. The food was good, home-baked – the spaceship kitchen was more than a showpiece. Mrs Staveley knew how to cook. She was in every way an exemplary farmer's wife, once she shut the door on the appalling farm outside.

The atmosphere was just beginning to ease when Jean came out with her little bombshell. Looking hard at me, she said flatly, 'You must be crazy, leaving London to come to a dump like this.'

Frozen silence. I wondered whether she was referring to her farm or Keldreth in general. 'London isn't all that wonderful,' I began.

'I'd sell my soul to live there,' she said vehemently.

She was slumped in her frilly chair, eating a piece of sponge with exaggerated disregard for the crumbs falling onto its immaculate fabric. Her face was hard, and very, very old. It was as if a switch had been thrown, transforming Dr Jekyll into Miss Hyde. My mind worked furiously, looking for a way to salvage the situation.

Effie got there before me. Dear pragmatic matter-of-fact

Effie. 'You don't have to go that far,' she said cheerfully. 'Keep your soul and sell a few sheep instead. That's all you need, you know: money.'

Jean gave an uncertain laugh. 'And a job.' Then she turned her hard direct gaze on Effie. 'Will you take me back with you?'

Effie's face betrayed no emotion whatsoever.

'I can paint, and hang wallpaper,' said Jean. She waved a contemptuous arm to take in the room. 'I'm the muggins who did most of this, you know.'

'I don't have any staff,' said Effie smoothly, 'apart from a secretary. I hire piecework. But you get yourself somewhere to live and the equipment and show me you can do the work and sure, I'll hire you.'

It worked. Jean's aggression wavered. She finished chewing a piece of sponge and said finally, 'I may just take you up on that.'

It was probably a bluff, but Effie's plain speaking had defused a potentially explosive scene sufficiently for Richard to intervene and change the subject.

*   *   *

That night, Effie and I post-mortemed the tea party over a glass of whisky.

'Is that all it is?' I said. 'Country girl suffocated by boredom and longing for the bright lights of London?'

'No,' said Effie. 'You were right first time. There's something fishy going on. Probably your Druids. She would like to leave, no doubt about that. But it's not the bright lights. She wants to get away from the whole scene. And so should you.'

'You haven't even met my other neighbours,' I said. Then, 'Would you like to?' After the awful tea party, the thought of The Folly was irresistible and I said excitedly, 'Look, why don't we take a walk over there tomorrow – I promised Belle ages ago that I would.'

'*Walk*?'

'It wouldn't kill you.'

'Yes it would. That's what I pay my gym an exorbitant subscription for – to make me fit without suffering the ignominy of walking.'

107

I laughed, 'Honestly, Effie!'

'Honestly yourself. First tea, then walking. You're getting so wholesome I hardly recognise you. Here, give us some more whisky.'

I topped up her glass. 'Seriously. I'd like you to meet them.'

'It's raining.'

'It might not be tomorrow. Effie . . . '

She sighed and took a contemplative sip of her whisky. 'If I must.' She rose, yawned, stretched luxuriously.

I rose, too, and banked up the fire, taking care not to disturb Tarzan, who was snoozing in front of it. She looked so soft and peaceful. The tea party seemed far away. Tarzan breathed a benediction over my house quite out of proportion to her size. Just looking at her made me feel serene.

Effie's voice jerked me back to reality. 'Hey! What the hell is going on up there?'

She was standing by the uncurtained window, looking out into the blackness.

Not so black. As I joined her, I saw again the pale orange glow above the moor.

'Is that supposed to be some kind of witches' coven?' Effie demanded. 'Jesu! I was *joking* when I said I was coming up on my broomstick to haunt you. Someone's taken me seriously.'

Of course. Halloween. Samain.

'Samain,' I said.

'Sam who?'

'Samain,' I repeated sleepily. 'The Celtic new year.' I'd forgotten all about it. I hoped Effie would let me forget it again.

'Jesu Christus,' Effie was muttering. 'A houseful of nut-cases on one side, a commune full of ageing hippies on the other and a bunch of loopy Druids on the moor. You do pick them, Charlotte. You really do.'

*   *   *

It wasn't the ley line, I'm sure of it. There were plenty of other reasons for a sleepless night. I turned restlessly in my bed like a pig on a spit, unable to find comfort for mind or body. The tape of the tea party rewound in my head and played itself back in slow motion. The other 'party', the one taking place on the moor, didn't help either. Both events jarred with the landscape. Both shrieked against my sleepless brain like chalk on a blackboard.

I got out of bed and went to the window.

The glow was more lurid than before. Clearly the party was hotting up, literally. Who were these idiots who trekked to the moor in the rain to play boy scout round their campfire? They must have had a hell of a time getting the fire going on a night like this. I supposed there was a scoutmaster in charge, he with the matches. Did they drink hot chocolate while invoking the spirits? The whole thing was so childish.

It wasn't the ley line that made me suddenly pull on my clothes, tiptoe past Effie's room and creep downstairs. It wasn't any fear of mystic forces either that made me write a brief note and slip it half under her door. Most likely I would be back long before she woke up, but it was only decent to let her know where I'd gone if – improbably – she discovered my absence.

Tarzan hopped to attention when I passed through the living room. I let her run up me and gave her a cuddle, but when she tried to scramble up the last stage to my shoulder I plucked her off and set her down by the fireplace. 'No, puss. This isn't a trip for you. You're too sane.'

I put on my anorak and wellies and went outside.

I walked through my grove and remembered Richard's remarks all those months ago. The oak, sacred to the Druids. Oak leaves were used in their rituals. Did they get them from my grove? David's forest? I wondered if David knew about the shenanigans on the moor and, if so, what he thought about it. Not much, probably. In his quiet matter-of-fact way, he was the one in harmony with nature. These others were just playing at it, making a mockery of what they claimed to believe in.

The wind intensified as I left the grove, throwing bucketfuls of water into my face. I didn't mind. In the four months I'd been at Cappelrigg I'd become so used to being outside in all weather that I almost felt uneasy in the comfort of my house. The rain was cold and fresh, a great antidote to the suffocation of Graegarth. I felt like a child released from school. The feel of the earth beneath my wellies exhilarated me and I ran all the way to the little gully for the sheer joy of it. I hardly cared anymore about the Druids. I was simply enjoying being outside.

The gully dampened my spirits a little, as always. I could never see the place where John Jowett had died without my pleasure clouding. It was the one blight on my love affair with Cappelrigg: that I'd gained it through someone else's death.

The land rose after the gully and I slowed down. I slowed down even more as I climbed up the green track.

With no cliff face to throw the land in shadow, the open moor was that little bit lighter. In addition, the cloud cover was patchy, allowing the moon an occasional watt or two. None the less, I picked my way with care. It was difficult to see the little peat channels which webbed the moor and I'd feel a right fool breaking an ankle on such a silly errand.

I headed straight for the table and its standing stones. I didn't care if anyone saw me. I felt no fear whatsoever. Indeed, I felt a twinge of slightly malicious pleasure anticipating their faces when, common sense personified, I would stride blithely into their midst. If only I had one of those trays used during intermission at the cinema. 'Ice cream! Ice cream!' I would sing out.

I shelved my fantasies when I reached the base of the scree. The scree was hard going; I had to concentrate on where I put each hand and foot. I could hear the chanting now. The voices were all male. I'd started reading up on Druids after the Midsummer's Eve bonfire, but I'd become bored with it before learning what role, if any, was played by women. Well, here was my answer. None.

I reached the top of the table. There were clumps of bush-height heather between me and the stones. Feeling rather childish myself, I darted from bush to bush and reached the shelter of a stone without being seen. I peered out from behind it.

A huge flat stone lay like an altar between the pond and

the fire. About twenty men, robed in white, stood in a neat circle around the stone. The circle was so neat, the men so evenly spaced, that the whole thing seemed rehearsed for an audience. How shocked they would be to discover that they had one.

There was one man separate from the rest. He stood in front of the altar, his arms raised, obviously leading the chants. I thought of a choirmaster and had to stifle a nervous giggle.

And it was nervous. What I hadn't anticipated was the hoods – white, like the robes, and triggering in me an automatic spasm of fear as I thought, inevitably, of those terrible photographs of the Ku-Klux-Klan. These hoods weren't pointed, but the analogy wouldn't go away. Nor would the thought that anyone taking the trouble to conceal his face is up to no good. I stayed behind my stone and kept very, very quiet.

I needn't have bothered. The chanting swelled into a chorus so loud as to drown out the roar of the wind, the crackle of the fire, the sloshing of the rain against stone. The sound was unmistakably fervid. This was no game. And it certainly was no outing for overgrown boy scouts. These men were in earnest.

I thought, briefly, of slipping away while I could. Then I gave myself a sharp mental kick. This was the 1990s. Stripped of their robes, these men were nothing but local bank clerks, schoolteachers, shopkeepers. I did not – emphatically did not – believe in the power of the ley line to turn these foolish but inoffensive men into monsters. The disturbing strength of their chanting was nothing but the frustration of their dull daily lives being let loose for once. There was no harm in it, and certainly no danger to me.

But an icicle shot down my spine as the chanting suddenly burst into a single manic shout and then ceased. The silence was truly deafening. And when the wind and rain and fire finally filled it, they, too, sounded a little frenzied.

The man by the altar was wearing a leafy crown over his hood – clearly he was the leader. He made a swooping gesture towards the earth – earth, air, fire, water; all were present –

111

and then thrust his arms up in triumph. While the chanting broke out again he held aloft a wicker cage. In it was a hen.

Again the impulse towards nervous laughter. A *hen*, for God's sake.

But my laughter never had a chance, for the next thing I saw was the man swooping earthward again in a dramatic gesture accompanied by stronger and more rhythmic chants. He must have removed the bird from its cage unseen, because he then swooped up bearing the hen in both hands while the men emitted another chilling shriek. My guts twisted as I heard a different kind of shriek: the poor terrified hen, struggling frantically to escape, its tiny brain going haywire as it tried to make its pitiful strength prevail against that of twenty or so men.

That was the moment when I should have sprung out of hiding and called a halt to the whole awful thing. But, like in a nightmare, I was rooted to the earth. My legs had turned to stone, my voice, which wanted to scream a protest, was shoved back into my throat by the wind. I watched, paralysed and helpless, as the leader, with horrible slow-motion deliberation, wrung the hen's neck.

The chorus roared.

The leader placed the still-jerking bird on the altar, drew out a knife and, after holding it high so that the fire glinted from it, plunged the knife into the hen.

The chorus roared louder.

Then he slit its belly on the altar and placed what looked like a small round stone in it before criss-crossing the corpse with thongs to tie it up again. At this point the men divided into two lines and raised their arms to form an archway. The man with the hen came round the altar and walked solemnly through the archway, holding the hen high above his head. Blood streamed from the corpse all over the white hood of its killer.

The chorus changed to a shrill series of rhythmic stabs, as if imitating the death of the bird, as the man reached the edge of the pond. Then, with a final swirl of his blood-stained robe, he wheeled round once and threw the corpse into the centre of the pond.

The chorus gave one final ear-shattering roar before falling silent at last.

I sank to my knees behind the stone and vomited.

I was too busy being sick to notice how the ceremony ended. The next thing I knew, the men had formed into a single line headed by the blood-stained 'priest' and were marching straight towards my stone.

There was no way I could escape, so I made myself as small as possible at the base of the stone. There were enough heather bushes round me to form a sort of nest; with my dark anorak and jeans, and with the men's eyes unconditioned to the dark by the firelight, I might just get away with it. I drew my anorak hood round to cover as much of my face as possible. Then I held my breath and waited.

I should have kept my head down. With my head down and my hands drawn up into my sleeves, there would be no light patches to disturb the dark of my nest. But some primitive fear of being taken unawares prevented me from doing the sensible thing. I couldn't bear to crouch there with my head down and my neck ready for the knife, just like the hen's. I had to see what was coming. And so, breathing as shallowly as I could, I raised my head a fraction and waited.

Just as he was approaching my stone, the priest stumbled. I thought briefly of drugs or alcohol, then realised that some of the hen's blood must have trickled into the eyeholes of the hood. He couldn't see where he was going. Still walking, though unsteadily, he reached into the recesses of his robe and drew out a handkerchief. Then he raised the hood just long enough to wipe the blood out of his eyes.

It was Richard.

15

I didn't want to tell Effie what I'd seen. It would only fuel her efforts to persuade me to leave Cappelrigg. But one look at my haggard face over breakfast told her more than enough; silence now would lead her to even worse speculation: attempted rape or murder at the very least.

'All right,' I said, 'but only if you promise not to over-react.'

'That's a matter of interpretation,' she said pedantically.

And so I told her. I tried to make light of it, use my jokiest language, turn it into an amusing if slightly gruesome anecdote.

She was not amused. She was even less amused when, after some hesitation, I revealed the identity of the 'priest'.

'Charlotte!' she exploded. 'You're coming back to London with me *today*!'

'That,' I said mildly, 'is over-reaction.'

'That,' she said rather less mildly, 'is common sense. I'm not leaving you to the mercy of someone like that.'

'It was only a hen,' I reminded her. 'You may not want to hear this, Effie, but I did exactly the same thing to the hen we dined off so well two nights ago. Wrung its neck. I'm afraid that's what one does to hens.'

This checked her for only a moment. 'Yes, but not all that other stuff.'

'True. What they performed was the whole Celtic "triple death" for sacrificial victims. First you strangle or hang the victim, then you burn or stab it, and then you immerse it in water. Remember the Lindow Man in the British Museum? That's what they did to him.'

'A long time ago,' she said.

'Yes, well.' I could think of no way to excuse what I'd seen.

'You stay here much longer and you'll end up as Cappelrigg Woman.'

'Don't be ridiculous.'

'First a hen, then a sheep, then a succulent young virgin.'

'I'm disqualified. Neither young nor a virgin.'

'This is serious, Charlotte. What would have happened if they'd discovered you spying on their fun and games?'

'Well, they didn't.'

'How *did* you get away?'

I poured us a second cup of coffee and finished the story. 'They didn't see me. The moor is pretty rough, and the wind and rain made it hard going for them. Also, their eyes were still dazed by the fire. They could hardly see where they were going, let alone notice a slightly larger clump of heather beneath one stone. I just stayed put until they disappeared. Then I followed them.'

Effie enunciated very precisely, 'You . . . are . . . an . . . idiot.'

'Not really. They never looked back. If they had, I would have hit the ground like in a western – I was so soaked by then that it wouldn't have made much difference.'

'So where did they go?'

'Straight down the ley line, of course.'

Effie's coffee mug came to an abrupt halt halfway up to her mouth. 'Charlotte. The ley line goes through this house. Richard said so. I remember distinctly.'

'I know.'

'Are you telling me . . . '

I laughed. 'That they turned into spirits and melted through the walls? No. When they got to the grove, they divided into two lines again and made a wide detour around. Moss wouldn't have seen a thing – I'd shut the barn door because of the rain.'

Effie's hands were shaking as she took a gulp of her coffee. I knew what she was thinking.

'When I think . . . ' she said. Another gulp of coffee. 'There was I, peacefully snoring in my bed, with visions of sugar plums et cetera. While outside . . . '

'Yes,' I admitted. 'It was rather a bad moment. But you see, Effie, they didn't do anything. The last thing in their minds was any prank that would mean discovery.'

'Prank!'

'I mean, the whole point of these rituals is secrecy. They don't want to be discovered. If I leave them alone, they'll leave me alone. There's no danger.'

'But you didn't leave them alone. You spied.'

'Well, I won't do it again. Now let's forget the whole thing and get outside. It's stopped raining.'

'Hang on a minute. If they left via the ley line, they must have arrived the same way. Why didn't we see them then?'

'They probably saw the lights and came some other way. See? They really do want to avoid people.'

'What about the hen?'

'Hens aren't people.'

'Don't be so obtuse. Where did they get the hen?'

I hadn't thought of that. My stomach gave a nasty little lurch as I realised that there was only one person up here who kept hens.

I ran outside. It was no use looking in the hen hut – I'd let them out that morning and knew who was there and who wasn't. The one who wasn't had been missing for two days. I hadn't been unduly worried – she was an independent little cuss forever wandering off to make unofficial nests in secret places. Usually I found them and shooed her back to the flock. Now I made a thorough search. There was no sign of an unofficial nest or of the hen.

I tried to hide my anger and dejection when I returned to the kitchen. Effie's face wore a maddening I-told-you-so look. I nodded.

'Phone the police this instant,' she said.

'For a hen? Hens disappear all the time. Usually it's foxes, sometimes it's Druids. Anyway, there's no proof. One hen looks much like another, and this one's at the bottom of that pool in any case. Come on – it's lovely outside, and there aren't any Druids in Farleton Forest.'

'You're taking it all very calmly,' said Effie.

'Not really. But there's nothing I can do. You do see that don't you?'

I hurried round the kitchen gathering up the breakfast

116

things and dumping them in the sink. I didn't want to waste any more of the morning – we'd had a late start already.

'Did you get any sleep?' Effie asked.

'Nope.'

'You must have been in quite a state when you got home,' she said sadly. 'Why didn't you wake me up? At least we could have talked it through over a whisky.'

'You need your beauty sleep.'

'Thanks a bunch.'

'And there was no point disturbing you. It was all over by then.'

'Solidarity, chum. That's what friendship is about.'

I gave her a brief hug in passing. 'I know. I do appreciate. I'll appreciate even more if you'll pull on those special "visitor wellies" I bought for you and come outside for a walk.'

'I don't know whether to admire your spirit or despise your folly.'

'Neither. Come and see the *real* Folly.'

*   *   *

It was a beautiful morning. The rain of the last few days had left the landscape with a scrubbed-clean face turned up to greet an Indian Summer sun. The wind had stopped showing off and contented itself with an occasional playful puff which lifted armloads of fallen leaves in my grove only to whirl them about and set them down again somewhere else. Gems of leftover raindrops were strewn lavishly across the grass, their tiny prisms catching the sun and throwing little rainbows everywhere. The air was full of the bittersweet scent of autumn.

Even Effie was impressed.

'Come on,' I said. 'Admit. It's sensational.'

She turned round slowly to take in the whole view. Her face wore the professional look she had when scrutinising a room she was about to transform. 'Not bad,' she admitted.

'Meanie.'

'But we could do with a clump of trees over there. Saffron. A little accent point.'

Oddly enough she was right. I filed it away for future reference.

'That's what David Farleton does,' I said. 'Trees for profit and beauty. He's more or less re-designed his part of Keldreth.'

'Hmmm,' said Effie, thoughtful. 'Yes. I wouldn't mind designing a piece of landscape.'

'You do surprise me.'

'Good. I'd hate to be predictable.'

We went through into the field containing my freshly-tupped ewes. They were due to return to the moor in a day or two. I didn't want to think about the moor, nor did Effie. She'd promised not to raise the subject again during our walk. Instead she frowned at the coloured blobs of dye on the rumps of my sheep. 'I don't much care for *those* accent points.'

I explained that the different colours indicated both the tup who had served the ewe and when she was due to lamb.

Effie didn't like that either. 'Not very discreet.'

'Farming isn't.'

'I like David Farleton.'

The *non sequitur* caught me off balance and I stopped, staring at her. 'You've never met him.'

'Designing landscapes,' she explained. 'He sounds my sort of guy.'

I burst out laughing. At the same time a whoosh of joy shot through me. That surprised me as much as Effie's remark. I hadn't realised until then how important it was that Effie should like David Farleton. I hadn't even realised how much I myself liked him. He had crept up on my mind. I suddenly saw him as a dark benevolent shadow brooding over the great expanse of Farleton Forest, its power and his so strong that it overshot the boundary to give a little leftover blessing to my own land. Like Tarzan. A good spirit. Yes. 'I rather like him, too,' I admitted. 'But I'm not sure you will. He's terribly grumpy.'

'So am I. We're obviously made for each other.'

The land crackled with life and energy and a sense of the future really going somewhere at last. We were approaching the forest. It hummed a little tune of welcome. Of course it was just a puff of wind through the leaves. Of course the fog that had enveloped Olwen and myself on our wild ride was just fog, not primeval mist. And then again, perhaps not.

We climbed the stile and dropped down onto the public footpath. It was the same one I'd taken that first day, when David Farleton had plonked a tree on me. Now, as then, I could hear a chainsaw, but this time far away, probably the other side of The Folly.

The forest was different, too. Last night's wind had plucked many of the leaves off and dropped them in a confetti carpet over the path. The leaves were still bright and clean: butter-yellow hazels looking good enough to eat, elegant pale-green fingers of ash, beech leaves glowing a rich warm russet. In one place a birch had showered down a treasure trove of bright gold coins. A little further along Effie picked up a leaf neither of us recognised. It was large and shaped rather like an oak but its colour was an intense soft red.

Above was a different picture altogether. The poor half-stripped trees reminded me of a dressing room full of women caught *déshabillé* by a man blundering through the wrong door. Their embarrassment seemed less a matter of prudery than pride. Neither naked nor dressed, they knew themselves to be temporarily unlovely, and they blushed. I realised with a pang that I'd missed the best of the autumn colour, too busy messing about with my sheep. Farleton Forest, with such a variety of trees, must be stunning at that time. Next year. Next year I would manage things better. For now, I contented myself with the leftovers strewn at my feet.

We arrived rather abruptly at a sort of crossroad, a junction with a broad forest ride which ran from north to south. We glanced up the north part of it and then stopped, both of us, enchanted.

A Renoir was coming to life. Two figures – strangers to me – were strolling along the vibrant sun-dappled carpet: a woman in an elegant riding habit and a small boy holding her hand. Both were dark-haired and darkly dressed. Making their outlines sharp against the gilded leaves, there was a timeless serenity about their motion, then the boy swung his leg and a froth of gold sprayed up rustling before them. Their laughter sang down the ride, hers dark and rich and warm, his a piccolo descant.

As they approached, I fully expected them to vanish, to melt into the trees which framed them in such an exquisite picture. But they were real. I could see their faces now: strong, handsome, happy. The riding habit was an illusion, though. It was just a fitted jacket and a longish skirt above a pair of dark leather boots.

The portrait came to a stop in front of us. 'Hallo!' said the woman. 'You must be Charlotte? I am Astrid, and here is Matthew?'

I announced Effie's name and we all shook hands. The formality was incongruous to the setting but quite in keeping with the woman's manner and continental accent. She had high cheekbones and long dark eyes which swept slightly upward. Her dark hair, by contrast, swept down and back from a centre-parting into a smooth knot. She was very beautiful.

In the few moments of easy silence that followed, it occurred to me that there was something a little odd. She had pronounced my name 'Karlotta'. That she knew of my existence wasn't surprising; there were so few people in Keldreth that I might well be mentioned. But such mentions would use the English form. It was as if she had known about me *in writing*, before coming here, and her mind had automatically used a foreign pronunciation. I didn't think I was significant enough to warrant a written description.

'The morning is so beautiful, yes? We go to see David and the horses work? You will come with?'

There was a charming little upward tilt which made each phrase sound like a question. It gave a touch of playfulness to her speech and contrasted with the dignity of her appearance. She wouldn't have been out of place in a nineteenth-century salon.

And so Effie and I, turning southwards, eased ourselves into the painting, and the four of us proceeded down the ride. There should have been music accompanying us. A chaconne, perhaps. Instead, we listened to the crisp rustle of our footsteps and the wind puffing some remaining leaves off the trees to dance down before us.

The boy touched Effie's hand, the one holding the red leaf. Effie held the leaf up. 'Odd, isn't it? We can't work out what it is. Do you know?'

'The American red oak,' he said. '*Quercus rubra.*'

In any other child it would have sounded like showing off, but the boy wore his knowledge lightly. I hadn't really noticed him before. Now I saw how attractive he was: small and dark and with a curious combination of delicacy and strength. I don't know much about children and so couldn't judge his age – perhaps somewhere between seven and nine? He was as clean-lined and definite as the woman I assumed was his mother. They were a devastatingly handsome pair. No wonder I'd seen them as a painting.

The boy smiled impishly at Effie. 'But *you* should know it.'

The kid was bright. Whether his knowledge of trees was precocious I didn't know, but he'd picked up Effie's American accent after only a phrase or two.

Effie returned his smile with a wry one. 'There aren't a lot of trees in Manhattan.'

'Central Park?' the boy tried.

Full marks for geography, too.

'You're right,' said Effie. 'It's probably crammed full of *Quercus rubra.* I'm just a dumb city slicker who doesn't see them.'

'Oh, no. You're not dumb. Hardly anyone knows the red oak,' the boy said magnanimously. 'We plant it because of the colour. Daddy says there aren't any English trees as red as this.'

We? Daddy? The boy was clearly more than a casual visitor. I tried to remember what Richard had told me about the younger brother, Hugh. I turned to Astrid. 'Actually, we were just on our way to The Folly. Belle asked me to come ages ago, but I've been so busy with the sheep – '

'Ah!'

There was a dark dramatic quality to the simple word.

'But Belle is not there,' she continued woefully. 'She has gone to the town. She will be so sorry to miss you.'

'I should have phoned,' I said. 'My fault entirely.' I had to work at keeping my own sentences grounded, so contagious was the lilt of her inflection.

The boy, I noticed, had no accent at all. But then, school would counteract the home influence. He was looking at me

121

so avidly that I wondered what on earth I'd said to arouse such attention.

'You have *sheep*?' he asked. He made them sound like quadrupedal miracles.

'Yes, that's why I haven't come sooner. First the dipping, then the sales, then the tupping. I'm taking them back up to the moor tomorrow, so that'll be the end of it for a while.'

The tragic quality vanished from Astrid's voice as she laughed the most extraordinarily musical laugh I've ever heard. 'Poor Matti – he adores every animal and here we have only the horses and a few cats. Otherwise, only trees.'

'Sometimes I wish I had only trees,' I admitted. 'At least they stay put, they don't have to be carted up to the moor.'

'Oh, please, may I come with you?' said Matti. I scarcely had time to wonder at the intensity of his plea before Astrid chided him.

'Matthew! This is impolite, to invite along!'

No upward lilt there. The earnestness of good manners cancelled it out.

I rushed to the boy's rescue. 'But I'd be delighted! You have no idea how boring it is trudging behind a bunch of slow-motion rugs all alone. I'd love to have your company.'

I meant it. Effie was leaving early next morning, and I knew her absence would leave a painful gap. The child was charming, and I could be sure he wouldn't rush about scaring the hell out of my sheep.

The boy's face glowed.

Astrid's looked doubtful. 'Are you sure?'

'Positive. What time can you bring him over?'

'Oh, most surely the time is for you?'

It took me a while to untangle this one. 'Oh. Yes. Well, normally I'd set out about nine, but if that's too – '

'Nine he is there – but only if you are truly sure he is no nuisance?'

'The pleasure is mine,' I said.

Matti exhibited his rapture by kicking a shower of leaves into the air. We all laughed, erasing his unspeakable social gaffe.

Up ahead a long flat trailer piled with logs seemed stranded by the side of the ride. With no cab attached, and no one about, it looked a bit desolate. I'd been wondering about it for a while. But now, as we approached, I heard noises issuing from somewhere deep within the forest and deduced that the trailer was in the process of being loaded. This must be where David was.

A flicker of pleasure went through me at the prospect of seeing him again. It was followed by apprehension. I'd just remembered Belle's remark about his desire to close the public footpaths. This ride wasn't even that. It was strictly private. Like David. How extraordinary that I'd forgotten. In my wild vision of David Farleton as a benevolent presence brooding over the land, I'd ignored the reality of my encounters with him. The real man was at best intensely private, at worst downright aggressive. There was no reason to believe he would be pleased to see myself and Effie making ourselves at home here. It was Belle, not David, who had urged the invitation, and now she wasn't here. I could only hope that Astrid and Matti would mediate our presence.

My apprehension vanished as the trees up ahead seemed to part and a magnificent black Shire stepped into the ride. The Renoir became a Constable. The magic had returned in full force. This must be how forests were a century ago, or two or three. Time had no place here. The scene gave off a powerful sense of ageless unity between horse and tree and man. Nothing could shake it, not even the appearance a moment later of the men in their twentieth-century jeans: Wolf, miniscule at the end of the long reins; Paul walking beside him, clearly giving instructions; and, far behind, David, watching their progress. I supposed that Paul was teaching Wolf, while David oversaw the process from a distance, just in case he was needed. Probably he wasn't. Each part of the vignette seemed to know its role and play it flawlessly. The whole scene breathed a sense of ineffable peace.

It was Matti who broke it with a joyous cry as he sprang away from us and ran towards the group.

'Daddy!'

David turned towards him and towards us, and I saw with a shock Matti's own face three or more decades on. Then David opened his arms and scooped up his son.

123

16

At nine o'clock precisely they arrived, Astrid and Matti, their approach foreshadowed by the same sense of distant thunder out of which Olwen had materialised from the fog. It brought me flying to first a window, then the porch and then the yard.

It wasn't Olwen. It was a black mare almost as large and equally regal. She made Astrid – herself of queenly size and bearing – look petite. As for Matti, perched in front of Astrid, he was the tiniest of elves. Time whizzed backwards again. I was in the Middle Ages; Astrid was a noblewoman mounted on her palfrey, albeit a rather large one. I felt awed and suddenly shy in front of these magicians who had such grand forces at their fingertips.

Astrid broke the spell with her rich dark laughter. 'We arrive in the style, yes?'

'That you do! I didn't realise the horses were used for riding as well.'

'Oh, David likes that the horses are handled all ways, so that nothing can ever surprise them, you see? Also, the walk on the moor is long for Matti, so we save the legs for that.'

I hadn't thought of that. A walk which was several miles for me would be doubled or trebled by Matti's little legs. I hoped he was up to it. I felt a little nervous being in charge of the squire's son.

Astrid seemed unconcerned. Her strong arms plucked Matti off the horse and handed him down to me. I don't think I'd ever held a child before and that, too, felt strange. A moment later, however, he was on the ground and looking sturdy enough. He scanned the yard eagerly for those wonderful creatures, sheep. It seemed absurd that a boy raised among mythical horses could be interested in sheep, but I suppose the horses were as ordinary to him as the sheep were to me.

'We won't be going far onto the moor,' I reassured Astrid, in case she needed it. 'Just enough to get the sheep on. Then we'll head straight for The Folly. Is Belle home today?'

'Yes, and she looks forward much to seeing you.'

My spirits lifted at the prospect of being welcomed back at The Folly. The gap left by Effie's departure an hour earlier would be filled. The twinge of regret I'd felt on learning that David was a married man and a father was now overlaid by a soothing sense of continuity. David's son would inherit the estate. Farletons would continue bringing this land into harmony with itself, and I would be one of the beneficiaries.

The squire-to-be seemed unimpressed by his destiny. He was obviously dying to get rid of his mother and see my fabled sheep. Astrid lifted a hand in farewell, then wheeled round and cantered magnificently down the track. I had only to fetch my jacket and change into my wellies before rejoining Matti in the yard. Together we went to the barn and untied Moss. Matti seemed surprised to see a dog, and I suddenly realised I'd neither seen nor heard one at The Folly.

'You don't have any dogs at home?' I asked.

He seemed slightly puzzled by this. 'You mean The Folly?'

Well, yes. Wasn't that his home?

'Daddy hates noise,' he explained.

I could see his point. The dogs at Graegarth had become increasingly noisy. 'Well, this is a quiet one,' I said. 'He's very well trained.'

Matti greeted the dog rather solemnly, which suited Moss's own sense of dignity, and we set off for the fields.

I soon realised how handy it was having Matti with me. 'Would you like to run ahead and open that gate?' I asked.

Matti flew across the field and then stood to attention as a wave of sheep surged through the gateway. Moss and I brought up the rear. We had two other gates to pass through before coming to the base of the cliff. Each time, before resuming his role as gateman, Matti walked with me a while and quizzed me about the sheep – what kind were they, what were the coloured marks on their rumps, how long did it take for the lambs to be formed? He was very down-to-earth but at the same time impressed. I was impressed, too, with his eagerness to learn. His teachers must adore him. In fact, he had altogether a sense of being a much-loved child. Belle had alluded to a period when David's personal life had gone wrong, much to the delight of the locals. Whatever it was, it had clearly left his son unscathed.

We reached the green track and paused a moment, watching the flock flow up the side of the cliff in unison. Perhaps I wasn't so blasé after all. There *is* something imposing about two hundred or so tightly run sheep all moving as a single woolly carpet across the land. Matti certainly thought so. I wondered if I should give him a pet lamb next spring. I would have to ask David first.

As we trudged up the green track behind the sheep, it seemed incredible that I'd been here only two nights ago on quite a different mission. At the top, too, standing at the edge of the endless sea of heather, it was as if the wind and the rain and the moor's own nature had simply wiped clean the ugly scene which the Druids had imposed on it. It was one of those rare moments when I had a sense of the vastness of time. What was one night of nonsense compared to the lifetime of the moor?

It was more beautiful than ever today. Billions of tiny heather bells had bloomed and died to leave a cinnamon blanket stretching into the distance to meet, finally, a pewter sky. Both colours were plain, with no variation of shade to mar the simplicity. This was the moor at its most dignified.

My sheep ambled off to create creamy accent points in this festival of neutrality. 'You've been up here before?' I asked Matti.

Silly question. The Folly was built in the shadow of the moor. He must have scrambled up that cliff hundreds of times.

'Oh, yes,' he said.

Doubly silly. Not only did he know the moor, he owned it, or at least his father did. The moor was part of Farleton Estate. The rest of us only had rights, ancient ones of grazing and turf collecting. It was strange to think that this tiny person would someday own something as vast as the moor.

'But not there,' he said, pointing to the flat table of land straight ahead. 'What is that?'

Ah. I had to say something, so I gave as boring a description as I could, droning on about rock formation and the movement of glaciers.

I should have known I couldn't fool him. His eyes positively glittered with excitement. 'This is where the stones are!' he exclaimed.

So, he knew about the stones. Well, I couldn't lie, but 'They're very boring,' I said in a last attempt to squash his excitement.

'Please can we go there? Please?'

A question in the imperative. He was a Farleton all right. Further, his little wellies were already dancing in anticipation. It would have taken a greater killjoy than me to deny him.

Even so, I felt uneasy as we started towards it. We were, of course, on the ley line, but that wasn't the problem. More a sense of dread at seeing the beastly place again. My imagination wanted to slide a giant trowel beneath that flat table, lift it up and fling it away somewhere where I wouldn't have to see it and be reminded of that night.

'What do you know about the stones?' I asked.

'It was a Druid temple – Nana discovered it. She wrote a book about it.'

'A book?' Nobody had told me anything about a book.

'Well, a little one. A pamphlet. Daddy doesn't like it.'

I should have known there was something fishy about this little expedition. If David disapproved of his mother's pamphlet, he would hardly thank me for taking Matti to the place itself. I tried to think of an excuse for turning back. A downpour would have been welcome. Then we could rush back down to the protection of the cliff. I looked skyward. Solid grey. Not a hole to be seen through which might fall even one welcoming drop. I sighed, looking down at Master Farleton's shaggy brown head. You little brat, I thought. You've really landed me in it.

He smiled up at me, innocent as hell. It was impossible to be angry for long. Very probably he sensed my displeasure, for he suddenly put his hand in mine. My own closed round it without thinking. You couldn't dislike someone with such a trusting little hand, even knowing the cunning behind it. 'That kid's really got the smarts,' Effie had said. Too right.

It was only as we scrambled up the scree that I remembered the bloodstain. The hen – my hen – had bled onto the altar stone before draining the rest of its lifeblood all over Richard's hood. Matti didn't miss a thing. Unless I was lucky and the rain had washed away the stain, Matti would see it and ask awkward questions. I could tell already that this wasn't a child one lied to.

I didn't have a chance to test it. As we came over the edge I saw that we weren't alone. David Farleton was there. He was kneeling before the altar stone.

I closed my eyes for a moment and fought a resurgence of the nausea from two nights ago. Not David. Not him. The sight of that dark mane of hair bent over the altar made me see how much I relied on him. I needed David Farleton to be the calm dark centre holding this plateau together.

David and I looked up at the same moment, straight into each other's eyes. Then he sprang to his feet. 'Matthew!' he said sharply. He strode across to where Matti and Moss and I had frozen in a stunned tableau. His walk was as decisive as his voice. He showed none of the embarrassment I expected of a man caught unawares worshipping at a primitive altar.

Of course. The bloodstain. He hadn't been worshipping at all; he'd been inspecting the bloodstain. The relief that flooded me was so intense that it blotted out my caution. I smiled at him rather inanely.

He wasn't smiling. A face like a thundercloud is no cliché. David Farleton was a one-man storm bearing down on us with awesome speed. Then he was standing before us, dark and implacable.

'*I told you never to come here.*'

Each word was a bullet aimed at his son. I looked down at Matti, expecting to see him crumple at our feet. He looked tense, certainly, but not annihilated, despite his father's terrible anger.

'It's not his fault. I brought him here.' My voice sounded stronger than I felt.

David's anger wavered only a second. Then, 'You weren't

to know. Matthew did. He knows the stone circle is off-limits.'

'I'm not sure he knew the stones were here,' I said. It was partly true. Matti hadn't known until I'd told him. I suppose I was hoping to divide that anger so that Matti's portion would be bearable.

It seemed to be working. David's face softened a fraction. He looked firmly at his son. '*Did* you know?'

I held my breath. I'd offered Matti a twig of half-truth to save himself with. Now I hoped he wouldn't use it. If it was important to me that David Farleton remain the calm dark centre of Keldreth, it was equally important that lies should play no part in it.

Matti's voice was small but firm. 'I knew.'

He had offered his neck to the chopping block. I waited for the axe to fall. There was a long pause. I became aware of a flock of seagulls circling overhead, their raucous cries out of place on the moor. I looked up at them, unwilling to witness the scene between father and son. If David had any decency, he would acknowledge his son's honesty and courage, make at least some small gesture of forgiveness. But anger isn't a decent emotion, and I'd seen plenty of it from David Farleton already.

'Matthew,' he said at last. 'There's a reason, you know. That pool's deeper than it looks. The bottom is nothing but soft sludge, there's no footing. One gust of wind or a shove from a panicky sheep and you'd be in there without a chance. Do you understand?'

Matti looked down at his feet. Forgiveness was harder to bear than anger; there was no footing there either. 'Yes,' he said, his voice smaller.

'Will you promise me never to come here again?'

The voice smaller still. 'Yes.'

David smiled. I was sorry the boy didn't see it. 'All right, then. Let's go home.'

He took Matti's hand, and now the boy did look up, and there was a small shared smile between them.

I wasn't sure if I was included in this homeward trek. Matti must have sensed my uncertainty. He reached out his other hand and took mine in it. The three of us walked along the edge of the table, while Moss followed discreetly behind. The seagulls couldn't suspect that a few moments ago a drama had been enacted among this sedate party now having a promenade.

We split up to scramble down the scree. At the bottom, Matti raced off to inspect one of those dark craters in the peat known as a hagg, Moss close at his heels.

Something was bothering me. David's explanation of why the stone circle was forbidden was reasonable enough if the boy were on his own, but he wasn't. Also, David had been intent on inspecting that altar stone. There was another motive behind it, I was sure of it.

'The pool isn't the only reason, is it?' I said flatly.

'What do you mean?'

'For declaring the stone circle off-limits. It's the circle itself.'

'The stones are harmless enough.'

I wasn't fooled. 'But the "Druids" who use them aren't.'

He gave me a sharp look of surprise.

'I saw you looking at the chicken blood,' I explained.

'How do you know it was a chicken?'

'I was there. The night they killed the hen. I think it was my hen,' I added rather foolishly.

He stopped and stared down at me. 'You were *there*?'

I kept walking. I suppose it was a bit provocative, as was the cool matter-of-factness with which I said, 'I saw the bonfire and couldn't sleep, so I came up here to see what was happening.'

He caught up with me. 'That was rather foolish.'

'Why? It was only a hen.'

Matti's dark head popped up above the edge of the hagg, then the rest of him. He scrambled out and came rushing towards us, holding aloft something large and white.

It was a sheep's skull, bleached white and washed clean by a season or two on the moor. A few of my own sheep would probably die on the moor this winter.

Matti held it up to David. David took it and turned it round in his hands. 'It's a good one,' he said. 'Complete.' He wiggled a loose tooth in the jawbone, then gave it back to the boy.

130

'Can I take it back to school?'

David smiled. 'Your teacher won't be well pleased.'

'Oh, she likes all that nature stuff. She likes us to bring things to class.'

'By "nature" she probably means pebbles and flowers,' I said. 'Not sheep corpses.'

Matti shrugged. We walked together for a while, Matti chattering on about his new find, all of us diagnosing the sheep's age by its teeth. It should have jarred – David's casual attitude towards the skull juxtaposed with his anger over the stone circle, but it didn't. Sheep deaths were a part of life up here. Druids weren't.

When Matti raced off to another hagg, David lost no time in saying, 'Please tell me everything you saw.'

He sounded like a magistrate questioning a witness. Accordingly, I gave my evidence. I didn't, however, mention Richard. I'm not sure why. Something about David's manner. Richard had enough to cope with, coming to terms with John Jowett's death. I didn't want to add to his problems by turning this stern judgmental man on him.

'I see,' he said when I finished. 'I'm sorry about your hen, but there's no point in going to the police. They're too busy with pub brawls to bother about a hen.'

'I know. I haven't told them.'

'There's not much I can do either,' he went on. 'Trespass isn't an offence.' He paused and I saw that splendid face light up in a smile. 'As you once pointed out to me.'

I'd almost forgotten our first inauspicious meeting in the forest. We seemed to have come a long way since then, without either of us knowing it. I had to resist an urge to press my hands on his face to preserve that rare and welcome smile. I did nothing and watched the smile fade and a concerned frown replace it.

'I don't even think their "ceremony" is illegal – apart from stealing your hen, and there's no proof of that. Even if it was, there'll be a lot of sympathy in town for these "Druids". I'd just make matters worse by interfering.'

That was true enough. Given the locals' dislike of him, they would most certainly side with the Druids. I felt sad that none of them ever saw that wonderful smile, or the

131

easy affection with which he bent down yesterday to scoop up his son. Belle was right. There was a human side to David Farleton. I wished he would be less perverse, would let the outside world see it.

'All I can do is keep an eye on things and hope to be around if it gets out of hand,' he concluded.

Generations of Farletons were speaking to me now. The squire. The moor was his, and even if a few patches of Keldreth had passed out of his ownership, centuries of inculcation made the whole place his responsibility, regardless of what the law said.

'Charlotte . . . ' he said suddenly.

It was the first time he'd used my name. It sounded wholly new, coming from him, and made my spine weaken dangerously.

'Charlotte, I can't prohibit you from going to the stone circle, as I can with Matthew. But I hope you'll keep away from it, at least at night.'

The squire protecting the people in his domain. I was too touched by his concern, even if it was automatic, bred in the bone, to give the cheeky retort that came to mind.

'Don't worry,' I said. 'I don't get a thrill out of mangled hens and bloodstained robes.'

He nodded, evidently satisfied. We walked in companionable silence for a little while. Then he said, 'I gather you don't take the ley line too seriously.'

'Not too,' I said. 'Though I did wonder about *you*, when I saw you kneeling at the altar . . . '

He laughed. 'I'm not surprised!'

'I gather it was your mother who found the stone circle.'

'She was an extremely lively person. She never really liked being "the squire's lady" – too independent. So she took up archaeology as a sort of hobby. People did in those days. And Britain's crammed with ancient remains; she was bound to find something sooner or later. I just wish it hadn't been the stone circle.'

Matti joined us, skull in hand, his seemingly inexhaustible store of energy finally faltering. He looked tired but contented as he took his father's hand. I thought David would change the subject in Matti's presence, but he didn't.

'These things are harmless enough in themselves. It's the use people make of them. I hope this one doesn't get out of hand.'

Matti was slowing down. It was tough walking, stumbling over the clumps of uneven heather, and his legs were going on strike. In one powerful sweep, David swung the boy up onto his shoulders. The movement had the grace and vigour of a ballet and was clearly as well practised. The easy love between the two of them made me feel a bit lonely.

Then Matti grinned down at me, as if again sensing my thoughts and anxious to include me. I grinned back and felt better. Matti placed the sheep's skull on David's unruly hair. The effect was of an ancient head-dress which wouldn't have been out of place in a Druidic rite, but neither of them seemed to see it that way. Their entire relation to the chunk of nature they owned was so down-to-earth and reassuring that the skull ceased to worry me.

'Where do you go to school?' I asked, thinking of the poor teacher who would have to deal with the sheep's skull.

Matti named a school in Islington.

'London? I didn't realise.'

'I live with Astrid during school and Daddy in the holidays,' he explained. 'It's half-term now,' he added.

So. David and his wife were separated, perhaps divorced. It was characteristic of Matti to be so down-to-earth about even this. So were his parents. They'd joked together so easily yesterday that it was hard to imagine the storms which must have preceded their separation. A few of my London friends were already divorced. None of them took it as calmly as this.

I put it down to The Folly, magicking even the trauma of divorce, and dropped the subject. David was ominously silent, his face blank. Probably he thought I was prying. I didn't want to ruin the beginning of what I hoped would be a long and happy friendship.

We were approaching The Folly now. The battlements of the crazy building had come into view, and now the whole rear façade was being unpeeled by the edge of the cliff. I couldn't shake off the sense of a time warp, of being flung back into a medley of past eras.

133

What happened next only confirmed it. David took Matti firmly by the ankles and twisted him off his shoulders in one fast and powerful movement. He swung him round several times, the boy shrieking with delight. Then he let go of his ankles for a fraction of a second during which the boy was suspended in the air. Instantly David's hands had grasped Matti's waist, and with a little flourish he set the boy down. Matti, quite unruffled, was still clutching the skull. A pair of medieval jugglers, itinerant acrobats.

I did the only thing possible. I applauded. David and Matti bowed. The skull grinned. We began the descent down the cliff.

As we wound our way through the curved paths of the enchanted garden, I could feel a long gown sweeping the grass, a conical hat on my head and from it a gauzy wisp of material wafting in the breeze. In the courtyard would be, surely, a knight in shining armour astride a mighty war horse.

Actually, it was Belle, court jester in her vivid skirts.

'Charlotte! How lovely to see you! I could kick myself for being away yesterday!'

The warm welcome of The Folly enfolded me. The sun, visible only as a paler-grey fuzz in a dove-grey sky, focused all its efforts on the sun-trap of the courtyard and turned the autumn into high summer.

'Come and have a coffee now, and then I'll show you The Folly, and then we'll all have lunch, and then . . . '

Belle's chatter plumed behind her as we proceeded towards the kitchen. Near the door, Belle caught sight of the skull.

'Ugh!'

I laughed. 'I know. His mother won't think much of that.'

The sun froze. All motion ceased. Four statues plus dog stood by the door.

'His mother?' said Belle blankly.

David turned and went abruptly into the stables. Matthew went inside, seemingly oblivious.

Belle smiled and shrugged. 'Never mind, love. You weren't to know.'

17

'You weren't to know,' Belle said again when, after coffee, we were alone in the great hall, having the long-promised tour of the house. 'I should have told you. Only you didn't stay very long last time.'

The hall was a marvel of early Victorian eccentricity: huge, dark with floor-to-ceiling oak panelling and littered with the spoils of hunting. Not content with the indigenous deer and fox, the Farleton who had furnished The Folly had hauled out his predecessors' trophies from hunting trips abroad. Lions and tigers and unidentifiable beasts scowled down at me from the wooden plaques which made them look as if they'd just blundered through the wall and got stuck. I imagined their bodies still stamping impatiently behind the oak panelling, but as their skins littered the parquet floor, I suppose that was out of the question. To anyone with even a tinge of Green in their blood it was a gruesome sight.

'I know,' said Belle with a grimace. 'David doesn't much care for it either. We keep meaning to sort out the house, but there's so much work out of doors that it doesn't get high priority.'

The hall opened out from the front terrace. Its saving grace, apart from the panelling, was a broad graceful staircase opposite the door. On the landing where it branched was a huge oil painting of a woman who seemed to be presiding over the carnival of animals below. I couldn't see her face from this distance.

Belle gestured me towards a corridor and up some steps and round a corner into the library. It had the same dark oak panelling, but the south wall was a bank of tall thin gothic windows with the exquisite tracery of a cathedral. They flooded the room with warm light, illuminating a hodgepodge of deeply comfortable chairs, tables littered with books and magazines and loose papers, and a homely scattering of sweaters and suchlike which had probably been peeled off against the heat of the fireplace. The fireplace was magnificent, its carved wood echoing the tracery of the windows. The same theme continued in the tall built-in bookcases which covered the rest of the walls. Some of the books were the leather-bound volumes one would expect in such a place, but more were obviously modern and obviously used, as was the fireplace, set in readiness to blaze up this evening. The room was nearly as cluttered as Graegarth, but here it was for use, not show. It was the most welcoming room I'd ever seen, and I sank uninvited into a big worn leather armchair simply because it was irresistible.

'This is where we all live,' she said. 'Here and in the kitchen. In fact, the kitchen's just the other side of that wall. You're probably lost already.'

I was. The house was a confusion of corridors, little half-flights of steps in unexpected places, rooms all at different levels. That explained the peculiar placing of the windows I'd seen from outside. There was indeed no ground floor, first floor and so forth. The whole house was a perverse but lovable jumble.

'It's a maze,' said Belle. 'Literally. We have to issue a map to new students, and even then they keep getting lost the first few days. Sometimes we have to send a search party to find the poor souls.'

'Was he mad – the Farleton who designed it?'

Belle laughed. 'Mad with anger when he found out he couldn't have a maze in the garden. Something about the winds up here being so strong that they would bend the greenery in one direction and that would let you know where you were and ruin the frisson of terror at being lost.'

'So he built the house as a maze instead?'

'Exactly. Yes, I think he was a little mad. Not for nothing is it called The Folly. Though its original name was simply The Lodge. Locals started calling it The Folly when David took over, and one day, in a rage, David had all the signs redone to make "The Folly" official. One of his perverse thumbing-his-nose-at-society gestures which hurt him much more than society. Sometimes I think it's David who's mad.'

136

She sat down heavily in a chair opposite. 'Charlotte, I must tell you about Ros before we get distracted or interrupted again.'

'That's his wife?'

Belle nodded. 'Ex-wife. Ros Rawlinson.'

I had been sinking into the comfort of the chair. Now I shot up straight. '*What*?'

'You've heard of her?'

'Has anyone not?' Ros Rawlinson was the darling of the Royal Shakespeare Company. In the last few years her name had suddenly begun appearing everywhere. She was regarded as something of a phenomenon even within a theatrical tradition famous for such success stories. She was the new Peggy Ashcroft/Judi Dench/Maggie Smith/Glenda Jackson, depending on which reviews you read. Her house was as littered with rejected scripts as The Folly's library was with the sterner stuff of forestry books and papers. The conjunction of Ros Rawlinson and The Folly was impossible. For a moment I wondered if Belle was joking.

'But that's incredible!' I said. 'I had no idea. No one's said a word about her being David's ex-wife.'

Belle nodded. 'I know. I keep telling David. The gossip stopped ages ago. Even something as spectacular as SQUIRE'S SUPERSTAR WIFE FLITS MARITAL NEST gets shoved aside eventually for something fresher. But David is convinced people are still laughing behind his back.'

No wonder he was so touchy, so anxious to keep people away from him. 'Oh, shit. I've really put my foot in it, haven't I?' I said, remembering David's abrupt departure when I referred to Matti's mother.

'Not really,' said Belle cheerfully. 'Probably he just remembered something he'd forgotten to do in the stables. He's like that – so obsessed with his work that he forgets other people are around. He probably didn't mean to be rude.' Belle got up. 'Anyway, I just thought you'd better know. "Matti's mother" is a taboo subject round here. It's the only one. Otherwise David's a joy to live with, believe it or not. Here in the bosom of his weird little ersatz family. Come and see the rest of the house.'

Belle led me back to the hall and up the stairs. My mind

was so full of Ros Rawlinson's face that I almost expected the portrait to be of her.

'David's mother, Rhiannon,' Belle explained. 'Unmistakably Welsh.'

She was also unmistakably David's mother and Matti's grandmother. I'd never seen a picture of any other Farleton, but it was clear that the dark brooding Celtic element had started here and taken over the family appearance. The portrait was impossible to date. The squire's lady wore a midnight-blue velvet dress of such classical plainness that it could be from any period. Her hair, too, was wound in a series of voluptuous dark coils which said 'elegant' rather than any date. The only part of the portrait that seemed old-fashioned was a rather striking ring: a huge emerald badly cluttered by smaller stones and a fussy setting. The woman's face was as handsome as David's, rather heavy and grand but with a restless impish look to the black eyes. This splendid woman must have hated wasting her time sitting for a portrait, was patently impatient to shed the grand gown, climb into a pair of muddy trousers and rush off, trowel in hand, to excavate another bit of ancient Keldreth. I felt a sense of loss at not having known her.

'This was the last family portrait,' Belle explained. 'Ros wanted to have herself and David "done" but he refused. He hated the whole family history bit. She loved it. She never really forgave him for selling the Hall and moving up here. She was very young, of course – both of them were. They were students together in Cambridge – they met at a first night party after *As You Like It*. That was the first time she ever played Rosalind – at the ADC.'

'Matti seems remarkably unscathed.'

'Praise be to Astrid. Astrid is a miracle. If it weren't for her taking over the boy he'd be a right mess by now.'

'Who *is* Astrid?'

'David's sister-in-law, wife of his younger brother, Hugh. Ex-wife.' Belle smiled ruefully. 'As David once said, "The Farletons aren't much good at marriage," though personally I think he's being a bit hard on himself.'

'What about his own parents?'

'Oh, they stayed together, but only because Rhiannon

threw herself into archaeology. Her husband was, frankly, a real bastard, which probably goes a long way towards explaining why David is so antagonistic to the Farleton heritage.'

'In what way a bastard?'

'Chronically unfaithful just for starters, and an alcoholic. He would have been a wife-beater too except that Rhiannon could run faster. Seriously. It was that basic. I never met him, of course – he was long dead by then – but I did meet Rhiannon when David brought us home for a holiday a few months before she died. She was wonderful. Tough as hell, or she couldn't have put up with the squire. But she never lost her sense of fun and sheer joy of life, despite him. And she was beautiful, even in her old age, with that fabulously exotic bone structure. Actually, I'm not surprised you thought Astrid was Matti's mother. That heavy grace, very dark and eastern and mysterious. In fact, Astrid's Swedish, would you believe it? If you take the left stairs we'll see some of the bedrooms. And if you think the house was confusing before, wait till you see this hive!'

I had to shelve all the unasked questions as the tour continued. There would be time. I would be coming here often, and gradually I would piece together the enigma of David Farleton.

But it was difficult to concentrate on the tour with Ros Rawlinson's face constantly before me, she who had been mistress of this house. She, too, was beautiful – the Farletons obviously had impeccable taste in wives – but in a way unusual for an actress. Hers was an off-centre kind of beauty, so striking that once seen, never forgotten. She stood vividly apart from the puddingy mass of starlets with their interchangeable blonde blue-eyed blandness. What's more, she was immensely talented, and bright. I'd seen her several times in London and been struck by the way she played the role as if she were truly inventing it, speaking the well-worn lines for the first time ever. It's not a unique ability, of course. Most of the greats have it. But that was the point. She was great, not just a pretty face. If the Farletons had a taste in beauty, they were equally attracted to talent. I began to see why Farleton Forest's benevolent power felt so strong. It was grounded, solid, it went deep beneath the surface appearance. It was the real thing.

'Brendan and I have the Chinese Room, if you can imagine anything more inappropriate,' Belle was explaining. 'It's just round the corner and up those four steps.'

She flung open a door and we stepped into a dream of oriental vases, prints, screens, rugs. The wallpaper looked hand-painted, old and valuable.

'It is,' said Belle when I asked. 'Some of the junk here is quite valuable. David keeps meaning to make an inventory and sell some of it to expand our forestry. Probably we should – the house is hell to clean. A girl comes up from Kirkby daily but even so it's a bit like the Forth Bridge.'

'It's quite a trek from Kirkby,' I said.

'Oh, she could live in – we offered. She looked at me as if I'd made an indecent suggestion. This place spooks the locals. Or rather, we spook them. People regard The Folly as a den of iniquity. In fact, the whole place is run like a ship. Locals would be terribly disappointed if they knew.'

I laughed. 'Richard Staveley said it was a commune.'

'Did he? Yes, well, I wouldn't take anything he said very seriously.'

'How do you get help at all, if the locals are so skittish?'

'Money,' said Belle bluntly. 'We pay a decent wage, unlike most. Bren and I get paid pretty handsomely, too.'

'But I thought – ' I stopped in confusion. 'I just assumed you were a part of the place. Equal partners or something.'

Belle laughed. 'It does feel like that. And quite honestly, we'd work for a pittance just to be here. We've told David that, but he's funny about not exploiting people. So we just set most of our income aside for retirement. Though I hope to God it never comes to that. I hope we drop dead in our traces. I couldn't stand to retire to some nice seaside bungalow after this.' She waved an arm to take in not just the exquisite room but the whole of the estate.

We moved on to the rest of the house, circling round irregular corridors, going up and down bits of stairs. The student rooms were together in one area. She opened the doors, one after the other. Moorish, French Empire, Renaissance.

'There was a rage for exotica at the time The Folly was built,' she explained. 'All the rooms are thematic.'

I'd seen thematic rooms in stately homes, but never on such a scale. The crazy diversity of windows I'd noticed from outside now made sense. The design had taken the themes to such an extreme as to include even the windows, regardless of the hodgepodge effect it made from the outside.

'It's Grade One Listed,' said Belle, 'and rather special, because nothing's been changed apart from installing a few discreet mod cons. We've been approached about opening it up to the public, but of course David hit the roof. He's right. It would interfere with our work, and in the end it's the land that really matters. The house is just where we live. David's room is behind here, but I'd better not show you because I haven't asked him. Do you have any idea where you are, by the way?'

'Not a clue. If you abandon me now I'll scream like hell till the minotaur arrives.'

Belle laughed. 'Would I be so cruel? You're at the back of the house. You know that big stained-glass window that looks rather like a Russian icon?'

I nodded.

'That's one of David's.'

'The whole place is utterly bizarre.'

'I know,' said Belle. 'David was quite right to rename it The Folly. Now, if you go up this circular staircase you come to Astrid's room. She told me it was all right to show you.'

Belle opened the door onto a perfect Queen Anne world. A sense of dignity and serenity greeted us, appropriate to its occupant.

'Nice, isn't it?' said Belle. 'It used to be Hugh's as well, but now he has a room of his own. He doesn't come often, thank God. He hates David, says he's ruined his heritage by turning it over to us hippies. We keep him in the furthest corner so he can grump by himself.'

There was a beautiful writing desk under one elegant window. I remembered Astrid's strange pronunciation of my name, as if she'd read rather than heard it. 'Is there a lot of correspondence between The Folly and Astrid?'

'Come again?'

'I mean, when she's in London. Does someone here write to her?'

Belle laughed. 'We're not that primitive – we do have a telephone! Why?'

'Oh, nothing.'

'I suppose it's conceivable that David writes – he and Astrid are very close. Their marriages broke up about the same time, and they were both the injured party, so to speak. It makes a kind of bond. I'm sure David tells Astrid things he wouldn't dream of saying to Brendan or myself – we're too close on a daily basis. What makes you think they write?'

Probably I was imagining things. I could see no reason for David writing to Astrid about me. But if he had, no doubt he would want to keep it private. 'Just seeing that,' I gestured towards the writing desk. 'By association.'

'Oh. I see. Yes, it does cry out for a graceful old-fashioned correspondence. But then, Astrid would be in London and David here, so it wouldn't be that desk anyway.'

'Yes, of course. It was a foolish notion.'

'This place does do that. You enter one room and you're in a different time or country. Quite disorienting. Come and see Matti's – it's right next door.'

Matti's room was Romany, what I could see of it beneath the debris of a whirlwind life.

'You'd never guess he was such a little slob, would you?' Belle had to kick aside some discarded clothing before she could shut the door again. 'Ros is next along.'

My head jerked up in surprise. 'But I thought – '

'Oh, yes, she comes from time to time, preferably when David's not here. Now that she doesn't have to live here she quite likes the occasional visit. And to see Matti during school holidays. She sees him when she's working in London too, of course.'

'What happens if everyone turns up at once?'

Belle laughed. 'The atmosphere can get pretty crackly. Fortunately, the house is big enough to keep people apart. This is her room – top south-east corner.'

Belle opened the door onto a huge round room with a circular staircase leading to a sleeping gallery. It was Tudor, rich with tapestries and magnificent carved oak furniture. It was grand and the furniture undoubtedly authentic, but I couldn't dismiss the notion of an upmarket stage set.

'From here you can see our best field,' Belle was saying, 'where we let the horses loose for romps in the summer.'

I went over to the window and quickly located the field Olwen and I had flown across. I could see now the route David had taken to intercept me, and the path we had walked up to reach The Folly. I could also see, near the place where it widened onto the gravel, the back of a person darting out of view. The glimpse was too fleeting for even an attempt at identification, but a quick mental inventory told me it was unlikely to be anyone from The Folly.

18

A few weeks later Richard phoned and asked me out for dinner. Richard puzzled and intrigued me. Here at last was the perfect opportunity to ferret out some information, stitch together some of the inconsistencies of his behaviour and that of his family:

We drove down the winding road towards Kirkby Langham in style, that is to say, in a Rover, only two years old, which I hadn't even suspected him of having. It began to answer one of the many questions I had lined up for the evening: why was Graegarth Farm such a dump, while Mrs Staveley presided over a beautifully maintained house crammed with expensive furniture and knick-knacks? Clearly Graegarth's income went into other things – things of show – while the land and its buildings starved.

Our dinner date was at Farleton Hall, which was another reason for my eagerness. I was dead nosy. Having seen The Folly, with its weird leftover splendour, I wanted to see the place David had abandoned in favour of it. I wanted to piece together David's past. This was his ancestral home. It was where he was born and raised, and it was where he first brought his wife, Ros.

As we walked through the magnificent rooms on our way to the Long Gallery now serving as a restaurant, it was easy to reconstruct the past. The consortium which had turned the Hall into a country hotel had done it so discreetly that it maintained the illusion of still being the ancestral hall. That was, of course, what the customers paid such outrageous prices to experience. For one evening, or weekend, or week, they could play the role of squire and lady.

The Long Gallery was breathtaking. It was panelled with the same beautifully carved dark oak as The Folly's library. Massive chunks of tree blazed in the two fireplaces on the

144

long inside wall. The opposite wall was pierced with a row of fine windows uncurtained to show the park by day and the windows themselves by night. There were no lights to mar the splendid ceiling, only wall sconces with real candles and hidden lighting to display the paintings which were the room's original purpose. The tables were all beneath them, leaving the rest of the gleaming oak floor free for the waiters.

The one who showed us to our table clearly knew Richard. 'We've reserved your favourite table for you, sir.'

So, he was a regular, or at least regular enough to have a favourite table. I wondered vaguely who his other dinner companions were – with his charm and extreme good looks, he could have his pick.

Richard was familiar with the wine list, and the menu. I chose fresh asparagus in wine sauce, Richard paté. I sipped my wine sparingly and contemplated Richard.

The soft candlelight turned him into an icon glowing gold. It was hard to believe that this was a Yorkshire hill farmer. His appearance, dress, behaviour and tastes all made him seem more like the natural squire of Farleton Hall. I looked at the well-tended hand round his wine glass. David's hands were stained with resin which no amount of scrubbing could remove in the short intervals between one work day and the next.

'Penny for them?' he said.

'I was thinking that you don't really like being a hill farmer,' I observed.

'Does anyone?'

'I do.'

'You've chosen it. I haven't.'

'Thousands of people would sell their soul to own Graegarth,' I said, 'and have the chance to turn it back into a decent farm.'

He took up the challenge without hesitating. 'It's a mess, isn't it?'

'Yes.'

'My father,' he said simply. 'He drank. Whether he was an alcoholic I don't know, but he was at the Golden Oak just about every night. Not that I minded. I was glad to have him out of the house. So were Mum and Jean.'

'Was he violent?'

'Only with words. There was a row most evenings. Then he'd storm out and drive down to the Golden Oak. I'm told he was a great raconteur. His cronies paid him with rounds of drinks.'

'Then he didn't spend much on it himself,' I said.

Richard grinned. 'You're quick, aren't you? No, that wasn't the problem. There was money enough, just no interest. Mornings he was so hungover he couldn't work. Afternoons he was too busy thinking of the good time he'd have that night.'

The first of the food arrived. I dropped my questioning while the waiter hovered and while we took the first few bites. My asparagus was good, though whether it justified its price was another matter. I'd never given a thought to such things in London. That I did now showed me how much I had changed already.

I returned to the subject as soon as I could without appearing too intrusive. 'I gather you weren't terribly fond of your father?'

Richard grinned again. 'Why pretend? I hated him. I couldn't believe he was my father. We didn't even look alike. He was small and dark and wiry, a foxy little type.'

'Lots of people don't look like either of their parents.'

'This was rather extreme.'

I couldn't see why the lack of resemblance was so significant to him. Jean didn't look like Richard's description of their father either. 'Did Jean get on better with him?' I asked.

Richard finished his paté and leaned back. 'I suppose so. Poor Jean was a late child, an accident. Mum never really took to her, but Dad was rather pleased to have a daughter. He called her "nut brown maiden" and "little pipit", spoiled her rotten when she was young. Later he lost interest even in her.'

I could barely recognise the Jean I knew in those endearments, and I wondered yet again what had happened to make her grow old and harsh so quickly. 'She was much more upset when her father died?' I suggested.

Richard shrugged. 'Not much.'

Clearly he was getting bored with the subject, and as I wasn't learning much, I dropped it. We talked idly of farming matters for a while. Then, suddenly, my mind did a computation so obvious I wondered why I hadn't thought of it before. Richard was in his early forties. All those years when his father was drinking the farm into dereliction, Richard was young and fit and perfectly capable of doing the work himself. He even had the greatest incentive to do so; he would inherit it in the end. And now he had. And two years later the farm was still a slum.

Our next course arrived – smoked trout mousse for Richard, scallops and wild rice for me. I barely tasted my food. I was too preoccupied with the main thing I wanted to find out. It required more aggression than I cared to use, but it seemed the only way to get through. I had ordered roast chicken in madeira and walnut sauce for my main course. 'Delicious,' I said after the first bite. 'It must be free range, like mine.'

Richard finished chewing some of his roast sirloin with marinated grapes and said, 'The sirloin's good, too.'

'What was the ritual all about anyway?'

'What ritual?'

'On the moor. Samain. The hen at the bottom of the tarn.'

'Someone's found a hen in the tarn?'

'Of course not. It was weighted with a stone.'

He took another bite. Possibly he was eating to gain time, to concoct a story. I chewed my own chicken and waited.

'Then how do you know it's in the tarn?' he said at last, smiling at my feminine lack of logic.

'I saw it being thrown in.'

'When was that?'

'Samain. As I said.'

'Samain. Oh, yes, the Druid thing. It's the festival of the new year, isn't it? Yes, I did see the bonfire. I didn't give it much thought. It was the same night that you and your friend came to tea. I'm afraid Jean was rather rude.'

'I rather liked Jean.'

His face lit up with such obvious pleasure that I felt ashamed of my inquisition. 'I'm glad you like her,' he said.

'She's rather sweet, really. She's just been a bit restless lately. I don't blame her – what future is there for her at Graegarth? Obviously I'll look after her, but it's not her farm and she's tired of being stuck in a dead end life. Would your friend really help her if she went to London?'

Ashamed but undaunted. I'd gone too far now to pull back. 'Quite possibly. I wonder where the wood came from for the bonfire. That's an awful lot of wood to haul up to the moor.'

'What? Oh, the bonfire. I wouldn't take that sort of thing too seriously. It's harmless enough.'

'My hen didn't think so.'

Blank stare. 'Your hen?'

Did he really not know it was my hen? Perhaps it wasn't. I wished I hadn't said it was mine. I was beginning to wish I hadn't started the whole line of questioning. None the less, 'The one you used for the Celtic triple death,' I said.

'*Me*?' His eyebrows shot up. 'What on earth makes you think it was me?'

'I saw you.'

There it was. I'd played the final card. I could hear warning bells ringing all the way from London, Effie's voice saying, 'Charlotte, you birk!'

Then, to my amazement, Richard began laughing, a soft and rather affectionate laugh. 'My dear foolish Charlotte,' he said, 'do you mean to tell me that you actually went up there?'

'I did.'

'Well, well,' he said, still chuckling softly. 'I really do admire your spirit. When you came to Cappelrigg, people said you wouldn't last the winter. I think they're wrong. You're a plucky lass. If I had a hat on I'd take it off to you.'

Whatever I'd expected, it wasn't this.

'But you should be more careful,' he went on. 'The moor's a dangerous place at night.'

'Why? You said yourself that the Druids are harmless.'

'I meant the moor. It's full of peat haggs and little channels you can't see at night. You could easily break your ankle. But I'm sorry if you've lost a hen – perhaps they did take it.'

'Not "they", Richard. You. I saw you.' I hoped I sounded more confident than I felt.

'Stealing your hen? I most certainly didn't steal your hen.' He looked rather hurt.

'Not stealing it. Killing it. I was there, Richard. I saw you.'

His frown deepened. 'You couldn't have, Charlotte – I wasn't there. In any case, don't they wear costumes to disguise themselves?'

'Robes, yes, but not usually hoods. This lot were wearing hoods. Clearly this lot do want to disguise themselves.'

The frown remained a moment, then vanished in an impulsive smile. 'But Charlotte, if they were wearing hoods, how could you see anyone?'

'You moved yours aside for a moment to wipe the chicken blood out of your eyes,' I said. 'I was hiding behind a stone. I saw you, Richard. Why are you denying it?'

Effie's warning bells were clanging so loudly by now that I feared I might miss Richard's reply. Then Richard's hand moved across the table and placed itself gently on mine. His voice was gentle, too, and a little concerned.

'Charlotte, I'm sorry you had a bad experience on the moor. But you must understand that I wasn't involved. It was dark; probably the firelight blinded you a little, too. I don't doubt that you were there and saw the things you say you saw. But it wasn't me. Honest. You only had a glimpse, and you must have mistaken whoever it was for me.' He smiled a little ruefully. 'I'm not so striking that dozens of men couldn't be mistaken for me in such circumstances, you know.'

I shut my eyes and conjured up a picture of that night. Richard was right: it was dark, there was the firelight, my glimpse was brief. I could easily have been mistaken. If so, I'd done him a terrible injustice.

I opened my eyes and saw at least two men in the room who could as easily have been the man I had glimpsed that night. Of course. Kirkby Langham had been a Viking settlement. It was full of big fair-haired men, many of them bearded. How could I have been so stupid?

I pushed away the uneaten chicken. Richard had finished

his sirloin, his appetite seemingly undiminished by my horrid interrogation. What a fool I was. Richard's slander of the Farleton ménage was mild compared to my accusations tonight. I sighed, then pulled myself together to assure the waiter that yes, everything had been lovely. 'I don't think I could manage a dessert – just some black coffee, please, and some cheese,' I told him.

Richard smiled. 'I'm going to be greedy. I'll have the pear and frangipane tart with butterscotch sauce.'

When the waiter left, Richard leaned forward, put his elbows on the table, rested his head on his hands and gave me a direct look, intense and full of charm. 'Charlotte, I didn't ask you out to talk about Druids.'

We had changed gear so quickly that I had to think fast. 'Stocking ratios on LFAs? Indoor lambing sheds versus mobile outdoor units? Come on, I'm all agog.'

He laughed. 'What a little minx you are! You must know. All right, I'll spell it out. Have you finished with this "stripping bare" nonsense? Including men? If so, may I put in an application to become the man in your life?'

I laughed easily, or at least I hoped that's how it sounded. His question threw me into a greater quandary even than my *faux pas* over the Druids. For the truth was, I hadn't forgotten that unexpected kiss. I didn't want to accelerate a relationship I still didn't feel I could fulfil.

The waiter arrived with our coffee and gave me time to think. Why was I so neutral towards this handsome and likeable neighbour of mine? I must be the only woman in Langhamdale immune to his attractions. Surely I didn't begrudge him that violent kiss way back in August? There's no one on earth who hasn't done some impulsive thing and then regretted it, and Richard's behaviour since then had been exemplary.

The waiter glided away, leaving our table full and my mind still empty of an answer. 'I'm afraid I'm still feeling dreadfully independent,' I tried.

The disappointment on his face was so strong that I felt sorry for him.

'After all,' I said lightly, 'if people are saying I won't last the winter, then I'd better concentrate on proving them wrong.'

'You know as well as I do that there's hardly anything to do on a hill farm in winter,' he said with a knowing smile. 'There's plenty of time for a social life.'

I pictured his neglected farm. 'Repair work?' I countered.

He raised one hand as if fending off a blow. 'All right, Graegarth could do with a bit of attention. But during the day. These are long dark evenings, Charlotte. I'd like to have your company. Please?'

What excuse could I give him? I looked round the room, hoping idiotically for inspiration somewhere, anywhere. The room was lined with paintings. I'd paid little attention to them when we'd arrived, I'd been so intent on my questions. Now I noticed that they were all portraits. I appealed to the long-dead faces for help. They stared back at me with the mute arrogance of their class.

'Richard, I'm sorry. It's difficult to explain, but I just seem to need an infinite quantity of solitude these days. Perhaps it's all those years in London, being crowded in with millions of other people. I need space, and time. A lot of it.' I took refuge in my coffee.

'You seem to have enough time for the people at The Folly.'

I looked up at him guiltily, then at the portraits again, still hoping for inspiration.

'They're not as grand as you think, the Farletons,' he said, following my glance and dismissing the portraits. 'Or as rich. They sold out. Or rather, *he* sold out – David Farleton. Sold the Hall with everything in it. Didn't even have the decency to take the family portraits with him when he flitted up to the hills. He turned his back on all this, destroyed his heritage and the heart of the community with it. He's nothing but a small-time forester now, Charlotte. You're too sensible to be dazzled by phoney gentry.'

My jaw dropped at the unexpected assault. What did David Farleton have to do with whether or not I went out with Richard?

Then I saw. Quite a lot. *Richard was jealous.* It was absurd. I'd seen David only a few times, and mainly in fraught circumstances.

'The one up there was the last one worth anything,' he

151

continued, looking up at the portrait hanging above our table. 'That was the last *real* squire.'

I glanced at the painting. It was larger than the others, and I suddenly saw that it was the companion picture to Rhiannon's at The Folly. So this was David's father.

I looked back at Richard. 'The Farletons, past and present, are no concern of mine,' I said. 'But my own life is. I want to be alone. I want to find out who and what I am. It's as simple as that.'

Richard sipped his coffee, then smiled winningly at me. 'And how long will that take?'

'I have no idea.'

He nodded and took another sip. 'And will there be space for me at the end of it?' he said quietly.

'Nobody can predict their future.'

'People make their own future,' he said. 'They don't just sit around waiting for it to happen.'

'Some. Not me. Not now.'

'I make my own future, Charlotte. And I want you to be in it.' He leaned back and contemplated the portrait above us. 'He made his own future – the last of the real squires.'

Suddenly, the words of the waiter came back. The waiter, as he led us to our table. *We've reserved your favourite table for you, sir.* Richard's favourite table, beneath the portrait of the old squire whom he so clearly admired. Why? And why did he keep coming back to the subject of the Farletons? It was *he* who was obsessed with them, not me.

I had scarcely glanced at the portrait until now. I was too close to see it well, from where I sat the light above it turned the squire's face into a glossy blank glare. I leaned to one side until the puddle of light shifted to reveal the squire's face.

He was better looking than I'd expected. Belle's remarks about him had sketched a character so disagreeable that I'd assumed without thinking that his form would mirror his content. It didn't. He was a big blond handsome man, a little florid, perhaps – that would be the drinking. He must have been in his early forties when it was painted, his flesh ample but firm, his beard thick. Clear blue eyes looked out at me from a smiling face. The smile was full of confidence, possibly a bit arrogant but no more so than one would expect in such an old family.

I looked back at Richard, then froze.

Richard was smiling, too. It was the same smile. They were the same eyes. The same hair, the same beard, the same face.

I looked back at the portrait, then at Richard again.

There was nothing to differentiate the two men except the scar.

19

That night was one of patchy sleep filled with visions on the border between dream and hallucination. Richard and the portrait merged, dissolved, reconstituted themselves in strange combinations, with David flowing in and out of the images to make a dissonant trio. I would have brooded for days on that awkward dinner date if the following day hadn't wrought such a change in my life.

The morning began innocently enough. Indeed, innocence was the touchstone of the whole day, transporting it and me back to some nostalgic past. Not so far back as that primeval morning when Olwen emerged from the mist, perhaps, but far enough to give a touch of unreality to everything that happened.

I awoke to the first hard frost of the year. My cold toes told me that something was up, and I flew to the bedroom window to see a translucent silk coverlet, sprinkled with diamonds, laid lightly on the land as far as I could see. After the first sharp intake of breath, I had to smile. The frost had tried so hard to cover all with its delicate white film, but beneath it the grass, palest sea green, was making a statement. And over it a newly-rising sun was trying just as hard to turn the silvery waves to gold. The trees of my grove had overnight exchanged their few remaining tatty leaves for a smart new ermine cloak. They looked terribly pleased with their accomplishment.

Tarzan was licking my icy toes to life. I scooped her up and plonked her on my shoulder. 'Come on, puss. This is your morning.'

The boundary between the fresh white walls of my kitchen and the landscape beyond was blurred. Only the steady warmth chugging out of the Aga distinguished indoor from out. Breakfast felt like a banquet, Tarzan and myself presiding over a courtly event, smug as hell, as if we were the creators of all this wonder. I slowed down all my movements in an effort to preserve the moment. 'Take your time,' I said to my crazy cat. 'This very second is the culmination of your life.'

But she wouldn't listen. She gobbled her food and raced about the kitchen in utmost determination to share the world outside with me. 'All right, you win.' I opened the porch door and she flew out, then skidded to an astonished stop and looked back at me. 'Frost, you silly puss.' She sniffed an ivory cobblestone, licked it, then exploded in a series of acrobatics.

Moss watched her with the disdain of One Who Has Seen It All. A big yawn, a stretch, and then he settled down to a sedate breakfast, oblivious of the beauty around him.

The hens were not amused either. They tumbled out of the hut eager for the day's pickings only to find the ground frozen and the goodies therein locked up from their beaks. A great deal of disgruntled preening followed. There is nothing so withering as a hen's glare.

I refused to be ruffled. I stood in the centre of the yard, hugging my jacket to me and breathing in the transformation. The rough track leading from the yard was a soft furry blanket. To either side the fields had turned into bowls of pale lime sherbet. Beyond the council road was another field, then the edge of the forest before it began its descent into the vale. How artful David had been. The winter trees glowed with all the fullness of the vanished summer: the medley of different greens in the pines and spruces and firs vied with the gold of larches which hadn't yet shed their needles and the rich tracery of the deciduous trees, all of it softened to exquisite pastels by the frost. Above it rose a whitish sky trying its damnedest to force a bit of blue into the scene.

A single robin sat on a nearby fence post, chittering like a thumb run across the teeth of a comb. It was the only sound in the landscape. Even the hens had gone quiet.

I started to drift down the track, reluctant to go in. A pile of washing awaited me. To hell with it. My footsteps gave back tiny rhythmic crunches to compete with the robin. Tarzan, alarmed at my desertion, came skittering up to me, adding her own dwarf sounds to this minimalist composition.

And then, another sound. Wheels. Wheels, but no motor. Instead, an uneven riff of hoofs giving a percussive bass. And was there just the faintest hint of tiny fairy bells? I craned my neck in the direction of the sound, as if a few more inches would make all the difference. It was somewhere on the road, just beyond my east boundary, where the trees of the forest began. I waited, breathless with childish excitement as the sound crescendoed coyly, just out of sight.

And then, as if riding a ray of slanty sun, it appeared: a matched pair of great grey horses pulling a bright green cart piled high with wood. The driver was dressed in the darker green of what looked from here like a loden jacket. A hat was pulled down low onto his head, but I knew who it was: Brendan, delivering my firewood. I'd told him to come any time and told him where to put the wood if I happened to be out. How awful if I *had* been out! I would have missed this lovely moment. It was a strange gift they had, my friends at The Folly, for subverting time and transporting this whole plateau into whichever piece of the past took their fancy. Today, the nineteenth century. I watched, both amused and enchanted, as the reincarnation of a long-vanished farm worker hup-hupped his team along the road. I, too, would play my part: kitchen maid to the house, stealing a moment from my chores to fly down the track and open the gate for him.

I stood to one side, smiling demurely. I was out of breath from running and the cold air forced into my eyes a pair of incipient tears which clouded my vision. I snapped them away with a jerk of my head just in time to see not Brendan but David, sweeping his hat off to release the mass of perpetually tangled black hair. I was too startled to speak.

David wasn't. Cap in hand, he half rose on the seat to bow. 'Much obliged to ye, ma'am,' he said in an excruciatingly bad imitation of a rural accent. 'Be the mistress of the house at home?'

Was it he, or me, playing this trick with time? I recovered my wits to return a curtsey. 'Aye, that she be,' I said in what I hoped was a more plausible accent.

'Might ye be minded to have a bit of a spin?' he said, moving aside to make room on the seat.

I tried to blush. 'Such light ways would displease the mistress.'

'And it would displease me to ride while a lady walks,' he said, dropping his accent but not the idiotic language. He fastened the reins and jumped to the ground with the same strong easy grace I'd seen in his play with Matti on the moor. An intensely physical family, I thought. And intensely happy. Even David's great bulk could barely contain the sheer joy of being alive on such a morning that seemed to radiate from him as he stood on the track beside me. His eyes, that had seemed so black and opaque and forbidding before, now seemed to gather into themselves the whole of the landscape and give it out again transformed by love. His love for the land was so clear and naked that I almost feared for him – and for the land. What a terrible responsibility, to be the object of a love that intense. I hoped the land appreciated it. Considering the beauty of his forest, I thought it did.

All of this flashed through my mind in less than a second. In the next, Tarzan had scuttled up her former owner to perch on his shoulder.

'She remembers you,' I said.

'And Olwen remembers you,' he said, as the great mare 'nudged' my shoulder, almost knocking me over. She didn't know her own strength.

It was the first time I'd seen her in harness. I expected her to seem diminished by the trappings of work, after the freedom of the field. Not a bit of it. She looked like a *grande dame* showing off the spoils of a Paris shopping spree.

It was also the first time David had referred to the incident which had so infuriated him. But there, too, I was wrong. His dark eyes, moving back and forth between Olwen and myself, reflected a heady mixture of respect, amusement and that strange intensity of love he felt for everything in his domain, including, apparently, me.

To hide my confusion, I stepped in front of the team and said, 'Who's her friend?'

'Sif. Olwen's half sister. If you look closely you can see she's about an inch shorter, but nobody notices.'

157

They were indeed a wonderfully matched pair, in character as well as appearance. 'Your horses are very proud,' I observed.

'They enjoy their work,' he said simply.

Their coats, a little rougher now with the extra hair grown for winter, had been brushed to a fine gloss, and the long silky feathering of their lower legs must have been combed hair by hair. All the complicated bits of leather in the harness were well oiled, the brasses and bells shone with fresh polish. Even the cart was recently painted. The whole ensemble looked set for the Lord Mayor's parade rather than a firewood delivery.

David took Olwen's rein, I took Sif's, and we processed up the track. Tarzan maintained her perch on David's shoulder, looking absurdly small. The fierce contentment of her purr added a countermelody to the morning soundscape. She was playing with a ragged piece of David's collar as if it were a toy put there for her amusement. It no longer surprised me that David, who took such meticulous care with his estate, ignored himself. Though private, he looked outward rather than inward. He probably had no idea how outrageously handsome he was. He probably used a mirror for shaving and nothing else. The slight scruffiness of his appearance was strangely touching. I stole a glance at him from under the archway of Sif's neck, looking for some resemblance to the portrait of his father I'd seen the night before. None.

'What's the lord of the manor doing delivering firewood?' I asked lightly.

He had to duck down a bit to peer at me from under Olwen's neck. 'My turn,' he smiled. 'Brendan's working one horse with Simon, Paul's working another with Wolf.'

I refrained from pointing out the obvious: that any other squire would be in his estate office letting others do all the physical work. 'I didn't realise you used the horses for delivery, too.'

'It's good practice for them. It's something they need to know before they leave us.'

'I'll bet it wows the customers – having their wood delivered in such style.'

He peered at me, his eyes dancing with amusement. 'Are you wowed?'

'I am.'

'Good.'

I laughed in simple enjoyment at his pride. Belle had grumbled about his pride and the barrier it made with the locals. True, no doubt. But there was another side. Not to feel proud of what he'd accomplished would be demeaning.

'I suppose "Sif" was a giantess, too?'

'Of course. And she was married to Thor. That's a god's wife under your hand. I hope you're wowed by that, too.'

'I am.'

'Good.'

'I'm wowed by everything you've done up here,' I said. 'You've created something very special, you know.' I wondered if I'd gone too far. A bit of light banter was one thing; to approach the heart of what really mattered to him was another. 'Not many people even have the chance,' I continued regardless. 'And then they don't always use it. Artists, perhaps. To paint a great picture, perhaps. Or write a great book.' Why is it so difficult to pay a compliment? If I'd said something rude, David probably wouldn't have minded, but I'd silenced him with a compliment. 'But to take a raw material as poor as this land and turn it into something so good . . . ' I petered out, embarrassed.

There was a long silence. Then his head appeared again in the frame formed by the horse's neck. He looked at me for some time, very seriously. Then, 'Thank you, Charlotte,' he said simply.

Nineteenth-century dignity. He looked so vulnerable at that moment, under the weight of my unexpected praise. I gave him an impertinent smile to relieve the burden. 'The one thing I'm not wowed by is your stables, because I haven't seen them yet. Can I come over some day and have a look round?'

He laughed, dispelling the awkwardness. 'Come today! I can even give you a lift, if you don't mind making a diversion – I have another load to deliver. Then I'll show you around myself.'

I caught my breath. Was this really David Farleton, the

159

hermit who shunned the outside world, tried to close down public footpaths, stalked the farm dispersal sales with his head down so he wouldn't have to greet anyone? He who had sworn at me after squashing me beneath a felled tree?

David was waiting. 'Thank you,' I said. 'I'd like that very much.'

We arrived in the farmyard in an explosion of activity as the hens scattered, squawking, in every direction. Olwen and Sif seemed oblivious of the consternation they'd caused. They stopped and stood neatly, necks arched, as if posing for the cover of *Country Life*.

'Where's it going?' David asked.

I pointed towards the long low shippon on the west side of the yard. In the past, when even a hill farm as high and poor as Cappelrigg had a dairy, the shippon had housed cows. Now I used the empty stalls for the Aga's coal, the firewood and anything else I didn't have space for in the barn. I crossed the yard and opened the big double doors. As I fastened them back against the outer walls, the sun, which had just cleared the top of the barn opposite, whooshed in to fill the shippon with golden light. Tiny gilded motes danced in the doorway. That they were merely dust from old hay didn't diminish the loveliness one bit.

David walked the horses in a wide semicircle and then backed them up near the entrance.

'Can I help you unload?' I asked.

'No reduction in price,' he said. 'You've paid for my labour already.'

'You old meanie!' I laughed.

'If you really want to play the skivvy, you could give the horses a bucket, once they cool off.'

He plucked Tarzan from his shoulder and set her down. She raced towards me, skidded, then noticed a small stone she'd dislodged from between two frosty cobbles. She batted it with one paw. As it skipped across the ground, she pounced on it. Then she batted it, pounced again. Endless pleasure from one little pebble.

Years ago someone had put, or left, a single bale of hay near the doorway to the shippon. Now too old and dusty to eat, it remained as an informal seat. I sat myself down on it, feeling strangely grand, as if long graceful skirts draped the bale. The nineteenth century wouldn't go away. The farmyard was filled with such an intensity of time past that I had to keep reminding myself that this was merely an illusion, a bit of the magic of The Folly turned portable and come to pay a visit to my farmyard.

From where I was sitting, the horses and cart were in full profile. Olwen and Sif maintained their *Country Life* pose long enough to impress me, then relaxed a little. They turned their heads towards each other, bumped noses gently – just keeping in touch, literally. Such a simple gesture and yet so moving. The gentle peace of their companionship descended on the farmyard like pentecostal doves. The first faint warning of tears began to prick the back of my eyes, the same reaction I felt when hearing an unbearably moving piece of music. It *was* almost unbearable, this sense of peace and love and simple goodness.

Tarzan tried to break the spell. She batted her pebble so far away that she lost it. In compensation, she trotted up to Olwen and batted the silky feathering of her leg instead.

'Tarzan,' I warned.

She gave me a haughty look, then abruptly curled up in a furry grey ball between Olwen's forelegs. Olwen lowered her head to peer at this odd midget. Then she blew softly, a plume of frosty breath spiralling into the clear air. She consulted with Sif, who gave an enigmatic toss of her head. It set off the little bells on the harness, making them jingle like Christmas come early. The robin, staring down from the eaves of the shippon, scolded. I smiled, settled my invisible skirts round me on the bale, and waited for the next episode in this charmed festival.

David was unloading the wood at the back and stacking it in one stall of the shippon.

'You don't have to stack it,' I said. 'Just throw it in – the air will circulate and dry it.'

He tried to look offended. 'Would I sell you unseasoned wood?'

'I beg your pardon.'

The stack made a pretty pattern against the weathered wood of the stall. Little puffs of dust rose and danced, golden in the uneven patches of sunlight. The sun, trying to stream into the shippon, was thwarted by the horses and cart which threw their dusky silhouettes into the building. David passed back and forth through the chiaroscuro, parts of him shining a rich dark gold while other parts merged into the charcoal shadows. The dramatic play of light and shadow gave even more power to the movement of his body. Hercules, handling the wood as if it were so many matchsticks. To rejoice in one's body, isn't that the phrase? The same body which had so exuberantly tossed Matti rejoiced now in the humble shifting of firewood. I could almost hear the muscles, shrouded by the tatty jacket, singing out in pleasure at being well used.

Hercules, or a peasant. The picture changed and I saw a roughly smocked peasant going about today's work in the same way as yesterday's and all the days' before. The simple enjoyment of work, of a body and mind being used. David had no need of Farleton Hall or all the trappings of tradition. His own went back further than mere landed gentry, right back to the beginning of time.

A huge bundle of wood in his arms, he paused, for no apparent reason except perhaps to listen to some distant sound. The abstract shadings of light and dark that had been playing across him stopped at the same time, frozen in the stillness, to give me a portrait of – what? No longer Hercules or a peasant, he became for that heartbreaking few seconds the simplest picture of all. Man. Just as Olwen had separated herself out of the primeval mist to become the first horse, now David stood before me, the first man.

And then it happened. The tears that had been pricking my eyes before returned, this time with such unexpected force that they streamed down my face. I stood up, turned abruptly and hurried towards the house in a mad confusion of sensations. My body felt saturated with richness and at the same time seemed to be dissolving, while my mind emptied of everything except the desire to shed this pleasurable pain and at the same time preserve it forever.

I was aware of nothing, not even where I was going, until suddenly I felt a weight – not heavy but firm – on my shoulder. I whirled round and looked directly into David's face and knew without thinking that this was the source. His face wore a look of anxious concern but even that couldn't erase the first man I'd seen in him only a few seconds ago. All the magic and beauty which had transformed my farmyard swept at once into that face with a concentration so fierce that the rest of the world seemed emptied and pale.

'Charlotte, what's wrong?'

I barely heard the words, only the voice, rich with the winter sun and more beautiful than any singer's could ever be. Wrong? What was he talking about? Then I heard my own voice, low and furred at the edges with tears. 'There's such a thing as too much beauty.'

As soon as the foolish words were out I wanted to take them back. How could he possibly understand the turmoil of sensations that had gone into them? They must sound as cryptic to him as a sybil's garbled prophesy.

Or did they? His head was slightly tilted, the look in his eyes far away but clear. There was a strange touch of sadness to his smile but no confusion and certainly no trace of the condescension which such words would have produced in anyone else.

'Yes, I know,' he said.

But he didn't, not completely. To him, beauty meant the landscape he had created. To me, it also meant its creator. Because the real name for this explosion of exquisite pain disguised as beauty was love. And the real words used since the beginning of language to express it were the simplest words of all: I loved him.

20

Nothing could ever be the same after that. When David resumed his stacking of the wood I went into the house and prowled from room to room, not trusting myself to be in the same landscape as him. But it was still there, surging into the house through every window. What had before been merely beautiful had now shifted to a new plane. It was as if a careless god had breathed over the world and infused every object, however humble, with a portion of his own massive life force. Nothing was too banal for it. Through one window I saw a cobweb with a spider toiling to make some repair. The cobweb wasn't even a good one. It was broken, tatty and dusty, and the spider was no great shakes either. And yet both of them glowed with supranatural majesty and I stared at them, as enraptured as if I'd stumbled upon a great treasure.

Through other windows I saw David, working away as if nothing very remarkable had happened. I tried to pull myself down to the same earthy level. That is only David Farleton, I told myself, a nice forester who happens to be your neighbour. He is not a god. He is a human being. If you must love him, love him as a human being. And for heaven's sake, please be sensible about this whole absurd business.

It didn't work. Each glimpse I had of him through the windows repeated the image which had brought me to tears. Adam, the first man, radiant with the joy of being the beginning of the human race, god and man fused into the greatest work of art ever created. How could I pretend otherwise?

And how could I pretend that this was some new revelation sprung on me this morning? I could see now that some portion of me had fallen in love with him in storybook style: at first

164

sight. It all came back to me now as I paced the rooms trying not to explode with love. That first glimpse of him through the tangle of twigs and leaves when he'd felled the tree on me. Why else had I been so uncontrollably furious? It was myself I'd been furious with. That hidden part of me had known already that this man *mattered*, and had fought against the knowledge. That same night, I'd dreamt us as Adam and Eve making love in the Eden of Farleton Forest. I'd been furious then, too, when I'd awakened and realised that my unconscious longing had sneaked through into my dream. And my anger when Brendan had thwarted my buying of the tractor? Poor Brendan had nothing to do with it, nor did the tractor. There were dozens of secondhand tractors that would do as well, and I knew it. It was David, standing beside Brendan. David – silent, unimpassioned and achingly desirable – who had aroused my defensive rage. And, after Olwen and I had created the world anew, I had accused David of destroying the magic of that world. False. I knew even then that *he* had created the magic, and I was terrified of succumbing to it.

I paused at another window that framed a portrait of David. I tried to control myself. Control, that was it. I had lost control of my life. Even as far back as May, in the auction room, some force had taken hold of me, bypassed my reason and bought Cappelrigg. I'd been shaken then at the loss of control. Now I could see it was only the beginning, the symbol of a greater relinquishing to come.

Fate? Rubbish. I did not – emphatically did not – believe in some supernatural thing called Fate that drove us to fulfil a destiny designed by someone else. I was designing my own destiny at Cappelrigg, and the irrational business of Falling in Love had no part in it. I would have to control myself somehow, turn him back into that nice forester and neighbour.

I stiffened as I saw that the picture outside my window had changed. David had finished stacking the wood. He walked to his horses and caressed them briefly, a sort of thank-you, perhaps, for standing still so long. Then he looked towards the house. He must have seen me, frozen in panic by the window, for he smiled.

I tried to smile in return, while my mind whirred. Somehow, Adam and Eve would have to vacate the scene, make room for plain old David and Charlotte, mortals both. Somehow, this lovesick idiot trying not to swoon at the window had to do a quick change back into a hill farmer acknowledging a delivery of firewood. I prayed to the gods of banality to send me a big supply, fast. Then I stepped away from the window, took some huge gulps of air and went outside.

*　　　*　　　*

Flying through the magic forest with my lover. That's how it felt when we climbed aboard the cart and made our way through Farleton Forest. I suppose if I must try to be sane about it, the cart was hardly a magic carpet and our 'flight' was pretty bumpy. I'd never been in a cart before, didn't anticipate the roughness on a council road in need of repair.

Did I care? Like hell. The cart seat was narrow, and each slight bump nudged us that bit closer together. The horses' pearly backs were the screen for a light-show, displaying a kaleidoscope of silvery-gold patterns from the sun sifting through the half-bare canopy above. It was hypnotic, dazzling. They scarcely seemed real, Olwen and Sif, more like figments of an imagination trying to conjure up the notion of Horse. The workaday harness, far from destroying the illusion, added its own dark-brown bars to the pattern, while the brass bounced rays of gathered sunlight into the forest beside us. The jingle of fairy bells, scattered about the harness, would have lulled me into an enchanted sleep had I not been so excited by David's presence and all the events of that morning.

It was still the same morning. I could hardly believe so much had happened. In physical terms, not much: a delivery of firewood. It could scarcely be more banal. But the emotional changes wrought in that brief time had changed the landscape of my life forever.

It was difficult to contain my joy, especially when each small movement of the cart bumped our arms together. I counted the layers between us: two jackets, two sweaters, two shirts. Six damnable barriers. I willed them to dissolve – to hell with the frost which was decorating the air with our plumes and the horses'. On the pretence of gazing into the forest, I looked at David's profile instead.

David turned a questioning gaze on me. I smiled. Poor David; what would he think if he knew I'd captured his image, usurped it to hold against me in lieu of the real thing which was separated from me by six layers of mundane clothes.

We had reached the crossroad where Effie and I had stopped all those months ago. Without pausing, Sif and Olwen trotted across it, down the road through the eastern side of the forest. I'd never been on this road before and had only penetrated a few bits of the forest it served. I'd never been sufficiently interested, either, in the houses that lay beyond.

'How many are there?' I asked. 'Houses, I mean.'

'Four. Two original farmhouses and one barn conversion each. There's a third barn being converted now, with a fourth planning application going through the council.'

'Quite a hamlet,' I observed. 'Do you know them well?'

'They keep to themselves,' he said. 'They only buy our firewood because it's better than anyone else's.'

Of course. In my new-found passion, I'd forgotten how much David was disliked by others. It seemed incredible. Even if I disregarded my own love – after all, love is a personal thing – how could others fail to appreciate the beauty he'd created around them?

And the forest *was* beautiful that morning, glowing in the mysterious winter sunlight. I could see now how clever David had been in planting it. The blend of deciduous and conifer was perfectly balanced, giving a sense of harmony I'd not seen anywhere else. However pragmatic, he was an artist, too, painting with trees. A bough of Scots pine drooped over the road just above our approaching cart. I reached up and slid the long needles lightly through my hand. It felt as good as it looked.

David smiled at me.

'Nice,' I said. I smelled my hand where the resin had touched it. Then I put my hand up to David's nose. Silly, really. He smelled it every day, his hands were stained by it. But he smiled again, sharing it today.

We reached the boundary between the original forest and the newer part which David had reclaimed from farmland. There was a wide forest ride separating them – acting, I suppose, as a firebreak as well as access. On the other side of it, the trees were smaller, some only ten or twenty feet high. Already, though, the new forest was seductive. The trees had passed the awkward adolescence when few trees look their best. They were just coming into the grace of early adulthood.

'Hup hup!'

The horses' trot became brisker; the bells tinkled with a festive air. 'Where are we going?'

'Whinfell – one of the original farmhouses.'

'Who lives there?'

'A family called Dearden – Douglas and Nicola, I think, and two children.'

'Weekend?'

'No. The husband works from home. He owns a company based in Leeds, but he's rigged up the house so he can run the business from home. He goes in just one day a week now, to keep an eye on things.'

'Are they nice?'

'Nice?' he echoed blankly.

I looked at him sharply. A change had come over him. The heavy features, so strong and vigorous before, had settled into the slightly surly planes I remembered so well from our early fraught encounters. His eyes, which had been radiant with the reflection of his love for the landscape, had retreated, almost physically, further back into his head. He looked out now from a great depth, wary, defensive. I shrank back before realising that I wasn't the target. At The Folly he could be himself. But here, even though the hundreds of acres of trees belonged to him, he was in hostile country, on guard. Each house contained someone opposed to him, and he knew it. His next words confirmed it.

'The husband's all right. The wife's a bit shrill and the kids are awful.'

168

I laughed a little uncertainly. 'Thus spake David Farleton. What a stern judge you are.'

'Am I? I'm sorry. Well, you'll have a chance to judge for yourself – the wife, at least. The kids are at school and this is the husband's day in Leeds.'

He slowed the horses as we approached the big gateway to Whinfell. 'Oh, hell,' he said.

I looked at him anxiously.

'I've just realised,' he said. 'I shouldn't have asked you to come with me.'

'Why ever not?' I said in astonishment.

'Mrs Dearden detests me. It would have been better if she didn't see you with me. I'm sorry, Charlotte. I didn't think.'

'This is ridiculous,' I said. 'If Mrs Dearden takes against me because I'm with you, then I don't think much of her opinion anyway.'

'What a stern judge you are,' he said softly, mocking me with my own words to him.

I think it was at that moment that I began to understand the faint film of melancholy that lay, however lightly, over The Folly. That sense of separation, of being misunderstood and disliked, must wear one down like the persistent work of water on stone. However lusty and full of life they were – David, Brendan, Belle – however passionately they believed in what they were doing, the odour of public disapprobation came to meet them whenever they stepped outside the fairy ring of the forest.

Well, I was one of them now, and I had no regrets. I looked hard at David. 'I do appreciate your concern. It's sweet of you to care what people think of me. But believe me, I can look after myself. Not for nothing was I in the City all those years.' I smiled at him. 'All right?'

'It's too late anyway,' he said gloomily.

I had to laugh. 'And stop being such a grump.'

We'd come to a halt before the gate. I climbed down and opened it. David went through and waited. I waved him on and, after shutting the gate, walked behind up the short drive to the house.

The house, set in about an acre of well-tended garden, was sumptuous. Extensions had been added to each side – one a three-car garage with rooms above, the other probably the office space. Richard had told me that his father demolished the old outbuildings at Graegarth and sold their stone to newcomers extending their houses. I supposed this was one of them. It looked good, but I remembered the hideous new concrete block and asbestos sheds Graegarth now had in their place and felt sad.

David stopped the horses in front of the house and jumped down from the cart just as I caught up with him. At the same moment, the porch door opened and a woman came out. She was about thirty-five and beautifully dressed in the expensive tweeds which pass for rustic among outsiders. She was also beautifully made up. For the dogs? Two red setters came bounding out of the house after her. Olwen and Sif eyed them warily but maintained their aristocratic aloofness.

'How nice!' said Mrs Dearden with what sounded like forced gaiety. 'I wasn't expecting the delivery so soon!'

Evidently not. A shadow loomed behind the glass door before it opened a second time and a man came out. Richard. I stared. Dear God. Was this really a bedroom farce being played out in this improbable setting? I think so, because Mrs Dearden seemed startled and annoyed to see Richard. She recovered quickly, though.

'Dear Richard's brought me some manure for the roses,' she explained.

Dear Richard had patently done nothing of the sort, not in the Rover which I now saw parked in the garage. Surely she'd lived in the country long enough to concoct a better excuse than that?

She came across the neatly raked gravel towards me. 'I'm Nicola Dearden. And you are . . . '

'Charlotte Venables – from Cappelrigg.' I smiled and put out my hand. If we were going to dislike each other I would make sure that no blame could accrue to me. Her own smile was spectacularly false. I wondered if mine was, too.

'Ah, yes, Richard did mention that someone had bought it. How nice to meet you.'

David ended the small talk by asking where she wanted the wood. She gestured towards a flagged area just below a set of mullioned windows. David expressed surprise – didn't she want it stored indoors? No, it looked more picturesque stacked against the house wall. David pointed out that it would get wet. Mrs Dearden said that practicalities weren't the be-all and end-all of life, that appearances mattered, too. The wet wood would wreak havoc with her woodburning stove, said David. That was her problem, said Mrs Dearden. It would indeed be her problem, said David, but he wished to point out that he never sold firewood that wasn't thoroughly dried and seasoned. If it got wet afterwards, he wished it to be quite clear where the fault lay.

I listened to the exchange with sadness and amusement. PR certainly wasn't David's strong point.

She cut him off with a peremptory gesture. David backed the horses towards the space indicated and began unloading the wood. His face was set and sullen. I wanted to take it between my hands and kiss the irritation away. Instead, I stood by the horses' heads. Olwen gave me a conspiratorial look, I'm sure of it.

Nicola Dearden strolled round the corner of the house, followed by her dogs. I don't know whether she expected Richard to follow her too, but he didn't. He came and stood beside me.

'I hope I didn't keep you up too late last night,' he smiled. His voice was just quiet enough to sound private but loud enough to be heard by David.

'Not at all,' I said.

David must have heard, but he hid any reaction behind that dark sullen mask.

Then Richard lowered his voice further. 'I thought you said you weren't interested in the Farletons.'

'I'm interested in good relations with all my neighbours,' I said, 'as you obviously are too.' I nodded towards the house.

Richard gave me an awkward smile. He reached up his hand to caress Olwen's forelock, but Olwen was having nothing of it. She raised her muzzle high to brush away his hand. The gesture had nothing to do with the intuition animals are meant to have about humans – she merely expected that the hand would contain a treat for her and went out to get it. But the effect was very like rejection and seemed to discomfort Richard.

171

Then Nicola Dearden's voice sailed across the frosty air from the corner of the house. 'Richard, I wonder if you could give me your opinion about something.'

I noted that she hadn't even bothered to invent an item requiring the opinion. She must have realised that her affair with him was obvious and given up all but the faintest pretence. The currents of hostility criss-crossing between the four of us were increasing. Then Richard went to meet her and broke the circuit.

I went to David. 'Can I help?'

'It wouldn't look good,' he warned.

'How so? That I'm a navvy? Or that I'm too chummy with you?'

'Both.'

'To hell with it.' I grabbed an armload of wood, and we finished unloading the cart together.

David took a pad from his jacket pocket and scribbled a delivery note. He slipped it through the letterbox and we left. As soon as we drove through the gateway the air seemed to lighten again and I smelled the gentle healing fragrance of resin.

'Will you come back for lunch?' David asked. 'It's only bread and cheese, but the bread will be fresh – this is Belle's baking day.'

'Wonderful!'

David hup-hupped the horses into a trot. They didn't need much urging – no doubt their own equivalent of freshly-baked bread was waiting for them at the stables.

'I couldn't help overhearing,' said David.

I didn't pretend to misunderstand. 'I think he meant you to.'

He hesitated. Then, 'Charlotte, I don't want to interfere – what you do with your life is your own business – but will you let me say just one thing?'

I nodded, feeling a little sad at the freedom he allotted me.

'Richard Staveley may not be quite what he seems to be,' he said.

'What do you mean?'

There was a long pause. Then he said quietly, 'It's a fair

enough question, but I can't answer it. I can't even say why I can't answer it.' He smiled ruefully. 'That doesn't sound very convincing, does it? I warn you against someone, then refuse to tell you why.'

I sighed. I was tired of secrets. The Druids' secret rituals. The secret which I was sure lurked behind Jean's old-young face. The secret Belle had been about to tell me that first euphoric morning at The Folly before Brendan had appeared at the window. I tried to remember what had led up to it. Something about footpaths, David wanting to close down the public –

'Is this something to do with the footpaths?' I asked. I was watching him closely but needn't have done. His surprise was easy enough to see.

'What do you mean?' he said warily.

'Belle mentioned that you were wanting to close the public footpaths. She didn't say why,' I added quickly. 'I just wondered if one of the people you want to keep off them is Richard.' It was a wild enough guess – I couldn't see why Richard's presence on a footpath could have any significance – so I was startled at David's response.

'Yes,' he said simply.

'*But why?* What can he do that's so awful that you have to close an ancient right of way just to get rid of him?'

'That's the other thing I can't tell you. I'm not free to tell you. There are other people involved.'

Then I did something which shocked me as much as David. I took the reins from his hands and stopped the horses. I did it gently – I'd never driven a team and knew David would be enraged if I ruined a good horse's mouth. Gently but firmly. Then I turned round on the narrow seat and made him face me.

'David,' I said, 'you trust Belle and Brendan. Why not me?' It was an audacious question really. Why should he? He barely knew me.

He turned his face away. I knew he wasn't having an idle look at his forest. Finally he turned back and reclaimed the reins. 'I'm sorry,' he said. 'You're right. Let's go and have lunch. Belle will be there. We'll tell you everything.'

21

Belle was as vibrant as ever in her glorious palace of food. As we entered the kitchen, great yeasty waves billowed out to meet us and envelop us in the magical fragrance of fresh bread. The white witch herself was crouched before the Aga. She waved an oven glove in greeting, then plunged both hands deep into the Aga to extract another loaf. When she'd set it on a rack beside the others, she turned to greet us again.

'The last loaf – what timing! Charlotte, it's lovely to see you again! Do sit down, both of you. I'll put the kettle on!'

And so forth. If Astrid's sentences ended with the sweet little lilt of question marks, Belle's were finished off with the exuberant flourish of exclamation marks. I listened contentedly as they jabbed the soft waves of bread scent, accompanied by her cheerful chatter and the clatter of the table being set. It was strange how her *perpetuum mobile*, far from damaging the peaceful atmosphere, conferred on the kitchen her own form of calm.

Finally she sat down and pulled towards her one of the loaves. 'They say you shouldn't eat bread straight out of the oven – indigestion or something – but to hell with it! It tastes too good!'

I accepted a steaming slice. 'Where's everyone else? Don't they come in for lunch?'

A large chunk of butter melted into David's bread. 'Not in winter. There's too little daylight to waste it coming back with the horses. It's sandwiches and nosebags in winter – I told you I was a slave-driver.'

I nodded and bit into my own slice. It was exquisite. The freshness of my love for David and that of the bread combined to make a feast.

Finally we pushed away our plates and, with a second mug

of tea before us, David said to Belle, 'It's time for Charlotte to know everything.'

'Well, thank God for that!' She let out a great sigh of relief and smiled reassuringly at me.

'It's a long story – I hope you'll be patient,' David began. 'It goes back a long way, to when my father was the squire. I hated my father. The personal reasons are irrelevant, but there was a less personal reason, too. In those days, the family lived at Farleton Hall. Keldreth was just a distant spur of the estate. As for the forest, that was just a playground where he and his cronies went shooting a few times a year. The rights and wrongs of shooting don't concern me. I'm not a vegetarian, I can't afford to be moralistic about it. What did concern me was the use of the land. Half of it was artificially farmed and the other half was used for artificially rearing game birds. What "management" there was of the forest was done solely for the pheasants – some parts hacked down, other parts allowed to become overgrown and useless for anything except pheasants.'

He paused. His face that I loved so much was knotted with emotions I couldn't fathom. 'I love this land,' he said quietly. 'More than anything in the world, *I love this land*.'

I'd heard similar words many times before, mainly from farmers who said them because that's what the public wanted to hear. This was different. I realised now that I'd seen only a fraction of it this morning, shining forth from his eyes as they swept over the landscape. I'd seen the benevolent side. But now I saw that there was another side to it: a passion so intense as to pass, almost, the bounds of acceptability.

'So you can imagine,' he continued, 'how I felt about this land being used as my father's toy. Rhiannon – my mother – felt something of the same thing, though for her it was more a matter of the trees. She was Welsh, she'd grown up respecting trees. She didn't like seeing them messed about. When he died, she tried to do something about the forest, but her love of trees was too romantic. She knew nothing of the practicalities and neither did I. Neither did the keeper who "managed" it for the pheasants. He was used to my father's ways and couldn't have changed if he'd wanted to, which he didn't. I read everything I could on the subject, a kind of do-it-yourself crash course on forestry. But it wasn't until I got to Cambridge that I really started to learn. Even there, the Land Economy course was pretty conservative. Except for Brendan.'

He smiled at Belle, then turned back to me. 'You probably think Brendan's just a nice good-natured fellow, a kind of sidekick carrying out the gaffer's orders? Well, you're wrong. He's brilliant. Beneath that grizzled skull is one of the most phenomenal brains I've ever known. Incredibly, he had never been promoted. It took me a while to realise that he had ideas of his own that had no outlet in the course. When I did discover it, though, things started to happen. I still did the required work for the course and finished with the right letters after my name – it's useful in dealing with other people, it makes them take me seriously. But the real education came from Brendan.

'It's easy enough now to say what Brendan was on about. Now there are words like "ecologist" and "green" to explain it. But at the time, his ideas were revolutionary, and even now we don't fit in. We didn't want to create an artificial wildlife preserve, but we didn't want the other extreme either: using the land as a commercial forest. We wanted somehow to combine the two. We knew it wouldn't be easy. If we'd known just how difficult it would be, we probably wouldn't have tried it at all.'

'That's not true,' said Belle. 'You were fanatics, both of you. Nothing would have stopped you.'

David shrugged and went on. 'Then two things happened. I finished my course at Cambridge . . . and Rhiannon died. I sold Farleton Hall and all the junk in it. What was left after death duties went into the forest. We moved up to The Folly and got down to work. None of it would have been possible without Brendan and Belle. They dropped every bit of security and every job prospect they had to come up to The Folly.'

'Brendan dropped a dead end job he'd hated for years,' said Belle. 'He wanted action, and you offered him just that. As for me, I was a second-rate actress going nowhere. I had nothing to lose.'

Actress. Of course. It was all coming together now –

her easy grace of movement despite her size, the ringing voice that would carry to the back of the stalls, her theatrical taste in clothes, even her gestures, bigger than life, trained for the stage. I had vaguely wondered before. Now I knew.

'You had your whole career to lose, and you lost it,' he said bluntly. 'There aren't exactly a lot of opportunities to act up here.'

'Thank God. I wouldn't have made it, and I knew it. You gave me a graceful way out. Cut the praise and get on with the story.'

And Ros? The other actress, the one who wasn't second-rate and who did make it – where did she fit in? Both Ros and Richard were conspicuous by their absence from the story so far.

'As I said,' David continued, 'Brendan and Belle made an insane leap of faith and came with me to The Folly. For several years we worked like hell trying to salvage what there was of the old forest and replant the new. When the bulk of the work was done, we were euphoric with what we'd accomplished. We had laid the foundations for the new Eden, we thought, and we thought it made us into gods. Hubris, Charlotte. The real snake in the garden. We dared to play god, and we're paying for it now.

'The situation was simple. Our renovated forest was already attracting a lot of wildlife back into it. If we'd left it at that, nothing would have happened. But we were ambitious. We wanted more. Brendan had belonged to conservation groups for a long time, before I even met him. He knew all the schemes for reintroducing endangered species to the wild. He also knew that our place was perfect for such schemes.

'Think about it. We have a vast stretch of inaccessible moorland right next to a forest. Further, that forest is mixed. Most are either coniferous or deciduous. Ours is both. There's hardly a bird imaginable who isn't catered for. In addition, the forest is unusually fragmented; as well as the rides, we have several little fields for hay and to give the horses a bit of freedom in the summer. The whole forest is full of edges – hell to fence but perfect for birds. Best of all, this is one of the most remote places in England. There are plenty of good sites in Scotland, but not England.

'So that was it. We offered ourselves as an experimental site and started taking on endangered birds – mostly peregrines. We did pretty well, too. They settled down and bred with reasonable success. Of course there were failures. There were eggs that disappeared, ringed birds that never turned up again. But you expect that. Crows sometimes take the eggs, a certain number of fledglings die of natural causes. There was nothing suspicious about our losses, nor were they worse than anywhere else.

'Hubris again. Again we were euphoric with our success, and again we couldn't leave it at that. After all, if peregrines did so well here, surely other birds with similar needs would do equally well?'

'Kites!' I cried. 'Red kites! Of course!'

They looked at me with amazement. 'You've seen them?' David asked.

'Once. Just one. I decided it must be something else – I thought there weren't any kites in England, and I only had a glimpse. I was walking along the edge of the moor with – ' I broke off.

'With Richard?' Belle asked.

I nodded.

'Well,' said David grimly, 'then you can probably guess what's coming. There's just one part of Wales that has a small natural colony of red kites left. The RSPB and the Nature Conservancy Council started reintroducing them into Scotland, using birds brought in from Sweden. Then they decided to try a few sites in England as well.'

He smiled rather sadly at me. 'I suppose they're guilty of hubris as well. England's just too overpopulated for a bird like that. We all should have known. But it *seemed* possible here, and at first it went quite well. Only this time the stakes were very high. It's a complicated business, and very expensive, bringing the birds in from abroad, and kites are particularly awkward about adapting. A lot of time and money – and not just ours – went into the project.'

'And the stakes are equally high for the other side?' I suggested quietly.

'Yes,' said David. 'A single egg can fetch thousands. A stuffed bird – if it's been killed cleanly – is worth a lot, too. But the real coup is a live bird.'

'What for?'

'Falconry. In this country it's monitored. Falcons are reared for the purpose, and the buying and selling is controlled to make sure they're the only ones used. But there aren't any controls in the Middle East, and a rich sheikh will pay a very great deal of money for something as rare as a red kite.'

'And as special,' Belle broke in. 'Charlotte, if only you could *see* these birds you'd understand. There's nothing in the world like them! They really are the most spectacular creatures! Look!' she laughed excitedly, showing me her arm. 'I've got goosebumps just *remembering* the last time we saw them! Do you remember, David? Up at the first site? David, you must take Charlotte to see them – there's no way she'll understand what the fuss is about unless she does.'

But I did understand. I didn't need to see them to realise that the red kites were the culmination of David's vision. It wasn't a matter of time and money wasted. Nor was it a sentimental love of nature. They were potent symbols, these birds.

I tried to remember the time I saw the kite – when I met Richard on the moor. The scar. It was the obvious conclusion to jump to: that it came from a kite resisting capture. 'You think it's Richard, don't you?' I said. 'That's why you want to close the footpaths.'

David nodded. 'It wouldn't stop him, of course, but it would make things more difficult. As it is, he can stroll about as he pleases – legally – looking for the new nests, and there's not a damned thing I can do to stop him. There's not a scrap of evidence, never mind proof.'

'Even if the police caught him red-handed, it wouldn't make any difference,' Belle added. 'The fines are ludicrously small. He'd just pay them out of his profits and then carry on as usual. He's here for life, Charlotte. And there's nothing we can do.'

The clock ticked very loudly in the silence that followed as I began to comprehend the enormity of it all. This wasn't just a case of a few casualties in one reintroduction programme. David had, in a crazy euphoria of idealism, brought these birds to a lifelong slaughterhouse.

'Do the students know?' I asked.

'No,' said David. 'They're good lads, but it would be unfair to expect them not to slip up and say something. Staveley's not the only dealer in this kind of thing. If word got out, the place would be swarming with them, the whole colony could be wiped out in a year. Which is another reason we keep clear of the police.'

I looked at David's face, almost white with suppressed anger. I thought again of his passion for the land, that passion that almost passed the bounds of acceptability. Slander was one of those boundaries. I had passed beyond it myself, last night with Richard, accusing him of leading the Druids and slaughtering my hen. Perhaps it was my own guilt, anxious to make amends, that spoke when I said quietly, 'I think you're wrong. Richard's a lousy farmer, but so are a lot of others. He wouldn't do a thing like that. I'm sure of it.'

I looked at Belle, and at David again. It was clear that they hadn't expected this. I felt confused and disturbed. They'd put a great deal of trust in me by telling me about the kites. I felt almost as if I'd broken that trust by refusing to believe that Richard was the culprit.

I smiled awkwardly. 'I won't tell anyone about the kites; that I can promise. No one. Not even Effie.'

Belle's smile was awkward, too. 'Charlotte, I'm sorry. We shouldn't have expected you to – I mean, you have no reason to – We don't want to bully you into thinking – What I mean is, you must make up your own mind, of course. Anyway, regardless of what you think, it would help if you could see the kites. I'm sure David would love to take you up one day.'

'Up?'

Belle looked uncertainly at David.

He nodded.

'There's a place on the moor which no one knows about,' she said, 'a hidden valley about four miles from here. There's a stretch of bogland before you get there, so it's inaccessible except by foot. That's where we released the first kites. From there, fledglings moved on to colonise two or three other hidden valleys which are also inaccessible, so whatever happens all those should be safe. The problem birds are the ones who move south into the forest. Anyway, David will show you.'

22

The frost held, and one December night David phoned to say that tomorrow was the day. 'It's an eight mile walk there and back, and there isn't much daylight, so be here an hour or so before dawn.'

I was, gripping a little haversack of sandwiches and flask and wrapped up in so many layers of clothes that I felt like a stuffed sausage. A larger sausage, with cap pulled down over ever-unruly black hair, came out to meet me. He took my haversack and then my hand and led me through the pitch-black forest. Either he had cats' eyes or he knew every inch of the way.

After some time we emerged abruptly into a shallow gully I hadn't known existed. It ran north-south and cut through the edge of the cliff which everywhere else made a sharp separation between moor and forest. Here, we simply strolled from the forest into the gully, following a beck which glittered in the strange light. There was a sharp crescent moon just thinking of setting. Above, a navy-blue sky shaded, by stages too subtle to see, into a pale aquamarine fringing the eastern side of the gully.

'Do you know where we are?' David asked.

'Somewhere east of The Folly,' I said, 'but other than that, no.'

'This is the route we used when we established the colony,' he explained. 'The lie of the land makes the part of the moor it takes us to invisible. Even if there'd been anyone on the moor, they wouldn't have been able to see us. You'll see what I mean when we get up top.'

The soft light made the gully so magical I didn't care if we ever left it. Much of the beck was frozen over. Pretty little swatches of icy lace reached from the sides towards the narrow channel of still-running water which showed glossy black by contrast. The water gurgled in different pitches: dark resonant notes where it moved secretively under the ice, fluting little trebles where it scrambled over the iced rocks. The melody was varied, unpredictable and wholly pleasing. No harmony of the spheres but an anarchic little composition which seemed to be performed just for the fun of it. At the sides, clumps of frozen fern and rough grass made an appreciative audience.

About halfway along the gully we left the beck and began a long oblique climb up a sheep path which ended just above a waterfall. Coming out was a surprise. Dawn had arrived without bothering to tell us. Up here, on the open moor at last, the aquamarine was streaked with filmy banners of pale apricot on the eastern horizon. Elsewhere, the sky was assuming the clear blue of a perfect winter day. The only sound was the tumbling tune of the waterfall, and even that was soon left behind as we struck out across the moor.

David looked as remote and self-contained as the moor itself. It was his territory. A big man for big spaces. It was impossible to imagine him in a London flat or office, confined to hearth and bounded by walls. He strode across the moor as if it were his living room, utterly at home.

I didn't. I stumbled across the tough terrain like a hedgehog in the wake of a panther. My feet ski'd down the frozen hummocks of heather and threatened my ankles with each landing. At last I discovered that the boggy bits between were frozen, and I began to pick a meandering path along it. Even so, I felt clumsy. Did one have to be born to it in order to glide effortlessly through this maddening landscape like he did? Probably. Several times he had to stop and wait for me to catch up.

'I'm sorry,' he apologised. 'I'm so used to being alone up here.'

'That's all right.'

Several times we had to cross little cuttings too wide to jump, scrambling awkwardly down and up, avoiding the iced rocks jutting out of the peat.

'This is why it's inaccessible,' he said. 'Not even a Land-Rover can make it across here.'

I nodded, puffing great clouds of white breath into the air.

It was full daylight now, the air as thin and pure as at the top of a mountain. 'Wait a minute,' I said. 'I want to see where we are.'

I looked round. There was nothing to see, nothing but wave upon wave of land undulating more markedly than I'd ever expected. The effect was strange. I felt I was seeing a never-ending vista of uninterrupted moorland, but in reality there were dozens of little hills and depressions stitched together by distance into the illusion of a smooth moor. I could barely tell in which direction we were walking. I'd never been this far into the moor and felt completely lisoriented.

David pointed in one direction. 'The Folly's over there.'

I couldn't see a thing.

'Over there is the stone circle,' he continued.

Nothing.

'And we're heading for the valley up there.'

'Do you have a compass?' I said nervously.

'I do, but we won't need it. I carry it just in case the fog comes down. It won't today.'

True enough. The sky was now a clear picture-postcard blue, a Mediterranean effect ludicrous on a midwinter moor. Here and there a neat little cloud hung poised for action, like a sailboat becalmed and waiting for a puff of wind that never came.

Suddenly David gripped my arm. 'Up there,' he said quietly.

It took me a while to see what he meant, it was so high up; not even a shape, just a vague sense of interruption to the plain blue of the sky. But as I focused, it began to take the shape of an angular cruciform silhouette. It was moving – I could tell by its changed position to a nearby cloud – but its flight was so effortless that it was easier to believe that it was the sky moving like a piece of stage machinery behind the motionless bird. I'd seen hawks before, all kinds of hawks, but nothing like this.

It was making a wide circle. Or rather, a descending spiral, for it was just that bit closer now, and I could see the forked tail at last, the famous forked tail of the red kite. And now I could see why it was forked. Astonishingly, the bird seemed to use sometimes one fork, sometimes the other, quite independently, to achieve its strange mobility. The wings, too, were independent of each other, giving the bird a breathtaking freedom of flight. Now and again it simply soared, with its wings held forward and slightly arched. Then it would glide, angling the wings back.

It was hard not to believe the bird was showing off, putting on a performance for us, two tiny earthbound creatures staring enraptured at its unbelievable virtuosity. And the illusion increased when, maddeningly, it shot high up again and disappeared behind a cloud, for all the world like an actor with the curtain down. I wanted to applaud, but David's pressure on my arm kept me quiet.

'Wait,' he whispered, though how it could hear us at this distance I couldn't imagine. 'It should appear again. I wish there were two of them,' he added.

'Greedy old thing.'

'You'd know what I meant if you saw it.'

We waited. It seemed weird that the bird could disappear just like that, but after witnessing its magical flight, I felt it was capable of anything, even dematerialising. Perhaps it hadn't been there at all, perhaps it was just an illusion. I might have thought so, if David hadn't seen it, too.

'Patience,' he whispered.

'What goes up must come down, right?' I felt the need to be a little flippant, it was just too beautiful.

And then, patience rewarded. Suddenly it was there again, though I hadn't seen it emerge from its cloud. But it wasn't until David squeezed my arm hard that I saw that there were two.

'I don't believe it,' he whispered. 'We're lucky enough to find *one*.'

They were higher than before, and it took a while before they floated near enough for me to see their shapes again. Even so, they must have been a hell of a distance away. I knew they were big birds – the biggest of all the British hawks – but at this distance their six-foot wingspan was irrelevant.

Not so their grace. Not even a Nureyev or Fontaine could rival the combination of grace and strength spread across this remote sky. I remembered the time I'd seen David and Matti play, how much I'd felt in David that same grace and strength. No wonder he loved these birds so much. They were, in some way, his kin. Would he be reincarnated as a red kite? Very likely.

As if on cue, the birds began to play, approaching and separating with great sweeps across the sky. It had to be for pleasure. It was too early for a mating display with all the fraughtness that entailed. This was pure exhilarated enjoyment of their astonishing abilities.

Suddenly, they were falling out of the sky. Without the steadiness of David by my side, I might have cried out in alarm and ruined everything. But I clamped my mouth shut and watched, breathless, as the two birds tumbled down together, wings closed and gaining speed alarmingly. And then, at the last moment, a sharp upward turn and they were climbing into the sky again, far apart and seemingly oblivious of each other.

David said nothing, and I was glad. The moment had been too precious for words. I knew now what he had hoped against hope that I would see, and it had happened. I felt privileged beyond belief, and terribly humbled. I could feel, too, David's love of the birds transmitted to me. No one could witness such grandeur and remain unmoved.

They were picking up speed in their climb, their wingbeats deep and strong and fluid, their glowing chestnut bodies gaining height and losing colour as they resumed, finally, their place in the high regions which seemed their natural home. And again, the flight-play, as they soared towards each other and moved apart in their stunning *pas-de-deux*. I watched greedily now. Would they do their amazing nose-dive a second time? It seemed too much to hope for.

But what I got was even more. For this time, instead of closing their wings for a freefall, they suddenly locked their talons together and then, as I held my breath and pushed back tears of awe, the birds gyrated slowly – oh, so slowly – downward, their wings full open, the four great wings seeming to belong to a single mythical creature. The two birds were one, cartwheeling through the heavens, the sun striking sparks off their glowing bodies, turning the birds into a majestic wheel of fire. I wished it would never end, I wanted to slow down the camera of my brain, make the moment last forever. But finally, just before they would have hit ground, they separated with one great powerful lunge and sped off, close to the ground now, to disappear in some secret place on the moor.

We stood there, David and I, for a long time, long after we'd given up hope of their return. No doubt they'd gone off for the day's hunting. Fervently I wished them luck. I shut my eyes and tried to press the image of that last magnificent flight onto the back of my eyelids where it would be caught forever, ready for recall the next time I felt life to be a little grey. I could feel the cold seeping into my feet and up my legs and I didn't care. I didn't care if I turned into a frozen pillar, just so long as I could remember. I could understand now why everyone at The Folly felt so passionate about these birds. Belle had been right; they had to be seen. And I had seen them.

When finally we started walking, we still said nothing, not until we reached the edge of the bog. Then David seemed to shake himself and wake up. He looked at me, almost as if surprised to see anyone there. 'I've never seen that,' he said quietly. 'I've heard about it, but I never thought I'd see it.' Then he smiled. 'Perhaps you're a good luck charm.'

It was a lovely thing to say, however untrue.

How does one come back to earth after an experience like that? Easy. By trudging across a bog. This one stretched as far as I could see, a great frozen mass of peaty ice and reeds. It was, David explained, the reason he'd waited for the frost to do its work before bringing me up here. The bog was impassable even on foot unless it was frozen. There was a way around it, but it would add several hard-walking miles to our journey. In fact, the bog was the easiest part of our walk that day. Compared to the roughness of the moor, it felt like a superhighway.

'Your birds are certainly safe up here,' I observed. 'It's like Sleeping Beauty's castle, with the bog instead of a thorn hedge keeping out all but the prince.'

'That's the idea,' he said. 'You can see why we volunteered

ourselves for the scheme. The habitat couldn't be better if we'd designed it just for them.'

About half a mile of rough moorland separated the far shore of the bog from the valley. The place was so hidden that we had to be this close to see the first signs – a few scraggy tree tops seeming to perch like bushes on the moor. As we drew nearer, I could see a big dark mass in one of them.

'That's the original nest,' David explained. 'If a site is successful, they use it year after year and extend the nest. You can get some idea of how long they've been here by the size of it. They can grow up to a metre in diameter. That one still has a way to go, but the fact that it's still growing means they've been undisturbed for some years and bred successfully from it.'

'Won't they mind us trespassing?'

'Not at this time of year. Anyway,' he smiled, 'they've gone out for the day.'

There's something strangely thrilling about a secret valley, even if you know there's nothing in it but the same things that are in any little valley. It's like hidden treasure, special for being where it shouldn't be. David had already described this one to me: the usual little rift carved out of the moor and colonised by the usual rowans, hawthorns, ashes and – in this case – the big old Scots pine in which the kites had made their nest. At the bottom, a gill, small and slow flowing. The usual tumble of boulders with the usual lichens making themselves at home on them. Other than that, just heather and cotton grass and sedge.

One doesn't expect to find anything out of the ordinary in such a place. Above all, one doesn't expect to find signs of a human presence other than one's own.

We saw the trap as soon as we reached the edge. It was large, and it sat beneath the pine containing the kite's nest. For a moment we said nothing, did nothing. I could feel the magic of the morning crumble with each motionless second.

Then David scrambled into the valley. I followed close behind. We stood beside the trap, staring at the bird inside. It was a partridge, ludicrously tiny for the cage that held it.

Then I realised. Of course. Bait. What's more, the trap had been baited very recently. Involuntarily, I looked round the valley but could see no one.

David stooped down and opened the trap. The partridge, not recognising its liberator, flapped about for some time before making a comical dash for freedom. It was so funny, this little wind-up toy of a bird, that I had to work hard at not laughing. A little like the hysterical laughter that bubbles up at funerals, I suppose.

I was still dazed by the shock of seeing the loathsome trap so soon after the magnificence of the wheeling kites. I hardly noticed David walking to the bank of the gill. I watched, only half attentive, as he selected a large rock and brought it back. He raised it high above his head. Then, with one powerful heave, he crashed it down on the empty trap. It shattered into a mass of twisted wire and wood.

His face was twisted, too, into a rage far more fearful than the one with which he'd confronted me after my ride on Olwen. There was no doubt in my mind that at that moment he was quite capable of killing.

23

A few days later I received the first threat.

I wasn't entirely surprised. I'd thought a lot about that kite trap. I'd also thought about the Druids. I couldn't believe that twenty or so grown men, quite respectable in their daily lives, would organise themselves for such a silly purpose as enacting old rituals without some other reason urging them on. It had to be the kites. After all, what better cover for being innocently on the moor? Those days spent hauling wood up to the stone circle, for example.

On the other hand, I couldn't believe either that all twenty were involved. The group must have been formed by the one who was trapping the birds. Whoever he was, he'd managed to whip up enthusiasm for the old Druid cult and persuaded the others to join him in performing the rituals. He'd also persuaded them that I was blocking the ley line. The truth was that the 'priest' didn't want me anywhere around the place, and especially not on the moor where I might see something a good deal more significant than their rituals.

I even had a hunch, though nothing to back it up, that the whole cult was centred on the Golden Oak. I'd noticed for some time that the atmosphere whenever I entered the pub was quietly hostile. At first I'd thought it was just because I was a newcomer. Now I wondered. Further, there were several regulars there who could easily have been the 'priest' I had glimpsed. I was beginning to wonder if I myself had been glimpsed that night. But if so, why had the threat been delayed so long?

The threat contained two words only – LEAVE CAPPELRIGG – composed of individual letters cut out of the *Langhamdale Gazette*. My name and address were similarly composed. Whoever it was was taking no chances with a traceable typewriter. The paper and envelope were both ordinary, equally hard to trace. It had been posted in Kirkby Langham. First class.

'I'm flattered,' I said to Belle on the phone that morning. 'Second class would be a real slap in the face.'

'It's not funny. You get on the phone to the police the minute I hang up – you hear, Charlotte?' And she hung up to make her point.

Detective Sergeant Tyndall was a plump young fellow with a cherubic face and altogether too good-natured for his trade. He was clearly baffled. We chatted comfortably over a coffee and went through the possible suspects.

None.

I was barely known in Kirkby itself – only a few tradesmen. I knew a few farmers in the vale from the autumn sheep sales, but none well enough to generate a grudge. Keldreth itself was even less promising. David and Richard were both known to have bid against me for Cappelrigg, but we agreed easily enough that neither would resort to threats to make me sell up and leave. I was outraged that he should even consider David. As for Richard, it turned out that he was on very good terms with the local constabulary. The only person I knew in Yuppyville was Mrs Dearden. She might have detected Richard's interest in me, but she seemed too silly a woman to be overwhelmed with jealousy, not to that extent anyway. In any case, I kept quiet about her. If she was having an affair with Richard, that was her business.

When finally I mentioned my suspicions about the Druids, Detective Sergeant Tyndall was amazed. Did I really expect him to search out twenty possible suspects from among the town's citizens with nothing more to go on than some daft business about a ley line? I couldn't, of course, mention the real reason – the kites – if their presence was to be kept a secret.

Then the second threat came – a phone call this time. Just two words again, the same two: LEAVE CAPPELRIGG. The voice was unfamiliar, though with only two words even the most familiar voice would be hard to guess. But I was pretty sure it was a woman trying to disguise her voice to sound like a man's. I phoned the police again, feeling baffled myself. It didn't fit in with my Druid theory or anything

191

else. Unless it had been a man trying to sound like a woman disguised as a man to throw me off the track? It all seemed unnecessarily complicated. Detective Sergeant Tyndall made a few inquiries and then let the matter drop again.

By now I was inclined to see it as a practical joke, though that still begged the question. None the less, I was pleased when the rug-curtains Effie had commissioned arrived and I could at least shut out the night. I also had locks and bolts put on all the downstairs doors and windows.

Luckily I had other things to think about. Christmas was coming and so was Effie. We'd spent Christmas together for several years now. Her parents were divorced, living in California and New York. Both had spouses who cared little for Effie's abrasive presence in their cosy new lives. My parents had always given her a huge welcome in our Sussex farmhouse, so much so that at the end of her first Christmas Day with us, Effie's chin had wobbled uncharacteristically and she'd sniffled, 'This is the best Christmas I've ever had.'

When my parents died, Effie felt almost as orphaned as I did. We spent that first Christmas alone together in my Docklands flat. We didn't do too badly, for two bereaved solitaries. But this year would be better still. If one couldn't have a family for Christmas a big old farmhouse was the next best thing.

I prowled round the house on the morning of Christmas Eve, inspecting my handiwork. It's no joke, decorating a house for a guest who's an interior designer. As I couldn't rival her ingenuity, I went for the opposite extreme and put the house into its most traditional finery. There was a lovely little Christmas tree decorated with the best of my parents' ornaments. There were swags of fragrant fir and pine smothering every beam and mantelpiece. There were jars of holly everywhere, and candles, and bowls of nuts, and oranges and chocolates. There was a holly wreath on the door. There was Tarzan, spruced up in a red bow. The makings of our Christmas Eve punch stood ready by the Aga.

The only thing missing was the turkey, for we were going to The Folly for Christmas Day. Effie had been overjoyed on the phone. 'I *adore* other people's families. It's just my own I can't stand.'

I was pretty pleased about it, too. I hoped that David's general affection for me would turn to something more. I saw myself as a slow and steady candle flame that might in time throw a little light into some dark corner of his mind that was waiting. Perhaps, perhaps. In the meantime, I loved being with him, and with Brendan and Belle. Astrid was coming for Christmas, too, and Matti. I was eager to see them both.

The only thing I wasn't so pleased about was the snow. The long cold period had ended a week before, bringing in its place high winds, rain and snow. A modest fall or two was fine with me, doing its White Christmas bit and completing the traditional decor. But I had to be alert for an early blizzard, ready to rush out and bring my sheep down.

I was prepared for it. I had cheated. All through the autumn and early winter I'd taken little treats up to the sheep – a bale of hay one day, a scattering of sheepnuts another. Not a lot, just enough to keep them interested. I distributed my goodies at the foot of the moor, just beyond my boundary wall, thus ensuring that they wouldn't stray too far. This was contrary to normal practice. Other farmers wanted their sheep to spread themselves all over the moor to find every last blade of grass. But I still regarded the moor as a death trap. I wouldn't have put my sheep on it at all if I hadn't feared other farmers' contempt. My reputation was at stake. I had to keep those sheep up there as long as I could.

None the less, if it came to a choice between my reputation or my sheep, I knew what I would do. And so I hovered, ready to spring to the rescue at the first threat of serious snow. Starting with 'Farming Today' in the small hours, I listened to every single weather report until broadcasting shut down for the night. They were surprisingly accurate. I was comforted. Nothing would happen as long as I kept listening, kept myself at the ready.

Then my radio broke down. It was two days before Christmas. The man in the shop was sympathetic. It was an old-fashioned shop which prided itself on total service. When he understood my plight, he loaned me a radio someone had just brought in as part exchange. He was very apologetic – the radio wasn't up to the standards of the posh ones he sold – but I assured him it would do very nicely.

There was nothing particularly alarming about the weather report that night. I went to bed with a clear conscience. I awoke the next morning to the gentle snow flurries that were predicted. Nothing alarming there either. I turned on the radio.

Silence.

I twiddled the dials, I shook it, I turned it upside down, I gave it a thump.

Nothing, not even static. No wonder the customer had traded it in. It had been on its last legs and had chosen the worst possible moment to kaput. For a moment I thought of the ley line. They were meant to affect electricity. In certain conditions they were meant to interfere with currents other than their own. But batteries?

I got up, dressed, and finished my Christmas preparations, keeping an eye on the snow all the while. It was meant to be slowing down and stopping by mid-morning. It had always done what it was meant to do, but what if there'd been a change in the night and I hadn't heard about it this morning?

At mid-morning it was still snowing. Further, the wind had risen. I phoned The Folly. No one there. David and Brendan would be felling, everyone else was probably in Kirkby doing their last minute shopping. Oddly enough, I never thought of phoning Graegarth.

By lunchtime it was snowing harder – not a lot, but I couldn't risk it now, now that I was out of touch with the weather reports. I put the spark guard on the fire, wrote a note for Effie just in case it took me longer than expected, climbed into several layers of clothes and went out. I was perfectly calm. I remembered to leave the door open in case Effie arrived early. I even took a torch, also just in case, though it seemed improbable.

'Come on, Moss, put your glad rags on. Time to play knight in shining fur.'

We set off through the grove. The snow was lovely, coating the east side of every tree and snaking its way unevenly

194

along the horizontal branches. Here and there a little blob accumulated at the end of a twig, making the dormant bud seem to accelerate its growth like in a Walt Disney film: from bud to snow-white flower in a few seconds. Then the wind would come along, knock it off and send its petals disintegrating downward, crystals once again, spring turned back to winter with one flick of the wand. The wind had whipped the thin covering of snow beneath the trees into miniature drifts, the highest no more than a few inches, leaving yellowed grass exposed. Fading trails of pheasant prints ambled aimlessly, only to vanish into a mini-drift. I had visions of the birds shrunk to insect size, hiding beneath, tucking into a meal of manna in their white caves. Everything was so small of scale, hugging the ground. It never crossed my mind that there could be any danger.

The snow was only a fraction thicker as we crossed the first field. The land sloped slightly upward here, presenting me with a canvas of graceful white swirls against a background of faded grass. It looked just like an abstract painting, very beautiful. I wondered what a human painter would do faced with a canvas that size. Moss trotted ahead to put himself in the picture, like a geologist's hammer to give a sense of scale. The black patches of his coat made a pleasing contrast.

'Very handsome, Moss,' I called.

He nodded sagely.

In the second field I was surprised, going down the slope into the dip by the syke, to find myself welly deep in a rather high drift. But of course the wind was funnelling the snow there, it was only to be expected.

If the field had been a painting, the tiny gully was a sculpture. Boulders, mottled fresh white and grey, loomed up through the undulating ground. On some of them a particularly strong gust of wind had whisked clean a patch through which a lichen showed, its deep ochre colour startlingly vivid against the white. All the colours were intensified here, twigs which were normally just shades of brown were here turned into purples and reds. A clump of reeds was shockingly green. The swollen water of the syke was shiny black, as if a clumsy writer had spilled his ink pot and the contents were now rushing across his pristine blotter. I almost expected great black stains on my wellies when I forded the syke, black footprints trailing up the opposite slope until they faded into grey and then white.

It was only the contrast with the relatively bright colours in the dip that made the next field so muted, or so I told myself. Here the swirling patterns of drift and bare field showed only as different shades of white. And yet, as I trudged up the field, the bare patches seemed the same faded yellow as before. I squinted ahead, puzzled by the discrepancy. It took me a while to see that what muted the canvas was not on the ground but in the air. Snow. Rather more of it than before. In fact, rather a lot of it, making its own counterpatterns against the pale sky. The difference in altitude between the fields wasn't all that great, surely not enough to explain the increased thickness of snow? It occurred to me, uneasily, that it might simply have started snowing harder. But it wasn't supposed to. The snow was meant to be easing off, and it had always done what it was meant to do.

I squinted harder, and needed to, because the wind had also picked up and was blowing fistfuls of snow at my face. I was looking for the familiar dirty-grey bumps on the cliffside that would tell me my sheep were near at hand and my journey nearly over. Surely they would be there, come for their usual treat?

No dirty bumps. Indeed, no cliff at all, until my eyes, continually adjusting, managed to pick out the faint hairline which separated the top of the cliff from the sky.

I was walking faster now, taking advantage of the wind-swept patches to trot along after Moss, knowing that the drifts between them would slow me down. I couldn't afford to waste time admiring the view, such as it was. There was no doubt about it now: both the snow and the wind were increasing. I couldn't pretend it was my imagination anymore, or the difference in altitude. No doubt the radio would have told me so this morning. I cursed myself for not guessing, not having a hotline to God. I should have gone out first thing in the morning. I should have been super-cautious instead of merely common-cautious.

I caught the rising panic and snatched it down. Don't

be ridiculous. The sheep will be there, just the other side of the boundary wall, waiting patiently for their treat. Their amber eyes will glare *Where the hell have you been*? I will apologise, and together we'll all swarm back down to the farm, none the worse for our little outing.

I rushed for the familiar gate, then cursed aloud as I found that a particularly deep drift had glued it shut. My mittens and wellies whirling, I cleared the snow and heaved open the gate, whistling in advance to round up the sheep.

No sheep.

I looked hopefully for the trampled area where I left the food.

Not a mark. Not a single little hoof print to tell me they'd even been there. I looked down the length of the boundary wall, east and west. The snow was beginning to pile up against it. I knew that was the real danger: the sheep moving to the wall for shelter and being snowed into the drifts that could trap them for days. But the drifts weren't anything like that deep. Any sheep beside the wall would be visible, as visible as I was to them. If they were there, they'd come. Their absence could mean only one thing. They were on their way, probably just at the top of the cliff, about to make their way down.

Well, I wasn't going to wait.

'Come on, Moss. Mountain Rescue,' I said cheerfully, and made my way to the old green track which was now white. The snow had left the cliff face itself almost entirely clear. It was just too steep for the snow to cling. The jutting rocks were as grey as ever, the tufts of rough grass self-sown in the crevices bristling all over it like a sloppy beard.

I kept to the cliffside. The track was rougher there and I stumbled quite a bit, but at least I knew where I was. On the other side, the track fell away unevenly, and as the snow swirled about me, the edge disappeared from time to time. I wasn't taking any chances for the sake of an easier walk. Moss, more confident than I, clambered up ahead of me. Absurdly, I tried to read in his movements what he was feeling about our situation. Exhilaration? Fear? Earnestness? I wanted him to tell me what *I* should be feeling, too.

When he disappeared round the curve at the top, I had to

quell a spurt of panic. The sudden aloneness was appalling. This wasn't the time to lose my black and white chum, my only companion on this ridiculous mission. 'Moss!' I yelled sharply. 'Come here!'

He came, and together we toiled our way up the last stretch and onto the moor. A big fat gust of wind was there to greet us, smack in the face, with a fistful of snow. I scooped it off with mittens already sodden and noticed in passing how much my face hurt with the rawness of it. When I could see again, I took my bearings.

I wasn't at all surprised that the flat table with the standing stones had vanished. It was half a mile away, and I knew already that visibility was down a good deal less than that. Even so, I could see far enough to the east to notice a sense of movement there, a slight darkening of the snow. There was only one thing that could cause that: my sheep, waiting as I'd suspected. I had only to summon them and they'd come running and we'd get this foolish business over with. Was I looking forward to that log fire! I wondered if Effie had arrived yet. Would she throw a few more logs on, brew up the punch while she waited?

I whistled. The sound, normally a shrill intrusion I hated to make on the quiet moor, disappeared, and I realised that the moor was no longer quiet. The wind and the snow between them had upped their decibels, perhaps to compensate for the lack of trees to act as amplifiers. There was instead a strange roar of empty space in motion. I whistled again, louder, or so I thought.

But of course. The wind was blowing the sound to the west, behind me, far away from the sheep. Of course they couldn't hear. I would have to go up to them, present my familiar self to lure them away.

I set off as fast as I could in the direction of the shadowy movement. It was hard to measure either time or space, so I don't know how long it took me to reach the spot where the first peripheral prints began. Never have I been so pleased to see a humble hoof print. And I was overjoyed when the prints converged and then turned into a huge trampled area where hundreds of hooves had milled around.

Had. They were gone. Only their prints remained, so fresh

that I had no doubt that the movement I'd seen had indeed been them. The idiots had moved on only minutes ago, while I was making my way towards them.

'You idiots!' I roared. 'Come here!' I whistled again before remembering that both whistle and shout were useless. I sent Moss to fetch them. I watched him disappear into the blank whiteness ahead, then reappear, bounding up to me as best he could in the deepening snow. Then he gave a single bark before starting to make his way back the way we'd come.

He'd never done a thing like that before. I didn't know how to interpret. I didn't have time to find out. The sheep were somewhere just ahead, just out of sight. We had to round them up, fast.

'*This* way, Moss!' I shouted. 'The sheep are *this* way! No, we can't go home, not till we've got the sheep!'

He stopped and barked again. His behaviour, utterly out of character, disoriented me as much as the swirling snow. It made me realise how much I depended on his solid predictability. And now, when I needed it most, he was letting me down. Impatiently, I set off in the direction of the hoof prints, calling him to me as I stumbled across the ghostly hummocks. '*This* way, Moss!'

He followed with utmost reluctance. I wasn't too keen either. The little stab of panic returned. If Moss wasn't going to cooperate, the simple job of rounding up the sheep could take some time, and time was the one thing we didn't have. The snow was thickening fast, blowing straight into my face and blurring my vision. I could see the churned-up snow which marked the direction of the sheep, but I couldn't see much more than that. I couldn't understand why we weren't catching up with them. They couldn't be moving all that fast, and they shouldn't be moving at all. It wasn't their instinct in a –

The word 'blizzard' sprang to mind. Ridiculous. It was only a snow shower, that's what the radio had said. Heavier than usual, but nothing to worry about. If only the sheep would stand still and let me find them.

Suddenly I understood. They were running away from *us*! That's why we weren't catching up. All we were doing was pushing them further and further east, away from home.

We needed to get *around* them, to start driving them the other way.

I plunged off to the left, into fresh snow unmarked by the sheep. If we could make a wide arc around them, they would turn. It was difficult to know how wide an arc to make, though. After all, the last thing I wanted was to move into the heart of the moor. I'd never find my way back. And with no trampled snow to guide me, I had little idea where I was. I tried to use the direction of the snow instead. It was blowing from the east. As long as it didn't change, I could use it as a compass. My face would be my compass. As long as the snow blew at this angle, it meant that I was walking north-east.

Walking? Lurching. The terrain was rough enough in fine weather, its hummocks an obstacle course. Now the distinction between hummock and flat was disappearing, the snow drifting in weird shapes to form a brand new topography of its own. Several times I put my welly confidently on what looked like a hummock only to have it sink two feet through soft snow, almost unbalancing me with the surprise.

Then I fell. My leg went straight down into nothing for what seemed a great distance. When finally it hit land, the impact crumpled my body in an untidy heap around the folded leg. It was a peat channel. Incredibly, I'd forgotten that the moor was booby-trapped with them, snaking their way round the hummocks with total unpredictability. Even in summer they were a hazard, their narrow sides disguised by the thick heather clumps which grew right across them. In the snow it would be impossible to guess.

I picked myself up and tested the leg. It seemed all right; it was the rest of me that was shaky. What if I broke a leg? It was bad enough up here fully mobile, but if –

I brushed the fear away along with the snow which now covered my clothes. I couldn't afford to think of such things. I would manage better if I kept my wits.

I stood quite still, breathing deeply for calm, and took my bearings. From the snow on my face I deduced that I was again facing east. But why couldn't I see the forest? Surely I had long since entered the part of the moor above the forest? And I couldn't be that far in from the edge. Even in the snow, the mass of trees should show as a great dark shadow to my right. But there was nothing there except snow. Nothing in any direction except snow. I couldn't even tell how far ahead I could see. The great white swirls refused to give me a sense of distance. The madly patterned curtain in front of me could be a few feet away or several yards, there was no way of telling. I could scarcely even see which parts of the white belonged to the land and which to the air, it all seemed to merge into a single seasick blur of white.

Still standing motionless, I found myself tilting to one side and almost lost my balance. With no distinction between land and sky, it was difficult to remain upright. Where was up, and where down? I hadn't realised until then how constantly my eyes monitored the world to maintain something so basic as my balance. My eyes could no longer perform this function, and the roar in my ears was no help either.

Direction. The wind. I closed my useless eyes and felt the snow blowing straight on my face. I must still be facing east. As long as I kept going east – But why did I want to go east? Oh yes, the sheep.

The sheep? Was I mad? Surely it was obvious that I had no chance whatsoever of finding them now, let alone guiding them through the blinding whiteness when I myself had no idea where I was or where I should be going. No, I would have to abandon them, make my way home as quickly as I could before I broke a leg or dropped from exhaustion. Already I could feel the seductive giving-in of my legs that wanted only to stop, let myself comfortably down into the snow for a little rest. People died that way.

I wasn't going to die, there was no need to be melodramatic. All I had to do was turn round, get the wind on my back and let it guide me back to the cliff above Cappelrigg. After that, the cliff itself and the stone walls of my fields would take over and let me know where I was.

I turned round at what I judged to be about 180 degrees, but still the wind blew in my face. I must have turned too far. I tried again. Still the snow spattered my numbed face. And again, and again. No matter where I stood, always it was there, the hateful snow hurling itself into my face.

It was then that I realised what was happening. The wind had, without my knowing, increased to such a velocity that it was now blowing the snow off the ground as well as through the air, blowing it up and around in mad circles which hit me from every direction. I had lost my 'compass'. I had lost my sense of what was up and what was down. I opened my eyes as wide as I could and strained to see. I don't know what I hoped to see, but there was nothing, nothing but the monotonous blur of blinding white wherever I looked.

My first crazy reaction was indignation. How had this happened? I had set off, not that long ago, on an ordinary winter day with a few snow flurries decorating the landscape and had ended up lost in a blizzard on the moor. It was impossible. Surely I would have noticed? But it had happened so gradually, the wind and the snow increasing step by tiny step, so smoothly and without transition that I hadn't even noticed.

So this was how it happened. I'd always felt contempt for people who got caught in blizzards in the Scottish mountains. I'd always assumed they were foolish feckless people risking not only their lives but those of the Mountain Rescue. Now I saw how easy it was. It crept up on you like a sneak thief, taking away your senses and leaving you alone.

Alone. Moss. Where was Moss? Had I lost even him? I prised my frozen jaw open and yelled his name with such force that it must surely awaken the sleeping giants in the earth. I yelled it again and again, knowing I shouldn't squander my fading strength but conscious only of the terror of being alone. I didn't know what Moss could do to help, but it was imperative to have him with me, whatever happened.

A yelp, distant but distinct. And then another, closer. I kept yelling as the noise drew nearer, fighting hysteria as well as the wind and snow. Finally I saw a tiny shadow. Or did I? I had seen shapes and shadows before and they'd turned out to be hallucinations. No, this was real. The little shape moved unevenly towards me. Hallucinations weren't jerky like that. The poor old dog was floundering towards me with the same instinct against aloneness that made me lurch towards him. I didn't care anymore what direction I was going in, where I was, what I was going to do. Only the one thing mattered: to get to Moss, to make ourselves two living creatures lost on the moor instead of one. My world had shrunk to just that, and I felt my limbs flailing wildly as I propelled myself towards that single goal, my legs, near exhaustion, pushing violently through the resisting snow.

And then nothing. Suddenly, all resistance was gone. I was weightless at last. For a split second I felt relief at the effortlessness of it all. Then I realised I was falling. It seemed to take a long time, but time, like distance and direction, had been abandoned in this mad white world, and very likely it took only a second or two before suddenly I was falling no longer, and the world was white no longer, and then, mercifully, I too existed no longer. There was one exquisite moment, a warm dark sense of comfort, and then I lost consciousness.

24

'Lottie . . . Lottie, please don't be hurt, please be all right . . . Lottie . . . '

Warm, dark, soft, the voice and me all swirling about in the darkness together. And then, alone, only the darkness, for a long, long time.

'Lottie . . . please . . . ' The voice again, just for a moment, until the darkness took over.

And then something rough, like an unshaved cheek against mine. I struggled out of the darkness with the pain on my skin.

'Don't . . . ' The voice was mine this time, soporific, thick. 'Hurts . . . ' I opened my eyes to a grey blur against the darkness. I turned my face away from it. A moment's reprieve, and then the pain on my cheek again. I moved my hand towards it and felt something soft and warm. Fur. Grey.

'Tarzan?' I whispered.

She made a tiny sound and resumed her work, her rough tongue scraping my cheek and pulling me into consciousness.

Another sound, rustling, and then another voice. 'Charlotte, are you awake?'

Effie's face loomed over mine, bereft of its sharp edges and peppery urban smile.

'Cat,' I whispered. 'Hurts.'

Effie's hands closed round the fur and plucked the cat away. 'I'm sorry, I should have realised – your face is still raw. Other than that, how do you feel, Charlotte?'

Charlotte. Lottie. The voice. 'Is David here?' I mumbled.

'Not for ages. Why?'

'Thought I heard . . . ' But of course I hadn't. The voice had been low, dark and male, but not David's. It couldn't be. He'd never called me Lottie. No one did. Not even as a child did anyone use a diminutive for me. I wasn't that sort of person.

'How do you feel?' Effie's voice again, anxious.

I shifted my body slightly, an automatic response to the question, and felt the smooth sheets rustle round me. Sheets? 'Why am I in bed?'

Effie smiled for the first time. 'You've had a rough time of it.'

Something was wrong. Slowly my mind fixed on the present. Christmas Eve. Effie was coming. Why was I in bed? Had I overslept? I struggled to get up but could hardly move. A sharp pain shot up from one foot.

'Don't you remember anything?' Effie asked.

'What's to remember?' I mumbled. 'Overslept.'

Effie laughed nervously. 'That's one way of putting it. Do you really not remember? The blizzard? Going up on the moor and getting caught in the blizzard?'

Blizzard. The warm dark softness ripped away, in its place the blinding white of the snow. It was coming back now, bringing me with it. I'd gone to get the sheep down, and then, nothing.

'Sort of,' I mumbled. 'Don't remember coming back.'

'I'm not surprised! You were out like a light.'

'What happened? How did I get home?'

'You didn't. You're at The Folly.'

'*What*?' I woke up at last. I tried to push myself further up the bed, ignoring the pain in my foot. Effie rearranged the pillows and propped me up against them.

'You're in the Scheherazade Room, I think it's called. Have you ever seen such a crazy place?'

I looked round. The walls were completely covered with gauzy silk curtains, all different colours and all moving faintly, though there couldn't be a breeze. On the floor, a Persian rug; on the rug, a sea of silk cushions. The colours were vibrant but soft – amethyst, amber, topaz, rosy reds, lapis lazuli – all glowing softly and mingling their hues in the light cast by several lamps. The lamps, wrought-iron and a riot of arabesques, stood out black and definite in this room of shifting colour. One of them flung a pattern of stars

205

onto an ultramarine ceiling which seemed as insubstantial as everything else. The bed, I now saw, was at floor level, as was a luxurious couch in one corner made up like a sultan's divan and heaped with yet more cushions.

'Almost worth getting lost in a blizzard to wake up in a room like this,' Effie laughed. 'No wonder you were so slow to come round – you must have thought you'd copped it and landed in paradise.'

'But *how* did I get here?'

'Well . . . ' said Effie. She brought some cushions over and settled herself into them. Then she began. 'I got to Cappelrigg feeling pretty heroic myself after the poor old Porsche and I battled through the start of the blizzard. Only to find that mine hostess had done a flit. Left a note, the churl, saying she'd just popped up to the moor to fetch her sheep. Not even had the sense to say *when* she'd left,' Effie added sternly. 'Anyway, the snow was thickening fast, and I wasn't taking any chances, so I phoned The Folly straightaway and raised the alarm. As it happened, while I was on the phone they had an alarm of their very own, viz one bedraggled sheepdog by name of Moss, who suddenly turned up at The Folly yapping his head off and making unmistakable 'follow me' gestures towards the moor. The message was clear, and lucky for you there was someone here to take it. Charlotte, whatever made you do a crazy thing like that?'

'It wasn't crazy. It wasn't snowing at all, hardly, when I set out. I got caught, that's all.'

'Well, our two jolly woodcutters got caught out as well and came home early. Otherwise you'd still be languishing in a bed of snow instead of this scrumptious pasha's den. But be warned: the Lord of the Manor is hopping mad, and I don't blame him. He and Brendan got home just in time to find out they had to go out again and rescue some damsel in distress.'

'Oh, God . . . '

'Oh, God indeed. Though I must say I don't understand why he's *so* huffy. Anyway, lucky for all, you'd landed up very near The Folly – which is another mystery we're waiting for you to answer. Evidently this room we're in is at the back of the house, and if it weren't pitch black out there now and

206

snowing a cauldron you'd almost be able to see the very spot where you fell.'

'Fell?'

'Fell, Oafling. Smack into a stream. The very stream, I'm told, that feeds the waterfall at the back of the garden. And if you'd been just a few metres south you would have waterfalled yourself right into the garden. In little pieces.'

'Oh.'

'Yes, oh. Actually, I'm beginning to see why m'Lord is so narked. You really are a liability, Ms Venables. When you're not plonking yourself under falling trees or dashing across the countryside on wild horses you're doing a slalom down waterfalls. Why don't you retire and come back to the peace and quiet of London? It'll save the NHS a lot of trouble.'

I smiled. The subdued and anxious Effie who'd hovered over me a few minutes ago had been an alien creature. I much preferred her stroppy.

'If you hadn't been so near The Folly,' she continued, 'they probably wouldn't have found you. As it is, David had a hell of a time lugging you down off that cliff. I don't know who's more heroic, David or Moss.'

'Where is he?'

'David or Moss?'

'Moss.' I didn't want to think about David, not just yet.

'In the stables, having medals pinned on his hairy chest and being spoiled rotten by everyone, right down to the stable cat.' She laughed. 'You should see him; he's got a pasha's bed of his own, a heap of clean straw practically up to the ceiling, and they must have emptied out the kitchen to fill all the food bowls around him. He eats a fraction of that and he'll burst.'

'Poor old Moss.'

'Poor Moss hell. He's got a grin on his face to make the Cheshire cat green. He'll probably be off to Hollywood next – big takeover bid for Lassie, Rin Tin Tin et al. Don't think he'll ever stoop to playing around with your crummy sheep again.'

'My sheep!'

'All tucked up in a field nearby with a mountain of hay around them. Brendan brought them down. They were right

207

there, right where you'd fallen. When Moss saw Rhett Farleton sweep you into his arms he decided to switch movies and went off to help Brendan herd the sheep instead. All very efficient, à la Folly. I must say, they *do* do things well here,' she said, looking round the room admiringly.

Then she sprang up and went to an ornate little table by the divan. She came back clutching a piece of paper. 'Map,' she explained. She studied it for some time, frowning. 'If I don't find my way back to the kitchen soon, you'll be stranded here instead of on the moor – you must be starving.'

I hadn't thought about food. I was still trying to piece together Effie's story. There were pieces missing, I was sure of it, but my mind was too foggy to find them.

'Right,' said Effie, moving towards the door with her map. She struck a manly pose in the doorway. 'I may be gone a little while,' she intoned. Then she laughed. 'A bit near the bone, that. Belle said that if I got desperate I should just stand still and yell like hell and someone would be despatched to find me. Ciao!'

As soon as Effie left, Tarzan hopped back onto my bed. Ah. One of the missing pieces. What on earth was Tarzan doing *here*? No wonder I'd been disoriented when I awoke.

I could picture the place where I'd been found: a wide but fairly shallow channel which narrowed at the mouth before plunging down the cliff into The Folly's garden. How on earth had I walked so far in the blizzard? But then, I'd lost all sense of time as well as space up there, so perhaps it wasn't so surprising. I could picture, too, the track just east of The Folly which Brendan must have used to bring the sheep down. How had he done it, when I'd seen nothing but white? Perhaps the trees helped, crowding up to the cliff and lining the paths, perhaps they gave a sense of direction.

But the thing that puzzled me most was David. His anger seemed unfair – he hadn't even waited to hear my story before passing judgment. Clearly I was a silly twit who'd put herself and others in danger. The trespasser beneath the felled birch. After all that had happened since, it was hard to accept being rudely pushed back to square one.

'Hallo? Mountain Rescue here!' Effie's voice sailed

through the corridors. Then she flung the door open and stood aside as Belle entered bearing a tray. 'I've found a friendly St Bernard for you – complete with brandy barrel.'

'Not quite,' Belle laughed. 'Only soup. Would you like a brandy, too?' She crouched down to floor level, tray and all, and looked into my face, suddenly earnest. 'How do you feel, Charlotte?'

'The better for being here. Though I feel awful about causing so much trouble.'

'Pooh! It's lovely having you here! If you hadn't arrived when you did, you probably wouldn't have got through tomorrow – it's a proper blizzard now, the real thing. Let me have a look at your foot.'

'My foot?'

'Didn't Effie tell you? You've sprained it – it was so swollen we had to cut away your welly.' She peeled the bedclothes away, talking all the while. 'We phoned the surgery in Kirkby – they have one of those miraculous vehicles that does everything except fly – but it was out, up in the hills east of Kirkby. The usual thing – some hill farmer's baby arriving prematurely. So I strapped it up myself.'

I peered over a mound of bedclothes at my foot, swathed in bandages.

'Don't worry,' she said. 'I've done it before. I took an intensive first aid course when we started having students up here. Forestry's a bit tricky that way. David's fanatical about safety, but even so there are bound to be little accidents. Does this hurt?'

She poked and prodded very carefully, asking my reaction at each move.

'I'm pretty sure nothing's broken,' she concluded, 'though we'll have to wait for an X-ray. Meanwhile, don't move it at all. If the pain gets too bad, take one of these.' She indicated some tablets and a jug of water on a low bedside table. 'We managed to get one down you before I strapped you up. You've been semi-conscious several times since you arrived – do you remember?'

I shook my head.

'You were a bit delirious,' she admitted. She settled the

bedclothes back. 'There. Do have some soup now. Min-
estrone with dumplings – a bit of a hybrid but it should get
you going.'

Her manner was brisk but affectionate. Like everything
else at The Folly, she inspired confidence. I sipped the soup
gratefully. It was wonderful and reminded me with a pang
of that other simple meal, when we had fresh bread together
and talked about the kites. It all seemed a long time ago.
'How did Tarzan get here?'

'Ah. We've taken a liberty,' she said. 'When I realised
you had a sprain, and when the snow kept coming, I sent
Brendan over to fetch a few things. I hope you don't mind,
but at this rate we'll be snowed in good and proper for a few
days.'

'It was quite a trip,' said Effie. 'Brendan and me and a
load of suitcases in the front of the Land-Rover with Tarzan,
and a heap of hens squawking in the back, the snow whizzing
round us – '

'*Hens*?'

'The lot,' said Effie. 'They're in an outbuilding now. I
don't think you realise, Charlotte – you're going to be out
of action for a week or two at least. No way could you look
after a farmful of livestock. So we did the obvious: brought
the livestock here.'

'I see.' I sank back against the pillows. It wasn't they who'd
taken a liberty. It was me. In one act of folly, I'd landed
them with myself and my entire farm for the whole of the
Christmas period. It was a gross abuse of hospitality. No
wonder David was angry. However friendly we'd become,
he was at heart an extremely private man. Independent.
Self-sufficient. Unlike me, barging into his life this way
and trailing my whole farm behind me. It was little con-
solation that I hadn't done it on purpose. The fact that I'd
blundered into this situation was almost worse. People at
The Folly didn't blunder. I felt small, stupid and horribly
humbled.

Not that anyone else saw it that way. The rest of the
evening was a mixture of dozing interspersed with visits,
everyone coming to see me, everyone treating me like an
honoured guest. The sumptuous room didn't help. Propped

up in my silk-swathed bed, I couldn't but look like a queen receiving her courtiers.

When Belle arrived the second time, bearing a tray full of dinner, she pointed to a tasselled rope hanging by the bedside. 'I forgot to mention – if you need anything, just pull. It's linked to a bell in the kitchen. It's the only one that still works – that's why we put you in this ridiculous room.'

The lady of the house summoning a servant. Oh God. 'I'm sure I won't need anything, honest. I feel fine. Just a little overwhelmed, that's all.'

I think she understood. 'Charlotte, you should know by now that I adore fussing over people. The worst thing about Christmas is that the students all go home. Thank heaven I've got a houseful this year to compensate!'

Astrid was next, gliding magnificently to the bed to give me a welcoming kiss, as if I were part of the family. Behind her came Matti, full of excitement about my adventure, full of praise for my heroism. He gave me no chance to disabuse him. I'd never seen him so talkative. The little boy, sandwiched between the thrill of my exploits and the anticipation of Christmas, was almost hysterical with excitement. He burbled away in a torrent of words as confusing as any snowstorm. Finally Astrid scooped him up and propelled him towards the door. 'Bed.' His face registered horror at the prospect of being obliterated by sleep, though it seemed improbable that he would be. That wonderful musical laughter of hers echoed through the corridors for some time, accompanied by plaintive protests from Matti.

Effie came and went. Now that I was out of danger, she was exploring the house and reporting back, her enthusiasm as exhausting as Matti's. It was an interior designer's dream, she said. The slow accumulation of oddments for each thematic room was something no designer could do today, she said. Any attempt to do that kind of thing these days always looked contrived. Here, everything had its own glorious higgledy-piggledy rightness. I should marry David, she said, and come and live at The Folly. I winced.

The last to arrive was Brendan, his shambling shape and grizzled hair incongruous in Scheherazade's den.

'They say the animals talk on Christmas Eve,' I said to him. 'If so, there are a lot of sheep singing your praises.'

He laughed. 'No four-legged article ever thought to be grateful to the likes of us humans, and that's a sure thing.'

'Well, *I'm* grateful anyway. I don't suppose I'll ever understand how you managed it.'

'Easy enough, with a good dog and a tree-lined path. It'll be you that had the hard bit, up there on the moor with nothing but the snow and all.'

'It was rather awful,' I admitted. 'Solid white wherever I looked, no distinction between ground and sky or up and down. I didn't know things like that could happen.'

'It'll be a white-out you were having,' he explained. 'It happens in the Arctic often enough, but you don't expect a mendacious thing like that in Yorkshire.'

'Brendan, I didn't expect anything at all,' I said, eager to explain. 'Honestly, it was hardly snowing at all when I set out. My radio broke down this morning so I didn't hear the forecast. I know it all looks hideously irresponsible, but it wasn't like that. I feel awful, causing all this trouble, and – '

'Don't you be talking like that,' he said. 'You did right. If this snow carries on like this, there'll hardly be a sheep on the moor to survive it.'

'It's only thanks to you that mine will. Brendan, will you do one more thing for me?'

'State your item,' he smiled.

'Will you keep track of how much of your hay you use for my sheep? Then when the roads are clear I'll bring you some of my own.'

'Did you ever hear of such nonsense!'

'Not to me it isn't. I'll feel better about this whole mess if I can at least repay the hay. And,' I continued cautiously, 'it might make David a little less annoyed with me.'

'Don't you be fretting about Davey,' he said. 'A fine thing it would be to begrudge your neighbour a bit of hay.'

'But he *is* annoyed,' I said. I knew Brendan would be too honest to deny it. I needed to know the worst.

'Have you ever known him not to be?' he said lightly. 'You know the lad – always thinking he can order the universe.

He with no humility on him, it's no surprise that he gets a trifle tetchy when some little thing goes contrary. And he was crucified with worry when he found you all crumpled up and so near the edge of the waterfall.'

Belle arrived with hot chocolate and shooed Brendan out. He was probably glad to leave. He was one of those men like David, bred for the big spaces outside and nervous of the confinement of a sickroom.

After Belle left, Effie arrived with another report from the outer reaches of the house. 'I've just discovered the most amazing room! It looks like a ballroom, though I can't imagine a bunch of dumb hunters dancing up here. It's a bit decayed, but it has the most marvellous potential! I'd love to get my hands on it. How about it, Charlotte? Can you get me a commission?'

I laughed. 'I thought you hated the wilds of Yorkshire.'

'I'm changing my mind. Anyway, Americans love eccentrics. This house is nothing if not eccentric. Seriously, I took one look at the room and instantly saw it filled with elegant dancers. I'm going to sound out Belle – I'll bet she'd love to put on a grand ball up here.'

'David wouldn't.'

Not long after she left, Matti sneaked in. He'd forgotten to tell me about the giant toboggan Brendan was hauling out of the attic. If the snow stopped tomorrow, we could all go tobogganing. My swollen foot writhed at the thought.

Then Astrid arrived to pluck him off my bed and march him off to his room again.

And so it went on, all evening a succession of visitors. Everyone came to see me. Everyone except David.

25

I awoke late the next morning, after being drugged into a long oblivion by the painkillers. My foot felt better, at least better enough to tempt me to ease myself out of the low bed and drag myself across the carpet towards the window. Brilliant light was filtering through the soft folds of the multi-coloured silk curtains and spreading throughout the room. It was like being inside a kaleidoscope where all the edges have melted, clarity of colour with none of the harshness. A wonderful sensation, wrapped around by pure colour. I parted the curtains and crawled inside, letting them billow out behind me to form a sort of tent.

Pure colour on one side, pure absence of it on the other. It had stopped snowing, but only recently, for the sky was still ominous, a soft, furry Tarzan grey. A neat line separated it from the sharp white edge of the cliff which was doing its best to look like a glacier. But the wind had flung the snow about in so random a fashion that it left streaks of hard grey rock exposed. Through it all cut the waterfall, frozen at the edges but still inky black as it plummeted down into the garden. I tried not to think of myself perched so near the edge.

Instead, I looked at the garden, covered with a thick fleece which glittered even in the absence of sunlight. The shrubs were bowed down into indistinguishable humps, but the wind, as if disapproving of too much smoothness, had whipped the ground snow into great angular ridges, sharp crested and lethal looking at this distance. Elsewhere there were areas that looked like ribbed sand, an incongruous beach stranded in the middle of Yorkshire. The winding paths, designed to entice, had vanished, replaced by new wind-carved paths that suddenly ended in a drift. I couldn't recognise a thing, could only guess at the location of the pond by the white-coated willow which kept it company.

No one had been in the garden, but closer to the house the courtyard had been roughly ploughed and that snow which remained was dirtied by the activity of many wellies. I could hear voices inside the stables, including Matti's.

And then another voice, Effie's, speaking quietly outside my door after a tentative tap. 'Charlotte? Are you awake?'

'Come in,' I called.

The door opened to a surprised silence as she surveyed the empty room. 'Where are you?'

'I am the Ghost of Christmas Present,' I said behind my rainbow tent.

Footsteps. The curtains parted. Effie glared down on me. 'Hey, you're supposed to be an invalid.'

'Not anymore. I want action.'

Belle brought in a tray of breakfast and then rearranged my bandages. I was annoyed to discover that the foot still hurt.

'The swelling's gone down a treat,' she said, 'but it'll still hurt for a while yet. Painkillers are a bore but useful.'

I popped another painkiller and nodded.

'Astrid's looking for some crutches. I know we have a pair, but heaven knows where. We need an archivist to keep track of all the stuff stashed in this place. Do you feel like coming downstairs? You've missed the Christmas morning bit but that's probably just as well; you'd just have got dizzy again with Matti rushing about like a lunatic. Effie can help you to dress, then give a yell and I'll send some transport up.'

It was Brendan, not David, who came to carry me down. I tried to tell myself that David was just busy somewhere else, probably feeding the horses, but I wasn't convinced. David was avoiding me, and I didn't blame him. I was dreading our first meeting. I'd rehearsed my explanation, but I knew I'd make a mess of it when the time came.

On the big landing where the two parts of the staircase came together for the final descent, Rhiannon of the gleaming green ring looked down on me. In both senses. Rhiannon wouldn't have sprained her ankle in a blizzard. Nor would anyone else at The Folly. Despite the occasional appearance of chaos, everyone and everything worked properly at The Folly. I had worked properly, too, in the City. I'd never made silly mistakes in the City. For the first time in many months, I wondered if the one mistake I'd made was buying Cappelrigg.

At the bottom of the stairs, we turned right and went along bits of corridor, up and down portions of stairway. Effie, preceding us, opened the library door and then vanished towards the kitchen. Brendan carried me to a *chaise-longue* beneath one of the tall thin windows. Draped picturesquely on it, I felt once again like a lady of leisure, pampered and useless.

'The Ice Woman cometh,' said a newspaper propped up in front of a chair. Then the newspaper crackled to the floor and the man behind it rose. He walked over to my *chaise-longue*, gave a sprightly smile and stuck out his hand.

'Hugh Farleton,' he said, clicking his heels together facetiously, 'at your service.' He glared amiably at Brendan. 'Since nobody in this establishment has the manners to introduce me.'

'Charlotte Venables,' I said, taking his hand. 'This is a surprise. I had no idea you were here.'

'Ah, the fate of the secondborn,' he sighed. 'No property, no existence.'

Brendan excused himself and left the room – rather mysteriously, I thought.

Hugh brought a chair to the *chaise-longue* and settled himself into it. He was tall, thin and so bendable that for once the term 'willowy' seemed appropriate. I could almost feel a breeze in the room making him sway slightly like a crafty young sapling that knows better than to resist. A swatch of fine fair hair flopped over his forehead, necessitating a frequent toss of the head to flip it back in place. His skin was fine and fair, too, and surprisingly smooth for someone who, according to Belle, was only two years younger than David. All his features were fine, as thin and precise as an etching: long, narrow grey eyes, long narrow mouth, and between them an extremely long narrow nose. He looked boyish, almost a cartoon caricature of an etiolated and thin-blooded English aristocrat.

And yet and yet. The whole effect was peculiarly charming, especially when the sprightly smile suddenly animated his otherwise languid face. There was something familiar about him, though he could hardly be more different from his brother. David's combination of burly strength and grace was missing. Hugh had only the grace. Neither of them looked remotely like the portrait of their father hanging in the dining-room of Farleton Hall, but while David had the Celtic intensity of his mother, Hugh lacked even that. So why did he seem so familiar?

'I suppose I'll be committing an inexcusable gaffe if I admit that not only did I not know you were here, but I had no idea you were coming.'

'Quite excusable,' he smiled. 'I didn't know myself until yesterday.' He pulled his features into a little moue. 'A disagreement with my live-in lady-love,' he said in a stage whisper. 'In short, she chucked me out, heartless wench, on Christmas Eve. Ski resorts were booked up, so I fled like a wounded fledgling back to the ancestral nest.'

'Yesterday?' I said. 'How on earth did you manage to get here?'

'By heroic effort, my dear, that I can tell you. Racing the storm, battling the blizzard, et cetera, and flopping exhausted onto the home hearth only to discover that my stupendous feats were quite overshadowed by those of a young slip of a thing who'd staged a far more dramatic entrance via the wilds of the Yorkshire moors. I'm quite cross with you, my dear. Stole my thunder, you did.' Again the amiable mocking glare.

I burst into laughter. His foppish manner and language were irresistible. And suddenly I knew why he was familiar. It was simple, really. I had met his type many times in the City. Not so much the brash young set but the older ones who'd been there before the youth invasion began: Lloyds underwriters, bankers, patent agents, some of the more respectable commodities dealers, people with a bit of lineage and the grace to go with it. No wonder I felt so at ease with Hugh. He belonged to the world I had left behind only a few months ago.

'My humble apologies,' I said with a slight bow of the head. 'I had no intention of upstaging you. In fact, my heroic efforts are no more appreciated than your own. You must

217

have noticed.' I leaned forward and whispered in imitation of his own confession: 'I'm in the dog house.'

'Such a charming dog,' he murmured. 'You're quite forgiven – by me at least. Indeed, you've made my Christmas. Had I known that a lovely Ice Maiden was lurking in the old homestead, I would have come sooner. Why did no one tell me of your existence?'

And why had no one told me of Hugh's arrival? All my visitors of last night had come and gone without a word. Even Effie.

'Ah, well,' he answered himself. 'That's what comes of being the black sheep. Nobody tells me anything. Tell me, Ms Bo Peep, have you any black sheep among that motley crew you rescued yesterday?'

I shook my head. 'Mainly Swaledales, some Rough Fells and Dalesbreds, and a lot of crosses between them. Oh, I do have a few Blackfaces, will that do?'

'Only faces?'

'Yes.'

'Then may I be your black sheep?'

I laughed again. His flirting was so outrageous as to nullify itself. It was an amusing game. I had enjoyed the same game myself, in my first few years in the City. I was enjoying it again, however incongruous the setting.

But how incongruous was the setting? Hugh, sprawled languidly in his chair, looked perfectly at home in the dark elegant old library. It was his heritage, too, as much as David's, and in a way he seemed more suited to it. If ever there was a natural aristocrat, for better and for worse, it was Hugh. The Folly was as whimsical as he. I tried to remember what Belle had told me about him. Not much. Just that Hugh hated David for 'ruining his heritage and turning it over to us hippies'. It was hard to believe that Hugh hated anyone.

The door opened and in the doorway stood Brendan and Effie, the mysteriousness of their earlier disappearance now augmented by sly smiles. Brendan was wearing the same big sweater and jeans, but Effie was bundled up in her outdoor clothes and clutched a similar heap in her arms. They came up to the *chaise-longue* and, their smiles turning into smirks, enveloped me in an ancient fur coat smelling of mothballs.

218

They eased several big thick socks over my injured foot and plonked a Lapland boot on the other. Then Brendan picked me up and carried me to the front door. Effie opened it and, to my surprise, I saw Belle and Astrid already standing just beyond, themselves wrapped up in equally voluminous clothes. Smirking.

'What on earth is going on?' I said.

More smirks as Effie and Brendan and I took our places in the little assemblage. We were now standing, four abreast with me a lumpish fifth in Brendan's arms, looking down the avenue that led to the main road.

'Are we posing for a photograph?' I tried again. It would certainly be a pretty one, with the white-capped Folly behind us, its crazy windows underlined by snow sills, its ivy variegated by the remains of the blizzard packing the spaces between the glossy green leaves.

But there was no photographer, nothing to disturb the whipped-cream vista through the forest, not so much as a camera click to punctuate the breathless air.

Except . . . perhaps the faintest possible tinkling of bells? It was a sound I hadn't heard since the magical autumn day when David had emerged from the forest with his cart of firewood and I'd fallen so utterly in love with him. And now, faster than words can tell, the second sound merged with the first to shoot through me with a pain of instant nostalgia so sharp that it brought tears to my eyes. That love, which had seemed so full of promise, had somehow gone askew. The scrap of reciprocity I thought I'd sensed in David had melted away, replaced first with the impersonal solicitude he felt for everything in his domain, and now with anger which even Brendan and Effie didn't deny. Why?

The bells were louder now, crisp against the crisp cold air. They were coming from the east. I looked in that direction, puzzled. Why would David be delivering firewood on Christmas Day, and why on earth would we be brought out to witness it?

And then, from round the corner of The Folly, it came: a troika, sleek and shining against the Russian winter background, its bright brass bells jingling, its red harness glowing against the flanks of the three horses. Two great greys on the

219

sides – Olwen and Sif – and a huge black stallion, bigger even than his companions, in the centre. It was Ymir. I'd met him during my autumn tour of the stables, but I'd never seen him working. As the proud black centrepiece of the troika, he was stunning, and he knew it. So did David, pretending to readjust the complicated set of reins so as not to show too clearly his pride. Beside him perched Matti, who had no such reservations. His grin nearly split his face open. He looked like a merry little grasshopper in the company of these giants, his father included. The effect of the whole entourage was both grand and touching.

And romantic. Unbearably romantic. It was difficult to believe we were in twentieth-century Yorkshire. Once again The Folly did its time trick, tossing us into the Russia of a century ago. Even the furry black hats with their warm earflaps – identical for David and Matti – were unmistakably Russian. So strong was the illusion that I was startled when my companions suddenly broke into excited English chatter.

Then, 'Good God, do we still have that old thing?'

It was Hugh. He'd come out onto the terrace behind us and now peered at the troika.

'The venerable ancestors used it for distributing Christmas cheer to the peasants,' he explained. 'The whole family was bundled into it, clutching their baskets of goodies, to do the rounds of the tenants. Dear me, I'd assumed it fell apart years ago.'

I felt a momentary dislike for Hugh. There was so little magic in the world; why did he have to puncture David's Christmas treat?

No one else seemed to notice. They were too busy climbing into the troika. It was a big one, much bigger than the pictures I'd seen. As well as the broad seat facing forward, into which Belle and Astrid and Effie were distributing themselves, there was a matching one just behind the driver's seat. Brendan placed me on it as if it were the *chaise-longue*. Then he disappeared into the house and reappeared almost instantly with an armful of fur. Two enormous old bear rugs, fragrant with cedar and mothballs. He draped one across me and the other across the three women opposite. Then he stood back to inspect his work.

'Sure and we should have had a camera,' he decided. 'You're a treat for the eyes and that's a fact.'

I was glad there was no camera. These beautiful moments conjured up by The Folly were too precious to be ossified into a colour print for posterity. It was their very transience that gave them so much charm.

David twisted his head round and smiled at us. 'Ready?'

It was our first meeting since he'd carried me off the moor. He made no reference to it at all. No Are-you-feeling-better? No Why-did-you-do-a-crazy-thing-like-that? The smile that glanced off my face was no different from those he gave to Astrid and Effie and Belle. The day had hardly begun and already I was confused. My gratitude for my rescue competed with the humiliation of having to be rescued. I also, ignobly, resented having to feel forever grateful. Everything was give on their side, take on mine. I felt passive, useless. Even my farming, so useful compared to the work I'd done in the City – no one at The Folly respected it. They were tactful enough, but I knew they saw it as a misuse of land that should be turned over to trees. Their trees, their horses, their dominion over Keldreth and over my life. And now Hugh, reminding me of the life I'd had in which I had been respected. And the momentary attraction towards him, the nostalgia for what I'd left. And then all of it swept away in the fairyland troika.

'Hup hup!'

The horses sprang into action drawing the big sleigh and its six people as if there were nothing at the other end of their harness. We made a wide arc before turning into the avenue. As soon as we entered its green and white aisle, I forgot my confusion and simply gave myself up to the beauty of it. Beyond the big beeches which lined the drive the forest proper began, with its seductive mixture of trees now looking so Russian that I gave up any attempt to pretend we were in Yorkshire. The firs were so obviously Siberian, their big lower branches weighed down heavily by a winter's worth of snow. The deciduous trees all became poplars and birches, no matter that in real life there were dozens of species in Farleton Forest. And surely those were the tracks of wolves leading into the dark depths? And didn't I glimpse a chimney or two belonging to a peasant cottage? I leaned back and breathed in the exotic scenario along with a lungful of perfect air. Yes, to glide along forever on these smooth runners, lulled into peace by the rhythmic jingle of the harness bells. Craning my neck, I could see the gleaming rumps of the horses, pale grey and black segmented by the bright red of the harness. Beneath them I could feel the powerful legs of the horses cleaving the drifts as if they were air.

Even the confusion when we reached the entrance gates couldn't damage the magic. A large drift had nestled up to the gates, making them immovable. David jumped down and shovelled it away while Matti stood in front of the horses and held them still. David glanced apprehensively at his stable-boy from time to time, but he needn't have worried. The horses had no intention of ruining their own outing by a prima donna display. They stood quite still for Matti, nearly three tons of horse acknowledging the authority of his skinny wrist.

Outside, we turned left and took the same route David and I had used to deliver firewood in the autumn. The old forest gave way to the newer plantings where the snow, less impeded, had drifted more freely. A big male pheasant, gaudier than usual in the white wilderness, flew up from the base of a small tree where he'd been pecking for food. His voice was raucous and unnaturally loud in the stillness. The horses' hooves made barely a sound on the thick snow. Only the bells, jingling hypnotically. We should have been gossiping, we four ladies ensconced beneath our bearskins – anticipating the samovar at the head keeper's house, perhaps. But the stillness was too beautiful to break. I opened my senses and let the beauty of the Russian forest rush in.

We passed by the gates to Whinfell. I barely gave it a glance. Just beyond was a second house obviously converted from a barn that had once belonged to Whinfell. A newish hedge separated the two and divided the original property awkwardly. Half a mile further along was another set of two houses, one the farmhouse and the other a barn conversion, also awkwardly divided. A little way off was a third building, another barn in the process of being converted, the ugliness of its scaffolding and heaps of building materials softened by the snow. None of it impinged. It wasn't real, only the forest was real.

I don't know how long we spent gliding over the snow-covered road and through the forest rides. In a world where time can be flung back at will, it can also be stopped. Everything was reduced to the smallest detail: a crow lifting off a laden fir branch and scattering a white waterfall of snow onto the ground beneath; a few russet oak leaves, left over from summer, rattling when a chaffinch landed. The scolding of a great tit. A bare thorn hedge seen in profile with a flock of fieldfares filtering through it as if propelled by a gust of wind. A beech tree silhouetted against the grey sky with a single bird flitting about like a fig leaf trying to cover the tree's nakedness. And all the while the hypnotic jingle of brass bells, the occasional snuffle of a horse, clouds of steam pluming over their heads and disappearing into the pale pewter sky.

They say a rider who falls must get back on the horse without delay, otherwise the thin shock of fear will spread and he'll never ride again. I might have hated snow after my nightmare on the moor. But that morning, gliding across its gentle surface, I saw its other side: calm, silent, protecting the evergreen branches from the cold. I don't think that was the intention – Belle even said that David, hating to shower his son with cheap material goods, gave him magic pieces of time like this instead. But the effect on me was powerful, erasing my fears and confusions and lulling me into a sense that the world would always be like this.

26

Christmas dinner materialised late in the afternoon and was a happy occasion – perhaps because the kitchen was Belle's domain and everyone in it succumbed to the easy contentment which floated about her like spirit vapour. Strife was unthinkable in Belle's kitchen. The eight of us around the big table must have been one of the least irascible gatherings in Britain at that moment. Even Hugh. His unexpected – and presumably unwelcome – arrival at The Folly was forgotten. It was difficult to believe that he and David hated each other. Difficult, too, to imagine the misery that must have preceded his divorce from Astrid. Hugh was witty, charming, lovable – the perfect dinner companion. For those two hours or so we were the embodiment of that great old myth, One Big Happy Family, though only three of those present were related by blood.

Afterwards Belle and Astrid and Effie stayed behind to clear up the kitchen while the rest of us proceeded to the library. I was now mobilised – Brendan had unearthed the crutches and I could hobble about under my own steam. My increase in contentment was in direct proportion to the decrease in dependency, and I was looking forward to the long luxurious evening with my friends.

The library was beautiful. I'd barely noticed the Christmas tree that morning, partly because I was preoccupied with Hugh and partly because the tree was deep inside the room, far from the windows. Now, however, with the red velvet curtains drawn against the dark, the tree came into its own. David and Matti had gone ahead of us to light fresh candles. It must have taken them ages, because the tree was huge and lavishly supplied with them, each in its antique holder. I'd never seen a tree with real candles before. It was exquisite.

Matti sat on the edge of my *chaise-longue* and gave me a

lesson on Christmas trees. 'It's a noble fir,' he explained. 'Sometimes it's called *Abies nobilis* and sometimes it's *Abies procera*.'

I remembered our first meeting on one of the forest rides, when he'd been so pleased to tell me all about the American red oak. He squirreled information about trees the way other children collected computer data. He was clearly thrilled to find someone as ignorant as myself.

'It's the best tree for candles,' he continued. 'You see how all the branches stick out and go up in a pyramid? So there aren't any branches above them in the way to catch fire.'

'So nature designed it for candles?' I said.

He nodded.

'What about all the ornaments? Where do they come from?'

'Oh, everywhere. Some are terribly old and some come from friends. Come and see.'

I hobbled over to a chair near the tree and he pointed out the ornaments, explaining the history of each. It seems that the Farleton Christmas tree had always been something of an event, and Christmas guests often contributed an ornament of their own as a souvenir of their stay. I looked forward to choosing the choicest of mine and presenting it next year. It seemed inconceivable that I wouldn't be here next year, and the next . . .

From close up the foliage was wonderful, far thicker and lusher and greener than that of ordinary Christmas trees. Farleton Forest, Matti said, had pioneered the growing of these trees and, through the years, succeeded in convincing fashionable Londoners that this was the only Christmas tree worth having. Matti tried not to take all the credit for it.

Throughout the lesson on Christmas trees, he consulted his father for arcane bits of information. David was in a big old leather armchair near the tree, sipping his wine, filling in the narrative. He seemed perfectly contented. Whatever anger he'd felt for my exploit on the moor was gone. Perhaps Brendan was right; it had only been his worry, translated into anger as happened so often with people who cared. And there was no doubt that he did care about me, but only as a friend,

225

a part of the household. I should have been content with that, but wasn't.

My foot began to hurt. I made my way back to the *chaise-longue* and laid the offending thing out horizontally again.

Hugh was in a chair just beyond the far end of the *chaise-longue*. He contemplated me for some time, head tilted, his boyish face quizzical. 'Tell me, Snow Queen, what makes a beautiful, intelligent and no doubt talented woman like you bury herself in a godforsaken patch of earth called Keldreth?'

This wasn't the Hugh of the Christmas table. There was mischief in his manner. I should have been alerted but wasn't.

I smiled. 'A whim.' It wasn't true, but his way of putting the question precluded a serious answer. I described my accidental purchase of the farm in a way I'd never done before, turning it into a lark, the impulsive kind of thing people did in the City. I could feel my past coming back to meet me as I talked. I might have been in London.

'And where will the next whim take you?' he asked.

David and Matti were fiddling with one of the toys beneath the tree. David's posture suggested a man pretending not to listen.

'How can I do the impossible?' I said with a smile. 'Whims are by definition unpredictable. But it won't be the City again, that much I do know. After the first excitement wears off, it's pretty tedious.'

'What did you do?'

'Commodities first,' I said. 'The natural extension of being a farmer's daughter, I suppose. Instead of growing the stuff, I sold it – in the abstract. Then some friends of mine switched to the money market instead, and so I drifted into that. It was fun for a while, but just making money can pall. What about you? D'you know, nobody's even told me what you do.'

He leaned forward and said in a stage whisper, 'That's because I'm the black sheep.'

'Sheep don't do anything,' I said. 'They just eat.'

He leaned further forward, conspiratorially. 'Property,' he whispered. 'I'm a property developer.' Then he twisted his extremely mobile face into a toothy cartoon snarl. 'I'm the big bad wolf.'

I had to laugh, he looked so funny.

'It's true,' he said with mock indignation. 'I'm the wicked fellow who turfs people out of their cosy slums and puts up nasty office blocks in their place.'

'Well, I'm hardly one to criticise. My own flat was probably one of your developments, and very nice it was, too. Anyway,' I yawned, 'what I'm doing now isn't much better: taking taxpayers' money to produce food nobody wants.' Why did I say that? It was true, in a sense, but that wasn't the reason. Some malicious part of me wanted to bring out into the open David's unspoken disapproval of my work. I wanted to niggle David, not Hugh, into a response. I wanted to crash through the bland friendliness to see if there was anything else beneath it. 'Anyway, who *does* do anything useful?' I added. David did. Why didn't he turn round and say so?

Brendan came in with a basketful of logs. He threw another one on the fire and stooped to prod it into position. Sparks were whizzing up towards the chimney, as hypnotic in their way as the harness bells. He turned to me suddenly. 'Isn't it just the like of me to forget: I had a count of those sheep of yours today. About fifteen are missing.'

I felt unaccountably irritated by his accent. He'd never told me anything about his Irish past. Nobody ever talked about the past here, except when they absolutely had to, as when they told me how the kites had come to Keldreth.

I shrugged. 'I'm surprised there aren't more gone missing.'

Hugh's face brightened. 'Fifteen less subsidies for those poor old taxpayers!'

I laughed, God knows why. Brendan looked puzzled and a little hurt. Hardly surprising, given the effort he'd made to save those sheep. What on earth was I doing? It was as if some deep-buried devil was slowly swimming up through the wine and taking control of my tongue. There'd been a fair bit of wine with dinner and we were still at it. I was conscious of this even as I reached to the floor beside the *chaise-longue* and retrieved my wine glass. I should have left it alone, but didn't.

A burst of laughter from the kitchen, Effie's the loudest of all. It was amazing the way she'd taken to The Folly, after all the disparaging things she'd said about my move. Disparaging, but never inappropriate, and never mindlessly malicious. Even Effie, whose tongue could be London sharp, saved her swipes for targets that deserved it.

The laughter drew nearer, and a moment later the three women arrived. The atmosphere lightened perceptibly as Effie told a story about a colour-blind client who insisted there were 347 different shades of white and he wanted every single one of them in his house. Belle went round with the wine bottle, topping up our glasses. I should have put my hand over mine but didn't. Matti listened impatiently to Effie's story, and as soon as she finished, comandeered her to play some new board game with him. They spread themselves out on the carpet by the fire. Astrid brought a low stool over and sat with me. Within minutes the scene had gone back a century, to a Victorian household. The big log fire, the magnificent Christmas tree with its real candles, the worn old furniture and friendly clutter. Even the clothes were in part anachronistic: Belle's voluminous rainbow-striped skirt, Astrid's long brown wool one with a black taffeta blouse and a cameo at the throat. True, Effie and Matti weren't dressed the part, but their absorption in their game was from a vanished age. I wondered what Matti was like in his other home, in Islington with Astrid. Did he do a Jekyll and Hyde, turn into a greedy little materialist and computer-game fanatic like his London school-friends? Keep up with the Jones kids? Probably. He must be something of a chameleon if he could adapt to The Folly, Islington and his superstar mother's home.

Hugh left the room. Astrid turned to me.

'If Hugh is become a nuisance, Charlotte, you must please be firm with him?'

Even the musical uplift of her voice irritated me just a fraction. 'I think he's rather charming, not at all what I expected.'

'Yes? He is wonderful company for some hours or even days – but a lifetime?'

She should know. I wondered, though, if she was referring to her own experience, or giving me a veiled warning. I felt unaccountably annoyed, just as I had about Brendan's Irish accent. All my good feelings towards my friends were going sour, blighted by my frustration over David.

Hugh returned, shivering. 'Christ, this place is a deep-freeze – why don't you put some heat in the old dump?' he complained to David.

'That is why we come into this room,' Astrid answered serenely.

He glared at her and refilled his wine glass. Tarzan had entered the room with Hugh. Now she stalked over to the board game and peered at the pieces laid out on it. The slow switching of her tail was ominous.

'Tarzan,' I said in warning.

'Where's the telly?' said Hugh. 'Why aren't we watching some revolting film like everyone else?'

'The television is put away until the students return,' said Astrid with the same serenity.

'Ah, of course. We mustn't let the twentieth century intrude into our olde worlde idyll, must we. Mustn't ruin the Victorian illusion. Soon Grandpapa and Grandmama will sweep into the room in their stiff cloth and taffeta to give us a little home entertainment. Home Sweet Home.'

I looked sharply at Hugh. His forehead glistened. He was drunk. Tarzan edged closer to the board and sat down, her rear end giving a little wiggle.

'Tarzan, come here,' I said.

'Matti,' said Hugh, raising his voice, 'give us a little tune. Entertain us. Show us what Auntie has taught you.'

'Busy,' he answered distractedly. He was clearly contemplating a difficult move, his little face screwed up in concentration.

'Busy?' Hugh roared. 'What kind of an answer is that? Some Victorian you are. Do as you're told.'

'Leave him alone,' said Astrid. Serenely.

Tarzan was seated neatly at the edge of the board, looking like the famous Egyptian cat at the British Museum. Her tail twitched once. Then, with no further warning, one paw shot out and swiped at the pieces, scattering them all over the board.

'Tarzan!' Matti's cry of hurt and anger.

Effie scooped up the kitten and held her close to her face,

giving her an authoritative glare. 'Tarzan, you wicked little beast!'

The kitten grinned. Now I knew how mothers felt when their children went wrong. Tarzan was growing up to be a problem cat.

'Tarzan decrees!' said Hugh. 'There! Play us a little tune, Matti. Tickle the ivories or whatever.'

'Never mind,' said Effie. 'We'll have another game later. And tomorrow. Whenever you like.'

'It is good if you like to play for us?' said Astrid.

Her smile cleared the air. Matti smiled back uncertainly. Astrid rose, and together they went over to the piano. There was a big untidy heap of sheet music on it. They rustled through it for some time, with whispered consultations. Then Astrid swivelled the piano stool up several inches and Matti perched on it, frowning at the music. Astrid took a seat nearby and tried hard not to look like his piano teacher. Was she his piano teacher? Nobody had told me even that much about her.

Matti began. It was one of those deceptively simple little Mozart pieces which sound like child's play and aren't. Matti gave a brave rendering but the result was lacklustre – inevitably so, unless played by a master.

'Once more with *feeling*!' Hugh roared when Matti had finished to applause from everyone else.

Astrid ignored him. 'That was *much* better,' she said to Matti.

'It wasn't,' said Hugh. 'It was rotten. The kid obviously hates the piece. Give him something with some oomph in it.'

Matti chose a second piece, a simplified version of Tchaikovsky's piano concerto. Oomph it had, and Matti put his all into it. The piece was awash with rubato the composer had certainly not intended, but Matti was enjoying himself so much it would be churlish to criticise, and nobody did, not even Hugh.

'That's better,' he mumbled.

Matti finished his concert with a Scott Joplin, again greatly simplified. This time he seemed to know what he was doing. Whatever he lacked in technique he made up for by a surprisingly sophisticated sense of rhythm. The applause at the end was genuine this time. The little boy slid off the stool and bowed sheepishly.

'Next!' Hugh roared, waving his empty wine glass. 'Well, Astrid? Or is the audience too big and scary?' He gave his toothy wolf's grin.

There was a long pause, while Astrid and Hugh looked at each other, both of them quite calm. Only then did I begin to see that something was going on between them, some reference to their shared past.

Astrid broke it with her smile, more serene than ever. 'I think I manage,' she said, and began rummaging through the sheet music. She twirled the stool down and seated herself on it with dignity. A single last look at Hugh, inscrutable, and she began.

It was one of the Bach forty-eight – like the Mozart, seemingly simple but impossible for anyone but a professional to play well.

Well? It was superb. After only a few notes, I could feel the goosepimples rise on my flesh. My jaw slackened, and just in time I managed to set my wine glass down on the carpet before it would have dropped from my paralysed hands. My scalp prickled. I looked at Effie. She was staring at me, her face as astonished as I knew my own to be. This was no piano teacher, no hack earning a living at second-best. This wasn't even a so-so professional, but a real musician, and of the highest order.

When she finished, everyone applauded except Effie and me, both of us too stunned to react.

'Jesu Christus,' Effie breathed.

'Astrid, I had no idea . . . ' I began and trailed off foolishly, too moved by the music to have any ideas at all.

'What?' said Hugh. 'Nobody told you about My Wife the Failed Pianist?' He corrected himself. 'My ex-wife the ex-pianist.' His voice was hard and ugly. He was very drunk.

'Hugh, do shut up,' said Belle.

Astrid waved aside the confusion she'd created. 'The story is small,' she said. 'I come from Sweden to London to study at the Royal Academy of Music, then I have third prize from Leeds Piano Competition – you know this thing?'

'Of course,' I said.

'Third prize nobody remembers, not even second, but I get some good engagements anyway and start to play for publics, and – '

'Ah ah ah,' said Hugh. 'You're leaving out the other prize you won in Leeds. Me.' He grinned at me. 'I was in Leeds on a business trip. Not much to do in Leeds between times, so I took myself off to the competition. There she was, big beautiful Astrid, giving hell to that Bechstein. Ever see a generously endowed lady play the piano in a sleeveless dress? The upper arm wobbles. Very sexy. Only thing to beat it is a lady cellist, ditto. The vibrato, you know. What could I do? I married her.'

He laughed. Nobody else did. The atmosphere was screwed up to the tension of a piano wire – I could tell without even seeing anyone's face. I couldn't look, though. I was riveted to Hugh's narrow grey eyes. He was watching me intently now and smiling in open mockery.

'Very cultured place, The Folly,' he continued. 'Very highbrow we all are. Everyone but Hugh. Poor crass businessman Hugh. Make money, not music. So? I married music. And what does the lady do? Quits. Some women use false pregnancy to trick their men into marrying them. Mine used music.'

'Hugh! That's enough!' David's voice, silent until now.

'No, it's not enough,' said Hugh. 'Our guests should know a few of our little skeletons. Not that my lady-wife was a skeleton, never that. But, soon after we married her poor old teeth started chattering like bones every time she climbed up onto that concert platform. Isn't that right, Astrid? Scared shitless you were. Scared the people who paid good money to hear you would throw rotten tomatoes.'

'Hugh!' David got out of his chair and started across the room. 'That's enough for one night!'

Astrid's arm shot out to stop his progress. 'Leave him,' she said quietly. 'Leave him to say.'

'You hear the lady?' said Hugh.

David stood still, his face almost black with anger. I'd never seen him so angry, unless it was up in the hidden valley on the moor when he smashed the trap.

Hugh smiled at Astrid, then looked back at me. 'Nerves,

it's called. Every musician gets them. Every musician takes drugs to get rid of them. Beta-blockers. Everyone except pure wholesome Astrid. And so it came to pass – this being Christmas, let's have a bit of the Biblical – that Astrid, my beautiful and talented wife Astrid, the ornament of my life, Astrid . . . quit. Just like that. Quit. To become . . . a piano teacher. My God.' He jerked his head to face her. 'You think I married you for love? That's right, Astrid, hold him back, don't let the squire get at me' – this as David made another lunge. 'No, my lovely, I married you to be my better half. My cultured half. What else did I have? No estate, no title, no talent. Second son, sans everything. Except you.' He rose to his feet and, after swaying a bit, started towards the door. 'And then even you finked out. What could I do?' He smiled, his hand on the doorknob. 'I divorced her.' He opened the door, gave his toothy wolf's grin and disappeared.

As if released from a magician's spell, the room awoke into activity. David stepped over the abandoned board game and poked the fire. Brendan added another log. Belle swept Matti into her arms and said soothing things – 'Poor old Matti, you shouldn't have to listen to such things. Try not to worry, darling, it doesn't mean anything. Hugh had too much to drink, that's all.' Effie came over to sit on the stool by my *chaise-longue*. Astrid moved to a rocking chair near the fire and looked at us both. She smiled. Incredibly, she smiled.

'What Hugh says is all true,' she said. 'This nerves? Sometimes I could play, sometimes not. Then the tension starts: which kind of night is this? Will I be able to play or not? The drugs work, but only for some time. Then they go weak, and also the drugs make you play not quite so good. Music is a ruthless job – so many good people, all waiting to be better than me. "Pure and wholesome" is wrong, though. I know that soon – very soon – the drugs stop to work and then? Nothing. Better to go with grace and make a new life.'

'I'm so sorry,' I murmured. 'I had no idea.'

Her smile brightened. 'Please, pity is wrong. I have a good life. To play the tragic heroine is maybe okay for a little time, but soon is boring. Before I did not so good work, now I do good work. I am repetiteur for dance company – you know

233

this word? I play piano for rehearsing and am very happy. To be part of a good big whole, this I like more than the prima donna on concert platform. And also the teaching? This I like, too. My house in Islington is full of music students – because Matti and me have no worry of the sound of practice. And good baby-sitting for Matti, too, yes? A happy house. The musician life is hard and only good if you are perfect. I am lucky to find out soon that I am not perfect. And now –' she jumped up and clapped her hands imperiously, twice. 'David! Sing!'

It seemed impossible that the evening could be salvaged after that, but it was. Astrid returned to the piano and played a run-in to *Shenandoah*. David hesitated only briefly before joining her. Leaning one arm on the top of the piano, he began to sing. He had a lovely bass voice – not professional, oh no, Astrid was the only professional among us – but deep and rich and firm. A good amateur voice, pleasing to listen to. It eased the frazzled atmosphere faster than I would have imagined.

Then Belle plonked Matti in the rocking chair, put Tarzan on his lap and joined David in singing a sappy Victorian duet that couldn't but make the rest of us laugh. After that, Brendan stepped up to the piano and, after a dramatic pause, the four of them sang the quartet from *Rigoletto*, Astrid joining in while playing a simple accompaniment. The voices were well matched, all good amateur voices, and the piece was so effective that Effie and I demanded an encore. They sang the exquisite canon quartet from *Fidelio*.

After that, they all rose and bowed to their audience of two – Hugh was still absent and Matti was slouched far down into the rocking chair, asleep. I wondered why Astrid didn't take him to bed. Clearly he was exhausted – with last night's vigil and all the excitement of today's presents, the sleigh ride, the big dinner, the long evening. It seemed odd that everybody just let him sleep on in the rocking chair.

'Good!' said Astrid. 'Now, your turn?' she said to Effie.

'*Me*? Jesu, I don't even sing in the bathtub. Honest. Even I can't stand the sound of it.'

'A poem? A little dance?'

'Tell you what I *would* like to do,' she said. 'Redecorate that

scrumptious ballroom. How about that for my contribution?'
She was talking to David. No matter how much she had to
drink, Effie never let her mind close down. I knew she was
in earnest or she wouldn't have directed her offer to the one
person who could yea or nay it.

'Ballroom?'

'That big room over there.' She waved an arm towards
the east side of the house.

'Oh, that. I don't think it was a ballroom, not in a hunting
lodge. Though the old man was so dotty . . . Anyway, it's
never been used, not for anything that I can remember.'

'Well, the ventilation must be terrific, because it's in good
nick except for the shredded wallpaper and a few kilos of
cobwebs. Seriously. Let me come back at Easter and do it up.
Free of charge, of course. Better still, as a token repayment
for your hospitality.' She made a graceful bow.

Effie was shrewd, and she already knew David well enough
to see ways of getting round his stubbornness. The same
suggestion made by most people would have caused an
explosion. As it is, David nearly scowled but at the last
moment turned it into a wary smile. 'And what would we
use the room for?'

'A ball, of course.'

'*Here*?'

'Where else? Where better to hold a Green Ball – for
charity, of course. Seriously. People are dying to see the
inside of The Folly. Let them – and let them pay a whacking
great entrance price for the privilege. You said yourself you
felt frustrated at having no more land to plant. Give the
money to the Woodland Trust to plant somewhere else.'

David stared at her. It was the crucial moment; the scene
could go either way from here. I wondered if Effie had
misjudged. Then, slowly, his big stroppy face began to shift
towards a smile.

Belle helped it along. 'It's not a bad idea. Is it?'

'At least think about it, okay?' said Effie. 'Meanwhile, I'll
do my party piece. Astrid, can you play a piece of jazz?
Something with a tricky rhythm – Dave Brubeck kind of
thing.'

Astrid returned to the piano and thought while Effie

cleared some chairs from the centre of the room. When Astrid began *Blue Rondo à la Turk*, Effie kicked off her shoes and began to extemporise a piece of modern dance. If the others were surprised, I wasn't – I knew Effie had taken dance lessons in her New York childhood. She hadn't kept it up, but she was still limber enough to do a passable job.

As she took her bow, a distant telephone rang. Instantly, Matti was awake, looking around, alert. I heard the muffled voice of Hugh through the book-lined wall separating the library from the kitchen. So that's where he was lurking. A little later, he arrived in the doorway. 'Belle.'

Belle hastened to the kitchen. Hugh strode across the room and sat down in the same chair from which he'd delivered his devastating attack on Astrid. Nobody paid any attention. Every muscle in my body strained, waiting for the reaction to his return, but there was none. Astrid continued to play Brubeck while everyone else listened.

Finally Belle reappeared. 'My sister in Edinburgh,' she explained. She nodded once to Hugh in acknowledgement of his return, then went to her chair. 'Right, who's left?' she said brightly. 'Charlotte, you're the literary one – how about a reading?' She waved an arm towards the thousands of books which were the room's main decoration.

How could she be so calm? How could Hugh sit there, smiling vaguely, waiting, like everyone else, for me to do a reading? It was as if the gruesome scene, straight out of *Who's Afraid of Virginia Woolf*, had never happened. Had it? I'd drunk quite a bit of wine, but not enough to fantasise that brutal outburst. The evening was growing unreal. Layers I'd never suspected were coming to the surface, my friends were revealing aspects of themselves that confused my easy assumptions. How could I think about a silly party piece after what had happened?

But, taking my cue from the others, I did. After some thought, I improvised a parody of Violetta's deathbed scene, with Astrid filling in snippets of music from *La Traviata* as a background. Delivered from my *chaise-longue*, it was quite effective and earned a fair bit of applause.

Finally, and more unreal still, Hugh rounded off the evening's entertainment with *Alfred and the Lion*. His

Stanley Holloway imitation wasn't bad and the piece was clearly rehearsed. Very likely it had been his party piece for many childhood years, just as the others had all played and sung their songs together for many Christmases since. It was the stuff of old-fashioned families and would have been unremarkable if the 'family' in question hadn't been so bizarre.

Matti was getting cranky. He'd figeted through my offering and Hugh's and now began to whine. I couldn't blame him; he must be exhausted. I wondered again why Astrid didn't put him to bed. Then the telephone rang again and I had my answer. Belle left and Matti followed her, as if this were another part of the evening's entertainment, well rehearsed and expected.

Belle returned alone. 'Matti's mother,' she explained. 'From New York.'

Matti's mother is a taboo subject round here, Belle had said, and here she was, out in the open at last. Of course. The ritual phone call to her son. It *had* been expected. There was a small awkward silence. Astrid covered it by playing some Chopin. I tried to listen – partly to keep from thinking of Ros, partly to prevent my eyes from straying towards David – but I don't think I heard a note.

It was a long telephone call – money no object. When Matti returned, he went up to David. 'Mummy wants to talk to you.'

This time I had to look, and the surprise on David's face told me that this wasn't a part of the Christmas ritual. He got up abruptly and left.

'Well well well,' murmured Hugh. He turned to me with his social smile once more in place. 'The great lady doesn't normally condescend to us lesser mortals,' he explained. He leaned back comfortably. His wine glass was gone but he was still visibly drunk.

'Bedtime,' said Astrid, rising from the piano and putting her hand on Matti's head. He didn't even protest as she led him towards the door.

'When's your mum coming to see us?' Hugh asked facetiously.

'Easter.'

Astrid froze. Clearly this, too, was unexpected.

'Well well well,' murmured Hugh again. 'Still has the spark for old David?'

Matti shrugged, not understanding, and let himself be led from the room.

I understood. Everything was clear now. Why David had never responded to me with anything more than friendship. And now Ros was coming back to reclaim him. I shouldn't have been surprised. I'd wondered enough how she could leave him. Clearly she couldn't. What I had suspected before, I now knew. I had never had a chance. Well, there was nothing more to lose. I turned to Hugh.

'I suppose you knew her well?'

'Ros? She was my sister-in-law.' He looked round for his wine glass, then gave up and turned his attention to me. 'Yes, I knew her. Very well indeed. Better than David. He never appreciated her the way I did. Too dull, our David. Good old solid David with his boring old horses and boring old trees. Not a spark of poetry in that muddy soul of his. How could he appreciate someone like Ros?'

Astrid returned – Matti had fallen asleep almost before he got into bed.

Hugh smiled up at her. 'Know something? We married the wrong people, you and me. You should have married good old David. You're a perfect pair.'

'Why don't you go to bed, Hugh?' she said calmly. 'We have enough skeletons for one evening.'

'No ambition, either of you. Plodders.'

'Go away, Hugh. We are weary of you.'

'You see?' He turned back to me. 'Changes the subject. And how about the way good old gallant David rushed to her rescue? One word against Astrid and he throws on his rusty chainmail and lumbers up to play the knight.'

Belle tried to intervene. 'Hugh, I hate to say the obvious, but it's lousy manners to play this kind of scene in front of guests. Basic courtesy.'

And there was another answer. This kind of scene *was* played over and over, every time Hugh came to The Folly. No wonder they were all so practised in ignoring him.

Hugh ignored her. 'Ah, but Ros! Now there was a real

woman! Fiery, passionate, oozing ambition from every delectable pore! She should have been mine, don't you think? What do you think, Snow Queen?'

'I've never met her.'

'We were made for each other, Ros and me. I think she knew it, too.'

'Nothing prevents you to go to New York,' said Astrid.

'Yes . . . ' he said contemplatively. 'Yes . . . '

For one wild moment I wished he would. To whisk her off her feet, take her away from David, leave him for me. But I couldn't fool myself. Hugh was, despite his sporadic charm, just a drunken buffoon. Ros could hardly be interested in someone like him when there was David. And what was the use anyway? Even if she didn't come back to reclaim him, he was hers, in spirit. I should have realised. David wasn't the sort of person who loved lightly. He had given himself to Ros in words of permanence, and meant them. There was nothing left for me except Just Good Friends.

David was gone a long time.

27

The next morning we straggled down to breakfast unevenly. No trace of last night's drama remained. Everything had been swept away by the fresh blizzard that had raged through the night and left the landscape clean and fresh again.

But I knew better now. The night's sleep had cleared my mind of alcohol fumes and a few delusions. I saw now that The Folly's success was built on failure. David's failed marriage, and Astrid's, plus her failure as a musician. Belle had failed to become an actress, Brendan had never been promoted and they'd both failed to produce the children to whom they would have been such wonderful parents.

Strangely enough, I respected them all the more. It was a strong and wonderful alchemy which had transformed these multiple failures into the vivid success of Farleton Forest. And Hugh was wrong about the poetry. There was poetry in abundance in the kites, and in the man who had brought them here. And how could Hugh be blind to the magnificence of Olwen and her stablemates, let alone the glory of the forest itself? Not that that stopped me from flirting with Hugh. He was, as Astrid had said, amusing company in small doses. I enjoyed sparring with him in the days that followed.

David was away much of the time. When weather permitted, he and Brendan went out to do some felling – students knew how to fell; what they were there to learn was the handling of the horses, and it saved time if the felling could be done before their return. In the evenings, he spent much of his time in his study, doing accounts and dealing with estate matters.

We were there for more than a week. I, of course, was immobilised, and Effie said trade was dead at this time of year anyway. She made herself useful round the house – not renovating the ballroom, though the subject did crop up from time to time. But her main contribution was simply the evident pleasure she took in being there. It still surprised me how well she fitted in, after her disapproval of Cappelrigg and all things rural. I suppose Cappelrigg was too bleak and bare for her. She loved to be surrounded by beautiful things. So did I, but for me the landscape itself fulfilled that role. Effie needed a beautiful house filled with fascinating objects, and that The Folly certainly was.

Why Hugh stayed on so long I don't know. There were one or two hints that I was the main attraction. I didn't take them seriously. I saw now how right Belle had been when she spoke of the antagonism between Hugh and David. If Hugh paid me a lot of attention, it was mainly to spite David.

Not that Hugh suspected my feelings for David. Nobody did. That, too, surprised me. I had thought, in the flush of love, that my face was unbearably readable. Apparently not. I was grateful to have come through that fraught period with no one the wiser.

It snowed on and off the whole week. No sooner had the council snow ploughs made their way up the hill to Keldreth than the sky dumped another batch on the newly cleared roads. Matti was overjoyed, and one of my happiest memories of that week is the day we all (apart from David and Brendan, off somewhere in the forest) spent in the garden building a whole cast of snowpeople, each one representing someone at The Folly, each one sporting a characteristic piece of clothing. Belle's was best, with a big disused rainbow skirt girdling the plump figure. That night a blizzard covered the lot.

I was becoming terribly fond of Matti. I'd never much cared for children, but Matti was different. He was bright, though not precocious, but the thing that distinguished him from so many children was his charming inability to see the difference between adults and children. All people were people to him, each one individual, each one responded to individually. With Astrid he was calm, with Effie he was crazy. With me he was contemplative and a little quirky. We had long philosophical discussions over the board games. His main preoccupation was the concept of eternity. He couldn't get his mind round the notion that something could have no beginning or end, just be, always. I don't know if this is usual in someone his age, but his ideas on it were always unexpected and interesting.

Yes, of course I had fantasies. David and Matti and myself forming a new family. Ros coming back, her brilliance extinguished, David discovering he didn't love her after all, turning to me at last. But I didn't take it seriously. It was David himself who prevented it. He was a long-term person, planting trees which wouldn't be harvested for a hundred years or more, spending years training just one horse. His friends, too, were the friends of his youth, apart from myself and Effie. He wasn't a man to change his mind, discard one woman in favour of another. Slowly, and with more anguish than I would have thought possible, I turned the future lover back into the present friend. There was nothing else I could do.

Not long into the New Year, I returned to Cappelrigg, and soon after that I brought my sheep home. Matti helped me. It was his last day before going back to London and he was feeling a bit gloomy. Shepherding was the perfect antidote. We did the first stretch by foot – from the field to the road where I'd parked my Land-Rover. The rest we did in comfort. My foot was much better, but too much exercise brought on ominous twinges, and I didn't want to compound my folly on the moor with a second and easily avoidable disablement. Matti didn't mind at all sitting high in the Land-Rover with me while Moss trotted on ahead, keeping his sheep on the straight and narrow.

Moss was probably superfluous. The snow ploughs had left a great bank of lumpy snow on either side of the road. My sheep, grown lazy in their field with daily deliveries of hay by Brendan, wouldn't dream of exerting themselves to jump the bank, but Moss didn't know that. He weaved back and forth, keeping the ladies in order, while the Land-Rover crawled behind.

When we reached my gate, Matti jumped down to open it and then stood by while the sheep poured through. It reminded me of the time we'd taken the sheep up to the moor and come upon David at the stone circle. We'd walked back to The Folly as a threesome that day, and Belle had shown me round the house. But then, everything reminded me of something. I'd been at Cappelrigg less than seven months and already every bit of the landscape was suffused with memories, some of them painful now that I had to dismantle my feelings for David.

After Matti had put the sheep into one of the lower fields, we had lunch together. I'd made up a casserole the night before and left it stewing gently in the Aga's slow-warming oven. It was delicious, and the little lunch was a delight. I realised that I was going to miss Matti, very much indeed. I tried to think cynical, tell myself that Matti was only a David-substitute, that I only responded dumbly to his resemblance to his father, but it wasn't true. It was Matti himself, in all his growing individuality.

Astrid came to fetch him in The Folly's Land-Rover that afternoon. Brendan had loaded it with the hens, and the unloading of these indignant birds provided some comic relief. But soon the time for parting came and the comedy was over. There were hugs all round, and when Matti said, in that straightforward Farleton manner, 'I'm going to miss you, Charlotte,' I had to clench my teeth to keep the tears back.

'Never mind,' said Astrid. 'We come back Easter, Matti. Easter is sooner than you think.'

But I wouldn't be there for Easter. At the next gathering of the clan, Ros would be among them. Even if they invited me over, I would make some excuse. I couldn't sit beside the dazzling Ros Rawlinson, inviting comparison, growing feebler by the second in the light of her radiance until I went out with a *pfft* like a used-up candle. No, I had far too much pride for that.

I didn't have much else. As the thaw came and my house became an island in a flood of melted snow, I began to see what a poor-quality farm it was after all. Its snug solid beauty at the height of the dry summer had been deceptive. Whether it was the nature of the land or John Jowett's repairs, I didn't know. But gaps were appearing in the walls and my sheep were sloshing about in fields that looked like rice paddies.

So I took my sheep back up to the moor. I had little choice. The land they were on was becoming so badly poached that there was no chance of the grass growing back in time for lambing unless the stock was taken off it again. I wasn't being reckless, though. The long-term forecast showed no sign of snow, and I now had two radios. I was taking no chances this time.

From then on I was busy gap-walling. I couldn't help noticing that the only walls that stayed firm were those on the boundary with Farleton Forest. I noted, too, that my contract stated that those walls were not my farm's responsibility but that of the estate. The conclusion was obvious: John Jowett had been a less good farmer than I'd thought, gapping his walls sloppily rather than taking the time to do it properly.

The worst walls of all, however, were those on the boundary with Graegarth, most of which were Richard's responsibility. I shouldn't have been surprised. If John Jowett's farming was sloppy, Richard's was almost non-existent. Three times I phoned Graegarth. Three times a surly sounding Jean said she'd pass on the message. I didn't know whether she did or not, but the walls remained untouched. In the end, I repaired them myself. It grated, standing out there in the raw winter, day after day, doing his walling for him.

I was losing patience with Richard. At first I'd felt attracted to him. Later, after discovering that he had regularly helped John Jowett repair his tractor, I'd felt sorry for him. That terrible weight of uncertainty and guilt, pressing down on him. But nothing in his manner ever suggested uncertainty or guilt. He seemed consistently at ease with himself, not unlike the men I'd known in London. And then there was his farm. There was no excuse for that. I hated to play the prig, but I was too much a farmer's daughter not to feel annoyed at the way he neglected his farm, spent his money instead on things of show.

*　　*　　*

In February came another of the Celtic festivals: Imbolc, the lactation of the ewes. I hesitated for some time before phoning Detective Sergeant Tyndall. There had been no more threats since the two in December and I didn't feel particularly worried for my own safety. But I was still convinced that the Druid leader was the person trapping the kites, and for this reason I wanted the cult exposed. This seemed an obvious opportunity. If a policeman could be stationed in or near my house, he would see the Druids pass by and be able to apprehend the whole lot at once.

Detective Sergeant Tyndall was not impressed. The threats had ceased, hadn't they, so why was I so keen to meddle with the harmless ritual on the moor? Was I really so uptight about a silly bit of trespass over my land? I still couldn't tell him the real reason without exposing the kites to even more danger. I wished I'd never phoned. He made me feel like a silly twit frightened by a few dotty men whose only fault had been (perhaps) to steal one of my hens.

And so I kept watch myself. After locking the doors and turning off all the lights, I waited at a darkened window for the men to appear. This time I saw the whole thing: the cars approaching and parking on the council road at the end of my drive; the robed men getting out, looking absurd in their converted sheets; the march up the drive; the dividing into two columns to go around the house; the reuniting of the columns to process up my fields and onto the moor. I saw everything except their faces, the one thing that mattered. The hoods, of course. I'd hoped – foolishly – that they might leave their hoods off until they arrived at the circle. I'd hoped at least to identify the leader.

And still I waited, while the fire burned and they did whatever they intended to do in the stone circle. After a long time, they flowed back down off the moor and past my house. I had debated whether to spring out and confront them myself. I didn't really think they would harm me. But when the moment came, I remembered the frenzy of their chants, the violence of their shouts, and my courage failed me. Perhaps if I'd done it while they were on their way up, it would have worked. But now, made wild by their ritual, they might forget the common decencies of their daily lives, such as not attacking a defenceless woman.

The next day I was furious with myself. How could I have been so cowardly? Perhaps I wouldn't have been so angry if I hadn't also felt frustrated over David. That, plus having to do Richard's walling for him put me in a high old temper. I don't know how else to explain my behaviour when, one rainy day, I found myself at a table with him at the Golden

Oak. Normally I avoided the place, but I had to wait for a spare part that wouldn't arrive until late afternoon. I was cold and hungry. Without thinking, I swept into the Golden Oak and ordered a hotpot for lunch.

No sooner had I sat down with my half of bitter than I noticed a change in the atmosphere. The conversation didn't exactly cease, but it changed down to a low murmur so striking that even those few customers who weren't locals noticed it. I could see them looking around, wondering what had caused it, and their gaze coming to rest finally on me. I felt naked, exposed and a little bit frightened.

The hostility was palpable, filling the room with bad vibes like a poor imitation of a ley line. How many of these big burly men had a white robe and hood tucked away in a corner where the wife wouldn't find it? And which of the hoods was stained with the blood of my hen? Suddenly I realised with overwhelming force that whatever was going on was indeed centred on this room. I stole a glance at the publican. Yes. He was almost certainly the 'priest'. I looked away and draped his after-image with robe and hood, smeared his face with chicken blood. I remembered the night I had accused Richard of being the culprit and once again felt guilt and embarrassment.

Just then, right on cue, the door opened and Richard entered. Instantly, as if a switch had been thrown, the atmosphere changed back to that of an ordinary market town pub. The customers lost the sinister robes my imagination had imposed on them and became amiable farmers amiably greeting one of their kind. The decibels increased, the conversation resumed. There was no doubting Richard's popularity, and as he slowly made his way to my table – waylaid several times to have a word with a friend – I could see my own reputation was rising with every step he took towards me. By the time he reached my table and sat down, I had almost been accepted, at least for as long as I remained in his presence.

I suppose that was part of it, for along with the relief I felt on seeing him came a surge of resentment. Why couldn't these people accept me in my own right? I'd worked hard at Cappelrigg – harder than Richard did at Graegarth, for that matter. And yet here I was, clearly regarded as a silly woman who needed a man's sanction before she could be taken seriously. Also, my hands were still raw from doing his walling.

'So,' he smiled. 'Back to the beginning, the circle complete.'

I realised that the table we were at was the same one we'd had on the day I'd bought Cappelrigg. 'Not quite,' I replied. 'I've put in several thousand hours of farming since then. Including your walling.'

He seemed not to hear. As I'd spoken he'd risen to go to the bar. He ordered some lunch and returned with a pint. 'I've been hoping to run into you, Charlotte. I want to talk to you.'

'Talking doesn't get the walls repaired.'

The door swung open and Detective Sergeant Tyndall walked in. At the same time, the hotpot I'd ordered was making its way towards my table. So was Detective Sergeant Tyndall. Richard glanced round, raised a hand in greeting and turned back to me.

'I've been very patient,' he smiled. 'You'll admit that, won't you?'

I was so annoyed about the walling and the locals' antagonism that I barely heard. The bargirl arrived with my hotpot and a supercilious smile in which I detected also a trace of envy.

'Did you hear me, Charlotte?' he said when the girl had left.

'Did you hear *me*?' I said. 'I did your walling for you. I spent *weeks* standing out in the rain and sleet, lacerating my hands to repair walls that are *your* responsibility.'

He held up his hands (not lacerated) in a charming gesture of surrender. 'I'm sorry, Charlotte. I meant to do it. If you'd just left it a bit longer I would have got round to it.'

'Richard, your sheep were coming across. They were eating what pathetic bits of grass I've got left. I couldn't wait.'

'I'm sorry, I really am. But I had other things on my mind. I've been doing a lot of thinking this winter. Serious thinking. I suppose you know what about.'

And, with a sinking feeling, I did. Richard had indeed

been patient, never pressing his presence on me. I'd asked him to respect my need for solitude, and he had done so, while I had blithely forgotten the whole business. I looked up at him now, feeling guiltier than ever but feeling nothing else. A friend and neighbour, yes. A lover, no. My eyes told me he was devastatingly handsome, coveted by most of the women of Kirkby Langham, but my emotions refused to act on this knowledge. It had been cowardly of me not to express something of this to him that evening we'd had dinner together. It would have been kinder. Instead, I'd left things to drift, and his own emotions had drifted further and further towards me at the same time mine had gravitated towards David. At the thought of David, my innards gave a lurch of despair.

'What I've been thinking about,' he said, 'is how much I love you.'

A sudden silence told me that everyone in the Golden Oak had heard this declaration. I could feel the colour rising into my cheeks. 'You barely know me,' I said quietly.

'Well, that's hardly my fault,' he said wryly. Then his face became more serious. 'Or maybe it is. I've been wondering if you've misunderstood me. If you've thought I was just playing around.'

Instantly I saw Nicola Dearden's face and knew he was thinking of her, too.

'It's not like that,' he went on, as if reading my mind. 'I'm serious about you. So serious that I want to marry you.'

The bargirl arrived with his ploughman's. She grinned and left. I barely saw her, hadn't touched my own food. The room was so quiet that the rain splashing against the windows seemed deafening. Every single person in the pub had heard Richard's proposal. Was he aware? These were private things he was saying.

'Do you hear me, Charlotte? I'm asking you to marry me.'

I closed my eyes in a turmoil of emotions Richard couldn't imagine, and in the darkness I saw David's face. Oh, the cruelty of it. How the gods must hate us humans, to be forever weaving their horrid triangles of mismatched feelings. There

248

was nothing I could do for myself, but I could at least minimise the damage to Richard, salvage his pride.

'I'm sorry,' I said, very quietly and with my face composed in a mask no one in the pub could read. 'I respect your feelings, Richard, but I can't return them.'

28

I didn't know what to think anymore, after the ghastly scene in the Golden Oak. I didn't know what was going on in Richard's mind. It occurred to me that he was much more cut off from the outside world than David was. I inclined to think that his proposal was genuine, despite the lack of passion behind it and despite the lack of encouragement from its object. But I did feel like an object. He seemed incapable of seeing me as a human being who might have feelings of my own on the subject. The whole business was so distressing that I couldn't bring myself to mention it to anyone at The Folly. They would probably hear anyway, I thought grimly, given the public nature of Richard's proposal. At least I had acted honourably this time, making a clean break. Richard had, in fact, taken it surprisingly well. So well that I wondered if he'd taken it seriously.

Luckily, I had other things to think about. The lambing season was looming and bringing with it new problems. I had deliberately spaced the tupping so as to spread the lambing. I still felt I'd done the right thing, but it did mean that someone had to be in attendance twenty-four hours a day for a whole month. There was no way I could do it alone.

I consulted Brendan. Brendan was not only a brilliant forester but a likeable man more in touch with the farming community than David could ever be. He gave the matter much thought and then produced Tom.

Tom was about my age, the son of a lowland farmer who had recently retired, sold up and taken the proceeds off to a seaside resort, leaving his son stranded. Tom had only basic education and no training other than that which he'd received on his father's farm. Like any other farmer's son, he'd assumed he would inherit the farm and never given a thought to his future. With the farm whisked out from under him, he had to think again. He did the only thing he could: hired himself out as a farm labourer.

He was, Brendan said, an excellent worker and especially good with sheep. In fact, he had already worked for me once, as part of the shearing gang last summer. I remembered him. Tall, thin and so angular that he seemed to be all elbows and knees, he had a shock of red hair and big calm hands which the sheep responded to magically.

And so began the long exhausting month. Tom worked a kind of nine-to-five while I, windows blacked out, slept through the day. Then, in the late afternoon, I would emerge and take over the night shift. For this, I filled the Land-Rover with lambing equipment and with comfy old cushions, blankets and food and a huge flask of coffee and drove off into the lambing field.

Much of the time I wasn't needed, except to daub my big green V of ownership onto the sides of the new lambs and tag their ears. Sheep are tough, they like to do their lambing alone and are usually pretty competent at it, but every so often a ewe got into trouble and needed my help. I found it much easier than I expected. My sheep, accustomed all autumn and winter to almost daily treats from me, and unharrassed by the neurotic dogs kept by so many farmers, trusted me and let me help them.

During the overlap between shifts, Tom and I would walk round the lambing field and discuss the day's progress before we herded the ewes with single lambs into one field and those with twins into another. We were, Tom said, doing quite well as regards the proportion of singles and doubles. But we were doing even better when it came to fatalities. Tom's ego was ferociously involved in maintaining this record and so was mine. It kept us going through the long lonely hours.

Tom also reported on other farmers' lambings. The Staveleys apparently weren't doing so well. Richard had lost a huge number of ewes on the moor during that blizzard. He had even boasted of it in town as proof to the lowland farmers of the hardship of hill farming. Reports of my heroic rescue of most of my flock had rather displeased him, but he'd dismissed it as beginner's luck. And now, even with fewer ewes to lamb, he was doing badly. Jean had the night shift and worked conscientiously enough, but during the day Richard did little more than stroll out into the field from time to time and mark the new lambs before returning to the comfort of his house.

Long nights they were for me. I don't think I've ever felt so lonely as during those long and largely eventless nights. I had made a sort of nest for myself out of old cushions and blankets in the back of my Land-Rover. When I wasn't in the driver's seat or prowling the field, I was in my nest. I read a little, hating to waste my waking hours, but the light was bad and my mind too disturbed to concentrate. There's something eerie about being awake throughout the night. Even when you imagine all the other people who, in their night jobs all over the world, are awake with you, you feel more profoundly alone than during the daylight hours. It's a time when brooding takes over. No matter how hard you try to keep it at bay, the gnawing negative wolf of the night will find its way into your mind and there perform its slow ritual destruction of your peace.

For me, it was the dismal triangle – being proposed to by the wrong man while the one I loved was indifferent towards me except as a friend. I tried to banish the wolf with proofs of my good fortune. I was young, healthy, financially viable and doing work I enjoyed in a beautiful piece of countryside. I had the friendship of Effie and of all the people at The Folly. Millions would envy me, and quite properly. I was no American with a constitutional right to happiness. If one piece was missing, so what? I should be grateful for what I had.

Then came the wolf, insinuating itself into my peace, flashing the image of the beloved face on the screen of my mind the moment I lowered my guard.

While the screen of my mind filled with his face, his no doubt still held the image of Ros. No doubt, too, her image was growing stronger with every day. Ros was coming at Easter. With the intuition of the failed rival, I could guess why. She had reached the height of her career. From now on she could only maintain her position and then, finally, begin to fade. How much better to make a dramatic exit now, consolidate her reputation and turn it into legend? And how better to do this than to return to family life?

It wasn't as absurd as it sounded. Families were fashionable these days; a lot of very successful people were, as they approached forty, renouncing their previous lives and starting again, rediscovering the deeper satisfactions of family life. Ros had a head start, with a ready-made family just waiting for her: a charming little son reaching the most appealing age, and a husband whose qualities were, I knew all too well, rare indeed.

As the lambing season drew towards its end and Easter came and went, I avoided the forest. It wasn't difficult. Everyone knew I was busy, nobody expected to see me during the most crucial month of the farming calendar. Nobody even suspected that I might have another reason, that I wished at all costs to avoid meeting Ros.

I would have succeeded, too, if it hadn't been for a bolshy ewe. One afternoon, during the change-over period, Tom and I discovered a brand new gap in the forest's boundary wall, the first ever. I was surprised, then annoyed. I'd lived with sheep long enough to know what it meant. We counted the sheep in the singles field, then counted again. Inevitably, one ewe and her lamb were missing. Tom offered to take Moss into the forest and flush them out.

If I'd accepted, my whole life might well have been different. Who ever sees the workings of chance? Even love sometimes needs a little kick in the pants, some trivial incident which no one could suspect will become the turning point of a life.

'No, I'll go,' I said. 'Moss is more used to me; it'll be easier that way.'

And so it was Tom, not me, who went back to the barn to fetch some corrugated iron for a temporary repair, while I clambered over the wall and disappeared into the forest. It was a section I particularly loved. Three species only: fir, beech and larch, each seemingly designed to be the perfect foil for the others, especially in the bleak months of winter and early spring. They were looking wonderful that day. The thin late-afternoon sunshine that filtered through turned the beech trunks into the gleaming silver columns of a pagan temple. Against them the crisp russet leaves of last autumn glowed with more than their usual intensity. The firs, ever green and watchful through the long dark winter, gave an illusion of perpetual summer and set off the silver and russet like the velvet cloth of a jeweller's shop. Here and there the tawny flash of sun-touched larch, its branches thick and luxuriant even with no leaves. Fir, beech and larch – the classic mix of German forests, David had told me. No wonder that country was so rich in forest legend.

I was enjoying my release from the lambing field so much that I almost forgot why I was there. 'Moss,' I said, 'go get them. You're faster than me.'

He trotted off, nose to the ground, while I wandered through the forest, looking more for the signs of spring than for the ewe. There was little breaking of bud yet, but everywhere the damp smell of growth rose from the forest floor, telling me in secret language that the roots deep down were starting their great work. I felt curiously excited, like being backstage just before the curtain went up and the stage filled with action.

Nature must have taken my metaphor seriously, for suddenly I saw up ahead a clearing, brightly lit where the canopy had drawn back to allow the sun through. And at the same moment, a voice, clear and ringing but at the same time intimate. A woman's voice. Intrigued, I moved quietly through the trees, my footsteps muffled by leaves made wet by the winter rains. At the edge of the clearing I stopped behind a young larch and peered through its branches.

It was indeed a stage, a theatre in the round grassy clearing with a knoll at the far end. On it stood a woman, facing me but not, I hoped, seeing me behind my densely twigged curtain. She spoke again:

> *'Hath not old custom made this life more sweet*
> *Than that of painted pomp? Are not these woods*
> *More free from peril than the envious court?*
> *Here feel we but the penalty of Adam,*
> *The seasons' difference.'*

The Shakespearean cadences rang out through the forest and caught at my memory: *As You Like It*. I'd seen it at

the Barbican and remembered it well. The part of Rosalind
had been played by her namesake, the dazzling new star who
had been discovered in that same play years ago in some
provincial theatre and had since made the role her own. Ros
Rawlinson.

So. This was my rival. I stepped a little closer and squinted
through the branches.

If I hoped that a closer view would reveal flaws unseen by
her usual audience, I was disappointed. She was stunning.
The bones of her small triangular face were so delicate that it
was difficult to believe she belonged to the same species as the
rest of us. All her features had the same exquisite refinement:
the unusually long brilliant eyes, the elegant nose, the finely
etched mouth, the pointed little chin. Above it floated a cloud
of strawberry blonde hair, beautifully cut to simulate a wild
and carefree mass. She was very tall and thinner than even
myself. Her gestures, as she continued her speech, managed
to seem both languid and full of barely suppressed fire.

Suddenly she swooped in a deep and graceful bow of the
sort made by ballet dancers, as if waiting for the applause.
She was smiling towards a spot screened from my view by a
prickly old juniper. I shifted to one side to see.

And saw David, kneeling at her feet just below the knoll.
I closed my eyes with the pain of it and cursed the damned
ewe that had brought me here. To see Ros was bad enough,
but David, subservient at her feet, was a sight I would have
done anything to avoid.

She was laughing now and gliding down from her knoll
towards him, her arms outstretched. I turned to leave. And
stepped on the one dry branch maliciously left over from the
long wet winter. It went off like a gun. Two faces jerked
round: hers the pale ivory mask of a goddess, his the rough
dark head of a primitive god.

I lurched into the clearing. 'I'm looking for a sheep,' I
blurted.

Two astonished faces.

Then the clear tinkling of her laughter. 'Little Bo Peep has
lost her sheep!' she cried delightedly, clapping her hands
together. 'David, you never told me that you stocked your
Forest of Arden with shepherdesses!'

I thought involuntarily of Hugh. Yes, they were similar, both carved out of the same brittle material. I remembered Hugh's malice, too, and waited for Ros to do her worst.

But it was David who scrambled heavily to his feet and came towards me. Perhaps he wished to be kind, hide my embarrassment from her shrewd eyes.

'I'm sorry,' I said to him. 'There's a gap in the wall over there – a ewe's got through, she'll have a single lamb with her. Have you seen them?'

'Ros, go and get Brendan, tell him there's some gap-walling.'

Ros Rawlinson an errand girl? She didn't move. She was watching us closely, her brilliant green eyes flicking from face to face.

'Oh, it's not urgent,' I said. 'Tom's put up a piece of corrugated iron. He's holding on in the lambing field till I get back. I have to go now. I'm sorry I disturbed you.' I turned to go.

'Wait.' Her voice was a little too imperious. She must have realised, because she added more softly, 'Please wait.'

She walked the few steps needed to join us, barely touching the ground. Then she was standing in front of me, smiling. From close up her eyes were hypnotic, like cut glass, faceted and sparkling with uncanny brilliance. Two pale green peridots, perhaps. Their long narrow setting made the effect even stranger. The green-eyed monster, envy. But of course she had no need to envy. I did, but I felt mesmerised like a rabbit by a stoat.

'You must be Charlotte,' she said. 'Everyone says such marvellous things about you at The Folly. I've been dying to meet you, but David insists you're in the thick of lambing and can't come over.'

I wasn't dying to meet her. Here was the moment I'd dreaded. Here we stood, side by side for gruesome comparison. Ros magnificent in a bulky Arran sweater which failed to disguise her sleek beauty, me scruffy as hell in the filthy old sweater and jeans I used for lambing.

She put out her hand. 'Well, I'm delighted to meet you. I'm Ros Rawlinson.'

Like a parody of a yokel, I wiped my dirty hand on my still

256

dirtier jeans and gave it to her. I tried to smile. 'I'm pleased to meet you, too. I've seen you on stage, of course . . . ' The usual banal remark. With every second I remained, I was sinking further into ignominy.

And then, rescue, from the most improbable source. I heard a thrashing of the undergrowth and a moment later the ewe shot into the clearing. Without thinking, I myself shot between David and Ros and flung myself at the ewe in a football tackle. As I sailed through the air, I realised the ridiculous sight I must be making. But instinct had been too strong. Sheep are damnable things to catch, you don't mess around thinking about your appearance.

When I picked myself off the ground, I was muddier than ever but holding the ewe triumphantly by one horn while Moss did a satisfied dance and the lamb skittered about its mother, bleating.

Ros captured the lamb and held it near her face in the classic pose of rural innocence, smiling with delight. David was smiling, too. I wished I could join in the amusement. I looked down, willing the earth to swallow me up.

Then I saw that it nearly had. By my feet was a little pit, about a foot deep and the same diameter. Beside it was what looked like a twig but turned out to be a tiny tree, with two unpromising forked roots. There were other things, too: a spade, a watering can, a piece of burlap with more tiny trees sticking out of it. And I realised that David hadn't been kneeling before her at all. He'd been planting a tree. The realisation brought with it the only small comfort of the whole awful episode.

There was a pile of soil at one side. I don't know why, but I couldn't resist bending down and plunging my free hand into it. It was cold but fine, a good tilth.

And then something strange happened. Ros and David disappeared, they didn't matter anymore. In the luminous little clearing another clearing appeared in my mind, and in it I saw only the tiny tree, its pathetic roots sticking up in the air. It wanted to be planted, and I wanted to plant it.

The sheep gave a lunge and startled me back to reality. I tightened my grip on her horn and spoke to her sharply.

Moss stationed himself in front of her and fixed her with a stern look.

David came to my side. I looked up at him. 'Do you know, I've never planted a tree. All those years on my parents' farm and I never planted a tree.'

My voice sounded odd. Perhaps that's why David was looking at me so intently. Or perhaps I had a smudge on my face from tackling the ewe. I reached up my free hand, but of course it was dirtier even than my face could be. I smiled awkwardly.

'Would you like to plant this one?' he said. 'I'll hold the ewe.'

He took her horn in his own rough hand. She recognised the hand of authority and stood absolutely still, glaring resentfully from her amber eyes.

'I don't know how.'

'It's all ready. I'll tell you.'

There was something odd happening. I was in a play where nobody had told me my role. The clearing had become extremely still. Even the lamb shut up. David's face was utterly inscrutable.

'Just set the tree into the hole,' he said. 'See that the edge of the hole is level with the planting line from the nursery – can you see it? Then scuff some soil under the roots and all around it. That's about enough. Ease it into contact with your fingers. Right. Now give it a little water, then add some more soil. Good. Pack it in gently and then some more water. Right. Make sure the soil's tight around the stem so it doesn't rock in the wind when it grows. Now cut a slit in that piece of loose turf, turn it upside down and put it round the tree. Firm it down and that's it.'

I stood up and looked at the bare twig I'd just planted. It seemed impossible that some day it would become a tree. A hundred years from now the tree would be a giant of the forest and I would be a heap of bones beneath some other piece of soil. And the extraordinary thing is, I didn't mind at all. In a hundred years it would be alive and I would be dead, and it was good that it should be so. Someone else would own Farleton Forest then, not even Matti. Someone else would come across this tree. He wouldn't know who had planted it and wouldn't care, and that was right, too. All that mattered was the tree itself.

I smiled at David but he didn't smile back. He was as inscrutable as before. Then I saw a flash of Arran sweater from the tail of my eye. I looked towards it just in time to see a smooth marble face carved with anger. It was so fleeting that I doubted my senses, because now the same face smiled across the clearing at me as if nothing had happened.

29

That night the scene in the forest clearing ran through my mind again and again as I kept watch over my sheep. I'd been too confused at the time to notice the significance of Ros's speech. If anything, I assumed it was one of Rosalind's and that she was reciting it simply to transport David back to their early days together. Now I realised they were some other character's lines. It was the words themselves that were significant.

Hath not old custom made this life more sweet than that of painted pomp? The message couldn't be clearer. Ros was, in the most charming and ingenious way, announcing her intention of giving up the painted pomp, returning to her old life – and to David. She'd even finished by descending from the knoll with arms stretched out to him. How she must have hated me, choosing that of all moments to blunder onto the scene! And how quickly her anger must have changed to satisfaction when I systematically made a fool of myself. I closed my eyes in pain at the thought of it.

The dismal memory combined with the dismal weather to make me thoroughly depressed. I was sitting Buddha-style in the back of the Land-Rover. The crackle of my anorak competed with the metallic sound of the rain beating down on the roof. Just beyond the open door, a curtain of the lousy stuff made vertical lines in the lamplight. Beyond that, a soggy field of soggy sheep contemplated whether or not to give birth tonight.

I rather hoped they'd wait. The few fatalities I'd had had been caused by the poor unsuspecting lambs coming out of that nice warm womb into a rain that chilled them to death in their first vulnerable hours. I'd tried my best, and saved some, but I couldn't avoid the conclusion that this was not the best of all possible worlds for a lamb to come into. I thought of their chums in Australia coming into a sun-kissed world and wondered why the hell anyone grew sheep in England, let alone on a hill farm. We should be growing rice. Or cranberries.

Or trees. The one memory that could ease my humiliation was the oak. It had really given me a thrill, planting that oak. When I tried to be rational, I saw that David had done most of the work and the tree itself would do the rest. None the less, it had been *my* fingers easing the tiny roots into contact with the life-giving soil. I wanted to do it again.

I looked out through the curtain of rain and saw the field ridged with open drains. Growing between them, a whole fieldful of little oaks. And then not-so-little oaks. And then enormous great oaks. The forest, come to reclaim the land.

I blinked and saw instead a sheep lying on the puddled grass and looking worried. I had the light focused on her, expecting trouble. Many of the Swaledales crossed with that particular tup were giving trouble.

I blinked again and thought I saw movement, far across the field, up against the forest. As I watched, the movement became more distinct. Someone was coming. Whoever it was was having difficulty negotiating the muddy field. It was a tall figure, and as it came nearer, I could see it was shrouded in a long yellow oilskin. There were a lot of those at The Folly. But why on earth should anyone from The Folly come to visit me at the dead of night?

Slim, too, despite the stiff folds of the oilskin. That ruled out everyone except –

And then she stood before me, rain running in great rivers down the oilskin and negating the warmth of her smile.

'May I come in?'

It was surreal. I should be in a New York brownstone, opening the door wide for my honoured guest. Would you like a cup of tea? Sherry?

'Of course.' I moved as far to one side as the wheelcase would allow and made room for Ros. She climbed in grace- fully and settled herself into a Buddha position like mine. Together we sat looking out into the night. I wondered if I should be asking for her autograph.

'Not much fun for you,' she said, waving a fine-boned hand towards the great outdoors.

'No.' Keep it short, I told myself. She's used to speaking great lines, don't give her yet another advantage over you. Then I wondered why I bothered. She wasn't really my rival at all. I was out of the running, had never been in it. Further, she had no idea that I loved David. Why should I be so churlish? She'd made quite an effort to come and see me – never mind what for. The least I could do was be hospitable.

'Would you like some coffee?'

'Mmm, lovely.'

I reached behind and fetched the giant thermos. There was only one cup – one doesn't expect guests in a midnight lambing field. I filled it and gave it to her.

'What about you?' she asked.

'I've just had some.'

She sipped the coffee gratefully. I couldn't see her very well – the light was trained on the expectant ewe. I could have put on the inside light but couldn't bear to reveal my bedraggled self to her.

'That sheep looks miserable,' she said.

'She is. She's supposed to be lambing, but she's having second thoughts. Trying to put off the dread moment.'

'I don't blame her. Couldn't this be done indoors?'

'It can, but there's too much risk of infection spreading.'

I couldn't believe she'd squelched her way here to get a lesson on hill farming.

'That was a brilliant piece of upstaging,' she said.

Her tone was no different from that in which she'd inquired after the sheep. I was caught unawares. 'Sorry?'

'This afternoon. In the forest. First that amazing display of acrobatics to catch the sheep, then planting the tree.'

Slowly my mind cranked into motion. 'I'm not sure I know what you're talking about. It wasn't intentional.'

She shrugged, drained the coffee cup and handed it back to me. 'I suppose you know why I came back?'

'More or less. Your speech made it pretty clear.'

She turned to me. I couldn't see her very well and was glad I couldn't see those eerie faceted eyes that had hypnotised me this afternoon. 'I never wanted to divorce David, you know.'

'Your personal life is none of my business.'

There was a long pause while she appeared to scrutinise me, though she, too, could see very little. Then she continued as if I hadn't said anything. 'It was a matter of logistics, that's all. David up here, me in London or touring or whatever. No marriage could take that kind of strain.'

Why was she telling me this? Whatever they'd said about me at The Folly must have included discretion. She was notoriously close about her private life, must have made sure that I wasn't the sort of person who'd rush off to Fleet Street with a scoop.

'But lately I've been wondering if some kind of compromise would be possible. Then it came to me. It was so obvious I wondered why I hadn't thought of it before. There are heaps of nice estates in the Cotswolds, and it's just about near enough for David and Matti and me to live there with a *pied à terre* in London while I'm working.'

Was she mad? 'What on earth would David do in the Cotswolds?'

'The same thing he does here. Plant trees. Train horses. If Farleton Estate isn't worth enough to exchange for something there, I could probably make up the difference. It wouldn't have occurred to me if Hugh hadn't come to New York.'

So Hugh had gone to New York. I'd thought he was joking, at Christmas, but apparently not. 'What does Hugh have to do with it?' I asked cautiously.

'Property. He's a property developer. He talked a lot about some properties he had his eye on in the Cotswolds, and suddenly everything clicked into place.'

Poor old Hugh! He'd gone to New York to woo Ros and instead given her the perfect plan for luring David back. I almost felt sorry for him.

'David would never go to the Cotswolds,' I said.

'I know that. Now.' She emphasised the last word. I felt her faceted eyes on me and was more grateful than ever for the dark. 'I didn't know, then, that there was anything keeping him up here,' she continued. 'He'd always been so blasé about the "Farleton heritage", I was sure it wouldn't make any difference to him where he planted his trees. If he planted them near enough London, we could get together again.'

I tried to imagine David on a balmy picture-postcard estate in the Cotswolds subsidised by his wife. Being a part of her kingdom, wheeling about the outermost reaches of her orbit. Would Brendan and Belle be there, too? None of it fitted, the picture refused to form. 'I didn't know then that there was something else keeping him here,' she continued.

I waited, unsuspecting, for her to go on. There was a long pause before she spoke again. Then:

'I didn't realise that he loved you.'

Cruel. Oh, monstrously cruel. How those uncanny green eyes must be glittering now! Why was she doing this to me? I'd never done her any harm, I'd never even met her before today. This was horrible revenge indeed for my clumsy interruption of her great scene. Then I pulled my thoughts together. I was being unfair. She didn't know I loved David, she didn't know how deeply her words had bitten. I said nothing for a while, busy gathering together some dignity.

'David loves everything and everyone on his estate,' I said at last. 'That's why the land responds so well to him. That's also why he wouldn't move to the Cotswolds, or anywhere else. It's only his ancestors and the whole business of "heritage" he despises. The land itself is different. He'd never leave that. If he's refused your offer, I'm sorry, but it's nothing to do with me.'

'That's not what Astrid says.'

'Astrid?'

'We're quite close, Astrid and me. She is looking after my son,' she reminded me. 'We keep in pretty close contact. She wasn't exactly forthcoming, but I finally convinced her that I needed to know what was going on. So she told me.'

I stared at the dark shape beside me. 'Ros, I can assure you that nothing whatsoever is going on between David and me.'

The shape shrugged again. 'That's David's problem. Mine is that he's so obsessed with you that he'd never leave while you're here.'

My mind flashed back to the threatening note, the phone call, the woman trying to disguise her voice as a man's. But that was long before Christmas, and anyway, Ros wouldn't stoop to something so crass. I suddenly felt tired.

'Ros, I'm sorry you're having problems, but I can tell you one thing: David isn't the slightest bit in love with me. Believe me, I'd know if he were. You must have misunderstood Astrid. Her English is pretty idiosyncratic.'

'David's English is fine. Astrid showed me a letter he'd written her last autumn, not long after he met you. David's English makes it perfectly clear.'

'This is ridiculous.'

'Is it? David and Astrid are pretty close, too. Who better to confide in than Astrid, safely in London for most of the year. He's got far too much pride to tell Brendan or Belle, knowing he'd have to suffer their well-meant sympathy every day.'

'He's got far too much pride to tell Astrid either – if there were anything to tell. It's totally out of character.'

'Exactly. He must have been in agony when he wrote that letter. Very likely he regretted it as soon as he sent it.'

'I don't believe a word of this.'

'Charlotte, I've *read* the letter. And when I saw the two of you together today, I knew it was true.'

My head was swimming. The idiotic spark of hope that had never quite died suddenly flared up again. I squashed it down as hard as I could. Nothing that Ros said made sense. If he had indeed written such a letter in an insane moment of infatuation, he must have changed his mind. If he did still love me, he had only to say so.

The brief battle between hope and reality had worn me out. My limbs were heavy and my mind was clouding over again. I said wearily, 'Well, if he was interested in me then, he isn't now, that I can promise you.'

Neither of us said anything for a long time. I wished she would go away. That first pleasure of having company, even that of my successful rival, was gone with a vengeance. I wanted to lick my emotional wounds alone. I wanted to be swallowed up into the peaceful dark of the night again, alone. 'What do you want of me?' I asked.

A long silence. Then, 'It must have occurred to you that it wasn't easy for me to come and see you.'

No, it hadn't occurred to me. I'd been too preoccupied with my own misery to see hers. Now the scene was forming in a completely different way. She'd confessed to me that she'd tried to get David back and failed. Yes, it must have cost her a lot. Why had she done it? 'Why *did* you come?' I asked.

Another long silence. 'To ask your help,' she said quietly.

'What do you mean?'

'If you were to make it clear to David that you're not interested in him, I think he might . . . change his mind. Be willing to leave.'

Her voice was hesitant. But then, she was an actress. And desperate. She must be, to ask my help. It was ludicrous. I nearly said so, then realised something else. She had no idea that I loved David. She'd left that out of her equation. I wondered briefly if I should tell her, but something – perhaps some age-old female instinct – stopped me. 'It wouldn't make any difference,' I said briskly.

'Then you refuse?'

'It wouldn't make any difference,' I said, more impatiently this time. 'It's much simpler than that. *David will not leave his land*. If you want him back, you'll have to come back here. I'm sure David would be delighted.'

The ewe was stirring. She gave a pathetic bleat and looked hopefully at the Land-Rover. I could feel my muscles tensing. As I'd thought, it was going to be a difficult birth. I unwound my limbs and got down out of the Land-Rover.

Ros followed me. 'What makes you think so? Has he said anything to you?'

'Of course not. You should know by now: nobody at The Folly ever talks about their private lives.'

'Then why are you so sure?'

I stopped halfway to the ewe. The rain was coming down hard, already seeping into an inevitable gap in my anorak. I faced Ros. It felt better to be out in the open, on the land. 'For someone who used to be married to him, you really don't know him very well. Have you ever thought what it feels like to have planted hundreds of thousands of trees? Do you really think he could leave them, just swap them for another bunch planted by someone else?'

'For love?' she suggested.

'There's more than one kind of love,' I said quietly. And rushed off to my ewe.

30

The next night the yellow oilskin appeared again at the edge of the field. I shouldn't have felt so agitated. I had thought calmly about the things she'd said and pieced together a plausible enough explanation: just as I had snatched at tiny signs of affection in David and magnified them into potential love, Ros had fastened onto the only explanation she could think of for David's refusal to leave Keldreth – another woman. I was the only candidate around.

But she had burst into my life in a most unwelcome way. I'd been trying to recapture my pre-Cappelrigg self, she who had shrugged off the whole notion of love. That earlier and more carefree self had rejected the importance of men – in women's lives in general and in mine in particular. It was ridiculous for women to be dependent on love. There were other things we could do with our lives. Biding our time before Prince Charming made his inevitable appearance was no longer acceptable. Yes, I could live without David, I'd decided.

But it was a precarious victory over my feelings, and here was Ros, coming along to destroy my fragile peace once again. I tried to think how to avoid her. It wasn't easy, in the middle of a lambing field. Nowhere to hide. Further, the field was nearly empty of sheep by now. Only one ancient ewe remained to give birth. She'd been a big mistake. She should have gone to market last autumn but had somehow escaped my notice. Now she was massively pregnant and overdue. I was sure there were a dozen lambs at least in there. Well, three anyway. The only other ewe in the field was one who'd lost her lamb this afternoon. I'd kept her there partly as company for the old lady and partly so I could coax her to take the old ewe's surplus lamb in lieu of her own.

Now I waited, my patience growing thin. I don't know who I resented more – the cantankerous old ewe or Ros, still progressing steadily across the field towards me. It was raining of course, the wretched stuff coming down like stair rods. I was cold, tired, bored, hungry, damp and angry.

I left the Land-Rover, my wellies hitting the soggy ground with a squelch so violent that mud sprayed up on my jeans. I strode across to the ewe, who'd found the one little hillock in the whole field that wasn't totally saturated. Years of experience, I suppose, and the same cunning that warned her to keep her head down last autumn when I was culling.

I glared down at her. 'Come on, you old devil. You can't keep them in there forever.'

She glared up at me. Oh yes I can.

Footsteps squelched behind me. Then a voice. 'Charlotte?'

I wheeled round and saw David, his hair plastered down like a swimmer just emerged from the ocean. My first reaction was irritation. He didn't even have the nous to put up the hood of the oilskin. My next was surprise. He was the last person I expected to meet in the lambing field. He should be snug and warm at The Folly, preparing for his reunion with his wife. Why else had I played the bitter role of matchmaker? True, it hadn't taken much doing. I'd only pointed out the obvious: that David would have her back as long as she didn't make him give up the land. Ah. Was he coming here to thank me? I felt like telling him what he could do with his thanks but instead looked at the ewe and said shortly, 'She's late. Do you have any magic charms? Maybe I should consult a Druid.'

'I want to talk to you.'

'Here? Now?'

'Yes.'

I sighed and we squelched back to the Land-Rover. At the last minute I veered away from the back. I didn't want a repeat of the two Buddhas and anyway my legs were cramped. I got into the driver's seat and curtly indicated the other side to David.

The whole vehicle stank of sheep. I'd had to persuade quite a few sodden lambs to accept the dubious gift of life. They'd left behind a medley of odours: birth fluids, wet wool, the astringent scent of antiseptic. An inauspicious setting for his speech of thanks, but I liked it. I was letting go at last and it felt good. It didn't suit me to be so dependent on a man, any man. The time would come perhaps when I could look at that big rough stubborn face without a scalpel cutting my innards into little pieces. Maybe now? Should I switch on the light and see?

'Put on the light,' he said.

I jerked my head round towards his silhouette. Was he reading my mind? I switched on the light and looked at him, then looked quickly away again. No, the time hadn't come.

He was fumbling in the pocket of his oilskin. I ignored him, watching the bolshy old ewe in the wing mirror. It was a false pregnancy, she was doing this on purpose because I'd thought to send her to market.

A crisp white envelope appeared in front of me.

'It's from Ros,' he said.

It was the first time he'd ever mentioned her name, even alluded to her existence. If it hadn't been for the others at The Folly, I would never have known she had anything to do with their lives.

'Why is she writing to me?' I asked.

'I don't know.'

I gave him a long hard look and decided he was telling the truth. How could I doubt? He never lied. The only deceit was in what he omitted to say. Then I realised. Of course. It was *she* who was thanking me. A spurt of anger died when I remembered she had no idea of my feelings for David. The letter wasn't meant as malice. Even so, I didn't want to read it in David's presence.

'Thank you,' I said formally. 'There's no need for you to stay.'

'Ros said I was to stay while you read it.' A ghost of a smile. 'People tend to do what Ros says.'

The smile told me nothing about their reconciliation or anything else. I opened the letter. I wasn't relishing this. I would have to do a neat piece of acting myself to remain composed. I took a few surreptitious deep breaths and began.

Dear Charlotte,

All right, you win. There are just two things I want to say. The first is to let you know that you didn't fool me. You may have fooled the others and even David, but not me. Within minutes of your dramatic entrance in that clearing, I had a pretty good idea of how things stood – both ways.

The second is to let you know that the estate is tied up – that is part of the divorce settlement. When David dies, the whole lot goes to Matti, and there's nothing anyone can do about it. You won't get a look-in, nor will any kids you and David have. If that doesn't bother you, fine. It would sure as hell bother me, and it may explain why David's been so slow: in financial terms, he's got nothing to offer.

One last thing. Please don't turn Matti against me. Astrid's been marvellous, and even David has refrained. If there's anything I regret about my life, it's what I did to Matti. It's a rotten lousy trick – bringing a kid into the world to solve his parents' problems. I wouldn't blame him one bit if he hated both of us. The only reason he doesn't is Astrid. Astrid's the only person I know who understands what totally unselfish love is. Hugh was an ass to divorce her. I told him so when he came to see me in New York. He was not amused. So please don't turn Matti against me. You may not believe this, but in my own way I love him very much. Leave me something for my old age, please.

You can let David read this if you wish. It's up to you.

Ros

Did I wish? I thought long and hard about it. In the letter she linked David and myself in an unmistakable way. Showing the letter to him would amount to a tacit agreement that it was true – on my part anyway. It would be out in the open at last. All my fine acting, which had fooled everyone, except Ros, would come to an end.

What if there was nothing there to match it? I had only Ros's word that he loved me in return, and she was hardly an impartial judge. If she had misunderstood, even Just Good Friends would disappear. David would become awkward, embarrassed, would avoid me. In time, my friends at The Folly would, too. I would be completely alone, farming a farm I wasn't even sure I believed in any more. My whole future was at stake. It would be so much easier just to put the letter back in its envelope, thank him for delivering it and send him away. If he did love me, it would come out in time, wouldn't it?

My friends at The Folly said they admired my spirit, but all they meant was a wild ride on a bridleless horse, a midnight trek to a Druid ritual, the rescue of some sheep in a blizzard. What did any of that matter compared to the courage it would take to show the letter to David? The danger I put my body in was nothing, the danger to my heart and soul was another thing altogether.

Anyway, slow and steady was my way. The unwavering flame rather than the fireworks. Fireworks were for people like Ros Rawlinson, not me. Should I toss a coin? Pluck the petals of a flower? No, that was too cowardly, even for me.

The answer, when it came, was stupendously simple. I would let David decide. I would look once more at that beloved face and ask myself just one question. Can I risk living the rest of my life with Just Good Friends? Or must I risk everything for the ultimate?

I looked at David. And gave him the letter.

As soon as he started reading it, a strange thing happened. A sense of peace came over me. It was a letting-go, but a far different one than I'd felt earlier that night. That one had been false: I'd been forcing myself not to care because I had no alternative. This time there *had* been a choice, and I knew I'd made the right decision. Either way, something had to be decided. Only a few more minutes of waiting left.

He finished the letter, folded it, put it back in the envelope and gave it back to me.

A few more seconds.

I waited, hands folded in my lap, looking straight ahead into the darkness. I had made my move. Now it was up to him.

And waited.

Finally, 'She's right, of course.'

'About what?'

'Everything. Our marriage, too. She was right to leave

me.' His voice sounded rough and disused. It must have been a long time since he'd let it talk about such things. 'It was my fault that it failed.'

I held my breath. I think it was then that I began to understand. It was so simple I hardly dared believe it. I let my breath out carefully and began. 'Isn't that a rather unsophisticated view?' When he didn't reply, I continued, 'Does anyone believe these days that the fault is one-sided?'

'When one side is a Farleton, yes.'

Ah.

'My father destroyed his marriage, Hugh destroyed his, I destroyed mine. Perfect record.'

'The Farletons are no good at marriage?' I suggested. 'I'm quoting Belle, who was quoting you. Don't be angry with her. It was the day I mistook Matti for Astrid's son. Belle simply sketched in the family history so I wouldn't put my foot in it again. She told me then that you blamed yourself, that you were convinced there was something wrong with the Farletons that made for lousy marriages. David, has it ever occurred to you that that's a pretty damn stupid analysis? We're talking about three completely different men married to completely different women. Do you really think there's some genetic fault that overrides – '

'Not genetic, but – '

'Or anything else. All right, I admit that your father sounds a real bastard, and even Ros says that Hugh was an ass to divorce Astrid. *But you're a different person.* There was nothing preordained about your marriage, David, and I'm not letting you out of this Land-Rover until you admit it.' A glance at the wing mirror – praying now that the old ewe would wait a bit longer.

'It's pretty obvious, isn't it? I was obsessed with my work; I neglected her. She was right to leave.'

'God, you're stubborn. Okay, I'll say it for you: Ros is and always was a charming but frivolous person with no imagination. She failed to see the significance of what you were doing on your estate, shrugged her pretty shoulders and did a flit. No? You don't like that one? All right, try this: Both of you were too young and stupid to have the slightest notion of what marriage is. Of course it failed, but that doesn't mean – ' I stopped myself just in time. *That doesn't mean a second marriage would fail, too*. The unsaid words hung in the silence. I hoped he hadn't heard them. There were limits to the amount of pride I was willing to jettison.

'That doesn't mean a second marriage would fail, too?' he suggested softly.

I froze, then glanced again in the wing mirror. Come on, you old devil, get me out of this.

'Charlotte, do you really think I haven't thought about it, over and over again? But I couldn't convince myself. I couldn't believe I might be given a second chance.'

I closed my eyes. The waiting was over at last. 'Why didn't you talk to me?'

'Cowardice.'

Dear clumsy David, unable to put on a smooth façade. Unable to lie. The only way he could hide the truth was through silence. I turned to him. 'Didn't it occur to you that *I* might have something to say about the matter?'

'Not for a long time. You weren't exactly very friendly the first time we met.'

'Neither were you.'

'Or the second. Or the third.'

'Hate at first sight.'

'I never hated you, Charlotte.'

'Not even when I purloined your favourite horse and risked her neck?'

'There was no risk. You've seen the field since then – it's completely flat. Olwen knows where to put her feet.'

'But you were so furious, I thought – '

'I was furious with myself. Charlotte, do you have any idea how you looked, flying out of the mist like that? Your hair streaming behind you, your face flushed with excitement? I'd never seen anything so beautiful. If someone had told me to invent the perfect woman, it would have been you. Then I saw Ros's face superimposed on yours and I thought no, never again. I won't let this happen again. So I pretended to myself that you were just company for Belle, that it was nice to be on good terms with at least one neighbour.'

It seemed extraordinary that we should be sitting in my

Land-Rover calmly discussing the past – our past. And then again, not so extraordinary. On some subterranean level, we'd been having this conversation for a long long time. Only then it had been two separate conversations. Now that the two were coming together, there was a certain inevitability about it. 'Ros said you wrote to Astrid. Did you?'

'A week or two after you rode Olwen. I was sending some money for a school trip of Matti's and I added a short letter. It was late at night. I suppose I had that mad urge that people do when they're in love, just to say the loved one's name.'

Which Astrid then mispronounced. How odd that I'd suspected a letter, way back then, when I'd no idea of David's feelings. 'Can I ask what was in it?'

'Not much. Just that we had a new neighbour, that you were extremely agreeable.' He hesitated. 'I think I might have said something else. Something like wishing I'd met someone like you instead of Ros, all those years ago.'

No wonder Ros had attached such importance to the letter. It was the supreme insult, his desire to annihilate her part in his past and put me in her place. I leaned back, feeling suddenly exasperated. 'David, didn't you ever think that I might feel the same way about you?'

There was a long difficult silence from the other side of the Land-Rover. In it the rain drummed on the roof louder than before. His hair was still very wet, forming little points which aimed trickles of water down his face. Irrelevantly I imagined myself rubbing that big stubborn head dry in a nice clean towel. It would feel so good. Perhaps the time would come when such things were possible.

'Once or twice I wondered,' he said at last. 'The day I delivered your firewood. When you burst into tears – "There's such a thing as too much beauty," you said. I know you meant the land, but – '

'I meant you as well. The two are the same, really.'

'That's what made it so much worse – seeing how much you cared about the land. Ros never did. It was just a great big stage for her. She wasn't interested in what went into it. It had no meaning for her.'

'It probably would now. Belle's right, and Effie. You've

275

cut yourself off from the outside world too much, you're out of touch. You'd be surprised how many people would care about what you're doing. I'm not all that unusual, you know.'

'Yes, you are.' He reached out and took my hand.

It was the first time he'd touched me since the day of the kites, when he'd led me through the pitch-black forest. It went through me like an electrical charge. 'Why didn't you tell me these things then? When you suspected that I – ' I couldn't use the word love, not yet. 'Cared about you?'

'Cowardice,' he said again. 'I knew you were different from Ros, but *I* was no different. Since it was my fault that Ros left, I couldn't believe that you wouldn't leave, too.'

All those months of misery, assuming he was comparing me to Ros. He *was* comparing, but in a way I'd never suspected. He *was* haunted by her image, but it was a negative one, the ghost of a failure he didn't dare risk a second time. His hand was a warm human link between us. I remembered the day of the kites, when we'd been so close in mind and body.

He turned clumsily in his seat. The look on his face was terribly serious and rather frightening. 'It was the day we watched the kites together – that's when I finally admitted to myself how much I loved you,' he said. 'I couldn't let it happen. The only way I could think of to keep you was to stop loving you. If I could turn the clock back and see you as just a friend . . . '

He took me in his arms and held me so close I almost stopped breathing. 'Lottie, I'm sorry, I never even thought of how you might feel. Ros is right. Astrid's probably the only person who knows how to love unselfishly. I only thought about myself and my own threatened feelings.'

His voice was muffled in the collar of my anorak. I could feel his breath warm against my neck. I held him tight, annihilating every scrap of space between us. It was better to be close than to breathe, all that mattered was to hold onto each other at last, after all the months of waiting. I think I mumbled soothing words, whether for myself or for him, I didn't know.

He was mumbling, too. 'And when Effie phoned and said

you were up on the moor in the blizzard,' he was saying into my collar, 'something snapped, I went berserk. I hated you, Lottie. I went up to the moor in a rage, hating you, almost wishing you *were* dead because then it would all be over and nothing would matter ever again. And then when I found you it seemed as if you *were* dead and I tried to make you come to life again, and you did. But then the pain began again, and I couldn't bear to see you. But there you were, day after day at The Folly.'

His wet hair was against my cheek, cold and real. 'I thought you were just angry with me for being so foolish. I thought you were comparing me to Ros. When she phoned on Christmas Day, I was sure she was coming back to claim you, that it was what you'd been hoping for all along.'

He released me a little and looked incredulously into my face. 'You thought I wanted her back?'

'Well,' I said foolishly, 'most men would.'

'Lottie, I stopped caring about Ros years ago. I don't think we'd been married a year before I realised it was a mistake. It wasn't her fault, we were far too young, we didn't know each other at all. Our worlds were completely separate. There was no communication between them. She did try at first, and so did I. I went to see her plays. But they didn't have any meaning for me, and my trees had no meaning for her.'

'But you seemed so agitated when she phoned – '

'Of course I was. Ros coming back like a ghost from the past to remind me that I had no future with you. Of course I was upset.'

I started to laugh, very quietly. It must have startled him, because he loosed his hold and I leaned back against the seat, laughing harder now. 'I can't believe how idiotic we've been. All these months of misery for both of us, all of it for nothing. If only – ' I sat up straight again and faced him. 'David, I won't ask you again why you didn't tell me all this ages ago. I think I understand why. But for God's sake, *will you please talk to me from now on*? In future, when you hate me, just say so. When you love me, say so. How the hell are we going to understand each other if you keep me out? And if you think for one minute that you *will* keep me out of your future, think again.'

'Lottie – '

'Not yet, I haven't finished yet. I want one thing understood right from the start: no more ghosts. No more taboos. No more "Matti's mother is a taboo subject round here", okay? If you hadn't banished her into silence, she wouldn't have grown into such a monster in your mind and mine. You know what? I think I rather like Ros. One thing I do know, she's no villain – '

'I never said – '

'I know you didn't. Big gallant David, taking all the blame on himself. Ros isn't so foolish. She knows it takes two. In her own way, she's probably been as lumbered with guilt as you have. And tonight she's finally shed it. This,' I said, picking up her letter. It was rather rumpled from being squashed between us. 'She didn't have to write this. She could have slipped away without saying a word. She knew. She wrote this letter. And sent you with it.'

He looked warily at the letter. 'It didn't strike me as a particularly friendly letter.'

'Why should it be? It's the act that counts, not how it's wrapped up. Leave her some pride.'

'She couldn't have known what would happen.'

'Perhaps not, but she knew *something* would happen. And she knew there was a good chance it would be this.'

He said nothing for a while. I could see it would be a long time before Ros Rawlinson became a name he could speak like any other, but we'd made a start. I could also see that Ros's letter, however sharp the words, was an act of love for David, probably her last. I wondered briefly if I should point this out to David, giving him his one last chance to reclaim her. But I knew he wouldn't take it. Where did all this confidence come from? David, of course. David who couldn't lie. There was no way, after tonight, that I could doubt his love. Whatever the future, it was *our* future.

I suddenly became aware that he was watching me. Smiling. 'You know why she really left?' he said. 'Her agent phoned – she's been offered Lady Macbeth at the RSC. Her first mature role ever, the first of the greats.'

'Do you mind?'

'No, I wish her well. You're right – it *is* a friendly letter.'

I raised one eyebrow.

'After all, she could have told you what I'm like,' he said. 'Could have warned you off.'

'And what are you like, David Farleton?'

'Stubborn.'

'That's for sure.'

'Obsessed with my trees. A workaholic. Selfish. Too dim-witted to see other people's feelings. Cowardly in expressing my own. Middle-aged. Scruffy. Antisocial.'

'And I'm sure you snore like thunder. Come here.'

31

The next day it was summer, or so it seemed, though I admit that after David came to me I lost all sense of time. The weeks tumbled by in a vortex of sensations, a crazy collage made up of exquisite happenings, each one a jewel with a lifetime's happiness cōmpressed into it.

Who was this lover of mine? Prince Charming he was not, though we played that game, too. But charm is too pallid a word for this ruler of my heart. He came from beyond the realm of mortals, bringing with him an intensity that belonged to the golden age when giants walked the earth. A giant, yes, like his horses and his trees and the huge sweep of landscape that surrounded us and played backdrop to our love.

Spring or summer, I don't know which, but the earth was waking up and I was waking up with it out of a long dark chilly sleep. This was no time for a cautious extending of hands towards a modest flame, take it easy, don't rush it. No, I plunged into the centre of the fire and gasped with joy as the heat seared me to sudden life. The time for the slow steady burning of my candle was over. Why shouldn't I, too, experience the explosion of fireworks lighting up the dark sky of our recent past? We had been apart far too long already, David and I, and in those months of misunderstanding suppressed an arsenal of passion. It burst forth now with a force which shook us both loose from the moorings of reason and we delighted in our madness.

Sometimes I lay in his arms and thought yes, I could die now and know I'd lived. It was almost as if we wished to destroy each other with love, as if only by annihilating ourselves could we dissolve the boundary which made of us two separate people. I remembered the morning when Olwen had thundered out of the grey mist of a dawn which itself was a dissolving of boundaries. She had seemed a giant being created out of the primeval earth. Then she had seemed to be the force of creation itself. I saw how much that awesome experience had prefigured what was to come. With each coming together, David and I were creating the earth and at the same time sweeping away that creation with our violence.

And yet at the same time we were simply two people, living our lives, getting up in the morning, doing our day's work, to all outward appearances no different from any other two people in the world. I suppose we even brushed our teeth.

*　　*　　*

Morning. Dashing to the window and drinking in a landscape suddenly gone green and steamy in the sun. Flying downstairs to find Tarzan irreverently playing with a note shoved through the letterslot. 'Give that to me, cat. You can't read.'

Reading:

Charlotte. I came early this morning and found a thorn thicket suddenly grown up round your castle. How can you do this to me? Meet me in the northwest sector. You know the spot. Do not pause for breakfast or I will throttle you. Yours ever, Prince Glowering.

The same route I'd taken on that first day, less than a year ago or was it a lifetime? I might indeed have been Sleeping Beauty slumbering for twenty years. Nothing looked or was the same. The oaks in the grove behind my house were still keeping themselves to themselves, playing at winter, but the trees in the little dip where the syke ran were less stingy. Rowans and birches and hawthorns were starting to leaf up, their tiny new leaves like green polka dots. I gazed at the landscape through them as through a dotted veil on an old-fashioned lady's hat.

My fields were full of sheep. Some of the earliest lambs were already quite big, their spindly flanks long since filled out and their sturdy back legs propelling them across the land at careless speed. A little gang of them suddenly shot into motion all at once. They made a feverish dash halfway across the field and then stopped just as abruptly, as if someone had pulled the plug on their electricity supply. Their too-big ears stuck out at right angles like propellers, and I thought that they might do a vertical take off. But they kept to the ground on their homeward dash, all except the smallest one which sprang into the air three times in succession as if on a pogo stick.

The ground was still sodden, but I barely noticed, didn't care. My feet hardly touched the ground these days. I floated across my soggy land in a dream of anticipation. The edge of the forest, once as dark and glowering as my prince, now drew me towards it. Even if David hadn't told me where he was, I would have found him as fast as any iron-filing its magnet. As mindless as that.

I climbed the familiar stile and dropped down to the other side so fast that I almost didn't notice the strange new leaf which had sprouted overnight: a piece of paper, terribly white, sticking out of a hole in an old beech tree by the stile. I plucked it down from its quaint postbox and saw the familiar writing of my lover:

> *Enter these enchanted woods*
> *You who dare.*

Who would have guessed that my lover, the surly squire, had a penchant for poetry? I recognised it, too: Meredith, from 'The Woods of Westermain'. I put the bit of paper in my pocket and filled in the next lines:

> *Nothing harms beneath the leaves*
> *More than waves a swimmer cleaves.*

And swam through the forest. It did feel like the sea, a green green sea above me, beside me, even under my wellies, so many different shades that I longed for a paintbrush and palette. The soft grey-green of the rowans just unfurling their brand-new leaves. The sharp apple-green of the birches. The larches had just achieved their most vibrant colouring, threatening to overshadow everything else in the forest. The spruces, in a show of one-upmanship, retaliated by thrusting across the path their two-tone branches, the bright new growth at the tips giving depth to the older and more sedate parts that had weathered already dozens of winters. Chestnuts unfolded like the great grassy hands of the Green Man of myth, and grass there was, too, brand-new blades bristling along the path, a giant's crewcut. From a thick swathe of emerald green leaves rose the varnished yellow flowers of the celandine.

The birds had ignored the morning curfew to continue their vocal olympics. Thousands of little throats strained to variations of 'I'm-the-greatest.' Right now a thrush was winning: 'Pretty-bird, pretty-bird' and a flourish of trills. Then a blackbird stepped in with a long sustained melody and overrode the thrush. The song ended with a piercing shriek which silenced the whole forest for a fraction of a second. Into the gap stepped a chaffinch with its siren song, a rich cascade of trills ending with a few sharp jabs at the end nearly as vulgar as the blackbird's shriek. And underneath it all, the rich bird-babble of countless voices making up the chorus.

Enchanted woods indeed. I hugged the forest to me, feeling immeasurably rich, then set my radar going. Where was my magus, the impresario who had laid on this lavish forest opera for my pleasure? I tried to remember where, last summer, I'd plunged off the path in angry pursuit of the chainsaw's whine. But the green wall on either side was anonymous. No little sign saying This Way Please.

And then, just beyond a bend in the path, there he was, my demon lover in scruffy jeans and plaid shirt. '*I* dare!' I shouted exuberantly. I ran to him and he to me, and at the meeting point I felt his hands on my waist and then myself being swung high up into the air with one great thrust of his arms. I was suspended above him, like a doll or a kitten. A single shriek of shock escaped, my contribution to the birdsong. Then I laughed and tried to retrieve my dignity – 'What will the neighbours say?' – but he held me all the more firmly in those big resin-stained hands. Finally he lowered me towards him and kissed me.

He took my hand. As if a green door had opened in the leafy wall, we slipped into the depths of the forest and padded softly along the pathless way to the place of our first meeting. Less than a year. I remembered how angry I'd been at the chainsaw and its owner. I gripped his hand more tightly in retrospective fear. What if I *hadn't* gone in pursuit of the chainsaw? So many what-ifs that might have prevented our meeting. The frisson that all lovers feel, knowing the multitude of tiny chances that brought them together, knowing that just one tiny break in the chain would have damned them to separateness.

Little gaps were appearing in the wood, places where single trees had been extracted. Then a bigger gap. We stood side by side at the edge of it. I stared. Whatever I had expected from Prince Glowering's note, it wasn't this.

A tiny clearing, neat and round and glowing green with the new moss which covered the ground like a velvet spread. On it, another spread: a blanket playing at being a tablecloth. And on that, a picnic breakfast. We sat down to eat. Musak courtesy of Farleton Forest Orchestra and Chorus. A robin perched on a small tree stump, his shiny black eye fixed on my bread.

Suddenly I realised. The stump was none other than the birch David had felled onto me. I tore off a piece of bread and tossed it towards the robin. He hopped down, retrieved it and flew off. I like to believe that the solo which followed was his thanks.

After we had eaten and cleared the remains of breakfast from the blanket, we found our own way of giving thanks, of celebrating the place of our first meeting.

*   *   *

It was time to take some sheep up to the moor again, those who had failed to produce lambs or lost them. There weren't many, but even those few mouths would deplete the grass I needed for the ewes with lambs. David came with me. 'Two humans and a dog,' I said. 'A lavish escort for so few sheep.'

'Should I go away again?'

I flung my arms around him. Oh, the freedom of being able to touch at last! Never again would I have to restrain my hands from roughing up that mass of black hair. Now my fingers could wander at will over that heavy face, memorising each carved crevice as much as my eyes. His body was mine and mine his.

Moss looked away in disgust. Very businesslike, Moss, no time for the frivolity of an unexpected embrace.

We had no time either, but we made it. Early morning, before our separate day's work began, and then in the evenings which were courteously lengthening for us. I would have despised a lover who dropped everything to rush puppy-like after me. David *was* his work. How could Ros have expected otherwise? I didn't. I loved him as he was, and he was Farleton Forest.

'My love is a mighty tree trunk!' I sang out to him as we toiled our way up the green track behind my silly sheep.

'Humph.'

'My love's hair is a wreath of laurel leaves!' The sun, low in the west, set the tips of his tangled hair ablaze, darkened his face.

'Humph.'

'My love's eyes gaze out into the night like a great owl from the branches of a tree!'

'My love should watch where she's going or she'll fall off the edge of the track. Come here, Charlotte.'

I came here. Entwined, we rounded the top of the track and were on the moor. The moor was ablaze, too, the sun sweeping across the vast expanse of last year's heather and making it glow a rich henna colour. The stones were tinted pink. Even my sheep, ambling off, had a touch of blush to their fleeces.

We sat down on a large stone, our backs turned firmly against the Druid site. Very probably the stone was on the ley line. I didn't care. I'd never taken seriously the power of the ley line, and now I had a power of my own that was stronger. Druids, demons, evil spirits – all of them crumbled like vampires into dust when faced with the day of love. The current between David and myself was enough to blow a stronger fuse than that of the ley line.

There would be another bonfire on the moor on May Day and no doubt one on Midsummer's Eve, too. There was nothing we could do about the first – there wasn't enough time. But the second we might be able to thwart. Effie's idea of a 'green ball' was gathering force at The Folly. Slowly we were all working on David, and slowly he was coming round to the idea. It would be held on Midsummer's Eve. It was this, as much as the idea of raising money for green charities, which would sway him, for if we held it on the same night as the Druids' biggest shindig, we would draw them to The Folly instead. The ultimate upstaging, as Ros might have said.

The stone was only just big enough for two, we had to squeeze up against each other to fit. No hardship. His arm across my shoulders, mine around his waist, our sides moulded to each other, we sat there, a single creature exuding electricity so powerful that the ley line went *pfft* beneath our feet. Down below lay Cappelrigg, the reeds burnished by the setting sun, the mottled green of its fields punctuated by tiny white specks which were lambs and bigger beige ones which were their mothers.

To the right was Graegarth's land, even worse than mine. And to the left, the forest, a great green sea undulating with the gentle ups and downs of the land. My eyes glazed – fatigue, the soporific caress of the sun, the sensual delight of David's nearness – and it seemed to me that the metaphor came to life. The forest *was* a sea, and as I watched, the big green waves swelled and began to move westward, engulfing my land. The vision was so vivid that I even saw little islands of grass left – quite literally – high and dry by the waves: those few small hills which were less soggy than the rest and to which the sheep invariably went for a dry bed at night. The pattern of trees and clearings was so lovely that I refrained from blinking, not wanting it to disappear.

'I'm going to plant it all,' I said dreamily. Then heard what I'd said. I hadn't meant to say anything at all, the words simply came out of me as if out of a dream. But now that they were out, I knew I meant them.

David stirred beside me. 'Are you sure that's a good idea?'

'What talk is this from my Green Man?' I teased. 'He who was so furious with the City chit outbidding him and thwarting his plans for the greening of Keldreth.'

'I don't want you doing anything you don't really feel is right.'

'Your trees would mutiny if they heard such talk from their master.'

'My trees have more sense than you. They know they're a commitment for life – theirs and mine. Seriously, Charlotte. You wouldn't make any money out of it.'

'So what's money? If I wanted money, I'd have stayed in the City. How about a merger, your trees and mine?'

I never proposed to my lover nor he to me. We didn't have to. After that night in my Land-Rover stinking of sheep, we knew without a word that we would always be together. Married or not, it didn't matter. No piece of paper had the power to bring us together or separate us.

'You might come to resent your trees,' he said. 'And me, for persuading you to plant them. I don't want to persuade you, Charlotte. I love your stroppy little mind. Decide for yourself. Don't let me sway you.'

'Does it occur to you that I might like trees, too?'

'It had crossed my mind.'

'The day I planted that oak. It did funny things to me. A kind of lust. Can one lust for trees? I can still feel my fingers easing the earth into contact with those roots. Very sexy.'

My lover laughed, a big open peal of laughter which rang out across my land. Then he placed his hands on either side of my head and looked deep into my eyes. 'I fell in love with those sexy little fingers of yours, my crazy Lottie. I was jealous of that oak. I wanted your fingers on *me*.'

I obliged by cupping his head in my hands. 'But I'm warning you, Squire. I intend to be promiscuous. I'm going to have intimate relations with thousands of trees.'

He scowled and tightened his hands. 'Then I'll exercise my *droit du seigneur*.'

'You terrify me,' I murmured, as he drew my face towards his.

*   *   *

I, too, could write notes. One evening when he was due to come to me, I grew impatient of waiting. I had been reading Shelley in a (futile) attempt to make the time pass. One line leapt up from 'Ode to the West Wind': *Make me thy lyre, even as the forest is.* I wrote it down, folded the note, put it in my pocket and set off across the fields.

There was indeed a west wind blowing. Soft and warm, it pushed me gently over the grass and to the old beech by our boundary wall. I slipped the note into the same crevice where his had been, then hid myself in a bed of bluebells behind the tree. A faint sweetness rose from my feet. I didn't realise that bluebells had any scent. Perhaps individually they didn't and only when massed could tinge the air with their pale perfume. Or perhaps it was the remains of the dappled sun coaxing it out of then. Or just another trick of the forest, another piece of enchantment. I breathed it in with all the intensified sensual awareness that had come to me along with the gift of my lover.

His footsteps were soft but firm on the path. I longed to peek but instead pressed myself closer to the trunk for concealment. The trunk was hard and warm. Pressed up against it, I felt like a dryad come home at last.

The footsteps passed. For a moment I feared he wouldn't see the note. Then there was a pause, a rustle of paper being unfolded. As he read, I pursed my lips and imitated the sound of the west wind blowing.

A shaggy head appeared round the trunk. Two shaggy black eyebrows rose in surprise.

'I am your friendly local dryad,' I chanted, coming out from my concealment and striking a balletic pose. I wavered, and he caught me. He held me close. He was hard and warm, too, and I pressed up against him with more than ever a sense of homecoming.

He took my hand and led me through a forest gone green and gold in the slanting sun. The blackbird and thrush were still fighting it out, their competing songs cutting through the gentler sounds of the smaller birds. Somewhere a great tit, undaunted, yelled its two-note 'teacher-teacher' while all around us was the flutter of tiny wings startled at our approach.

There were paths I'd never guessed at, deep in the forest, many of them concealed behind a feint of bushes and, when found, as narrow as the width of a foot – habitual routes of hares and badgers, he told me. One by one he took me to the green doors, opened them, and led me to the secret places, tiny pockets which the chainsaw rarely saw.

Today, a curtain of downy new willow leaves parted to reveal a tiny gill whispering its way through the forest between mossy banks just wide enough to take our passage single file. The moss had crept from bank to stone and furred the rocks at the water's edge. I stooped and ran a hand over one, delighting in the soft tickle. Here and there a patch of marsh marigolds caught the sun and flashed bright yellow through the green tunnel. Buttercups were straining towards the light at the edge of the trees. The water was dark and peaty except where stray sunbeams turned it bronze – moorland water.

It was easy to imagine elves lightly making their way along this mossy bank. Everything here was so small and delicate, scaled down for a miniature world which I almost believed existed. If there hadn't been elves before, surely these exquisite little secret places would conjure them into being, the landscape itself creating its creatures. Slender and silvery they would be, in the moonlight which would glance off their pale hair.

The banks were widening now, and the gill. We'd had to bend a little to accommodate the close-growing greenery arching above. Now the canopy lifted and we straightened up. The gill's whisper grew bolder and chattered over the rocks, while up ahead I could hear another sound, as of a waterfall.

And then we were there, at the edge of a clearing more beautiful than any he had shown me before. At the far end a wall of rock as tall as myself closed off the clearing. Over its smooth lip flowed a glossy sheet of water which shone like satin before plunging into the pool. The impact sent up a fine spray which caught a scrap of rainbow. The pool itself was large and deep, the water at the edge the colour of topaz but growing darker as it moved towards a centre in which only the faintest gleam of light remained.

I stepped into the clearing, onto a lawn of moss and grass dotted with wildflowers. There were bluebells here, too; a sprinkling of them had escaped from the great blue carpet which covered the earth beneath the hazels and oaks enclosing one half of the clearing. They were so thick, the blue so intense, that my eyes played tricks on me, made the carpet shimmer and shift through a spectrum of colour that was surely not there. The ones that invaded the clearing were competing with the fresh white stars of stitchwort, while lady's smock foamed pale lilac in whatever spaces it could find. Here and there a clump of campion added a vivid pink touch. On the other side of the pool the ground was spangled with wild violets and anemones in full bloom. Ferns sprang from clefts in the rocks at the base of the little waterfall and dripped sun-brightened drops into the pool.

I walked to the pool's edge, unloosed my hair from its plait, removed my clothes and stepped into the water. A first frisson of cold, and then the water wrapped itself around my body like a second skin. The pool's dark centre had soaked up the long day's sun and now gave it back to me. I stood waist-high in the welcoming water and saw the rest of my body turn gold and then shade darkly downwards before vanishing at my feet.

And then two bodies, his beside me. We were golden statues of the gods come to life, rising from the depths of the pool where we'd been hidden for countless millenia while the rest of the world grew around us, unnoticed by our sleeping selves. Awakening now from our long long sleep, we smiled at each other and gave ourselves to the water, floating on its placid surface while the waterfall thrummed its *basso ostinato* and the birds twittered a descant high above. Our limbs found each other and twined effortlessly in the unresisting water, a silent dance to the music of this world being created all around us.

I remembered the other pool, the dead black one between the standing stones. Now I understood the folly of the Druids. They had ritualised the place with their stones and ley lines, turned whatever magic it may once have possessed into something dead and formal, chanted the life out of it. Preoccupied with their place in nature, they had lost it. And the real magic had slipped away, found a new existence in this hidden clearing where it could spin its charm unseen except by the birds and trees which were its rightful priests.

And I knew that David and I would never come here again. Once only, the fleeting beauty of transience, and then we too would go our way, thankful for the brief blessing of the gods. It would graze our foreheads with the lightness of a kiss from the west wind, scarcely noticed and yet infusing our two lives with the benediction of eternity.

We never said a word in that enchanted place. The voices that praised were not ours. We laid ourselves in our fragrant bed of violets and let our bodies celebrate its mysteries and theirs. We were at the same time two ordinary mortals and two gods, and then one, a composite creature, a new mythical being, fused together, sinking, soaring, encircling the earth in mighty wingbeats, wheeling through the sky in a great golden cartwheel of joy.

Only later, much later, did I remember the dream that had come to me the night after I'd first seen David. When I had walked through all the grey pillars and people of my past and they had turned into the trees of the forest. And in it I had found David, and we had made love on the forest floor. Premonition? No, nothing so banal, just the deep-buried memory of something lost before we knew we had it, and then found again, if only in a dream. How did that dream become reality for us in the enchanted clearing? I have no taste for explanations, and neither does my lover. We are content to leave these mysteries unsolved, content simply to receive.

*   *   *

I should have guessed what the next note would be, but I have no supernatural powers and unfolded the note which the beech tree gave me unsuspecting.

> *How can I live without thee, how forgo*
> *Thy sweet converse and love so dearly joined,*
> *To live again in these wild woods forlorn?*

I stood as rooted to the spot as the beech tree beside me while Milton's great words thundered through the stillness of the early morning air. Then I smiled. The Folly's library had been working overtime. I pictured my big rough lover bent over it, searching for words better than his own to express his love. He didn't have to – I had sensed from the beginning that this was a landscape too big for any words – but I was touched by his willingness to play these games with me, to humour my foolish fantasies. And in a way, he meant it. These wild woods had been just a little bit forlorn, despite his friends.

Never again. No way would we forgo each other, whatever else might happen.

*   *   *

Another morning. Walking a path we knew well. The canopy was thicker now. The beeches had lost that first magic haze when some masterly hand seems to brush the bare branches with the faintest touch of colour. They were fully out now, a bright acid green as yet untouched by the wear and tear of summer. The oaks were just beginning, unfurling their leaves in flashes of bronzy gold. The ashes, stubborn as always, showed only a few ungainly tufts of green. All the other trees, though, were preening themselves in their new finery and greening the light that filtered through their branches.

The path was dotted with the bright blue of speedwell. At the edges clumps of sweet cicely infused the air with their aniseed fragrance. I crushed a few leaves between my fingers and inhaled the scent at full strength. Everywhere we went we heard the soft clumsy flap of fledgling wings in the underbrush. The sound of late spring, the forest at the height of its frenzy of renewal.

We walked aimlessly in our brief treat before our day's work. My arm was around his waist, his across my shoulders. So much of the day we had to spend separately, we clung the closer to each other while we could.

And then he was gone, lumbering through the underbrush, no doubt sending up a jungle telegraph of fear in a hundred miniature hearts. I peered after him and saw a flash of white beneath a tree. David stooped, picked it up and brought it to me.

It was a shell, or rather, fragments of one or two shells. The pieces were matt white with reddish-brown spots, and the broad curves suggested a fairly large egg. David put the pieces in his pocket, which I thought was rather odd. Why not let them break down on the forest floor? He searched the canopy for a long time. Then he motioned me behind some scrub on the other side of the path. From our hiding place he pointed to a high fork in a wych elm opposite. There were so many branches and leaves in the way that it took me some time to see what he meant. Then I saw the nest, a smaller version of the one in the hidden valley up on the moor. A kite's nest.

'Did you know it was here?' I whispered.

'No. The shells gave it away. They would have given it away to anyone else, too. This is a public footpath.'

Of course. The kites had shoved the shells out of their nest, not knowing that their bright white would catch the eye of any passer-by. No wonder David had removed the evidence. This must be a brand new nest, as yet undiscovered by the bastard who was stealing eggs, trapping the birds.

'Listen.'

I listened. The din of bird song parted to let through a shrill mewing that was unfamiliar. It seemed quite far away. Then, much closer, an answering call, the same *we-oo* with the emphasis on the second syllable. Not a very pretty sound for such a glorious bird. The calls became more frequent, the distant one drew nearer. David was no longer watching the nest but scanning the sky through the leaves. There was nothing to see for a while, and when it finally came, there was little more than a sense of movement, a shadowing of the sky, until the sun glanced off it and sent a chestnut flash through the leaves.

We stood very still, listening to the clumsy rustle of leaves as the bird landed, unseen, somewhere opposite. Its tree was a little way in from the path and largely hidden. Then, very briefly, it perched on a branch, very upright, its elegant tail hanging down, something that looked like a small rabbit held in its beak. It shuffled along the branch and disappeared from view. A moment later I heard a thin, high-pitched piping. The young bird, or birds, hysterical at the sight of approaching food. It was rather comical. However majestic these birds were in flight, their stomachs were no different from any others.

293

We waited until the male bird had left. Then we made our way through the dense trees for a while, until we guessed we were out of sight of the nest, before returning to the path.

'Who would have guessed they'd nest there?' David said. 'You see? You are my lucky charm.'

We were back on the moor near the hidden valley, David giving me credit for conjuring the kites out of the sky. Why disabuse him? Perhaps I was a conjurer, producing birds rather than rabbits from my magic hat. Anything seemed possible these days. The forest was charmed and so were we. It was easy to forget there was a world outside it. I wanted nothing more than to spend the rest of my life walking through its green cathedral with my lover.

David was frowning, though not at me.

'I was planning to take out some larch in there,' he said. 'Now we'll have to wait until they fledge.'

'Do you begrudge?'

'What do you think?'

*　　　*　　　*

I thought Keats wouldn't mind if I took a little liberty.

> *Happy is Farleton Forest! I could be content*
> *To see no other verdure than its own;*
> *To feel no other breezes than are blown*
> *Through its tall woods with high romances blent.*

I slipped the note into our leafy postbox and waited for my lover to come.

*　　　*　　　*

'Which way does it go?'

'Think about it, Charlotte.'

I was always Charlotte when we were being business-like, never Lottie. The business today: my first lesson in harnessing a horse. I stood stupidly holding the heavy padded collar. I could see the way it should fit on the horse but couldn't see how to get it there. Then, ingeniously, I turned

294

it upside down and eased it over Olwen's head. Once it was over, I could turn it the right way round again and settle it at the base of her neck.

'Good girl.'

'Olwen or me?'

'Both. You're very patient.'

'So's she.'

'That's why I keep her. She's ideal for beginners.'

'Liar. You keep her because you're crazy about her. Brendan told me. Should I be jealous?'

'If you wish. She *is* very beautiful.'

Especially this morning. We were in the old coach house, so high and airy that even the massive sleigh and cart and other paraphernalia of horsedom were dwarfed. The sun slanted through the windows like searchlights beamed on the horse who stood in the centre. Her coat, which I had lovingly brushed, caught the light and gave it back in a mother-of-pearl gleam. She appeared to be posing for a painting, though I knew in truth she was simply waiting for me to harness her up.

'What next?' I asked.

'Think.'

'The bridle?' This at least was familiar. With my right hand I touched the corners of her mouth. She opened it obligingly and I slipped the bit into it and drew the bridle on, bending her ears a little to fit the head strap over. I buckled the throat lash and stood back to inspect my handiwork. 'Why no blinkers?' I asked.

'Would you wear them?'

He was sitting on a bale of straw and leaning against one whitewashed wall. I thought of the day I'd sat on a bale of hay outside my shippon and fallen in love with the woodman at work. He had such a strong sense of belonging. Every inch of the estate was intimate with him. The bale of straw was his leather armchair, the coach house his sitting-room. If ever he were photographed for some famous deed, I hoped it would be just as he was now, in his jeans and frayed checked shirt open at the collar, the heavy mass of uncombed hair matched by the heavy boots at rest on the cobbled floor. It was hard to imagine him besuited for the Midsummer's Eve

Ball. Shuffling his powerful shoulders with the unfamiliar discomfort of the foolish clothes? Tugging at the restrictive tie? Probably.

'Forestry's dangerous,' he explained. 'Any horse so skittish that she needs blinkers is no use to me. I want a horse to be able to see everything I can see, to be ready to act intelligently in an emergency.'

I fed the reins through the rings of the hames. There was still an awful lot of harness to go. He'd brought it into the coach house, along with myself and Olwen, to avoid the amused eyes of the breakfasting students. They would have forgotten their own clumsy first lessons by now, scoffed at my mistakes.

'What next?'

'We're using a cart today, so the saddle is next.' He pointed.

'Doesn't look like a saddle to me.'

'It's not for riding, my dodo.'

I put it on as instructed and fastened the girth. The girth at least was familiar. My own horse had always puffed himself up at this stage. Then, when the girth was buckled, he would unpuff and gloat over the looseness. Olwen, aristocrat that she was, disdained such tricks.

'Do all these other bits go somewhere on the rump?' I asked.

He nodded and named the parts of the breechings: crupper, loin strap, hip strap, breech band. 'Try to work out for yourself where they go – you'll remember it better that way.'

Slowly, and with false starts, I assembled the puzzle on Olwen's sleek rump.

'Well done. We'll make a forester of you yet.'

I hoped so. I wanted to be a part of the estate, not some decorative wife who perpetually refurbished rooms and planned entertainments.

We left the hushed sanctuary of the coach house and entered the courtyard. I felt a strange thrill, leading the great horse, whom I had harnessed myself, into the light. All this power at the end of a lightly held rein. I could feel that harmony which comes to people who work these wonderful creatures. No master and subject here, the two worked together with mutual trust that brought with it a whiff of some imagined golden age when the barriers between man and beast had not yet risen.

The spell was broken as the students tumbled out into the courtyard followed by Brendan and Belle. The students were still a little shy with me. As a neighbour I was acceptable, but David-the-lover was something new and not quite dignified in their eyes. It was curious that the only bit of jealousy I encountered came from them.

Brendan and Belle had been ecstatic at the news. The first time we walked into the kitchen entwined, Belle had nearly dropped a saucepan in her shock. A moment later she abandoned the saucepan, rushed over to us and did her best to put her big arms round us both at the same time – 'And I never suspected, never suspected!'

Brendan did. I had a glimpse of him over Belle's shoulder, smiling with satisfaction. David was right. Brendan knew much more than his big amiable features let on. It crossed my mind that not only was this union expected, but just a little bit planned by him. I remembered that walk through the forest with him after my ride on Olwen. Was he even then plotting his benevolent work?

Toby – the newest student – stepped forward and inspected my work. He gave it a grudging pass. We were going out to work together – David and Toby and Olwen and I. I would only be an observer today, but sometime in the future David would take me out alone and teach me. I was greedy to learn every detail of the estate, not just in order to be the informed wife, supportive of her man's work. No, I wanted to do the work myself. David was inseparable from his trees and horses and students and friends, they were all as much a part of him as his own flesh and bones. Ros hadn't understood that. And if she had, she would have tried to winkle him out of his context. It wasn't her fault that she couldn't love his world, and it was no great credit to me that I could. Just luck. The same inexplicable force that had turned me from the City to Cappelrigg had simply moved on with utmost naturalness to include the forest which was a part of him. The search for something that would give meaning to my life had found its natural conclusion here, at The Folly. The fates had given me everything all at once: meaning and love and a future so rich that I could hardly contemplate it without feeling dazzled.

Toby wasn't dazzled. He'd found a fault at last.

'The belly band's too tight,' he said, and loosened it a fraction.

I apologised.

*   *   *

May Day. The anniversary of John Jowett's death. I spent the night at The Folly. Just in case.

*   *   *

And then it was June. Haytime was looming. Soon even the precious early mornings and evenings would be lost to us as I struggled to get a year's worth of hay stashed in my barn despite the best efforts of the weather, machinery and human fatigue to thwart that goal. Silage would have been easier, but I felt sorry enough for my sheep having to live on my cold wet land without making them eat second-best. However fraught and difficult, I preferred the hay that was their natural winter food to the slimy manufactured silage which they ate only grudgingly.

I skirted the edge of one of my hay fields en route to our postbox and inspected the grass. The heads were nearly ripe. Everything was ready, the tractor newly serviced, Tom standing by, keeping clear the space of time when we would work sixteen hours a day to get the hay in.

The evening sun and the breeze set the hay field in motion, a glimmering wave of gold above which the curlews sang and soared. I lingered at the stile, just taking in the peace and beauty of the scene. The edge of the field where no mower could reach was fringed with flowers all tangled up with the grass. The first few ox-eye daisies blushed in the slanted sunlight which deepened the pink of the ragged robin and campion. Tall and straight among them stood the foxgloves looking rather military in their posture compared to their graceful companions. Everything was tinted red-gold; even the delicate pignut lost its creamy whiteness and submitted to the dye.

I must have been standing very still, for a bullfinch landed not far away and began plucking the seeds from a dandelion clock. After each mouthful, he shook his head violently, trying to separate the seeds from the fluff which stuck out of his beak like a comical beard. Finally the fluff would let go and he would eat the seeds greedily and start all over again. I watched the process several times, then climbed the stile.

As I dropped down to the other side, a fountain of baby wrens sprayed up from the underbrush. They vanished and went silent. Perhaps they watched from their concealment as the giant crossed the short bit of land to the tree where I could already see the flash of white in the crevice. Perhaps someone else watched, too. But apart from the silenced wrens, there was no indication of anything untoward. The birds sang and the wind soughed softly through the trees as I drew down the piece of paper. The sun turned the paper gold as I opened it.

No lover's note, this. The big black handwriting which had become so familiar was gone. In its place a crooked line of letters cut out from a magazine. No lover's message either: LEAVE CAPPELRIGG NOW. THIS IS YOUR LAST WARNING.

32

The idyll was over. The princess of the enchanted forest became just plain Charlotte Venables, hill farmer, on the verge of haytime with an anonymous ill-wisher now upping the stakes. But this was the third threat. Whoever it was had cried wolf too often. Like a terrorist forever revising the ultimatum, he'd lost credibility, at least with me.

Not so with David. I had at last told him everything – not that there was much. He was horrified.

In any case, I felt obliged to hand over the note to the police. Detective Sergeant Tyndall took it more seriously this time. Druids playing around the stone circle were one thing, this extremely aggressive threat quite another. I still said nothing about the kites, of course, but I managed to convince him that a Druid who felt sufficiently fanatical about the ley line might indeed consider physical violence towards someone blocking it. Tyndall agreed that it was time to do some investigating, find out who belonged to the cult.

Meanwhile, I made a temporary move to The Folly – partly out of fear but also because Effie was making a flying visit to set in train the transformation of the ballroom. It would be convenient to have us all under one roof.

It was a surprisingly happy little interlude, despite the nagging oppression of the threat. Every morning I inspected my sheep and my hay. The rest of the day, while the men went off into the forest, Effie and Belle and I plotted the ball.

Effie was right about the room. It was in good nick, despite having little attention for the two decades or so that it had been in David's hands. All it needed was a massive scrub, new wallpaper and new paint for the woodwork. Effie understood the ethos of The Folly: however ornate and bizarre most of the rooms, any new work was to be simple, unobtrusive and good. The ballroom lent itself to this treatment. It was a long room, running north to south along the east side of the ground floor – in so far as there was a ground floor. A number of tall french windows opened out onto the terrace in front and the lawn which edged the forest on the east. The windows, plus a very high ceiling, gave the light and airy effect of a sundrenched woodland clearing, an effect augmented by the real woodland just beyond. The choice of wallpaper had been preordained: a delicate tangle of palest green trees against a white background, the design so subtle it seemed to have been breathed onto the paper by elves. It would, Effie assured us, echo the real woodland outside, and she promised us some equally subtle outdoor lighting which would bring the two woodlands together and make our Midsummer ballroom into a moonlit glade.

In the evenings, we got together with Brendan and David in the kitchen while the students watched the reinstated television in the library. Every so often a student would drift into the kitchen for a snack and linger. They were scathing about the ball, of course, but Effie they liked, and I'm sure these frequent forays into the kitchen had much to do with her presence there. With her spiky red hair, snappy talk and outrageous clothes, she seemed much nearer their age than I did. She also knew the world of pop music and fashion more than I and could speak their language. One evening they took her to a disco in Kirkby. She seemed to enjoy it as much as they did.

The students were becoming more used to me, too. No doubt part of it was Effie's aura rubbing off on me. For the rest, I fostered unobtrusiveness and took special care not to attach myself too conspicuously to David in their presence. They were used to The Folly being a masculine enclave with Belle as the sole female playing a role they could accept: the provider. Effie was both temporary and acceptable. I was more of a threat. They were, quite simply, possessive about David, and it was easy to view me as a usurper of his time and attention. I hadn't realised how much they idolised him. Once I did, I learned ways of signalling that I had no intention of upsetting the lifestyle they so enjoyed.

It was important to me to learn how to fit in, for the day would come when I would move into The Folly for good. Not for me the role of brash newcomer stamping my personality on the place. No, I wanted nothing more than to become a part of it, integrating my life and David's and The Folly's. For that, I would have to find a role of my own. David and I discussed it at night in bed, but mostly we made love, continuing the ecstatic exploration of each other's bodies which had begun so magically in the forest.

No question of the Scheherazade Room anymore. I moved in with David and shared with him the exotic world of nineteenth-century Russia. The room was full of onion-domed lamps, moth-eaten bear rugs and a number of rather beautiful icons. There was also a splendid samovar, unused. We were Anna Karenina and Vronsky, Dr Zhivago and Lara, the Russian forester and his peasant girl. We were madly and magnificently in love.

When the time came for me to leave, my Russian bear roared his disapproval.

'I need to be at Cappelrigg now,' I explained.

'Give me one good reason.'

'I'll give you several, if you'll stop kissing me and let me talk.'

'That's not much incentive.'

Later, much later, I resumed. 'Because Effie's gone. Because it's haytime. Because I have to show our friendly Druid that I won't be intimidated into leaving Cappelrigg –'

'Then let me intimidate you into staying at The Folly.'

I slipped out of bed just as he lunged at me.

'Seriously, David. You know the other reason. It's not time yet, things aren't right yet. I need to find my own niche before I can move in permanently. Look at me. I'm thirty-one. I've spent most of my adult life being extremely independent in London. I've spent the last year trying to be equally independent at Cappelrigg. I can't just give that up and become an idle serf on your estate, no matter how much I adore the master.'

'Ah, Lottie, sometimes I'm male chauvinist enough to wish you were stupid and pliable.'

'Then you wouldn't love me.'

'Very probably, my lovely Lottie. Get back into bed. I won't molest you for a few minutes.'

I slipped back into bed and kissed him. I dreaded the lonely nights at Cappelrigg. 'But don't you see?' I continued. 'That's part of what went wrong with Ros. She had no role here.'

Silence. Then David rolled over and took me into his arms. 'Don't ever leave me, Lottie,' he whispered into my hair.

'You know I won't. But I need to be here with you in every sense. Don't you see? Everything you've done here is so big and grand and good and right. I want our life together to be big and grand and good and right, too. That can only happen if I find a way of fitting in and yet being independent. There *is* a way, and I'll find it.'

'Please find it before tomorrow morning.'

I didn't, of course, and the next morning I returned to Cappelrigg.

In the days that followed, I had little time to miss David. We were both, separately, taking in our hay, working a sixteen-hour day. In the evenings, however, David came to spend the night at Cappelrigg. It wasn't only love that brought him to my side every night. No, we had a plan. The investigations into the Druid cult would take a long time. We couldn't carry on much longer with these threats hanging over me. I would therefore turn myself into a decoy to lure the culprit to Cappelrigg. Our hope was that we might also startle him into confessing his involvement with the kites – if indeed it was the same person. Beyond that, we didn't plan.

But David had no intention of letting me play sitting duck all by myself, and so, his day's work over, he would make his way to Cappelrigg across the fields under cover of darkness, on foot. No telltale Land-Rover parked to show his presence. With Effie's rug-curtains at the windows, no one would see David. And with the radio on to mask our *sotto voce* conversations, no one would hear him either.

As the days wore on, we began to think our plan would fail. Then, on the last night, something happened.

We had both of us brought in the last of our hay that evening. We were tired, dirty and disappointed in our crops. Over a late supper, and with Radio Three oozing a late night offering of baroque music into the kitchen, we compared notes.

The weather had been unkind, we concluded, but when is it not? Squally showers had flattened swathes of the standing hay, turning the fields into embossed carpets – interesting to look at but hell to harvest. When we did manage to get a field cut and the hay spread for drying, a day of sun would be followed by a downpour and we'd have to start the drying all over again. No wonder everyone had taken to silage. But David's aristocratic Shires were even less inclined to eat the stuff than my sheep were. In fact, David bought in most of his hay from areas more suited to producing it. The small amount he got from his own fields was supplement only. The fields were really there to act as firebreaks, exercise ground for the horses and forest edging for wildlife.

'Trees,' I said morosely. 'You're right. It's the only thing this land is fit for. Well, this haytime has convinced me. This is my first and last crop of hay *and* lambs. In the autumn I'll sell the lot. Then I'll get the ditching machines in and turn the land into Little Amsterdam. And then . . . the trees. Cappelrigg Forest. How does that sound? Quite a nice ring to it, don't you think?'

'I think I'd like some more chicken. Are you sure this is what you want to do?'

I pushed the cold carcass across the table to him. 'Yes. Absolutely. My brain is afire, my fingers twitching to caress those little roots.'

'You do that and they'll die. You've a lot to learn, my impetuous Lottie.'

'I'm smart.'

'I have noticed,' he smiled. 'And of course Brendan and I will help you.' Then he turned serious again. 'But will it satisfy you?'

'You mean will it make me move contentedly into The Folly?' I sighed. 'It'll have to. I can't think of anything else. But I do wish I could think of something I could do to help *you*. Don't you see? It's all so one-sided. It always has been.'

'You're the only one who sees it that way.'

'But my seeing matters, too, David. I want everything to be right.'

'Then you're not going to like what I have to tell you.

The nursery we use is going out of business. The other big nurseries are geared up for commercial forestry. They only stock a few of the main species. I'm trying to track down other sources, but it doesn't look hopeful.'

'I see,' I said softly.

'I don't think Cappelrigg Forest with just a few species is what you had in mind.'

'No. No, it most certainly isn't. I want something as rich and vibrant and beautiful as yours.' I smiled feebly. 'You've spoiled me for other forests,' I mocked, though I was feeling far from light-hearted.

'Brendan's thinking of starting our own nursery,' David went on. 'We've thought about it before but never had the time. Working with the horses and the students – we can't skimp that. Charlotte, what would you think about helping us start a nursery? Wouldn't that solve all our problems at once?'

My brain snapped to attention. The vision I'd had of Cappelrigg Forest vanished; in its place rose a new one, fresh and shining and ready made, as if it had been waiting in the wings all this time for its opportunity.

'Cappelrigg *Nursery*,' I cried. 'That's it! Oh, David, it's so obvious! Why didn't we think of it before? Look, those two fields in front of the house – they're reasonably good, I'll use them for the nursery. I'll grow my own trees for the rest of the land, and for you, and maybe even someday I'll go commercial and start supplying other estates! David, you're brilliant!'

The music ended to applause which, in my excitement, I thought was meant for us.

'Shh,' said David.

I'd almost forgotten our decoy plan. I lowered my voice and continued. 'Once I've done some drainage, those fields will be perfect. They're pretty exposed but I can plant some shelter.'

The BBC announcer came on to read the midnight news.

'Lottie, my love, you don't know a thing about nurseries,' said David.

'Pooh. I didn't know a thing about the City before I went there. Or much about sheep farming before I came here. I can learn. Don't be such a killjoy.'

My killjoy smiled, and I knew that he who thought in terms of centuries was, at amazing speed for him, coming round to the idea.

'Brendan could help,' he said. 'He knows more about that side of things than I do. Unless you're too proud?'

'Not a bit! I'll pick his brains ruthlessly. You see? – we'll even have the same teacher, you and I! And look, I even have the outbuildings just waiting to be turned into packing sheds or whatever! It's perfect! Oh, David, just think of it – '

'Shh,' said David, as the newsreader droned on unheeded.

I lowered my voice again. 'Think of it: our land, side by side, each complementing the other. Oh, David, my love, for once please stop being so damned sensible and cautious and steady and celebrate with me!'

I leapt to my feet in excitement. The newsreader signed off, leaving the faint sound of static on the radio. Over it, a second sound, that of the rain hissing down past the curtained windows.

And then a third sound. A knock at the door. Quietly at first, then louder. I froze. David and I looked at each other. It couldn't be anyone from The Folly. They were in on the plan, would use the phone if they needed us. It could only be one person.

Our plan had worked.

33

Our minds had been so filled with dreams of the future that it took some time to think straight. Then, quietly, David and I did what we had worked out in advance. David took up a position behind the door leading to the porch, ready to spring out if needed. I went through into the porch, pulling the kitchen door nearly-but-not-quite shut behind me.

I had long ago put roller blinds on all the porch windows. The door was solid. Beyond it, my visitor knocked a third time. 'Who is it?' I asked in a voice that I hoped sounded normal, though rainy midnight visits were far from that.

There was a pause. 'Jean. Jean Staveley. Let me in.'

'*Jean*?' I opened the door. Jean, bedraggled beneath her dark anorak, came in and shut the door quickly behind her. She scanned the shaded windows. Clearly it wasn't just me being furtive. 'I've got to talk to you,' she said. 'Are you alone?'

I avoided her question. 'Let me take your jacket. We can talk in the kitchen.' I hung up her dripping jacket and opened the door into the kitchen. David had, as planned, vanished.

Jean walked boldly into the room, but I had a feeling that she was less assured than she appeared. 'I was just going to make some coffee,' I said. 'Would you like some? Or something stronger? Do sit down.'

She remained standing. 'A whisky, if you've got it. God, this room is bare.'

'That's how I wanted it. Actually, I think I'll join you.' I poured out two glasses. 'Anything in it?'

She shook her head, still looking round the kitchen.

I put the glasses on the table. 'Shall we stay in here? It's warmer.'

She ignored me. 'Noreen had the place full of stuff, almost

as bad as ours. Mum's dying to see what you've done with the house. You never invited us back.'

I wasn't prepared for her staccato aggression. Also, I was concerned about the living-room wherein lurked David. I sat down at the kitchen table, hoping she would do the same.

She didn't. With stunning effrontery, she simply sailed across the kitchen and into the living-room. I sprang up and followed her just in time to see her first reaction to David, leaning one arm on the mantelpiece and pretending to read an out of date invitation to a London party. He nodded to her, rather gravely. She stared. Whatever her intention in barging into my living-room, it clearly hadn't been to check out whether anyone was there. Her face went white, the confidence sliding perceptibly from it.

'David,' I said, 'Jean and I are having a drink in the kitchen. Will you join us?' It was the best I could do.

But not good enough. 'I'm not talking in front of him,' said Jean flatly.

'Whatever concerns Charlotte concerns me,' said David.

'I had noticed,' said Jean. She'd recovered a little of her composure and with it that bitterness of the prematurely old.

I was unprepared for this meeting with Jean, hadn't expected it at all, didn't know what to do next.

David took over. 'Let's go into the kitchen,' he said, and led the way.

We followed in the same way that generations of tenants must have followed the Farletons. In the kitchen, David made no pretence of being a stranger. He poured himself a whisky and sat down at the table with it, indicating that we should do likewise. Jean hesitated, then walked past me and sat down. As she passed, I smelled a faint whiff of alcohol and realised that she'd had to augment her courage to come here. I suddenly felt sorry for her, despite her aggression and whatever her mission.

David didn't waste time. 'It was you who sent those notes, wasn't it? And made the telephone call.'

I sat down with a thump. How did David know that? Or was he just guessing?

'Of course,' said Jean. 'But if you tell anyone, I'll deny it.'

'Why?' said David. 'Why did you do it?'

Jean turned to me. 'To get you to leave, so we could buy the farm.'

'Threatening your neighbours is a rather unusual way of expanding your property,' said David.

'It wasn't a threat. It was a warning.'

'I see,' said David.

I didn't. As far as I was concerned, it was the same thing.

'And what is Richard planning to do?' David asked quietly.

I nearly bit my whisky glass. It was an outrageous remark, and I expected Jean to react against it as violently as I did. But after the initial shock, Jean seemed to slump, her muscles giving up their rigidity. She took a gulp of whisky. Her hand was shaking a little. I waited for her to refute David's words. Instead, she said dully, 'Why should I tell you?'

'Because I could phone the police right now and tell them you're here,' said David. 'Rushing across the fields in the rain at midnight to visit a neighbour you've never visited before is pretty unusual. The police would know something serious was at stake. They'd get you to talk.'

'Please yourself,' said Jean, and got up abruptly. 'I'm going.'

'If you do, I'll phone the police before you've got out of the door. I won't try to force you to stay, but if you do stay and talk to us, I'll try to keep the police out of it.'

Jean hesitated, then sat down again. Again I felt a twinge of pity for her, and sensed what sort of a person she might have been if whatever had turned her prematurely old hadn't happened. She must have been quite a gutsy little person before spirit had turned to aggression and bitterness.

'When did you first realise that Charlotte was in danger?' David asked.

Jean said nothing for a while. David had the sense not to prod her. Finally she spoke.

'Last autumn. I took some sheep up to one of the higher fields. Richard must not have known I was coming. He was in the little outbarn up by the boundary – it's derelict, we haven't used it for years. Nobody ever goes in there.' She stopped and drank some more whisky. 'Richard came out of the barn. He had a bunch of stuff I'd never seen before, and a live partridge. I asked what he was doing and he wouldn't tell me. When he left, I broke into the barn. There was all sorts of stuff hidden away there. I realised what he was doing, more or less.'

The kites. So David and Belle had been right. What a fool I was not to believe them, to try and defend Richard. Last autumn. It must have been around the time David smashed the trap in the hidden valley. The partridge had still been alive and active, it couldn't have been there very long.

'So I went back, but I kept an eye on the outbarn all day,' Jean continued. 'Finally I saw him coming down off the moor. I went up to the barn to meet him. He looked furious but he wouldn't talk. I said I knew what he was doing and I'd phone the police if he didn't tell me everything. Then he said he'd seen the two of you up there somewhere. He said you were interfering with his work. I wasn't sure what he meant, but there was something creepy about the way he said it. So I sent the first warning.'

She was obviously telling the truth. The first warning had come not long after that day in the hidden valley. Richard must have been there all that time, hiding behind a boulder, watching. I shivered.

Jean looked at David. 'After that, Richard went all quiet.' She made an impatient little gesture of dismissal with one hand. 'Not that he's ever talked to me much. But this was different. He also seemed watchful all of a sudden, and he was hardly ever at home. I got worried about what he was doing. And so I phoned and disguised my voice. I knew he wanted your farm and I guessed he would do something to scare you into leaving. But I didn't know how far exactly he would go.'

Jean finished her whisky. Automatically I reached for the bottle and refilled her glass. She looked down at it. 'Anyway, early in spring things seemed better, Richard seemed more like his old self. Then one day he was so cheerful that I asked him, and he said Cappelrigg was going to be ours, that he was going to marry you. Is that true?' she asked me. 'I mean' – glancing at David – 'was it true? Did he ask you?'

'Yes.'

'And what did you say?'

'I said no. It was a very public proposal – in the Golden Oak. I wasn't even sure how serious it was.'

'He didn't say anything about that. I thought you'd accepted.'

'I can't think you would have wanted me as a sister-in-law,' I said dryly.

'Not much,' she said. 'Not at first. You were just some Londoner who bought a farm we should have had. Coming up here with all that London money and pushing out the locals.'

'Is Richard's money any better?' said David quietly. 'Money from doing what he does to . . . hawks?'

I noticed that even now David wasn't going to admit there were kites here. Possibly Jean didn't know what kind of bird her brother was dealing in, how rare it was.

Jean shrugged, the shrug of indifference that most country people feel towards animals and birds not in their control. 'Anyway, when you came to tea that day, I thought you weren't so bad after all. And I liked your friend. Effie. Do you think she *would* give me some work, if I went to London and got myself set up as a decorator?'

'Effie never says what she doesn't mean. You should have sensed that much about her,' I said.

'Yeah, well, maybe I'll try some day. Anyway, one day – some time after Easter – I saw Richard looking through binoculars at something on the cliff. He didn't see me, but when he left, I had a look myself. It was the two of you, sitting on a stone up there. Well, it was pretty obvious that whatever Richard thought about you marrying him, he was wrong.'

'That must have been April or May,' said David. 'Why did you wait so long before sending the third warning?'

'I don't know,' she said simply. 'I didn't know what was happening. Richard started following you around and so I started following him. It took me a while to see that tree where you left notes for each other. I guess that was what gave me the idea. I got scared that he really might do something, and so I sent the note.'

All those blissful weeks of love in the forest, watched by Richard. I felt sick at the thought.

'At first I thought it had finally worked,' she continued. 'Soon as you got that note, you went off to The Folly to live. I thought you understood that there was real danger this time. Then you came back. I wasn't sure I really cared anymore. I thought if you were so dumb you couldn't get the message after three tries, why should I bother?'

'What made you change your mind?' David asked.

'Brendan.'

The answer was so unexpected that we simply stared at Jean. What on earth did Brendan have to do with any of this?

'Brendan's always been decent to me,' said Jean. 'About the only person up here who ever was.' She looked at me with open bitterness. 'I guess you don't know what it feels like to be invisible. You've always had everything you wanted. I didn't. Mum never wanted me, I was "a mistake" – she told me so herself. Dad liked me all right when he was sober, but that was hardly ever. Richard never noticed me except when he wanted some work doing. Brendan's the only person who treated me like a human being. Right from when I was little. I'd go to market with Dad or Richard and Brendan would always make a point of talking with me. "Jeannie" he called me. Nobody else liked me enough to give me a nickname. "Jeannie with the light brown hair," he'd say, and not condescending either, like you,' she shot at David. 'You just walked past with your nose in the air. I was too insignificant for you. Beneath your notice.'

David looked down at a spot on the table for a long time. Finally he raised his head and looked directly at Jean. 'I'm sorry,' he said quietly. 'I never meant it that way.' He tried, not very successfully, to smile at her. 'People sneered at me and called me a hippy freak. I took the easy way out – just withdrew from people altogether.'

I was astonished. David apologising?

I don't think Jean realised how deeply her words had bitten. 'Well, Brendan didn't. At least he talked to other people. Maybe we didn't know what you were all doing up there, but at least we knew *he* meant well.'

'I meant well too, Jean,' said David. 'If I'd known I was hurting your feelings . . .'

Jean looked slightly confused. 'Well, it doesn't matter anymore. I don't have any feelings to hurt anymore.'

'I don't think that's true,' I said quietly. 'Something Brendan said must have got through to you, to make you come here tonight. Will you tell us what it was?'

Jean drank some more whisky. 'Just before haytime, I saw Brendan down in Kirkby. We got talking and somehow the conversation came round to you two. Well, you must know – everybody's talking, it's hardly a secret. Anyway, he said you would be moving up to The Folly for good. And he said how happy he was that you would be there. That got to me. I hadn't realised he was so fond of you. I saw that if anything happened to you, he would . . . it would hurt him a lot.'

There was a long pause. It must have been difficult for her to talk about feelings, after years of denying her own.

'So I asked him if that meant you'd be selling Cappelrigg,' she continued. 'He seemed surprised. "Oh, no, she'll never be doing that," he said. "It's trees she'll be planting up there now." Well, then I knew. If you'd just gone off to The Folly and sold up, Richard probably would have got over his pride and left you alone. But if you weren't going to sell . . .'

The gap hung in the air. David filled it in: 'Richard would lose patience and do something serious?'

'I didn't say that. Neither did Brendan. All he said was, "You *know* something, don't you Jeannie?" He was terribly serious all of a sudden. Then he said, "I just hope you'll be doing something with what you know, before it's too late. It's your peace of mind I'm thinking of, Jeannie. As well as our Charlotte."'

One look at David's face told me he was as stunned as I was. Brendan had said nothing of this to us.

'And what *are* you going to do?' David asked.

'I've done it. Come and warned you. You can tell Brendan I've done what I could, and now I'll be going.' She drained the glass and stood up.

'Jean, please, stay a little longer,' I tried. I don't know what I had in mind, just that nothing seemed to have been resolved. The visit was somehow incomplete. She hesitated.

313

I poured some more whisky into her glass. Not a very noble bribe, but I didn't know what else to do.

She sat down again. 'So what else do you want me to do?'

'I don't know,' I said honestly. 'What do you think *I* should do?'

'Sell the farm,' she said flatly. 'That's all he wants. That's what he's trapping those birds for – to get the money to buy the farm. What do you need all that extra land for anyway? You'll have enough over there at The Folly.'

Sell the farm so that Richard Staveley could ruin it as he had done with Graegarth? Give up my dream of trees, and a nursery? 'I'm not going to sell the farm,' I said.

'Suit yourself,' she shrugged. 'Don't say I didn't warn you.' A hollow laugh. 'Four times now.'

'There's something else you could do,' said David. 'Tell the police what you've just told us.'

She shot him a look that was both vicious and fearful. 'You said you'd keep the police out of it. Anyway, there's nothing to tell. He hasn't done anything – except with those birds, and that hardly counts.'

'He *has* done something,' said David.

'It's news to me,' she said.

'No, it isn't. You know. You were in the house when John Jowett phoned. You heard the conversation. You saw Richard go off to Cappelrigg to "help" John with his tractor. You know what he did to that tractor, Jean, and why. That's what Brendan really meant. "I just hope you'll be doing something with what you know, before it's too late," he said. Will you?'

I gasped. Did David know this? Or was he guessing? And Brendan – that day he'd told me about Richard repairing Jowett's tractor. He'd hinted at 'responsibility' then. Had he had in mind a different kind of responsibility than I thought?

'I don't know what you're talking about,' said Jean.

'Yes, you do,' said David. 'And because your mother was out and Noreen Jowett was out and you were the only person who heard that conversation, you thought you could keep it to yourself forever. You think I never noticed you, but I did. Enough to notice that in the year since John's "accident" you've aged a decade or more. This knowledge you've had to keep to yourself has eaten you away, it's ruining your life. And that's why you were so frightened when Richard started behaving oddly. You knew just how far he might go to get what he wanted. It isn't too late, Jean, even now. If you go to the police now – '

'And what good would that do?'

'They would reopen the case,' said David, 'and arrest Richard. And you would get rid of the guilt that's been eating you up from the inside. You could start a new life, Jean. In London, if you like. I could give you the money to start up a decorating business. Or a loan, if you'd prefer.'

Jean's laughter was savage. 'Thirty pieces of silver?'

'For God's sake, Jean, Richard's no Christ!'

Jean raised her voice to match David's. 'And what if they find him not guilty? Hey? What then? Am I supposed to wait at home for him to come back and kill *me*?'

She jumped from her chair so violently that it overturned. Then she rushed through the porch and out into the rainy night.

34

The next day Jean had disappeared. I shouldn't have been surprised, but was. I was still numbed by shock. I couldn't assimilate everything that had happened, still couldn't quite accept the new portrait of Richard which events were forcing on me.

But at least David and Belle and Brendan had now told me what they knew. It wasn't much. Just that they had felt uneasy about John Jowett's tractor accident from fairly early on. But, as with the kites, there was no evidence. None the less, Brendan had on one occasion tried, in a casual half-joking manner, to broach the subject with Detective Sergeant Tyndall. Tyndall had made it clear that it was a joke in poor taste. Brendan knew there was no point in pursuing it further.

And he was right. Once again, by 'going green' before it was respectable and by shutting out the rest of the world, David and his friends had cut themselves off from normal society. Richard hadn't. He was a much-liked member of the farming community and charming as hell.

Even at The Folly they'd felt uncertain, reluctant to accuse falsely. But when Brendan had seen me bid for the fatal tractor, all his vague suspicions had burst out – hence the violence of his opposition which had so enraged me. Later, they had talked it over at The Folly, unsure whether I should be told. But what was there to tell? Finally it was I who had decided the issue, by refusing to accept that Richard might be the culprit interfering with the kites. If I couldn't even believe that, how much less would I believe that my charming neighbour might have lethal intentions against me to gain Cappelrigg?

And so the matter had rested until last night. David admitted that he hadn't 'known' what he said he knew, but the bluff had worked, surprising Jean into telling too much.

And now Jean's disappearance, confirming in the most frightening way possible everything she had said. It was Detective Sergeant Tyndall who told us. Fortunately, Brendan took the phone call. I wasn't the only one who'd seen Brendan as just a nice guy and a good worker. Only those who knew him well understood how shrewd he was. That night on the phone, Brendan expressed his genuine concern and his not-so-genuine ignorance of anything that might help the police. He said he would have a talk with the rest of us and phone back if there was anything to report.

As soon as the phone was back on the hook, the four of us huddled round the kitchen table and did some fast thinking. The dilemma was simple enough. We *did* have information, namely, the knowledge that it was Jean who had given those three warnings, as well as what she'd told us in her midnight visit. But if we told the police and they apprehended her – hiding in Leeds, perhaps – they would bring her back to Keldreth and into her brother's house. It would also mean that Richard would learn that Jean knew too much, and it was possible that he would find a way to silence her.

On the other hand, if Richard had already learned of Jean's midnight visit, he might well have harmed her by now. In that case, our refusal to tell the police what we knew would delay her discovery.

In the end, we decided that the first was more likely: that Jean, sensing Richard's growing awareness of how much she knew, had fled Keldreth of her own free will and gone into hiding. The best thing we could do for her safety was keep quiet and at the same time try to lure Richard to Cappelrigg and bring the whole nightmarish problem to a head.

Meanwhile, the police had discovered a woman who had last seen Jean near the bus station. This confirmed our hypothesis and set our minds more or less at rest.

And so we resumed our plan to trap the 'Druid', only now we knew who he was. Every evening David made his way to Cappelrigg just before Tom left. Every morning, David left just after Tom arrived. Our vigilance was heightened after Jean's visit. We now knew that the danger was real.

So why, one drizzly afternoon, did I blithely drive my

tractor into the fields while Tom set off for Kirkby, leaving me quite alone?

Stupidity, really. I'd decided to replace a couple of sagging field gates with new ones. One of these was already loaded into my tractor bucket, and Tom and I were just about to set off together when Tom noticed a ewe behaving oddly. He was pretty sure what the problem was and he phoned the vet immediately. The vet was out, and so the receptionist suggested that Tom drive into Kirkby to collect the medication, a standard one which she could dispense without the vet's confirmation.

Now, it so happened that my Land-Rover was in the garage for repairs. If we had thought about it, I could have driven Tom's car myself. Or we could have gone to Kirkby together. But our minds, distracted by this interruption of our planned work, functioned sluggishly. Tom hopped into his car, I into my tractor and off we went in opposite directions.

As I chugged up the first field, I had no time to think of anything except the gate, very long and thus rather precariously placed in the bucket. The land was uneven and I had to drive with special care to prevent the gate from bouncing out of the bucket.

I never gave Richard a thought, so hard was I concentrating. I never gave a thought either to the fact that I was driving straight up the ley line, heading towards the same little ford across the syke where John Jowett had been killed. Nor did I give a thought to last autumn's dream in which I'd been driving towards this very spot in my black and white dress, hurtling towards my death in an out-of-control tractor while Richard stood by. I didn't think about any of this until, suddenly, it was happening, only this time it wasn't a dream.

True, I wasn't wearing my black and white dress, nor was the tractor out of control. But there was the fatal ford, and there, not far from it, stood Richard. Smiling.

My first enraged thought was that I deserved what was coming; how could I have been so stupid? My second thought was that I would have to pull my mind together and remember the state of play – how much did Richard know I knew, et cetera. For I was no match for him physically. If I was to

318

get out of this encounter unscathed, it would be by my wits alone.

Then, inspiration. I gave him a cheery wave and, with my face screwed up in an exaggerated display of concentration, continued to steer the tractor down the slope into the ford. I'm not sure what I intended to do after that, but I never had a chance to find out. Richard, equally inspired, hastened towards the opposite slope and positioned himself in front of the tractor. At this point there was no way I could detour round him. Either I mowed him down or I stopped.

I stopped.

Richard came up to the cab. 'I've been hoping to see you for some time now,' he said pleasantly.

I made myself smile. 'You know how it is, haytime. Not the best time for socialising. How was your hay? Did you get it in all right?' Completely forgetting that the Staveleys never bothered about hay. They took silage.

'I didn't come here to talk about hay, Charlotte.'

'Well, actually, it's not a very good place to talk about anything. Why don't you come over this evening?' This evening, when David would be with me.

'And meet your guard dog?'

'Moss is very gentle, as you know.'

'I'm not talking about Moss.'

Play dumb, play dumb. 'Well, he's the only dog I have. Unless you're afraid of Tarzan?'

'It's your Welsh bulldog I dislike.'

Play dumb. 'Not a breed I've heard of.'

'Don't play dumb, Charlotte. I want to talk to you alone.'

So. He knew about David's night-time visits. Had he spied? Or had Jean told him? If the latter, willingly or not? 'Well, here I am. Talk. But I am in rather a hurry, and Tom'll be here any minute.'

'Then he must have gone into Kirkby by helicopter,' Richard smiled.

The state of play was defined. Half an hour at least before I could hope for rescue, and he knew it. Would my wits last that long?

'Well, will you say what you have to say and then let me get on with my work?'

'I want to know if you've reconsidered my offer.'

What offer? I was genuinely dumb this time. Then I remembered the scene in the Golden Oak. Ah. That offer.

'I'm sorry. The public setting, the suddenness – I didn't think you were all that serious. Anyway, you didn't ask me to reconsider,' I said, playing for time.

'You didn't stay long enough to let me. Well?'

'I'm sorry. I would need time to think.'

'You've had several months. I've been very patient. I didn't even mind you having a fling with the squire.'

I felt my anger rising. A bad sign. My mind worked best when calm, but it was difficult keeping calm with David described as a 'fling'. I breathed deeply, trying to get myself back in control. Richard spoke again.

'You must have had long enough to find out what he's like by now. You must be tired of him by now.'

My temperature zoomed off the end of the thermometer. 'I don't expect to be tired of him for a very long time. A lifetime, approximately.'

A curlew flew over, high in the grey sky, its mournful cry mingling with the second sound of the tractor engine. Richard watched it pass. I'm sure he wasn't seeing it. There's no market for curlews.

'So, it's like that, is it?' he said at last.

'It is,' I replied. 'Which means you have your answer.' I nodded curtly and engaged gear.

In a single motion of breathtaking speed he opened the cab door and sprang into the seat beside me.

'It's all the same to me if you want to come and help me put up the gate,' I said, 'but I would have thought you had better things to do.'

He took my hand from the gear lever and killed the engine. 'Does that mean you'll be selling Cappelrigg?' he asked.

His voice had changed. There was a hard edge to it that told me he was finally talking about something which mattered to him. His 'proposal' had been a farce. No wonder he hadn't minded the public setting in which he'd made it. There was nothing private about it, no love at all. What he wanted all along was my farm. I should have controlled my anger, mumbled something vague about not having given it much

320

thought, played for time. But there arose in my mind the vision of Graegarth, ruined by Richard Staveley. And beside it, Cappelrigg, his next intended victim. 'No,' I said coldly. 'I will not be selling Cappelrigg. Ever.'

What happened next took me by surprise. Richard simply nodded and smiled. 'That's what John Jowett said, too. I offered to buy it off him, you know. I would have given him a fair price. He could have bought another farm with the money. It wasn't as if the farm meant anything in particular to him, it hadn't been in his family for generations or anything like that. One farm would have done him as well as another.' He waited for me to respond.

'Well, then, one farm will do you as well as another, too,' I said. 'You can buy a farm down in the vale if you want to expand.'

'No, Charlotte,' he said softly. 'I want Cappelrigg.'

'Richard,' I said evenly, 'we're not children. Only very young children think they can have everything they want. Our wants clash in this particular case. And since I do own Cappelrigg, and intend to continue owning it, you'll simply have to buy something else.'

'No, Charlotte, I intend to own Cappelrigg. I'm offering to buy it. I can hardly be fairer than that.'

'Richard,' I said, 'let's be quite clear about this. I have no intention whatsoever of selling my farm, now or ever. This farm is *mine* for as long as I live. Do you understand?'

Would it have made any difference if I'd chosen my words more wisely? Probably not.

'Then I'm afraid you haven't got long to live.'

*   *   *

This isn't happening, this isn't happening, please God make it not be happening, make me wake up in bed beside David and everything will be all right it's only a dream a nightmare it's not real – Then I went quite still. It was real, it was happening. We had reached the inevitable at last, and at last I knew it was true. Everything. The kites, John Jowett's tractor accident, Jean's disappearance, the threat to my life. True. Every bit of it. Like a drowning woman's, my past flashed by, selective, just the bits about Richard, scene after awful scene. How *could* I have been so stupid, so naïve, so Pollyanna sure that no one as charming as Richard could possibly be what he was? I tried to think what that was. A con man. A brilliant ruthless con man. We all of us think that we would have some special insight that would let us know. But we miss the point. Con men are con men because they can con. Everyone.

All thought of rescue by Tom vanished. My anger vanished, too. And then, miraculously, my mind cleared. All the debris that might hinder me whooshed away, clean out of my head. I went utterly calm.

'How much time?' I said.

He looked at his watch.

'If you're thinking of killing me in the next few minutes,' I said calmly, 'there's something you'd better know. I made a will as soon as I bought Cappelrigg. In it, my entire estate is bequeathed to my best friend. Including Cappelrigg. Effie's never liked you. You're the last person in the world she would sell the farm to. And I think you know who she would sell it to. The other person who bid for it at the auction last year. David Farleton.'

And the wonderful, glorious, supreme beauty of it was that *it was true*. Every word of it. For once my wits had come to my aid in time. And I didn't even have to lie.

Richard said nothing for a while. My trump card had been truly unexpected. He was having to revise his entire plan. Finally he spoke. 'Then you'd better change the will.'

'I can hardly do that if I'm dead, can I?' I smiled.

'I'm willing to give you some time,' he offered.

Oh, very gracious. I felt the anger rise again. 'And what, may I ask, would give me the incentive? Or would you like me to make *you* my beneficiary, just to guarantee that you'll kill me?'

Richard was silent. He turned away and gazed over the fields, towards his own ruined farm. If I'd been more sensible, I might have thought of some way to soothe his wounded pride. For there was no doubt that my revelation about the will had surprised and humiliated him. Hell hath no fury. But, elated with the reprieve I'd gained for myself I was blind to everything except the present.

'Quite a few people have their suspicions about you and the Druids and John Jowett's accident,' I said. 'If there's a second tractor "accident", you'll not only give my farm to David but end up with a life sentence.'

'Druids,' he snorted. The amount of contempt he put into the word was startling. 'You don't really think I had anything to do with that bunch? All I did was tell them your house was on a ley line. They did the rest for me. It was coincidence, that's all, John's death happening on that day. But it was worth using. I thought there was a good chance they'd scare you into leaving.'

So that much at least was true: he hadn't had anything to do with the cult. But it was incredible. Here was a man who'd cheerfully murdered his neighbour fastidiously disassociating himself from a bunch of harmless Druids. What kind of a mind was this? And why was he so obsessed with Cappelrigg?

'Why are you so obsessed with Cappelrigg anyway?' I asked. It was a reasonable enough question. I had no reason to suspect it might be a fatal one.

He gave me his most charming smile. 'Because it's mine by right.'

I don't know which irritated me more, the smile or the words. 'Richard, nothing is anyone's by right. Land is bought and sold like anything else. I have bought Cappelrigg. What on earth gives you this idiotic idea that you have some kind of "right" to it?'

And now he turned to face me fully. If his smile had a touch of madness to it, I didn't notice, not yet. 'Look at me, Charlotte. Haven't you guessed?'

I looked. To me, that big blond head was the ugliest thing in the world and the only thing I could guess was that he had suddenly gone into second childhood, playing some silly game. 'Guessed what?'

'Where have you seen this face before?' he continued.

'What kind of a stupid question is that?'

'You've seen this face before, Charlotte. One place in particular. Farleton Hall. Don't you remember?'

'Of course I remember. I'm not senile.'

'The portrait, Charlotte.'

'What por –' I began, then stopped. The waiter conducting

us to 'your favourite table, sir'. The table beneath the portrait of the old squire, David's father, whom he so little resembled. And whom – I looked sharply at Richard.

He was still smiling, nodding his head encouragingly at me. Something had happened in the last few minutes to transform Richard's face. It wasn't Richard anymore. Only once before had I seen this transformation. When Richard had turned slightly sideways at the dinner table, lining himself up, so to speak, with the portrait. The two faces, so alike –

'My father,' said Richard, still nodding, still smiling.

My hands and feet went cold. I could feel the chill creeping up, numbing my limbs. 'You must be mad,' I said, my voice sounding hoarse. But was he? I remembered now how startled I'd been at the time, noticing the resemblance.

'Illegitimate, of course,' said Richard.

There was an ugly twist to the smile now. It made him look more than ever like the old squire. Oh my God. And Belle, telling me that the old man had been 'chronically unfaithful'. It was all coming together now. Richard's proud bearing. He'd never looked or behaved like a hill farmer. No wonder, if he knew –

'That's why I took you to Farleton Hall,' Richard was saying. 'I thought you would notice, would understand.'

The chill was creeping up towards my chest. I would have to think fast, before all my senses turned to ice. 'Richard,' I said, 'this may or may not be true. But Hugh Farleton is also the old squire's son, and he didn't inherit a thing. Younger sons don't, you know. Even legitimate – '

'Younger sons, no,' Richard smiled. 'But I'm not a "younger son". I'm four months older than David Farleton. So you see, I'm the real heir to Farleton Estate.'

There was madness in his face now, unmistakable and terrifying. Think. Think. Before it's too late.

'Richard,' I said gently. 'Even if you were the squire's son, even if you were older than David, you wouldn't be legally entitled – '

'Legally, no. But by right. By moral right.'

I felt the stirrings of anger stabbing through the chill. The murderer of John Jowett, talking to me about moral rights!

'This entire estate is mine by right,' he went on smoothly, 'and if the law won't recognise that, then I'll get it back in my own way. Now do you understand?'

Oh, yes, I understood. I understood I'd been a fool not to get out of the tractor and make a run for it. I understood something else, too. That day when I'd first seen The Folly and Richard had walked back with me and kissed me. I'd felt then that something was driving him, and that that something wasn't me. Now I knew what it was. Cappelrigg, which had once been part of Farleton Estate. I knew, too, that it was so powerful that no reasoning on earth could turn him aside from his righteous goal. To him, John Jowett and I were just impediments standing between himself and his rightful estate.

My brain was whirling. What could I say to get through to this madman? Reason – my speciality – was useless in the face of a force like Richard's. And to appeal to decency, let alone compassion, was equally absurd, with a man who had already murdered one neighbour. My only hope was to be direct.

'And so you intend to kill me to get it,' I stated.

He smiled again. 'I'd rather not. I'd much rather marry you. The offer still stands.'

'Big of you,' I said savagely.

He shrugged. 'Then sell me the farm.'

I turned to him, blazing with helpless fury. 'You bastard,' I spat, forgetting that it might literally be true. 'There's no way I'll let you get your filthy hands on this land and ruin it the way you've ruined your own. Ever!'

He looked calmly at his hands, which were not filthy. How could they be? He never used them to work his land. 'I'm going to give you one chance, Charlotte.'

'I don't need your chance! I've got my will – made out to Effie. Or have you forgotten? If you kill me, you kill any possibility of ever owning this farm.'

'I don't believe you're so indifferent to life,' he said quietly.

'What do you mean?'

'I mean, Charlotte, that I may kill you anyway.'

'And what would you gain by that?'

He shrugged again. 'If you refuse to sell me the farm, what have I got left? If you won't let me reclaim my inheritance, there's nothing for me to lose. Why shouldn't I at least have my revenge?'

So calm he was, so reasonable in his speech. The language of a psychopath. That was the right word. I knew it at last. That lovely smiling charm of his, that reassuring evenness of temper I'd once admired. Not a con man after all, or rather, the supreme con man. The psychopath. I could feel my muscles relaxing, giving up. There was no hope for me either. What could anyone do in the face of a psychopath determined to have his revenge?

And then, miraculously, a reprieve.

'Charlotte, I'm giving you a chance to change your mind. Let's say Midsummer's Eve. That's reasonable, isn't it? I'll give you until Midsummer's Eve to decide to sell the farm to me. I'll come to you then for your decision.'

He nodded pleasantly, like a businessman who'd just concluded a workaday deal. Then he jumped lightly down from the tractor and walked home across the fields. He didn't look back.

35

'You *what*?' David roared.

'I drove up the field and hung the gate,' I said.

'Are *you* insane?'

He was bellowing now. Everyone round the kitchen table was staring.

'It was the only sane thing I *could* do,' I said weakly. 'My mind was a pudding, I was shaking so badly I could hardly drive. I had to do something simple and mindless and physical or I really would have gone crazy.'

'With a psychopath just waiting to kill you, you – '

'Davey, be reasonable,' said Brendan. 'The lass is right. She's as safe as can be. You can be sure Staveley will be on his knees praying to the good Lord to keep Charlotte alive till Midsummer's Eve. He'd much rather have the farm than revenge. He's got nothing to gain by harming her now. And everything to lose.'

'Brendan's right,' said Belle. 'Now can we please calm down and decide what to do next?' She turned to me. 'How do you feel now, Charlotte?'

'I don't know,' I said honestly.

The rest of the day had passed in a trance. I'd done my day's work automatically, clutching at every shred of normality to counteract the horror of the scene in the tractor. Each banal action was precious. I kept thinking, 'Only a few more days to live.' I could see no way around it. At the end of the day, Tom had driven me back to The Folly. I'd sat down to dinner with everyone else. I'd even forced myself to eat. It was obvious something was wrong, but I'd said nothing until the students had gone to their television. They knew nothing about Richard and the threats. We'd all agreed to keep quiet about it.

Once they'd gone, however, I'd broken down and started

327

shaking all over again. It had taken some time to get the story out.

'We're going to the police,' said David grimly. 'Come on, Charlotte. Get up.'

I was almost afraid of David. If I hadn't known he loved me, I would have been terrified of his anger, his response to my story had been so violent. Even now his face was thunderous.

'Not so fast,' said Belle. 'You walk into that police station in the state you're in now and you'll just put them off. You're good at that, David Farleton. You're not leaving this house until you've calmed down. Sit down. Now, another cup of tea, both of you.'

'Tea!' He exploded.

'*Sit down*. And no, you can't have a drink. One whiff of alcohol on your breath and the police won't believe a word you say. We've got to persuade them to arrest the bastard. Sit down and *think*.'

It was another hour before David and I set off for Kirkby. We were as calm as we could be, in the circumstances. I faltered only once or twice as I told my story a second time. I told it verbatim. Words like those are engraved on your mind, there's no hope of forgetting them.

I was even calm enough to see that poor Tyndall was in a quandary. The picture of Richard which emerged from my story bore no resemblance to the Richard he knew. I could see him trying to put the two together and failing. I almost felt sorry for him.

'Please,' I said, 'I know it sounds incredible. But it's true, every word of it. What can I say? People like him *do* exist. Some of them exist in peaceful little places like Langhamdale. And they're often very charming.'

'We'll investigate it, of course,' was all he would say.

'*Investigate*?' David exploded.

I kicked him hard under the table.

'I'll have to talk to the Inspector first,' Detective Sergeant Tyndall said. 'We may try a charge of threatening behaviour.'

'*Threat* – '

I kicked David again.

328

Tyndall didn't notice. 'About this business of the portrait,' he continued. 'Is it true? I mean, could your father . . . ' He trailed off, quaintly embarrassed.

'I doubt it,' said David. 'And what if it were? It's hardly an excuse to kill Charlotte.'

'David, wait. Listen,' I said suddenly. 'If he *is* deluded, and if we can come up with some sort of proof to show him he couldn't possibly be the squire's illegitimate son, the whole obsession might collapse. Surely it's worth a try?'

That night they held Richard for questioning. He denied everything except the encounter in the tractor, and the conversation there, he said, had been completely different. According to Richard, I was a thwarted woman trying to get my revenge. He had proposed to me – Tyndall had even witnessed that – and then had changed his mind. Nothing personal, you understand; he'd simply realised he wasn't really a marrying man after all. I'd taken it badly. I'd also taken up with David Farleton on the rebound. Now, spurred by wounded vanity, I was spreading lies about Richard.

They released him, of course.

On hearing of Richard's release, David had to be restrained from storming over to Graegarth. I really think he might have killed Richard.

Belle thought so too. 'That'll be really helpful,' she said sarcastically. We were around the kitchen table again, again taking stock of the hopeless situation. 'You spending the rest of your life in prison. Charlotte's really going to love that.'

The only thing we could do was remind the police of the Midsummer's Eve deadline. 'Look,' I said to them, 'every word of my statement is true, whatever Richard may have said.' I was somewhat recovered now and feeling rather aggressive myself. 'If you don't take that deadline seriously and something happens, the Kirkby Langham police force is going to look more than a little silly.'

They looked rather uncomfortable at that.

'I'm going to be at that Midsummer's Eve Ball, which means that Richard Staveley will have no choice but to be there, too.'

The police finally decided to have a plainclothes man on duty at the ball. He would keep Richard in his sight at all times. Possibly, just possibly, he might overhear Richard's conversation with me. An even more remote possibility was that Richard would do something decisive, and the police would be there to move in.

I had moved to The Folly again, feeling rather like a ping-pong ball. Our plan to lure Richard to the house at night had failed. There was no reason for me to stay there, and no desire, when I could be with David and my friends instead. Nobody said so, but it was pretty clear that I would never live at Cappelrigg again.

One possibility we didn't discuss was selling Cappelrigg. By now we all realised that Richard was unstoppable. He wouldn't be satisfied with Cappelrigg, not for long. If he really believed he was the rightful heir to the estate, he would be driven until the entire estate was his. That would mean killing me eventually anyway. And David. And Matti. And Hugh. Whenever the conversation came round to this we went quiet. Then we busied ourselves with something banal.

I still felt, deep down in my guts, incredulity at the whole situation. Was there really nothing the police could do? But when I thought about how the legal system worked, I realised that there wasn't. How could they imprison for life a man who had merely threatened to kill, even if they believed it? And nothing short of a life sentence would solve our problem. I don't know what we expected the outcome to be, only that all our hopes were centred on the Midsummer's Eve Ball and the plainclothes policeman who might, just might . . .

We said nothing to the police about Jean's midnight visit. Her story – especially if she'd witnessed the fatal phone call between Richard and John Jowett – might lend credence to my own. But she wasn't here to tell it, and, as she herself had said, what would be the use? There would still be no real evidence that Richard had killed Jowett. Let alone that he intended to do the same to me. And, given the uselessness of the police in my case, we felt more than ever that Jean was safer in hiding.

At least we hoped she was in hiding. I felt so sorry for Brendan. I hadn't realised that he was so fond of her. Brendan and Belle had adjusted to their childlessness quite well, taking a caring interest in other young people instead – the students, Jean, even me to some extent. Jean was, quite simply, the daughter Brendan had always wanted. What a dismal irony. Her own parents had obviously cared little for her. If only the world were better ordered, she could have come to Brendan and Belle instead, been welcomed and loved so much by them.

Through all of this, work on the ballroom was proceeding at a frenetic pace. Effie had taken the whole thing in hand, long-distance, supplying the materials, engaging the labour. I hadn't seen her in action since she'd done my own flat and was again impressed. She was coming north two days before the ball – to check on what the workmen had done and to do the more temporary decoration for the ball herself. We were in constant touch by phone, so nobody was surprised when, the night before she was due to arrive, she phoned. But her first words made me think twice.

'You're not on a party line, are you?'

'Of course not,' I said.

'Is there anyone near the phone who isn't in on this whole Staveley business?' she asked.

We had, of course, told her the story by now. 'No, just the four of us. Why?'

'Extensions?'

'We should have but don't. This is the only phone. Effie, what's this all about?'

'Jean's here.'

It took me a few seconds to digest this. My silence must have worried Effie.

'Charlotte, are you there?'

'Yes. I'm here. Jean's *where*?'

'Here. In London. In my flat. She turned up last night in a pretty rough state. You wouldn't believe what she's been through the last few days – no money, no contacts, nowhere to stay, no nothing.'

'Effie,' I broke in, 'could you please begin at the beginning?'

'Sorry. Well, she did her flit right after that midnight visit to you,' Effie began. 'She was worried enough already about

331

Richard guessing how much she knew. Then she panicked, thinking you might go to the police.'

'But we promised her – '

'I know. But she's Richard's sister. Not much experience of people telling the truth, right? Anyway, she got to London without a thought in her head and hardly any money left after the train fare. Then she remembered me. But she didn't even know my surname, right? So she was living rough – the whole ghastly cardboard city bit – at the same time she was trying to track me down. Finally she found out my business address, but my gorgon of a secretary wouldn't let her through, wouldn't believe she knew me. Wouldn't even pass on a message. That's what I hired her for, she's great, but just this once – Well, anyway, somehow Jean then found out my home address, and I discovered her literally on the doorstep last night, just about to be harrassed by a couple of particularly thuggish-looking men in blue. Talk about the nick of time. Anyway, that's about it. She's cleaned up now and fed and she's been zonked out in the spare room ever since.'

'This is incredible, Effie.'

'Isn't it just. You know what? I rather like Jean. She's got guts, and she's no fool either. If she survives this whole awful mess I'm going to make damn sure she gets a job. I'll just put the screws on one of my decorating firms and tell them they take her on or I take my business elsewhere. She won't let me down, of that I'm sure. Meanwhile, she lives here. No problem. The only thing is, she's desperate to know if you've been to the police, and even more desperate to tell you to keep quiet if you haven't.'

'Tyndall says Mrs Staveley's frantic with worry.'

'Too bad,' said Effie. 'Frankly, from what Jean says, the only thing the old bag gets frantic about is tarnish on her horse brasses. I believe her. Don't tell, Charlotte. Promise?'

'Promise. But this can't go on forever.'

'I know. I've told her about your Green Ball plot. We're just hoping it'll all come to a head then. If not, God knows what next.'

'What happens when you come here tomorrow?'

'Jean stays here – couldn't be safer. I don't think Richard's got the smarts that his sister has – it would take him more than a few days to find where I live. Anyway, he's too busy plotting whatever he's plotting for the ball, right?'

When Effie arrived, she didn't have much to add. In any case, there was no time to talk tactics. The Folly was in well-ordered chaos. Effie had barely greeted us before she sped off to the ballroom to check on the work done. Watching her prowl around, invisible magnifying glass to eye, made me remember just how meticulous she was, which in turn made me see why she fitted in so well here. Quality. The hard-nosed demand that everything be done to the highest standards. The ethos that pervaded every aspect of life on the estate was Effie's ethos, too. Fortunately, the work passed.

The students had been given a long weekend off. They were eager to leave, scathing about the whole business which to them was just a bunch of silly twits dressing up to prance about to grotty music. I hadn't realised how macho they were. The steadiness needed to work with the horses normally disguised it. They considered themselves a tough élite and thoroughly disliked having their realm invaded by weedy outsiders.

There was certainly nothing weedy about Effie, going off into the forest with the men to dig up surplus saplings. These were brought back and potted up to form little groves of real trees around the ballroom. The pots were disguised by extremely realistic carpets of moss which made the groves appear to be on little knolls. There was other greenery, too, all of it real, lavish and yet discreet enough to blend with the fairy woodland wallpaper. It took ages to get the lighting – both indoors and out – exactly right, so that it would make the ballroom seem wall-less, as if it were simply part of the real woodland outside.

The final effect was utterly stunning. Even Effie was surprised at just how good it was. 'I can't *bear* to think of it all being dismantled after the night,' she wailed, greedily admiring her creation at the dress rehearsal on Friday night.

There were seven of us admiring it. Astrid and Matti had come up for the event. I don't think Matti thought much more of the ball than the students did, but he liked to be where the action was. Also, Astrid confessed, he was dying to see me again. I felt rather weepy when she said that. Matti had been ecstatic at the news that I was moving to The Folly for good, that David and I were living together. I don't think he understood the intricacies of our relationship. As far as he was concerned, I was simply a new mother, whether married or not, along with Ros and Astrid. Belle – and even Effie occasionally – augmented the roster still further. No doubt the time would come when this profusion of 'mothers' would rest heavily on his rebelling adolescent shoulders, but for the time being he thoroughly enjoyed his collection.

I enjoyed Matti, too. I'd feared that Charlotte-the-visitor might turn villain when she became Charlotte-the-permanent. I knew enough from my London friends to understand the trauma of this kind of arrangement. But once again my life seemed blessed, and the squalid black cloud called Richard receded from centre stage as I enjoyed the new relationship with Matti.

While Effie and the men had been raiding the forest, Belle had been cooking violently. A catering company from York was coming in, but Belle didn't trust anyone but herself to take the ultimate responsibility. She came to an agreement with the firm to provide much of the food herself, leaving them mainly to arrange the layout and service. I turned domestic and helped Belle. She was as merciless in her demands for quality as Effie was with her workmen and David with his students. I do not think the most expensive hotel in London could rival the food that was making its way into the dining-room which we opened up for the occasion.

Apart from the library and our bedrooms, which we locked, we opened up the entire Folly to our guests. We knew that was why most of them were coming, not only the better-heeled locals but many from as far away as London and Edinburgh. The Folly was known in architectural and 'heritage' circles. This might be their only chance to see it. Their green consciences alone wouldn't have made them pay the outrageous price we set. The tickets had sold out very quickly. We'd already sent the profits off to the charities.

By late Saturday afternoon everything was ready except us, still scruffy in our workclothes. The musicians had just arrived and were arranging their chairs and music stands on the largest 'knoll' at one end of the ballroom. They, like the caterers, had come from York, a trio of young men – violin, cello and piano – who were a few years out of music college and had set themselves up specifically to provide music for this sort of occasion. They were charming, intelligent and very talented, as we realised when we eavesdropped on their rehearsal.

When they'd finished rehearsing, we all had a light supper together in the kitchen. Then we put the cats out for the night and dispersed to dress.

I had chosen a green dress, of course. I knew many other people would, too, but I didn't mind. Mine was special. The cut was plain, even severe, to allow for the material itself: hundreds of tiny pale-green silk leaves overlapping each other and fluttering gently in the smallest breeze. Into my crown of black plaits, I wove a wreath of tiny white roses from the garden.

The wreath took longer than expected. I heard distant shouts of 'Where's Charlotte? Where's David?' coming from the direction of the ballroom. I hastened out towards the central stairs. David had, rather mysteriously, insisted on dressing in a spare room. I'd put it down to embarrassment – not at being naked, but at being seen climbing into the clothes he considered so absurd. I'd never seen David in anything but jeans and wondered how he would look.

My answer came as I began to descend the stairs towards the big central landing. There, on the other side, was David, matching his step to mine and looking unbelievably handsome in his dinner jacket, black tie and maroon cummerbund. To my surprise, he looked as much at home in the alien clothes as he did in his jeans. I suppose I'd forgotten about his life before he'd turned hermit.

I smiled euphorically as we descended the matching staircases and met on the landing beneath Rhiannon's portrait. 'You planned this,' I accused him.

He nodded, and a trace of unease touched his smile. Then he asked for my hand and put into it a small box. I opened it. It was a ring. Just one very large and magnificently cut emerald in a plain gold setting. I looked up at him, puzzled.

He cleared his throat. 'For you,' he said rather idiotically, 'in any way you wish. As a love token, or a symbol of our life together, or an engagement ring.'

Green. Large but simple and of the highest quality. Of course. I smiled uncertainly at him. 'Can I be greedy and ask for all three?'

He put his arms around me and held me close.

'Lottie,' he said.

'David,' I said.

Was there anything more that needed saying?

We entered the ballroom, still a bit shaky. The musicians were at the far end, tuning up. Everyone else was at the near end, clearly impatient for our arrival. I smiled weakly. Effie frowned, narrowed her eyes and came straight up to me. She saw the ring. 'And what is that?' she demanded.

'We're engaged,' I said.

Effie burst into tears. Belle rushed off for the champagne. Brendan sent the cork into a young rowan in one of the 'groves'. We all laughed and cried very foolishly. The musicians stopped tuning. The violinist who was their leader called across the room, 'Anything wrong?'

'Charlotte and David!' Astrid called back. 'They are just engaged!'

The musicians' heads leaned towards each other in consultation. Then they returned to their instruments. A few seconds later the strains of Lohengrin's Wedding March marched across the room, Palm Court style.

'We do weddings, too,' said the violinist hopefully when they'd finished.

The party began.

36

The first people to arrive were, by prearrangement, the detectives from the York CID. I was aware that plainclothes officers were clever at blending in, but even so I was surprised by the authenticity of these two. They were in their early thirties, stylishly dressed and lacking even the faintest whiff of authority. David and I had to see their documents to believe them.

The woman laughed as she put away her card and got straight down to business. 'Staveley may well suspect that someone from CID will be here,' she said, 'so we'll pose as friends of yours from York. Please call me Sally, and this is Greg. We'll have to check things out with you from time to time and we don't want it to appear odd,' she explained. 'Right, where's the library?'

We took them to the library, for which I alone had the key, and explained our plan. Sally, who appeared to be the senior officer, nodded her approval, then cautioned, 'You do realise there might be some risk to you. If he has a knife, for instance.'

I knew, but I wished she hadn't mentioned it in front of David. 'I'm sure he won't,' I said. 'He's too clever for that. He'll want to engineer an accident. A knifed corpse in the library would be rather obvious.'

'We'll keep you and Staveley in sight at all times,' she said, 'so bring him to the library whenever it feels right. Now, what about the rest of the house?'

We showed them round the 'maze'. We also gave them maps, though of course they couldn't consult them while anyone else was around.

'Does Staveley know the layout?' Greg asked.

'I doubt it,' said David. 'He's been in the house a few times, but only as a child. He couldn't possibly remember.'

337

By the time we arrived back in the hall to greet the first of our real guests, the four of us were chatting pleasantly of other things. I almost felt they *were* old friends from York. Their efficiency impressed me so much that I nearly forgot both the danger and the difficulty of our plan. They had never met Richard, never been subjected to his charm. It was clear that they took this more seriously than Tyndall, and that made me feel we had a reasonable chance of success.

That, plus David's ring. Being engaged shouldn't have mattered that much, David and I had no need of such formalities. But the ring itself, so symbolic not of love in general but of our very particular kind of love, felt like a magic charm. No harm could come to me, or to us, while the perfect green stone was with me. David had been a little apprehensive. 'I know diamonds are official,' he said, 'but the emerald looked better on its own.'

I agreed. 'We're not diamond people. We're big and green and plain.'

'Some people think green is unlucky.'

'They're out of date.'

'Green is the colour of the gods, that's why people are afraid of it.'

'I feel like a god tonight. Oh, David, we're going to change the world, you and I!' I cried, drunk on euphoria before half a glass of champagne had gone down. 'We're going to do something big and grand and glorious! We're going to live up to the promise of that emerald!'

'My crazy Lottie,' he said gently, 'we have to get through tonight first.'

'We will. It'll all happen tonight. And tomorrow we'll start our life together properly at last!'

People were arriving as early as they decently could, perhaps to give themselves time to see the house. I'd been to some pretty elegant parties in London, but none had generated such a powerful sense of excitement as this one. The huge hall doors leading onto the terrrace were wide open. Outside stood Brendan and Belle, officially collecting tickets and unofficially greeting the guests, trying to make them feel that this was a private party, that they were all friends of the household. They succeeded. By the time the guests arrived in the hall to be greeted a second time by David and me, they seemed surprisingly at home.

It was the first time I had played the lady of the house, the squire's consort. I enjoyed it. Up on the landing, Rhiannon smiled down on me. I could feel her approval wafting over me like another benediction, just in case my life wasn't rich enough already. I greeted my guests with genuine warmth, felt absurdly fond of these strangers who, it seemed to me, were gathering to celebrate our engagement. It did feel like an engagement party, and a wedding, all rolled into one great celebration. Even David seemed touched by the general sense of joy. Just as I'd expected him to appear ill at ease in his dinner jacket, I'd anticipated a grumpy squire grudgingly playing his role. Not a bit of it. He radiated his own dark happiness and seemed to take pleasure in introducing me to those locals he did know as 'my fiancée, Charlotte Venables'.

I was so happy I almost forgot Richard and was shocked suddenly to see him mounting the terrace steps with his mother. Brendan and Belle must have needed all their acting skills to greet them with the same enthusiasm as the other guests. I certainly did. I gripped David's hand as the Staveleys approached. 'Keep calm,' I muttered. 'Smile.' Then I felt the gentle weight of the green stone on my hand and, like magic, my own smile came, unforced. What, ultimately, did these hard twisted people matter? After tonight, it would all be over and they would recede from our lives, leaving us free at last.

Sally and Greg were positioned a little further along, apparently enjoying an intimate conversation with each other. As the Staveleys turned to join the people drifting towards the ballroom, I gave a little nod to Sally. And as the Staveleys passed them, she returned my nod. Not long after, I saw that Sally and Greg had joined the throng disappearing into the ballroom.

*   *   *

'May I have the pleasure of this dance, Miss Venables?'

I raised my love-besotted face to my squire. 'I would be delighted, sir.'

We swept into the dance on the waves of *The Blue Danube*. All the guests had arrived. The party was in full swing.

'I hope it will not be taken amiss if I express some surprise at the exceeding grace of my lord's dancing?' I teased.

'My lady's approbation pleases me greatly,' he smiled, and whirled me expertly through the crowded ballroom.

Where had he learned to dance so beautifully, he of the resin-stained hands and surly brow? He was a treasure house, my David, full of lovely surprises all waiting for my discovery.

'David,' I said, 'have I ever told you how madly, passionately and stupendously I adore you?'

'I don't believe you have, miss. Say it again. It sounds good.'

A grin perched on top of a shocking-pink satin dress flashed by. Effie, in the arms of a surprisingly light-footed Brendan whose grin matched hers.

They were by no means the only grins in the ballroom. When *The Blue Danube* finished and I stood with Matti while David danced with Astrid, I watched the couples whirling past. Happy smiling faces all. The evening was already a raving success. We hadn't thought much beyond this evening, but now I wondered if we should make this an annual event. We could have other events, too, daytime ones to show the public the work we were doing. People did seem to be interested, and much friendlier in their interest than David expected.

All except Nicola Dearden, who exuded the same chilled politeness as the day we'd delivered the firewood and encountered Richard. How much she knew about Richard's supposed parentage and his plans I had no idea, but she seemed to have absorbed his antagonism and made it her own. She was dancing with him now, the expression on her face transparent to her poor cuckolded husband if he'd bothered to notice.

Richard's face was opaque, the same bland blond mask I knew so well. Every time I saw him my guts gave a sickening lurch. Some time this evening it would happen – when, we didn't know. I was living two lives, one full of excited plans for the future, the other smeared with the possibility of extinction.

My tactic, such as it was, was to give Richard no encouragement. I would wait for him to approach me. That way, any suspicion he might have of a police presence would be lessened. I wondered how long he would spin out the suspense, carry on dancing with Nicola *et al.* I noted that he didn't ask Belle or Astrid or Effie to dance. Or me, thank God. The one thing I was not prepared to do was dance with Richard. The memory of that kiss on the moor sickened me.

'Quite some shindig,' I said to Matti, to cancel out the memory.

He was gazing at the whirling couples with cautious fascination. So like David, much more at home with the horses and the trees. I was glad that Matti would inherit it all. It was his in spirit already.

He looked up at me with unaccustomed shyness and, stumbling over his words, asked me to dance.

'I'd be delighted,' I said, and allowed myself to be led onto the crowded floor. Yes, so like David: full of surprises. Who would have guessed that all evening he'd been longing to dance?

As the sky outside the big windows began to darken, Effie disappeared to adjust the lighting, both indoors and out. The effect, happening so gradually, was wonderful, slowly turning the ballroom into a moonlit glade. The weather had been kinder to our ball than to our hay, soft and balmy with just enough breeze wafting in from the open windows to freshen the air. People drifted in and out, arm in arm, living their own idylls for one magical evening.

The dining-room was as lovely as the ballroom. Here, too, Effie had transplanted bits of forest to create leafy alcoves for the little tables, each one candlelit and centred on a small vase of woodland flowers. There was a bar at one end and an immense buffet running down one long side filled with countryside food: venison, jugged hare, game pie. The staff worked unobtrusively at clearing and resetting the tables. There was proper crockery – paper and plastic would have ruined the atmosphere – all of it being washed endlessly in the kitchen by more staff.

As I entered the dining-room I saw Belle at the buffet, filling her plate and trying to pretend she was just another guest while at the same time keeping a beady eye on the staff. I joined her.

'You have to admit they know their job.'

Belle nodded guiltily. 'I just can't get used to doing nothing. Come on – there's a table over there.'

We sat down with our laden plates. Belle touched my hand on which glowed the great green stone.

'Charlotte, I'm *so* glad.'

'So you should be,' I laughed. 'You plotted it all. You and Brendan. And don't you dare play innocent. I remember that first morning as clearly as if it were yesterday. *You're the one person who might get through to him*, you said.'

Belle laughed. 'Well, I hate to say I told you so, but . . . '

When we returned to the ballroom, the sky beyond the softly illuminated trees was nearly dark. Richard was dancing with Sally. The sight gave me a little shock, though I suppose it was just part of her job. None the less, I knew all too well the power of Richard's charm. Would she still believe him capable of murder? The pleasure that had held me up all evening began to drain away. Perhaps Richard wouldn't make his move tonight after all. What then?

I should have known. Midnight. Just as the big clock in the hall was distantly doing its count, Richard glided up to me. 'Midsummer's Eve is over, Charlotte. Shall we dance? Or shall we go somewhere quiet and talk?'

I nodded dumbly and walked towards the door, trusting him to follow. Oh yes, he would follow. His future and mine depended on this talk; he would let nothing waylay him now that the moment had come. I took care not to look at anyone in the ballroom, or in the passageways to the library. I had to trust, too, that Sally and Greg had seen. Richard was clever, would see any hint of a signal.

He raised an eyebrow as I took out my key and opened the library door. 'Some of the books are very valuable,' I said shortly, and ushered him in. While he was looking round, I partly closed the door, to exactly the place where the hinged side would provide a crack for viewing. Richard didn't seem to notice. First hurdle over.

'Have you made your decision?' he asked pleasantly.

'I have something to show you,' I answered, and went to the

bookcase where we'd put the diary. I held my breath as he hesitated, but then he joined me and stood just where we'd hoped he would, clearly visible from the crack in the door. I reached down the diary and opened it to the appropriate page.

'This is Rhiannon Farleton's diary,' I said. 'The relevant section begins here.' I handed the open book to him.

He barely glanced at it. 'What do I care about Rhiannon Farleton?'

'Not much,' I admitted. 'But you care a great deal about her husband. At least, you do if you really think he's your father. Read.'

He snapped the diary shut and handed it back to me. I opened it again and returned it to him. I made no effort to conceal my dislike. 'You'd better read this, Richard, because it's dated exactly nine months before your birth.'

He frowned. 'How do you know that?'

'You told me. You said you were born four months before David. It wasn't exactly difficult to work it out from there.' This was true enough, but not complete. Jean had also told us, and she'd been able to give us the exact date. 'Rhiannon kept a diary for the whole of her married life. Each day begins with the date immediately followed by the place where she was at the time. Look at this entry, Richard. She was in Nairobi, *with her husband*, while you were being conceived.'

He smiled. 'How do you know when I was conceived?'

'I don't,' I said smoothly. 'But I do know the biological limits of both early and late deliveries. I also know that during the entire period when you could have been conceived, the squire was thousands of miles away. You see, Richard, this was their honeymoon trip. They were away for six months. No amount of fiddling the figures can change that.'

I paused to let the full significance of my words sink in. I couldn't tell if I'd succeeded. Richard's face was a mask.

'Richard,' I tried again, 'do I have to spell it out even further? This diary is proof that you couldn't possibly be the old squire's son.'

I held the diary up to his face and began to page through the whole long section. The datelines stood out dark and clear, a gazetteer of all those African names stamped with the English aristocracy's mania for colonising. A sad chunk of history was

343

under my flicking fingers, but right then I didn't care. All I cared was that Richard's reluctant eyes were taking it in.

Suddenly he grabbed the diary from my hands and flung it to the floor. At the same time he wheeled round so that he was facing the bookcase instead of the door. 'It's a fake,' he said, too quietly to be heard by anyone but me. His anger seemed to have gone as quickly as it had arrived.

I picked up the fragile and now rather battered diary and held it out to him. 'You're welcome to inspect it,' I said coldly.

He put his hands in his pockets and stared at the rows of books.

'Richard,' I said, as calmly as I could, 'this whole ghastly obsession of yours is built on a lie. I don't know what made you so sure you were the squire's son. I admit I did wonder at first, after seeing his portrait. Then I realised. Blond bearded men look pretty much the same. You more or less said it yourself when you denied being the Druid priest. Well, now you know the truth. I suggest you take your filthy money and buy a farm somewhere else. You have no "right" whatsoever to Cappelrigg Farm. And I have no intention whatsoever of selling it to you.'

There was a long pause. The whole plan was going awry. I'd hoped to provoke him into a physical attack. That way at least there'd be a charge of assault to tide us over until we could persuade the police to reopen the John Jowett case. Instead, he stood quietly in front of the bookcase.

Finally he spoke. 'Is that your decision?'

'Richard, there *is* no decision to be made. There never was. Don't you see that now?'

'Is that your decision?' It was the voice of an automaton, with an automaton's mechanical smile spreading over the face. How does one communicate with a machine? This was my last chance to provoke him, to resolve the hideous nightmare forever, and my mind was blank.

'Is that your decision?' the automaton repeated.

'Yes!' I said furiously. 'Yes, that is my decision!'

He nodded, quite calmly, as if deeply satisfied with his evening's work. 'You're going to regret this, Charlotte,' he smiled. Then, just as calmly, he turned and walked out of the library.

37

'I'm sorry, but there's nothing to go on.'

Sally and David and I were on the terrace. Inside, Richard was dancing with the mayor's wife as if the scene in the library had never taken place.

'But you did hear everything he said?' I asked.

'Most of it. Enough to see that it fits with the statement you made to the police. We'll file our report, of course. It could be useful for future reference. But for the present there's nothing we can do. He didn't even make a definite threat. That bit at the end wouldn't stand up in any court.'

'"Future reference" isn't much use to us if Charlotte's dead,' said David bitterly.

'Mr Farleton, we have our rules and procedures. By the way, is the diary genuine?'

David nodded.

'Keep it safe, just in case.'

'For "future reference"?'

'We'll keep an eye on Staveley for the rest of the evening, of course, but beyond that . . . ' She smiled – rather sadly, I thought – and went in through the french windows.

David put his arms round me. 'We'll think of something, Lottie.'

I rested my head against his chest and felt momentarily comforted. David's nearness, the sweetness of the night air, the big green stone still giving out signals of hope. I had to grasp at everything to keep that hope alive. Without it, what future? 'Perhaps he'll still do something tonight,' I said, though I doubted it.

David nodded. 'Let's go in.'

We went in. We danced to *The Emperor Waltz*. I even managed to smile at the cellist, a rather jolly little fellow who showed no signs of flagging despite the late hour. The dancers seemed equally undaunted, though some of the dresses were looking a bit crumpled, the faces a little shiny with perspiration. Only a few people had left, older couples and one or two younger ones who no doubt had tyrannical baby-sitters. Other than that, the ball still seemed to be going strong.

It was some time later, while dancing with Brendan, that I noticed that Richard and his mother were both missing. So were Greg and Sally.

'They left a while back,' said Brendan. 'I think our coppers'll be giving them a discreet escort home. Headlights off, concealed car and all the rest of it. Not that any of it's much use to us.'

Later still, the detectives reappeared. David and I sat with them at one of the more remote tables in the dining-room, though there seemed little purpose in such discretion now.

'We watched the house for some time,' said Sally. 'Everything was as you'd expect. Lights on, then gradually being switched off. The house had been in darkness for quite a while before we left. Strictly speaking there's a possibility that he might make his way back here, but it seems unlikely.'

We agreed. It would be difficult to engineer my 'accident' during the ball. Much easier to wait, plan it at his leisure, do it properly.

None the less, when finally the last guests had left and the musicians and caterers had packed up and gone off into the night, we made the rounds of the house. We would have done this anyway, in case anyone had been lost in the maze. Throughout the evening, all of us except me had taken turns to go along the crazy twists and turns of the corridors and stairs to flush out any guests who'd become lost. Quite a few had, and seemed rather to enjoy it.

This time, however, we were more methodical, though the weird geography of the house put obvious limits on our effectiveness. But we did try to check each room in turn, and we locked behind us those rooms which were unused, something we wouldn't normally do. Some rooms had no locks, and there were also a multitude of little cupboards tucked away in odd places. We called loudly as we went along, just on the off chance that someone was having a drunken snooze. Once I thought I heard footsteps where none should be, but shortly afterwards we encountered our detectives and realised it must have been them.

We locked all the windows and all the outer doors as well and made sure there were no ladders about. I felt very silly about all of this, but the detectives wanted to finish off their assignment properly, and so we did as we were told.

The sky was already going grey when I pulled the curtains shut in our room and flopped into bed beside David. The house felt strange around me, both deathly quiet after all the noise and yet echoing with footsteps and scraps of music, as if the sounds had imprinted themselves on the very fabric of the house and were now letting themselves out again in a long breath.

I had, rather childishly, kept my ring on. In the brief time I'd had it, it had taken on a symbolism wider even than that of David's love. I couldn't explain it then and still don't understand why it seemed so powerfully imbued with good. I knew that a few famous jewels were reputed to have such powers – for good and for evil. Now, lying in David's arms, I wondered if this was one of them.

I could feel his smile in the darkness as he replied. 'Didn't you notice? It was Rhiannon's – she's wearing it in her portrait. The original setting was hideous – cluttered with a mass of other little stones – so I had it reset. The old and the new. The emerald had been in her family for generations, it's nothing to do with the Farletons. I thought you'd like that. Given the more recent history of the Farleton side.'

The old squire and Richard. Everything came back to that in the end. I pushed the cluster of ugly thoughts away and, comforted by the ring, said, 'I do like it. Very much indeed. You have a nice talent for symbolism, my love.' Then I remembered where he'd given it to me. 'David, the portrait – Rhiannon's. Was that a piece of your symbolism, too?'

'Of course. You and Rhiannon would have liked each other. Ah, my lovely Lottie, I wish I'd met you twenty years ago.'

'Twenty years ago I was a schoolgirl in pigtails,' I reminded him.

'Never mind. We'll make up for it now.'

And, tired as we were, we did.

I fell asleep quickly after that. And dreamed. It must have been a magic ring, infusing its benevolence into my sleeping mind, for the dream was a happy one, at least at first. It began as an uncannily realistic rerun of that September morning when Olwen and I had thundered across the mist-swathed field. How dreamlike the reality of that morning had been! And now, how real the dream, except that the dreamfield had no walls, no boundaries of any sort. Mile after mile we galloped, unimpeded, ecstatic, through the swirling grey landscape. So effortless was Olwen's gait that we seemed truly to be flying.

And then, in a mighty swirl of pearly arabesques, the mist heaved itself away and I looked down and saw that we were indeed flying. The flat field below soon gave way to a forest much bigger than the real one, a horizonless sea of swaying treetops which we skimmed in our flight; occasionally one of Olwen's hooves would graze the tip of a fir and I could feel the whole tree shudder with pleasure. The trees were brushed with the same silvery colour of the now vanished fog. And then it seemed that the trees *were* silver, a Fabergé wonderland of perfectly crafted trees. The sun, rising unseen, glanced off the burnished metal and made it gleam and I saw that Olwen, too, had turned to silver.

A moment later the sun made its appearance far over to the east, a brazen gold curve just rising over the tops of the furthest trees. At the same time, the silvery landscape began to brighten and the trees take on the harsher glow of gold. Olwen, too, had turned to gold. The brighter metal seemed to increase both her size and the power of her muscles, and we were two great gilded giants surging above the shiny gold forest.

Then I saw that all the other horses were flying behind us, all of them glittering with the same unnatural hue. Their manes and tails whipped behind them in a blinding flickering mass like palest gold flames. Olwen's mane, too, was ablaze. I had only a moment to thrill to the beauty of this fiery gold spectacle of which I was a part before I realised that the flames were real. The hairs of Olwen's mane lashed cruelly at my bare arms and I felt the fine hairs on them ignite.

My arms were on fire. Faster than it took to think it, the flames raced up my arms and ignited my hair. It blazed out behind me in an incandescent banner. The trees, too, were alight, a fiery furnace roaring beneath us. And then, with no transition, I felt Olwen lurch violently beneath me and we were plummeting earthward, down into the inferno.

I awoke – or at least I thought I did – with the stench of the flames rising to my nostrils and the neighing of the horses in my ears. I was – or seemed to be – in bed. I sensed rather than saw David sleeping beside me. Some part of my mind knew I was still asleep and tried to change the scenario, put the reel in reverse to take the film back to the first wonderful gallop through the grey field. But I was meeting with a puzzling sort of resistance.

And then I seemed to be gliding across the darkened bedroom, drawing aside the curtains and gazing out on the cobbled courtyard. More puzzlement. The courtyard was black, not a single feature visible. I heard myself say to David, 'Why is it night? It was dawn when we went to bed.' The logic seemed quite proper and I felt irritated to hear just a grunt from my sleeping lover. 'David,' I demanded again. 'Why is it night?'

There was a long silence in which I thought I heard a distant floorboard creak. Then David's voice: 'Charlotte? Is that you? What are you doing?'

His sleepy voice exasperated me. 'David, it's night. We must have overslept.'

Another silence. And then David was beside me, shaking me hard and saying in an equally hard voice, 'Charlotte! Wake up!'

I woke up. I still don't know what strange transitional state I was in when I glided to the window, but now I was truly awake and very angry. I started to say something like 'What's got into you?' but broke off coughing. I heard our door open and David's voice ring through the sleeping house: 'Fire! The house is on fire!'

I still didn't understand. Dream and reality slid together and I coughed out, 'Don't be silly, it was only a dream,' when I realised it wasn't. Somewhere in the dark room I could hear David scrambling into his clothes. 'Charlotte, get dressed!' I was still woozy enough to be hurt by the harshness of his voice, though I realise now that it had to be that way. This was no time for niceties. I hunted clumsily for my clothes and found the jeans and shirt I'd discarded for the leafy green dress. I put them on, and one shoe, and groped in panic for the other.

Before I could find it, David's hand grabbed mine and he pulled me into the corridor. All the time he'd been getting dressed he'd been yelling, 'Fire!' Now I could hear doors opening and voices answering. The corridor was full of smoke and the replies were interrupted by coughs.

'Soak towels in water!' he bellowed.

I broke free and rushed back into our room. I rammed the plug into the sink, wrenched both taps on hard and plunged our towels into the water. It seemed to take ages. Meanwhile, David was still bellowing, this time ordering everyone to shout out their name. Even now, the insistence on doing things properly. I had to smile. I felt comforted by it, and quite calm. Whatever was happening, it would be all right; David was in charge.

I raced across the room and thrust a dripping towel at him. We wrapped them round our heads. David was still calling out orders: 'Everyone go to the courtyard! Don't stop to collect anything!'

I think it was then that I knew it was for real. This wasn't just a little fire which my all-powerful lover would have under control in a few minutes. With one hand holding the towel in place, David grabbed mine with the other and we stumbled through the corridor. Then I stopped. 'Effie!' I yelled. She knew the house fairly well but in a panic might forget the layout. I heard a small voice behind say, 'Charlotte?' We called each other's names as signals until finally I felt her hand in mine. The three of us thus linked, we made our way through the maze of corridors and stairs and out into the courtyard.

It was as black outside as in. Thick black smoke oozed from every opening in The Folly, and a down draught pushed it all into the courtyard where we were – I hoped – all assembling. Again David demanded a rolecall. One by one I heard the voices. As the last name was shouted out – Brendan, saying he'd phoned the fire department – I could feel relief flooding over me along with a surge of love. They were all safe, everything would be all right, nothing else mattered.

Then David broke away from me and I felt a stab of incipient panic. 'Stay in the middle of the courtyard,' he ordered. 'We'll need you in a few minutes.'

Then he was gone. I could hear Brendan and David calling themselves together and the words, 'The pump!' Of course. I'd forgotten the pump, an ancient heavy monster of a machine stored in the outbuilding nearest the garden and pond.

It was becoming more difficult to hear their voices above those of the horses. I felt the same irritation with them as I had with the sleeping David who'd refused to tell me why it was night. If only they'd shut up, David and Brendan would be able to hear each other better and get on with the job of setting up the water pump. Then I froze.

The horses. They were trapped in the stables, their neighing becoming more and more panicky.

'David!' I shouted. 'The horses! We have to let them out!'

'Leave them!' his voice shouted back at me. 'They'll panic if you let them into the courtyard! Kill themselves and the rest of you! We'll douse the stables in a minute!'

He was right, of course. The one thing no horse can be sane about is fire. Already I could hear them plunging in their boxes. At least there was a limit to the damage they could do themselves in there. In the courtyard they would go berserk and probably foul up the attempt to set up the pump which would save them.

Effie still clung to me. Together we called Astrid and Belle and Matti to us and stood huddled uselessly in the courtyard, waiting. Matti had released Moss and was clutching him hard. I had to hope the cats were far away.

I don't know whether there was a wind, or whether the heat of the fire produced its own, but the smoke whirled erratically in the courtyard. Every so often a ragged gap would appear in it, and through it I would see rough-edged scraps of David and Brendan running towards the outbuilding. The outbuilding opening. An explosion of hens whizzing out of it towards the garden. David and Brendan lugging the ancient machine. All of it portrayed in funny jerky fragments. It was like watching a frayed piece of film where most of the frames had disappeared and the few remaining ones been nearly eaten away by some small animal determined that the audience should have to work at interpreting what was left. Another fragment: Brendan and David parting, David pulling the heavy machine towards the pond while Brendan unrolled the hose and started up the yard with it.

'Look!' yelled Matti.

We looked. The first flames had appeared, glowing orange through a window. I guessed it was the Scheherazade Room. It would be. All those silk hangings and cushions, how the flames must love it. Effie had been sleeping in that room. I don't think she realised which room it was we were watching. I wasn't going to tell her either.

The courtyard was getting noisier: the horses, David and Brendan still shouting instructions at each other, the eerie roar of the fire. And now, a strangely musical tinkling of glass as the heat forced its way through the Scheherazade Room and a flame shot out aggressively above us. It *was* aggressive, this first flame, and I couldn't help but see it as the leader of the fire just as David was the leader of the rescue.

The fire was winning. It must have been building up for some time behind all those locked doors and windows, building up and waiting for its chance to escape. Now a second window went, a little to the east and above the first. A third. And then a sound as if a whole china shop were disintegrating at once, as all the windows burst and the whole of the north façade burst into flame and simultaneously a moan burst from my throat.

Why was the pump taking so long? Probably it wasn't. There couldn't have been more than twenty seconds between seeing Brendan start up the yard with the hose and his arrival in our midst. He thrust the hose into Belle's hands, yelled, 'Water'll come in a minute! Stables first!' and raced back down the yard towards the pond.

The flames were racing too, and now there did seem to be a wind, pushing the hideous inferno eastwards. At least the flames had cleared much of the smoke. I almost wished hey hadn't. What I saw made me freeze with horror. The flames were making their way at high speed towards the eastern arch between the house and the stable block. There was an enclosed walkway above the arch, linking the two buildings, filled with a century or more of accumulated possessions that had overflowed the attics. All of it no doubt highly inflammable. And leading to the loft above the stables, in which was stored the whole of this year's hay.

And then I knew, as if my own pulse and that of the flames were one, that however soon the water came it would be too late. One spark alone would be enough to set the entire loft alight and the whole blazing mass would plunge through the wooden floor straight onto the trapped horses.

I didn't even need to think. The whole thing unfolded in my mind in one split-second vision, and I shouted to Belle above the roar, 'I'm taking the horses out! To the first field east! Is the gate open?'

'Yes!'

'I'll lead them out on Olwen! Soon as I'm on her, you open the other boxes! Astrid, you take the hose! Belle and Effie try to funnel the other horses behind Olwen and through the arch! Keep them following Olwen!'

Without waiting for a response, I ran to the stables and flung open the door. Immediately it was night again. The smoke had made its way into the stables and, with no outlet except the dutch doors through which it had come, been trapped inside with the horses. I groped my way to the central corridor, grateful that Olwen's box was near the main door. The noise was terrifying: the shrill whinnying, the crashes and thumps as the horses flung themselves against their boxes. Another noise: my voice ringing out, 'Olwen!' There was no fear in my voice because I had none. I was too busy working out the details of what I had to do. 'Olwen, I'm coming!'

I leaned against the big sliding door and heaved it open. 'Olwen, Olwen!' Her massive pale head loomed above me. I spoke her name over and over as I reached for her head before she could lurch away from me. My fingers grasped the leather straps of her halter. Thank God she was wearing the halter. A mad gallop freely chosen was one thing, but in the panic which gripped her now I would have been utterly

helpless without the halter. 'Olwen, Olwen!' I eased her
out of the box and into the corridor. For a moment I was
almost lifted into the air as she started to rear. 'Olwen!'
Sharp this time. She came down and I pulled her forward
towards the light of the doorway, crooning her name over
and over, hoping that somewhere within her terror she would
recognise my authority.

Then we were out in the courtyard. She was skittering
about; I could barely hold her. I raised my voice and by
talking and pulling and shoving managed to ease her against
the wall while calling to Belle. She rushed over to us.

'Leg up!'

Belle made her hands into a stirrup. I clambered into it and
pushed myself up onto the mare's back. Belle sprang back
and I pushed off from the wall so I could get my other leg
round Olwen. 'Stay, Olwen!' I said, loud but calm. Olwen's
ears swivelled back once, then forward, and she stood still.
That she could remember this one command, so crucial to her
work in the forest, was a miracle of training. I could feel her
quivering beneath me, desperate to break the command, and
yet she stayed. 'Stay, Olwen!' I had to quell her panic before
we could begin. The few seconds it took would be worth it,
I knew, just as I knew that there was no time to lose.

As soon as I felt her quivering diminish a little, I leaned
forward and, stretching hard, grasped the halter's cheek
pieces in both hands. Then I tugged gently on the near side
and, still talking to her, steered her away from the wall. I
would have given my soul for a bridle, but there was no time.
Out of the corner of my eye I glimpsed Astrid and Matti and
Effie well out of the way against the outbuildings opposite.
Astrid was now clutching the hose. Belle was poised near the
stables, waiting. I walked Olwen round till we faced the arch.
In the short time it had taken to fetch Olwen, the walkway
had ignited, turning the arch into a blazing circus hoop.

'Now Belle! The others!'

As Olwen and I moved towards the arch, I could hear Belle
releasing the horses. As soon as the first one plunged through
the doorway, I urged Olwen with a press of my knees and
a call, 'Now, Olwen! Hup hup!' She lurched forward, then
stopped just in front of the arch and reared up. My hands,

clinging to her halter, must have pulled back on her nose strap like a hackamore and acted much as a bridle, for she came down earthward just in time. A second more and I would have slid off. Two or three shapes now by the stables doorway. I pressed my knees harder against her sides and yelled, 'Olwen, *now*!' For a moment I thought she would refuse again. Then, suddenly, she shot forward under the blazing arch.

I couldn't afford to look behind and make sure the others were following. I had to trust that Belle would know what to do and somehow get them through the arch. As soon as they were through, I felt sure they would carry on behind Olwen.

Out on the gravel, I had to steer Olwen clumsily towards the right path and just hope the timing would work. I was shaking with the physical tension of my stretched-out body. If I lost hold of the halter, anything could happen. 'Ahead, Olwen! Hup hup!' I felt silly giving her the mundane command by which she delivered her firewood or hauled her logs, but I knew no special language to tell her that this was a rather extreme emergency and if she didn't do her bit nothing could save her or the other horses or me.

Then I risked a backward glance and saw shapes coming through the arch. Behind them, the smaller shapes of people with flailing arms. Olwen was moving towards the path. 'Good girl, Olwen! Ahead, Olwen, straight ahead, hup hup!' She was doing a bone-shaking trot which threatened my hold, but it was the right speed to match the following horses. The forest seemed so dark in front of me, the path so slender, and yet now she seemed to understand. There were no more attempts to toss her head, choose her options. She was moving straight, and behind her, the others. I could hear their hooves thudding, coming closer. 'Now, Olwen!' She broke into a canter. A moment later she entered the path.

The other horses were gaining on us. I don't know if Olwen sensed that the worst was over or whether the crazy fun of the race seized hold of her, but the canter became a gallop. What I did know was that this path was fairly straight and smooth and there was little danger of a horse stumbling on it even in the half light of dawn. I felt crazy, too, crazy with relief as we thundered down the path, the trees blurring past. So crazy that I wondered why the trees were beside us rather than beneath us, why we weren't flying. I had to shake my head to snap back out of the dream.

Was that it? Had my dream that turned into a nightmare been an uncanny rehearsal for what was to come? Was that how I knew what I had to do?

There was no more time to think. Ahead of us was the field, and yes, the gate was open. I would have liked to slow down, but we weren't safe yet, not until we were all through that gateway and into the field.

Olwen didn't ease her pace one jot as we flew through the gateway. But once in the field, I pulled back on the halter. 'Slow down, Olwen, slow!' She must have been used to our impromptu set of signals by then because slow down she did, just in time for me to glance back and see the other horses pushing through the gateway. I tried to count them but couldn't be sure. 'Olwen, stop!'

With utmost reluctance, Olwen came to a full stop in the centre of the field. I unlatched my hands, which felt like claws frozen on the halter, and slid to the ground. My legs gave way and I crumpled in a heap by her feet. Her great head swung down and her muzzle nibbled my hair. I could feel the laughter of hysteria and gratitude bubble up in me as she snorted softly at the foolish human. Once again I grasped her halter and let her half pull me to my feet. Then I put my arms round her neck and burst into tears. I don't know why, and I don't suppose she did either, but, just as I had calmed her down outside the stables, now she blew her soft horsy breath down my neck to tell me that everything was all right, she would look after everything.

I pressed my cheek to hers and whispered, 'Olwen,' one last time. Then I turned and ran towards the gateway. The other horses had collected round Olwen. They were milling about, still held by the fear that had propelled them to follow her and reminded of the danger by the black clouds of smoke moving high across the field. None the less, by the time I reached the gate and closed it behind me, they had settled just enough to try a few nibbles of grass. Apart from the smoke, and an occasional nervous toss of the head, the scene was almost pastoral. The big bodies were becoming more sharply outlined against the silvery grey dawn, and it seemed to me that a soft flash of silver glanced off Olwen's coat as I turned to make my way back up the path.

The scene before me now was dramatically different from the one I was leaving behind. Ahead of me the silver sky had turned a brassy gold. But it was no sun performing the transformation. It was The Folly, itself unseen but pushing its hideous flames high into the sky to stain the air with the colour of its own destruction. Against it the forest seemed unnaturally dark, black trees outlined as sharply against the sulphurous background as the horses had been against their softer sky.

Silver to gold. Again my dream flashed through my mind, but again I had no time to wonder. All my strength was turned towards the homeward flight. I don't know if I thought I could help, or if it was simply the homing instinct, but I ran blindly and unthinkingly towards the lurid sky above The Folly. It never occurred to me to stay with the horses in the field, this oasis which, whatever happened, would be safe. I'd brought them there because I knew that even if the fire spread to the forest, they would be untouched in their field, but I didn't think it would come to that. The thought of Farleton Forest destroyed by fire was unthinkable, and so I never thought it, not even now as I ran towards the centre of the conflagration.

Even when the heat began to sap my strength and slow me to a ragged jogging pace, I didn't think the worst. It was, after all, high summer; it had a right to be warm, even this early in the morning. And the sweat now running down my face was exertion, nothing more. It had been a terrible strain, stretched out on Olwen grasping her halter, and now, as I trotted up the path I was feeling the cumulative effects of a long night, little sleep and the residue of fear left over from the tense flight to the field. My mind was so set on the one thing – getting home – that I refused entry to anything which might interfere with it. The only thing that worried me was the excruciating slowness of my progress. The dash on Olwen seemed to have taken a few seconds, the return journey was a slow-motion nightmare, my legs refusing to go any faster, my breath rasping.

Finally I lurched into a fast walk, stumbling and cursing myself for my human weakness. Tears of frustration mingled with the sweat and stung my eyes. I began picturing the scene ahead of me. Surely the fire engines would have arrived by now, surely the pump had long since put out the worst of the flames and the Kirkby firemen would finish off the rest. Crazy with hope, I pictured a jubilant homecoming awaiting me: The Folly charred but still standing, my friends blackened with smoke but triumphant. They would laugh at me for prematurely moving the horses, but none of us would mind, we'd be so relieved it was all over. It would be an awful mess to clear up, of course, all those smoke and water damaged things in The Folly, but there, too, we would be so relieved that we wouldn't mind. Hard work didn't worry us, and if the school couldn't reopen for a week or two, it wasn't the end of the world.

I don't know when it was that I began to feel uneasy and allow the first unwelcome entry of reality. I don't know either when I saw the first fiery trees. They were somewhere to my right, at first just a sense of unnatural light glimpsed through the darkness of the nearer trees. But I was tired; my eyes were jerking with the strain of all that had happened. It wasn't unusual to see flashes of light where none existed. And somewhere the sun must be rising, no doubt it was glancing off some water on the cliff face.

At the thought of water, I imagined a huge glass of it dousing my burning throat. I hadn't realised how thirsty I was, and so hot. How could it be *so* hot? Surely the heat of the burning building wouldn't spread so far, so intensely? And myself so slow. I'd been running and walking for hours, it seemed, and still the coppery glow ahead was no closer. The colour was darker, more intense than before, and its hateful light seemed now to be infusing the sky to the north and east as well. In front of it the trees themselves were taking on the same colour. I could see now a stronger light to my right, the trunks of the nearer trees standing out darkly against it.

Was it then that I glimpsed the first burning trees? If so, it wasn't for long, and no doubt I dismissed that, too, as a hallucination, because now it was obliterated by a big black cloud that suddenly swarmed out of the forest across the path. I stumbled through it, coughing. My heart was crashing against my ribs. Even walking was an effort now, the heat was draining my muscles. The noise, too, was debilitating, a horrid roar which was rapidly becoming louder as I approached The Folly. My idiotic picture of a salvaged Folly and triumphant friends crumbled, and I admitted at last that the fire was as strong as ever. I could even hear a sinister descant above the roar, the crackle of the building and all its contents disintegrating.

The crackle was echoing throughout the forest. I could hear it, too, to my right. I glanced in its direction.

And saw the trees, a wall of them somewhere in the depths of the forest, shining brightly and exuding the hateful noise. No hope of a hallucination. The forest was alight. Further, the flames were advancing fast in the wind. Even as I looked my eyes gave a jerk and the flames were instantly closer. Through them I could see the skeletal shapes of a few trees bending and slowly falling earthward with a sigh audible even through the roar of the fire.

My brain must have been dulled by the smoke which was billowing faster now across the path, because it took a while longer to understand the significance of what I was seeing. Or perhaps it was simply the defence of the trapped, holding out hope against all evidence. I didn't want to know that the forest was burning and that the flames were bearing down on me at a terrible speed, a whole lurid wall of it closing in on me from the right. Instinctively I looked to the left. The forest here was utterly impenetrable. There was no way through it to escape the flames, they that could move so much faster than me. There were two directions only: onward, or back the way I'd come. How far *had* I come? I'd been so long on the path that I *must* be closer to The Folly than the field. I must be very close indeed.

Squashing my panic, I forced myself into a clumsy run. At least I could see better now; the smoke was clearing. But this time I knew what that meant: that the trees were so fully alight that they were burning cleanly, the force of the heat eating through the smoke. The smoke, I now saw, had been just the beginning, the sappy wood of the living trees refusing to catch just as in a fireplace. And, just as a log smoulders for some time before suddenly bursting into flames, the whole forest was acting out the process on a gigantic scale.

Whole forest? No, that I couldn't think. Surely the fire-breaks would do their job. If only I'd taken a different path! There was a lovely wide ride at the other end of the field; if I'd taken that I would have had more time. I couldn't hope that this narrow path would hold back the fire. No, my only hope was to get to the end before it arrived.

A second later I saw that it was too late. Ahead of me one of the trees fringing the path began its deathly lean and even as I raced towards it I saw that it was listing further and further, picking up speed in its descent which would in just a few seconds become a blazing curtain and cut off my last chance of escape.

How I forced my exhausted legs and heaving lungs to make that final spurt I'll never know, nor will I know how I willed myself towards the heat of that terrible furnace when every other instinct screamed for me to turn back. I remember nothing about it now except the vision of a second blazing arch under which I had to run, this time without Olwen, and this time the arch was in motion, sinking lower with every terrified lurch I made towards it.

I'm not even sure I really noticed when I burst through under the tree and came out on the other side just as it crashed noisily to the ground behind me. All I remember is a sudden sensation on my right arm as if a hundred tiny insects, themselves fleeing the flames, had rushed out to latch onto my flesh for one last feed. I remember flinging my other hand on the stinging arm and rubbing wildly and at the same time feeling the insects rushing up my arm and onto my neck and head. I remember the sudden feel of gravel instead of earth beneath my feet and the sharp jab as a stone went into my bare foot. I remember one last cry – 'David!' – and then nothing.

38

'Lottie. Lottie, wake up. It's all over, everything's all right now. Wake up, Lottie.'

The voice was calm and dark. It cut through the terror and lifted me, floating, above the inferno. I rose into the cooler air, still floating, seeking the source. Floating and then flying, on Olwen, above the gleaming gold forest below. 'David?'

'I'm here, Lottie. Everything's all right.'

'Why is it night? It was dawn when we went to bed.'

There was a long silence. Then, 'That's all over, Lottie. The nightmare's over. You're safe now.'

I was standing by the window overlooking the courtyard, the curtains open, David by my side. 'Why is it night?'

'Wake up, Lottie. It's day.'

I opened my eyes. I wasn't by the window. I was floating beneath a pure white hard expanse so bright I blinked with pain. Then, something dark in front of it, hovering above me and shielding me from the light. David. Lowering his beloved head and kissing me lightly on the forehead.

'Are you really here?'

'I'm really here. So are you. You're safe now.'

'Where is here?'

'The hospital in Kirkby.' David smiled. 'Belle's first aid isn't up to it this time.'

It took me a moment to understand the reference. Then I remembered. The last time I'd woken from a nightmare it had been snow, not fire. The rescue from the blizzard. The Scheherazade Room, the ankle wrapped in Belle's handiwork.

David kissed my forehead again. 'Lottie, please don't make a habit of this.'

'Habit?'

'Getting yourself knocked out by trees or blizzards or fires.

This is the third time, you know. Am I to make a habit of waking my Sleeping Beauty with a kiss?'

I started to smile but my face hurt.

'How do you feel?' he asked anxiously.

'I don't know. Why am I in hospital?'

'Burns,' he said. 'You were burned in the fire. Not too badly, but enough to keep you in hospital for a little while.'

'Fire? The nightmare?'

David looked puzzled. 'You were having a nightmare when I came in – that's why I woke you up. The nurse didn't want to let me in at all, she made me promise I wouldn't wake you up. But when I saw you were having a nightmare . . . Charlotte, what was it? Or would you rather not say?'

Now I was puzzled. Why was I in a hospital for having a nightmare? I tried to tell David but it came out in fragments. 'Flying above the forest on Olwen. She was silver, and the forest, and then it was gold and so were Olwen and the others and the trees. And then the gold was fire, and the forest was on fire, and Olwen's mane and my hair – '

David's eyes opened wide.

'And then I woke up in front of the window, that's all,' I ended foolishly.

'And then?' he asked.

'And then I was here. David, what's this all about? Why am I here?'

'Do you really not remember? The fire? It was real, Charlotte.' He touched my cheek softly. 'Perhaps you don't want to remember, is that it?'

It was as if he were giving me permission to forget, but as soon as he did, the memories began to seep through. Yes, I did want to forget. Hurrying through the corridors, out into the courtyard. The smoke, the flames, the plunging horses, Olwen's terror and mine. And that terrible path that went on forever, and at the end of it the tree, blazing, falling –

I whimpered with the unwanted memory and reached my left hand out from under the sheets. I groped for David's hand. When it folded round mine, so warm and comforting, my tears began. Foolish, really, now that it was all over.

David let me cry my fill, just holding onto my hand with both of his. When at last I finished, he found a handkerchief and wiped my face, so gently. Every gesture featherlight, as if I were the frailest porcelain. The burns, of course, which is also why he didn't take me in his arms as I so wished he would do. Instead, he touched my cheek again and said, 'My poor Lottie. I shouldn't have come so soon. You weren't ready to remember.'

I shook my head. 'I want to know what happened. Tell me what happened.'

'Are you sure?'

I felt myself go cold. 'The others – are they all right?'

'Yes, don't worry. Everyone's all right. And the horses.' He smiled, but there was strain at the edges, and I realised that he, too, was barely recovered from the ordeal. 'You do know that you saved the horses, don't you, Charlotte?' he said. 'I was wrong telling you to keep them in the stables. I didn't realise the fire was so far advanced. I thought there was time. If you hadn't acted so fast, if you'd waited just half a minute, they would – '

He stopped. He didn't want to say the rest, nor I to hear it, even though it was all over. I nodded and let him start again somewhere else.

'We got the pump set up very quickly,' he said. 'Everything seemed to be going fine, but when the first blast of water hit the stables it was already too late. The whole loft went up at once, and the stables were gone in just a few minutes. That's what set the trees alight just behind. By the time the fire engines arrived, the stables were gone and The Folly was obviously beyond hope. We concentrated on saving other outbuildings and the forest. The part of it that caught you was already well alight – we knew we had to let it burn itself out. But we saturated all the trees and ground everywhere else around The Folly to make sure it wouldn't jump.'

He faltered, and for a moment I thought the worst. A thousand acres of trees . . . 'David, tell me now, I have to know. The forest . . . '

'We managed to save all except the one section,' he said quickly. 'Thirty acres.'

How many thousands of trees on thirty acres? How many hours spent planting each one individually, all that love and care, all those years of growth, gone.

'Don't fret about it, Charlotte,' he said. 'The rest of the forest was salvaged, and the buildings with all the equipment.' He smiled. 'And the horses. My brave, foolish, wonderful Lottie. I don't know whether to curse you for your bloody-minded recklessness or pin a medal on that hideous hospital nightdress.'

I smiled feebly. Always giving me credit for luck, like the day we saw the kites. 'Belle had the worst of it. She had to let the other horses out. I don't know how she managed it, I didn't have time to see. And when I came back – '

David's face clouded. 'Try not to remember, Lottie. There'll be time enough when you're better.'

'But I do remember.'

He gripped my hand so tightly that I felt the ring press into my flesh.

'At least, I remember running up the path,' I said, 'and the tree coming down. After that, it all goes black.'

David's voice was hesitant. 'I think you fainted from the pain. Don't try to remember. Later.'

'No. I want to know, now.'

He hesitated, and when finally he spoke, each word seemed to be dragged out of him. 'I was in the courtyard. The arch you'd ridden through had collapsed. Beyond it I could see the path, and the fire sweeping towards it. And then you. And the tree. And then you running beneath the tree just as it fell, running onto the gravel.'

He stopped. Little beads of sweat had appeared on his forehead. It occurred to me that it was he who didn't want to remember. 'Go on,' I said.

'You were on fire, Charlotte,' he said, so quietly I almost didn't hear. 'Outlined in fire. Like some terrible avenging angel. Your hair blazing out behind you like a banner.'

Blazing out behind me like a banner. The words shot onto the screen of my mind an image I'd seen before, but before I could capture it, David went on:

'It was the most terrible sight I've ever seen. I felt paralysed. Then I scrambled over the rubble and caught you as you fell. I smothered the flames somehow. Charlotte, I don't want to think about it. I don't want you to think about it. It's over now, that's all that matters.'

Blazing like a banner . . . 'David,' I said slowly. 'My dream.'

'Lottie, try not to think – '

'No, I want to tell you.'

I told him the whole dream this time. It came back to me with the utmost clarity. When I reached the point where my arms had been on fire, and then my hair, David's hands went cold over mine. 'Don't you see?' I said. 'If I hadn't had the dream, I wouldn't have known what to do. I remember so clearly now, knowing exactly how I had to ride Olwen out and lead the others – it flashed into my mind straight from the dream, all complete and ready to be used.'

David smiled. It was the noise of the horses, already alerted to the fire, that had penetrated my sleep and formed the dream. I'd smelled the smoke, also in my sleep. My unconscious mind had simply used the external reality to compile a dream which would make sense of all these elements.

I suppose he was right. But I couldn't help think of the benevolence I'd felt radiating out from Rhiannon's portrait that night.

The portrait. 'Oh, David,' I whispered. 'The portrait. Rhiannon.'

He nodded. 'Gone.'

Words of comfort would have been useless, and I didn't even try. We sat quietly until the nurse came.

It wasn't until the following day that I began to wonder about other things. Most important, how had the fire started? The thought of fire had always been just beneath the surface of our minds, living in the forest as we did. Our awareness was heightened by the obvious danger, and we took pedantic precautions against it. It couldn't have been an accident. Couldn't.

'Haven't you guessed?' said David the next day. There was bitterness in his smile. 'Richard Staveley.'

'*What*?'

'He came back to The Folly after he took his mother home. He must have known there were police there, because he walked – the police found his car just where he parked it the night before, at Graegarth. He was still wearing the same clothes – probably so that if anyone did glimpse him in the corridors they wouldn't think anything of it. All the doors were open, it must have been easy enough to wait until no one was about and then slip in and lose himself in the corridors until everyone was gone.'

'But we searched!'

'Not very effectively; it wasn't possible in that house. And even the police didn't seriously believe that Staveley would come back. Why should he? It would be easier to engineer your "accident" later. You know how many little cupboards there are. He must have hidden himself until we all went to bed. Then he started the fire. You probably don't realise, but you and your dream woke us only about an hour after we'd gone to bed. The fire must have been burning quietly for much of that time, building up its power. That's why it was so far advanced by the time you woke up – why it spread so quickly to the stables. Lottie, it wasn't only the horses you saved. If you hadn't woken up when you did, none of us might have had the time to get out. I can see now that we were stupid not to realise. It was the perfect opportunity for Staveley. Not only could he kill you, and me, and Matti, but Effie as well.'

'Effie? But why should he want to kill Effie?'

'The will.'

'Oh, my God.'

David nodded. 'Your beneficiary. With her out of the way, the farm would have become crown property and been put up for sale. And with me out of the way, he would have no competition in buying it. The fire would even take care of my heir. Matti. Only Hugh would be left, and the last thing Hugh would want is to buy Cappelrigg. In fact, Hugh would probably sell the estate, and Staveley would be able to start accumulating that as well.' David grimaced. 'The "rightful heir" reclaiming his estate.'

'But he knew he wasn't!' I cried. 'He *must* have known – I showed him the diary. And he reacted so violently that I was sure he accepted the truth of it.'

'You caught him off-guard. He didn't *want* to accept it, and it probably only took him a few minutes to recover and start finding ways of not believing you. He'd believed it so long, based all his future plans on it. He couldn't change his course just because you proved that it was all based on a fantasy. I think he'd been planning the fire, too, for a long time – for as long as we'd been planning the Midsummer's Eve Ball. It was the one way he could get into the house legitimately. And with so many people around, an "accident" would seem plausible enough. As well as killing off all of us at once.'

'So,' I said grimly. 'He's still lying. No doubt he's charming the police again. Oh, David, when is it going to end?'

David was watching me closely, the expression on his face so disconcerting that, absurdly, I wondered about my hair. So much of it had burnt that the rest had been cut into short curls. I hadn't given much thought to it, or to the scars I would have on my arm, but now I wondered. Why was he staring so? This was hardly the time to care about such things.

Then it began to dawn on me, or at least I thought it did. 'David, you don't mean he *has* confessed?'

There was another long silence. Then, 'No, he hasn't confessed. He's dead.'

It was one of those moments of heightened reality, when everything irrelevant becomes vivid. A burst of laughter from somewhere down the corridor. A large bluebottle buzzing angrily against the window. A scrap of David's hair sticking out at a peculiar angle. My nose itched.

'Dead?' I said. It seemed as if we were talking about someone else, someone in a newspaper story.

'In the fire. And, God help me, I'm not going to pretend to be sorry. Ever.'

'In the fire?' I repeated stupidly.

'He was trapped in the maze.'

I lay back against the pillows and closed my eyes. In the maze. Yes, I could see it all now. How we'd searched and then locked all the rooms we could. Locking Richard Staveley out, we'd thought. But we'd locked him in. And I, too, couldn't pretend to be sorry. Seven people he'd intended to kill that night. Instead, he'd killed one. Himself. I opened my eyes. 'You don't think it was suicide?' I asked suddenly.

David shook his head. 'I think he tried to get out. Just as you and Olwen were racing through the arch, Matti thought he heard someone yell for help. He told Astrid but she couldn't hear anything – Matti must have heard it in one of those split-second lulls in the noise.'

'I see,' I said calmly.

'I wasn't sure whether to tell you so soon. I wasn't sure how you'd take it. I suppose he was a human being.'

'Was he?' I said shortly.

'Even if we'd known someone was in there, it was too late. It would have been suicidal to try to get anyone out.'

I looked at the big green emerald. We had a future now. We were free. We would rebuild, replant, the school would go on. And above it all the kites would wheel majestically, safe and free at last, living symbols of what even Richard Staveley couldn't destroy. We had paid hard for our freedom: The Folly and everything in it, the stables, the trees, a night of horror.

'I'm glad no one knew he was there,' I said quietly. 'I'm glad he died. Let's not pretend with each other.' I smiled. 'David, we're free.'

39

The next fortnight passed in a confusion of activity for my friends and a frustration of inactivity for me. My burns, though not bad enough to need skin grafts, did need frequent changing of bandages and a careful course of painkillers and antibiotics. Once or twice the painkillers wore off at the wrong moment. I appreciated, then, why I had to stay in hospital.

In any case, I would have been a nuisance at home. 'Home' was now Cappelrigg for everyone. They had commandeered my farm immediately after the fire. It made me extremely happy. It was the first time I'd been in a position to give them something important, and their taking it without a fuss showed me how firmly bound together we all were.

The house was, of course, pretty cramped. No sooner had Effie and Astrid and Matti returned to London than the students had come back. It was a tight fit, and would be even more so when I came out of hospital, but nobody complained. The students even seemed to like it. Trained to respond to emergencies far worse than cramped quarters, they settled into the new way of life easily enough. The horses were housed in my disused shippon, the forestry equipment which had been salvaged was moved into my barn. The horses were now eating my hay. Why not? I would be selling my sheep this autumn anyway when I began the work of converting Cappelrigg to a forest-cum-nursery. As for the shearing, now due, Brendan and Tom took it in hand, I wasn't to worry about a thing, I was simply to lie back and get better.

There were problems, of course, and would be for many years to come. The worst of it was that all the estate records had been destroyed. From now on the work was dependent on what was in David and Brendan's heads. Clothes had been destroyed, too, and all the silly little essentials one never thinks to think of. There were frequent shopping trips squeezed in between hours of work-as-usual. Life was chaotic indeed, but there was ample energy to cope with everything.

The source of that energy was clear to us all, though we didn't speak of it after the first few days. Richard Staveley. He had been a succubus, a deadly leech, sucking the life out of all of us. Now that he was gone, it was as if a terrible cloud had lifted and we could breathe again. The air felt good. We couldn't pretend that we regretted his death.

Mrs Staveley was another matter. She mourned loudly and bitterly. First her daughter had vanished, now her son was dead. She was left alone in the world with a difficult farm to run and it was all my fault.

My fault? Oh yes. For the story which she spread through Kirkby Langham was that I had seduced her son and then, enraged when he had refused to marry me, taken David Farleton on the rebound and plotted my revenge. I had lured him to The Folly that night, lured him to his death.

Jean knew nothing of these rumours at first. For reasons which she didn't explain, she refused to go home after the fire, despite the fact that the reason for her panicked flight had died in the fire with Richard. She wouldn't even let us tell her mother where she was, or the police. Because we had promised to keep quiet, keep quiet we did. We had our own code of honour at The Folly. Promises were for real. At first we felt rather sorry for Mrs Staveley, kept in ignorance of her daughter's safety. But as the rumours grew, we began to doubt her affection for both Jean and Richard. It was herself she was feeling sorry for, not them.

But when the rumours reached Jean, she took the first train back and confronted her astonished mother with the truth. She then went to the police and told the whole story, John Jowett and all. After that, she made her presence felt in every pub and café in Kirkby, telling everyone she knew what had happened. That tough streak in her which Effie had been the first to discern now came out with a vengeance. A lifetime of repressed anger was finding its outlet at last.

When Mrs Staveley had recovered from the blow, she

began to woo Jean back. It was all a silly mistake, she said, no harm done. But Jean was too much her own woman by now to give in so easily. She knew that what her mother really wanted was for Jean to come back and work the farm. Jean had had enough of working the farm for her mother and brother. It was time for her own life to begin, and she intended to begin it in London.

At this, Mrs Staveley dropped all pretence and told Jean bluntly that she would disinherit her if she didn't stay.

'Go ahead,' said Jean. And left.

All this I heard from Jean herself, in a visit she made to the hospital just before leaving. The transformation was miraculous. No longer prematurely old, she was a healthily enraged young woman who'd finally seen what she wanted to do with her life and was damn well going to do it. I couldn't help but admire her at the same time I played devil's advocate and cautioned her against rashness.

'There's a lot of money at stake,' I said. 'If she really does cut you off.'

'Oh, she will.' Jean smiled. 'I'll tell you exactly what will happen. She'll hire a succession of labourers to work the farm, and she'll pay them so little and treat them so badly that finally there won't be anyone left to work for her. Then she'll sell the farm and take herself and the proceeds off to York or Scarborough and set up a nice little tea shop and live happily ever after. Don't worry about her. She always lands on her feet.'

'And you?'

She grinned. 'I'm tough. And there's Effie. She says I can stay in her flat as long as I need to, until I get set up with a job and a place of my own.'

'You know David and I would be more than happy to help – if you wanted to start a business of your own.'

'I'll think about it,' she said. 'But right now I'd rather be dependent on as few people as possible. Nothing against you and David. You understand.'

I did. I also understood that part of that independence had been to cut herself loose from a mother who was indifferent to her and ally herself instead with the two people who'd shown her kindness without the strangling bond of blood:

Brendan and Effie. Her first act on coming 'home' had shown that; before even confronting her mother, she'd gone to the little outbarn and destroyed her brother's horrible 'workshop'. She'd said nothing to her mother or the police about the birds, knowing how important it was to keep our work with them secret. With a minimum of fuss, she'd become a part of our secret, and our friend.

When the 'Druids' discovered that they were implicated, however unwittingly, in Richard's plot to make me leave Cappelrigg, they came forward at last. They were furious that he had lied to them about the ley line, tricked them into changing their route to suit his own purposes. They were also rather sheepish. In the light of all that had happened, their cult suddenly looked a little foolish, even to themselves. Detective Sergeant Tyndall took advantage of the moment. 'Isn't it time you stopped this nonsense?' he said.

To this day, there's never been another bonfire on the moor.

*　　　*　　　*

The next week passed slowly, the only bright spots the evening visits from David and Belle and Brendan. Even the students came once, without prompting. They seemed, in my absence, to have accepted me at last. My wild ride on Olwen to save the horses ranked as a macho deed equal to the tough life they were preparing themselves for. It cancelled out my threatening femininity and made me one of the boys. I wasn't at all sure I should be pleased about that, but I couldn't help enjoying their awed admiration, at least for the time being.

But the long hours between visits left too much time to think. I tried to read, but over and over the image of The Folly as I had known it rose in my mind and with it a lump in the throat that hurt more than my burns. I was mourning The Folly. Now that it was gone, I was reconstructing it in my mind, a permanent memorial to everything David and Brendan and Belle had achieved.

I was also feeling guilty. If I hadn't been there, Richard would have had no reason to destroy it. All the ifs came tumbling out in the dreary hours between visits. If we hadn't held the Midsummer's Eve Ball. If Effie had never seen the ballroom. If I'd never brought her there, or brought myself there. I traced back the sickening succession of ifs, all the way to the auction room more than a year ago. If I hadn't seen the picture in the estate agent's window. If Brendan, rather than I, had made the final bid . . .

I talked about it with David, of course. The one thing I did know about our future was that there must be no more silences or misunderstandings, no more dark separate broodings left to grow and wreak their own kind of destruction. David was genuinely dumbfounded. He came up with a succession of his own ifs to cancel out mine. But the only one that rang true was Richard Staveley himself. We knew now that he really had been a psychopath. His refusal to accept the proof that he wasn't the squire's illegitimate son had shown us that much. His obsession was far too well advanced, long before I came on the scene, for anything to stop it. He'd murdered John Jowett before I arrived. He would have murdered again, and again, until he'd destroyed all the Farletons and gained his 'rightful inheritance'.

'Let it rest, my Lottie,' David said. 'The past is past. We'll mourn it and then leave it. We have other things to do.'

The biggest thing left undone for me was to see The Folly, face its ruins and acknowledge its destruction. In moments of weakness I was grateful to the hospital for keeping me away from it. At other times I felt impatient at the delay. Cowardice. It had to be done, the sooner the better.

The time came earlier than I expected. Though I wasn't due to leave for several days, Belle had brought me some clothes the evening before. They were neatly folded on the rickety chair by my bed. Real clothes, real life. Now David was here, showing me some rough sketches he and Brendan had made of the new buildings they proposed as replacements for The Folly. He was quite cheerful. The Folly hadn't exactly been environmentally sound, he said wryly. Hardly the best representation of the work they'd done from it. It had been a pig to heat, and peculiarities of construction had made it impossible to insulate. The new buildings would be just as beautiful – stone, of course, blending into the landscape – but more intelligently built. Strong, sound, the highest quality.

I was barely listening. I wasn't seeing the papers spread out on my bed. I was seeing The Folly, as it had been, as I had loved it. Suddenly I knew the time had come, 'I want to go home,' I said quietly.

David nodded.

The hospital made the usual fuss, but when I signed the papers discharging myself and taking full responsibility, they let me go.

Fifteen minutes later we'd reached the crossroads. To the left, the road to Cappelrigg and Graegarth; to the right, the road to the converted barns and houses. Straight ahead, the gates.

THE FOLLY
PRIVATE

'What will we call the new buildings?' I asked.

'We'll think about that later. Charlotte, are you sure you're ready? It's quite a shock the first time.'

'I'm ready.'

It was fairly late in the evening; the sun was sinking unseen, quite close to the horizon, I supposed. As we drove down the long drive, the sky above the trees to the left glowed a sinister red. I shivered. It would be a long time before I could see a red sky without shivering.

David stopped the Land-Rover before we'd reached the end of the drive. 'It's better to walk the rest,' he said. 'I don't know why, but it makes it just that little bit easier.'

We got out of the Land-Rover. I put my left hand through his arm – my right was still in bandages – and together we walked the short distance to the gravelled semi-circle.

David had, in order to prepare me, described in some detail what the fire had done, but no description could have lessened the shock. I remembered the first time I'd seen a dead goose on my parents' farm, killed by a fox. One day it had been a living creature; the next, a meaningless collection of feathers and flesh. The transition was incomprehensible.

And so The Folly. One day a living house, the heart of a

thousand acres' worth of activity, home to us all, the place where hundreds of people had danced the night away, where David had placed the green ring on my finger. And now?

The roof had crashed in, taking with it most of the chimneys and some of the walls. Those that remained looked stranded and ridiculous, a mockery. From the blackened jagged walls a maze of charred beams protruded at all angles like Pick-up Sticks frozen mid-flight as a malevolent player strewed them onto a mucky carpet. Windows gaped, glassless and ugly. Unidentifiable black lumps indicated that once upon a time there had been furniture. Slimy swathes had once been curtains. Filthy puddles were everywhere, the firemen's water mixed with soot into a horrid witch's brew. To the right, a long arm of inky skeletons that had been trees stretched into the forest. A few trees at the edges retained odd tufts of dirty green; they were alive, though barely, and would spend the next few weeks giving up the last pretence of life. I could feel their imminent death, and smell it: over everything, the charred stink of burnt wood. There was nothing majestic about these ruins, nothing to speak of the grandeur that had been. It was squalid.

'Oh, David.' I hid my face against his waiting chest and felt his arms reach comfortingly around me. A century and a half of life annihilated in just a few hours. The long-dead Farleton who'd lovingly designed each crazy feature; his descendants who'd filled the rooms with their bizarre collection of furnishings and with their own lives. And finally, David, lifting The Folly from its frivolity and building from it a paradise of trees and birds and horses and wildlife and purpose. It was those last two decades that hurt. I could feel David's own mourning through his inevitable frayed checked shirt, and I mourned with him.

'I know, Charlotte,' he said into my hair. 'It was your home too. We were happy there. But we'll be happy again. This is the worst. The worst of it is over now. We'll rebuild. And replant. And it will be even better. You'll see.'

I nodded dumbly, not quite believing but, as always, trusting his own belief.

'Don't hide from it, my Lottie,' he said gently. 'Look at

it. It's better that way. In a few years you'll remember this day and it won't hurt at all.'

I nodded again and turned my face towards The Folly. And for a moment, I saw past and present and future all fused together. David was right. Already it was just a fraction more bearable. The sun had gone down, leaving a bright mauve sky which softened the harshness of the ruins just a little. In the nearest trees I heard the faint rustle of birds settling down for the night. A distant curlew uttered its poignant cry.

I would like to say that at that moment, high up in the darkening sky, a pair of kites locked their talons together and, together, wings outspread, began their slow and breathless descending cartwheel over The Folly. But things like that happen only once in a lifetime, and then only if one is very lucky.

Epilogue

'. . . once . . . twice . . .' The auctioneer's hammer gave a prosaic thud. 'Sold . . . to Mrs Farleton.'

I rose and walked to the auctioneer's table. I signed the official papers which made Graegarth irrevocably mine. Then I walked to the head of the stairs, down the stairs, into the lounge of the Golden Oak.

The lounge was full of people chattering away. They stared at me as I walked towards the small table in the middle of the room. Several of them – tradesmen, farmers I'd met at the mart – lifted a laconic hand in greeting and an even more laconic eyebrow in question. I smiled in return and nodded. They didn't seem displeased.

I planted my handbag on the table, took my purse out and went to the bar to order half a pint. When I returned, two strangers were eyeing both the table and my handbag, unsure of procedure. 'Sorry,' I apologised. 'I'm meeting someone.' They wandered off towards the booth where my bank manager and one of his clerks were having lunch and where two seats were invitingly empty.

The pub was crowded; I was lucky to find a table. The auction, mainly. Several other pieces of land had been sold before Graegarth, and their new owners were now celebrating. Upstairs, the auction was still going on – the stock and machinery from the farm – but I had no need of any of that for Graegarth Forest.

The November sunlight slanting through the window was blotted out. I looked up to see David, smiling down on me with amusement and anticipation in his dark brown eyes.

'Yes,' I said in answer to his unspoken question. 'Not even any serious competition. Graegarth was just too derelict.'

But not for trees. In twenty years or so, the whole of the plateau would be one great gentle wave of green, broken only by the broad beautiful rides and the scattered fields where the horses would lift their heads and sniff the air before submitting to the harness and the day's work. It would be hard work for us, too, with failure and frustration along the way, but slowly the dream would take shape. I thought back to that first auction just eighteen months ago, to all the little chance events that had brought me to that room above the Golden Oak. Chance or fate? Who knows? I don't think it matters. There had been times when I'd regretted my folly, but not many.

My lover put his big resin-stained hand on my shoulder and squinted at the smudgy blackboard above the bar. 'How does shepherd's pie sound to you, Mrs Farleton?'

'Pretty good,' I said.